TELEGRAM HOME

KIRSTEN MCKENZIE

This edition published 2021
by Squabbling Sparrows Press

ISBN 978 0 9951170 99 (paperback)
ISBN 978 0 4734930 73 (ebook)

Squabbling Sparrows Press

ALSO BY KIRSTEN MCKENZIE

The Ithaca Time Travel Trilogy

ITHACA BOUND

ITHACA LOST

ITHACA FOUND

The Old Curiosity Shop Time Travel Trilogy

FIFTEEN POSTCARDS

THE LAST LETTER

TELEGRAM HOME

Standalone Paranormal Thrillers

PAINTED

DOCTOR PERRY

THE FORGER AND THE THIEF

Short Story Anthologies

LANDMARKS

NOIR FROM THE BAR

*This book is dedicated
to the real Nicole Pilcher.
Thank you for that first review.
You'll never know how
important that validation was.*

THE BEGINNING

THE MAHARAJA

*N*avin Pandya leaned back, abandoning his chisel and mallet on the ground next to his trusty boaster and rolled the kinks from his elbows and shoulders. In the haze of the afternoon heat he could see the clamour of activity around Maharaja Ram Singh, as he examined the work of one of his fellow craftsmen. Navin fantasised what it must be like to be part of the Singh family, the original builders of the great Jantar Mantar in Jaipur. Navin didn't understand how any of the instruments worked, given he was just a stonemason employed for his particular skill of finishing stone to an impossible smooth surface. But he was prone to fantasy.

The heat pooling among the astronomical devices didn't bother Navin, he worried more about the trouble he'd been having catching his breath over the past few weeks. He rubbed at his concave chest, bare under the Indian sun, his dusty fingers playing his exposed ribs like a harpsichord. Around him other stonemasons toiled away, repairing a century's worth of damage to the magical Jantar Mantar, replacing the crumbling plaster instruments with hardier stone replicas.

A fine dust danced on the shimmering warmth, tiny imperceptible particles worming their way into the lungs of the workers, tickling and clogging organs stressed by a meagre calorie intake and unsanitary living conditions. The work was hard but it fed their families, so the men kept their complaints to themselves. Navin coughed, fighting to control his ragged breathing. He cast fretful glances towards Ram Singh, willing him not to turn. Navin needed this job but understood he was ill. He had no idea it was his work which was killing him; him and his fellow stonemasons.

Muffling his coughing in the crook of his elbow, Navin didn't see the Maharaja approaching, untouched by the stark sunlight pouring through the site, minions tumbling behind his impressive strides.

'Are you ill?' asked Ram Singh, the Maharaja of Jaipur.

Navin froze. It was one thing to sneak glimpses of the Maharaja from afar, but to talk to him was unbelievable. He fought to control his coughing and shook his head, eyes watering from the effort.

'Give the man a drink,' directed the Maharaja.

A lackey ran forward with a cup of tepid water, which Navin gulped down.

'Thank you,' Navin mumbled, looking at the ground.

'I see you are working on the Nadi Valaya Yantra. One of my favourite pieces. I'm fascinated by the connection between the northern and southern hemispheres, as represented by this piece.'

Navin could only nod because he knew nothing of its workings. Beyond recognising that there were two sundials adorned with large bronze tablets and decorated with words in Sanskrit, his only goal was to finish the stone as smoothly as possible. How it worked didn't worry him.

Navin's eyes watered as he tried to stifle another bout of coughing, the strain casting him with a bluish hue. It wasn't the violent sun changing the colour of his skin, but the silicosis destroying him from the inside out.

'Here, take some,' commanded the Maharaja, pulling a jewelled betel box from the folds of his robes and offering it to Navin.

One of the Maharaja's courtiers protested, but the Maharaja waved him away.

Navin didn't know what to do. The foreman refused to meet his eye and the courtiers looked aghast that the Maharaja showed more concern for a mere worker than the diamond-encrusted and enamelled betel box. Finally Navin took the box from the Maharaja's manicured hands. Although small, it was heavier than he expected and he fumbled, the stunning trinket box falling towards the ground.

The crowd gasped as Navin lurched to catch the box, rescuing it an inch from the ground, sweat breaking out on his leathery brow as he flinched from the expected retribution from the foreman. Silence filled the nooks and crannies of the Jantar Mantar Observatory. No one spoke, all eyes were on the Maharaja who appeared unruffled by the near destruction of his valuable betel box.

'Chew the leaves, they will ease your discomfort. Return the box when your health returns. I need my workers to be healthy,' said the Maharaja, sweeping away, leaving the treasure in Navin's dusty hands.

As the crowd scurried away, the foreman cast murderous glances back at Navin, his thoughts clear — Navin's coughing and interaction with the Maharaja had brought shame upon them. Navin waited until the group disappeared from sight before opening the box to find fresh betel leaves wrapped around the nuts. The bright green waxy leaves reflected the brilliant sun over Navin's bare shoulder until a bank of clouds appeared on the horizon, chasing the sunshine away, lowering the temperature and sending uncomfortable shivers through his weakened body.

Navin shoved a handful of glossy leaves into his mouth, and chewed with his eyes closed, waiting for the promised pain relief, missing the arrival of the blackened clouds, only opening his eyes when the first rain pellets hit his emaciated body. Tucking the Maharaja's box under his arm, Navin scooped up his tools and ducked under the southern side of the equatorial double sundial, sheltering as best as he could from the torrential rivers of water running through the site. Triumphant thunder drowned out the shouts and screams of the stonemasons. Overcome by the effects of the betel nut, Navin leaned into the yellow stone of the Nadi Valaya Yantra; the rain and his illness and the side effects of the nut lulling him to a temporary stupor.

After the thunder came the lightning. Jagged and relentless, it lit the sky again and again, casting Daliesque shadows across the landscape, transforming the site to a surrealist's dreamscape.

Navin never felt the lightning curl around the corners of the astrological device he was sheltering behind, corners he had smoothed to an impossible level. The lightning flashed against the dial, illuminating the mysterious characters designed long ago by the true master of the Jantar Mantar — Jai Singh. Navin had no awareness of the electrical current conducted through his body by the elegant betel box under his arm. The current raced through his neurons short-circuiting every connection. His limbs jerked, pulled by unseen electrical strings, the gods playing cruel puppet masters with the workman.

Then the earth plunged into complete and utter darkness, the solar eclipse completing the work started by the storm clouds, removing any fragment of light. In that moment, Navin's life ended, his soul ripped from his body and pulled into the ether of the universe. The betel box slipped from his lifeless body, coming to rest in his lap.

A shadow emerged from behind another astronomical piece, and a boy darted through the blanket of rain. A street urchin, barely old enough to be out alone, wearing an outfit held together by nothing more than the whisper of a promise. Crouched on the lip of the structure, one hand against the bronze plaque for balance, the boy poked Navin with a skinny finger. When he didn't move, Sanjay the urchin reached for the jewelled box laying in Navin's lap.

A flash of lightning and a clap of thunder cut off the screams of the child, with silence following. The boy had vanished with the betel box. Only Navin's body remained under the angled southern equatorial face.

THE WORKSHOP

*T*he noise in the workshop was diabolical, filled with the relentless stamping of dies, the clanking of voices, over and over, as if the earth itself shuddered with every drop of the dozens of die stamps lined up against the red brick wall.

Sanjay was in a magical world. His mouth was dry and his head full of cotton and even the sound of his own breathing was foreign to his ears. And it was freezing, his body bound by a coldness he'd never known.

Tucked under a wooden workbench, Sanjay caught glimpses of white-coated men, business on their white faces, clutching pieces of silverware. None of them looked amenable to an urchin hiding in their workshop. He clutched his betel box tighter to his chest. If any of them found him, they'd be sure to accuse him of stealing the intricate silver box — which was the truth. But he hadn't stolen it from anyone here, in this other-worldly place he didn't recognise.

In Sanjay's short, short life, he'd never once left the confines of Jaipur. He'd ranged far and wide through the alleyways and back passages of homes who never knew he'd been deep inside them, stealing tiny trinkets no one ever missed. But he had never seen

5

anywhere where the people were all dipped in a lime wash—the colour flushed from their cheeks and bleached from their hair.

With eyes wider than saucers, he shrank deeper into the shadows, his tattered clothing no defence against the bitter English winter. He could see the red heat of the furnaces in the bowels of the workshop but their intensity didn't penetrate this far. A clap of thunder sounded above the building, causing the men at the workbenches to shrink from the windows. Lightning followed, splitting the sky the way a hot knife slices through butter. The rain outside sucking the soul from anyone foolish enough to venture out.

And still no one noticed the boy shivering beneath the workbench.

Only a second ago, Sanjay had been wiping sweat from his brow in the shadow of the world's largest sundial in Jaipur, India, and now... he wasn't sure where he was.

A horn sounded, like the hunting horn the Maharaja's court used. He'd seen them set off, a huge procession of *mahouts*, and riflemen, and minor royals armed with *katars* they didn't know how to use, carrying them as decorative pieces, passed down through the generations. And like those hunting parties he'd watched from afar, when the horn sounded, the workmen downed their tools and shrugged off their white coats, hanging them on a tidy line of hooks. A relative silence descended, allowing the wash of feminine voices to filter through to Sanjay's hiding place. The swish of long skirts filtered past him, as black leather-booted women followed the men from the workshop, abandoning their places by the frosted windows, each pulling gloves on over frozen fingers, tired from hours of work hunched over their scarred wooden benches.

The sharp angles of the silver betel box dug into Sanjay's exposed ribcage, but he hugged his treasure closer to his skinny frame. As the rooms emptied, dusk settled over the city. Paul de Lamiere's workshop was an eerie place after dark, the long rope pulleys swaying in unseen breezes, the heavy dies forming grotesque shapes where they lay, and the partially completed work took on animal forms with sinuous tendrils stretching towards Sanjay.

Sanjay's stomach growled, but experience said he'd survive a bit longer before he needed to eat. The hunger in his belly didn't bother him—he'd been hungry before, and would be again. Food could wait, hiding was more important because you couldn't eat if you were dead. At least he was inside and dry. The weather outside assailed the building like an army holding siege to a great fort. The rain on the roof had turned from pregnant droplets to icy hail. He'd controlled his own destiny for longer than he remembered. Left to fend for himself by an overwhelmed mother and an absent father, Sanjay had no problem caring for himself and scavenging, or stealing to survive. He also knew when it was best to scarper before they found him where he shouldn't be.

Other than the howling storm outside, which seemed to have followed him from India, the building was silent, yet still he waited, and waited. His mind filled with a thousand different thoughts and imaginations, but his innate sense of self preservation kept him alert, and when he was sure he was alone, he slipped out of his hidey-hole, his freezing body shaking from the cramped position he'd adopted. Sanjay pulled one of the white coats off its hook and wrapped himself up, the thick cotton a blanket of wool on his bare skin.

Sanjay wandered around the silversmith's workshop, the too-long coat dragged behind him, collecting tiny slivers of silver which lay in the cracks between the wooden floorboards, opening drawers and lifting lids, each movement as quiet as the blooming of a rose. The moonlight struggled to penetrate the frosted glass in the windows, making even the mundane piecework look elegant, but nothing he saw was as spectacular as a pair of giant candelabra posed on a polished desk, their monstrous arms reaching towards the heavens.

Still listening for potential threats, Sanjay stepped closer to peer at the shell and rock motifs common to the Rococo style. As he considered the practicalities of spiriting one away to sell, he ran a finger over the base of the nearest candelabra. A flash of lightning struck and lit the entire room at the same second he touched the candelabra, at the precise moment the polished silver absorbed a burst of pure energy from Sanjay's fingertip.

The exchange of energy so fleeting, that Sanjay was oblivious to the event. He was *not* oblivious to the monster of a man illuminated by the lightning flash, a man standing in the doorway, a white coat hanging in his hands.

The lightning vanished, and the giant lurched towards him, yelling in an unintelligible language.

Sanjay had only the barest of notions of the layout of the room, but ducked sideways away from the monster, the candelabra forgotten, his immediate concern being his own safety.

The man's accented words alien to Sanjay, who had no chance of recognising French any more than he did Arabic or Mandarin.

Then lightning flashed again, and for the briefest of moments the pair stared at each other, the man freezing in the electric light as he caught sight of the box jammed under Sanjay's arm. The light reflecting off the intricate golden leaves on the sides of the betel box, held the Frenchman in a trance, before the light faded to black, allowing Sanjay the smallest fraction of a second to run past the workman and through the doorway.

Sanjay ducked and weaved through the building seeking a way out. The silversmith grabbed the boy and Sanjay stumbled, slicing his face on the corner of a desk. Screaming in pain he dropped his enchanted box, clutching at the flap of skin. The hulking man hollered for help as he loomed closer, so Sanjay abandoned his treasure and ran for his life. Although petrified that the lightning would strike him the same way it had Navin at the observatory, Sanjay fancied his chances against the elements better than he did against the giant. So he ran, and ran, and ran. Away from the angry man, away from the building stuffed full of silver. He raced through the empty muddied streets until he found the half finished carcass of a new build, barely watertight and uninhabited except for the rats which sought their own shelter from the rain. Sanjay scuttled into a dark corner, panting and shivering, his face throbbing, the blood running freely down his face. And despite, or maybe because of, his ordeal he fell asleep, his dreams no more miraculous than the nightmare he was living through now.

THE SILVERSMITH

'*D*on't know how he got in, but he's scarpered now. Never seen him in my life, some urchin I'd wager,' said Arthur the silversmith to his supervisor the next morning, as he relayed the adventures of the night.

'And there's nothing missing?'

'Nought I could see.'

The men wandered through the labyrinthine rooms of the converted house, poking into long-forgotten corners and behind giant pieces of decaying furniture, devoured by hungry beetles. A haze of dust danced in the weak light coming from the covered lanterns the men carried.

'Perchance, was he sheltering from the storm?' the supervisor suggested, a kinder soul than the silversmith.

Arthur shook his head, his mind flicking back to the box he'd hidden in the chimney cavity of an unused room, waiting for him until he had a moment of solitude to examine it. *A masterful piece* had been his only thought when he'd rescued it from the floor last night. A stroke of luck, and one he wasn't going to share with his employer or colleagues.

'Then put it from your mind, Arthur, nothing is missing. Let's get back to those candelabra. The church is picking them up today and they need a final polish.'

Two hours later, Arthur threw his polishing cloth down and stretched his arms above his head. The more he'd polished the huge pair of candelabra, the more resentment gnawed at him, eating him up from the inside. His initials weren't around the edge of the candelabra, nor was it his name they'd praise for the fine workmanship. Oh no, it was the Frenchman who'd get all the glory, like usual. Arthur had a fair level of skill and an eye for detail, but the workshop wasn't his — he was only a tool of the famous Paul de Lamiere. de Lamiere was prolific in his output, but only because of people like Arthur doing the donkey work for him, and Arthur was over it. He'd toyed with incorporating his own moniker somewhere within the intricate design, but lost his nerve. That he hadn't made the candelabra wasn't relevant; he'd worked on them, for weeks. They all had. If only he had enough money to start his own workshop. His mind drifted back to the silver box, wrapped in a white coat, and stuffed up the chimney in the other room. They didn't bother heating the rooms no one worked in, and no one lived here now that de Lamiere lived in a fancy home in a better part of town, a place awash with servants doing everything for him, just like they all did here.

Somewhere a bell rang, the clergy come to pick up their candlesticks. Arthur retrieved his cloth and buffed an imperceptible mark from a Rococo arm. One candlestick would set him up for life, several lives. As the voice of de Lamiere came closer, Arthur made himself scare — his sort didn't mix with the clientele. His sort worked behind the scenes, like little church mice, but not for much longer; he planned to return home to Salisbury. He'd sell the box where people there would pay good money for it. And then he'd set up a workshop to rival de Lamiere. He'd passed his apprenticeship and had his Guild membership; he was only lacking the funds. Arthur's pride ran away on him as he considered his future good fortune, and the afternoon passed in a fuzzy haze of daydreams and fantasy. He never gave a thought to the boy; the owner of the valuable box.

There were no opportunities to rescue the box that evening. They were celebrating the award of a large order for a distinguished client — twelve sterling dinner plates with *gadrooned* edges, and a dozen matching salad plates, second course dishes and tureens, and sundry other items, for an Earl no less. As a group, they were off to celebrate the commission, so Arthur shelved his plans for the night. There'd be another night. Never one to miss an opportunity to avoid time at the workbench, he traipsed out behind his colleagues, leaving the heavy door to shut behind him.

Arthur expected someone else to lock the door which is why he didn't check it. They had never given him a key despite lesser men than him having one, which irked him. All his life he was a moment too late, a fraction too slow, the second choice. They needed to give him a chance to prove himself, and how could he if they refused to trust him with keys to the building? He bumbled along behind, hands deep in his pockets, protecting them against the bitter chill of the afternoon. He swore that Salisbury never got this cold. London was always frigid, with a fog you couldn't breathe through. It was like wading through stew, and tonight was no different. The sun hadn't even set yet fog nipped at his ankles and wormed its way through the heavy fabric of his trousers.

'Oi, wait up,' he called to the others as they rounded a corner, disappearing from sight, the gloom muting their convivial laughter, dulling their footsteps.

Arthur broke into a trot, trying to catch up with them. He hadn't bothered listening to which pub they were going to for their celebrations, and he didn't want to be the idiot turning up at the wrong one.

'Oi!' he called out again.

Running round the corner, Arthur caught his foot on a loose cobble, sending him sprawling to the ground, catching his chin on a curb stone.

The fog muted most things, but not the crack of Arthur's jaw breaking as it connected with the cut stone. He lay there, in the gutter still wet from the downpour the night before, the thick grey mist masking his existence. He could barely groan through the pain.

Broken, and dislocated, it would be a long time before he'd be able to use his teeth to tear the meat from a lamb chop.

Arthur struggled onto his elbows and tried calling out, the effort leaving him woozy. *Surely* someone would come looking for him? He probed his teeth with his tongue. At least he had lost none of those. A dark depression settled over him as he imagined the weeks ahead of him where he'd only be able to eat watery soup or stew. If his colleagues had only waited for him, this wouldn't have happened. The blame was on their shoulders.

Although slipping into the clutches of shock, Arthur heard the staccato clip-clop of hooves as a wealthy trader made his way along the fog-encrusted street towards his own home not ten doors up from where Arthur lay. The trader had enough trouble controlling a horse spooked by the mist, to identify that the pile of rags on the ground was a man. The horse did though and reared up in fright as Arthur raised his mangled hand to warn the rider.

And what goes up must come down, and thus the horses fine hooves destroyed the remaining shape of Arthur's jaw, caving in his skull. His dreams of owning a workshop disintegrating on the filthy cobblestones of the London street. His hopes of personal glory splashed up the young legs of a stallion and over the boots of his rider, who was oblivious to what had happened beneath his beast.

Even in death, Arthur missed out on his moment of fame. For although he made it into the paper, it was only as a footnote.

Man found dead on the road, struck by a horse. Identity unknown.

LONDON

THE GIRLFRIEND

'*B*ryce?' called the high-pitched American voice, the one belonging to Melissa Crester.

Bryce Sinclair paused at the threshold, both feet on the old black and orange tiles of *The Old Curiosity Shop's* entrance.

'Yes?'

'I'm tired, I don't want to go into a junk shop.'

'I won't be long. Just wait here,' Sinclair replied, his hand tightening on the door handle.

'Bryce, I'm serious. If you go in there, I won't be here when you come back,' Melissa said, pulling a cellphone from her designer handbag, tapping away at the screen. 'I'm booking an Uber now,' she added.

Sinclair backed out of the shop, like a puppy dog called to heel. He tried to ignore the syrupy smile on her face.

'Excellent choice. We'll go to my room, drop these bags, freshen up, if you know what I mean,' Melissa said, winking. She may have been able to move her eyelids but the rest of her face was as immobile as Stonehenge. 'Then we'll head over to the Savoy for cocktails and dinner. Yes?'

Sinclair nodded, his rugged scowl exciting her more than it should.

Treat 'em mean and keep 'em keen. That was her motto. Once she returned to America, he'd be a thing of the past. She never took her playthings home, they were purely holiday entertainment.

After another satisfactory tumble, Sinclair lay ensconced in the Egyptian cotton sheets and considered his options. Carry on with Melissa, enjoying her largesse, and spending his nights in a luxury he'd never imagined existed, or ditch her and continue tracking down that bitch Sarah Bell, or Sarah Lester as he now knew her. He should've ignored the frozen-faced cow when she threatened to leave him outside of *The Old Curiosity Shop.* So what if the place was a junk shop, it was where he was going to find Sarah. And after that he'd wring her skinny white neck and make her tell him how all this was possible. How he'd been in Bruce Bay in New Zealand one minute, a sack of silverware slung over his neck and the next minute, he was in London, where the shops glowed with sunlight every hour of the day. Where women dressed like prostitutes and no one batted an eye. And he hadn't seen a single horse, only carriages with engines leaching out fumes, filling every street. And the noise. There was music everywhere, and honking, and shouting, and thousands of people of a dozen different colours, speaking a hundred languages.

And here he was, Bryce Sinclair, who hadn't made it to school once since he was ten. Arrested more times than he cared to remember, but he had his own boat, a son, and a satisfactory life. No, that wasn't true. He couldn't claim satisfaction, but it was a comfortable life, one which suited him, or so he thought. He'd supplemented his income in a variety of ways, none of them legal, but it made things interesting. But once he laid his hands on Sarah Lester, and found out her magic, he would live this way forever, in luxury. He quite fancied staying in hotels and ordering whatever he desired whenever he liked. He ran his eye down the room service menu. With half of it in a foreign tongue, he couldn't decipher it. What the hell was *quinoa?* Or *dragon fruit?*

'Ready, lazy bones?' asked Melissa, resplendent in another gown too far north from her knees for comfort, and too far south from her neck to be decorous.

Despite Sinclair's proclivities between the sheets, he felt a flush creep up his cheeks. Being in public with a woman dressed like this didn't seem right, regardless of which century he was in. What she wore in bed didn't matter, but if she was going out with him, he didn't want her dressed like a brazen hussy.

After some quick thinking, he replied 'Didn't you already wear that?'

Puzzlement danced across her frozen features, before she shrugged and returned to the dressing room. Through the gap in the door he watched her throw the sparkly number to the floor. Good.

Sinclair stretched and got up to retrieve his trousers and shirt. They'd do.

'You ready?' he called out, his macho swagger back online. His smile widened as he took in the long dress she'd chosen to wear instead.

'That's better,' he said.

'This is Chanel, that other one was by Mizrahi.'

Her answer was as confusing to Sinclair as the menu had been.

Drinking cocktails at the Savoy were not the same as knocking back a pint at the pub in Bruce Bay. Sinclair suspected everyone knew he was an imposter, from the wait staff to the other diners. The only one oblivious to his comfort was Melissa, who'd hooked up with some friends upon their arrival at the hotel bar, and was guffawing loudly about the stupidity of the English currency and a comparison of the prices of the antiquities they'd purchased this season. Sinclair's collar barely restraining his belligerence as he swallowed his third shot of some fancy whisky she'd ordered him. He hadn't even ordered his own drinks.

Sinclair's gaze wandered across the crowd. Every single one of them dressed in outfits they'd never survive in back in his day. The shoes the women wore were lethal weapons, and the men just as perfumed. He couldn't stomach it anymore and made a mumbled excuse to leave the room. He was quite sure Melissa barely noticed him leaving, too tied up with her fancy friends discussing who the best dealer was selling Syrian artefacts — the hottest stuff in the market right now. Sinclair shook his head and stumbled from the bar, the doorman rushing to hold open the door lest he mar the polished brass with his meaty paws.

Outside was no better — the perfume replaced with car fumes and something else. Seeping odours of decades of pollution, absorbed by what little of the earth remained exposed in the heart of London, and as much a part of the fabric of every brick and every cobble in the city. The stench of the streets matching the dark stain of Sinclair's soul.

He knew he could carry on enjoying everything Melissa had given him with a twist of his hands around her neck. He'd watched her hand over a small card when she paid for something, and it hadn't taken long for him to realise he required one of those. His unusual gallantry had seen his cash reserves depleted more than he liked to think about and he needed to fix that before he gave up the golden goose holding court inside — he just couldn't get over how her face was incapable of movement. It was fun, but he had pressing issues to settle, and no bit of skirt would get in his way.

'Are you all right, sir?' asked the concierge, dispatched outside to check on the rough looking man loitering in front of the Savoy.

Sinclair glanced at the man, in his smart uniform and his polished shoes. He wouldn't have looked out of place if he'd come straight from the 1860s. Sinclair had never stepped foot in a place like this, but imagined the concierge looked exactly like a concierge back in the day.

'How long's this place been here?' Sinclair asked.

'This is the original site of the Savoy Palace, built in 1263. The site has been through several iterations, and the buildings have no resemblance to any of the initial structures. The only remaining historical structure is the Savoy Chapel, completed in 1512—'

'I didn't ask for a history lesson, I just wanted to know how long the hotel had been around,' Sinclair interrupted.

'1889,' said the concierge, checking behind him to ensure other staff were close enough in case he had need of them.

'Good, I might move here for a while. Depends what my lady friend wants to do though. It doesn't stink of shit like where I come from.' And with that Sinclair wheeled back inside the building to rejoin Melissa. And this time he'd order what *he* wanted to drink.

THE SHOP

*W*hen Sarah Lester stepped from her staircase into the eclectic gathering of people in her antique shop, her appearance was like the application of a defibrillator to the heart — shocking the frozen scene into life and nothing would ever be the same again.

Every person in the room began at once, the chorus of comments overwhelming the cramped space.

'Miss Lester?'

'Where have you been?'

'Sarah, when did you—'

'We've been waiting to interview you.'

'My statue—'

'I can explain,' Sarah said.

'Best to do that at the station,' Inspector Fujimoto replied, trying to diffuse the peculiar situation. 'I'm Inspector Fujimoto, and we've got some questions for you. If you'd be so kind to come with us to the station?'

With no way out, Sarah nodded. 'I'll get my things,' she said.

'No, no, no!' Shalfoon shouted, his face flushed. 'What about my statue? I need my statue.'

'I thought you said the statue belonged to the church? That you were reclaiming it *for* the church,' Fujimoto said, his eyebrows disappearing into his thinning hairline.

'Yes, yes, of course it belongs to the church. Please, it's very simple, they just need to hand it over. You have the required paperwork. I'll take the statue and leave it to you to sort out this... thief.'

'What?' Sarah said.

'Your accusations are without merit,' Brooke said, stepping out of the shadows.

'No one is taking anything,' Fujimoto said, dampening the tension in the tiny shop. 'Mr Shalfoon, you aren't helping things by remaining here.'

'But my statue—'

'No one is taking any statues today, apart from us as evidence of... of what I'm not sure yet. But that's what the law does, we analyse the evidence without jumping to conclusions,' Fujimoto interrupted.

Shalfoon stared at Fujimoto, mouth opening agape, his face the colour of fire.

'I am a bishop, a representative of the Archbishop of Canterbury, and through him, God. Are you saying that my words are not evidence enough?'

'We all know how good the church's word is,' Fiona muttered under her breath.

Fujimoto shot her a filthy look. 'We are aware of who you are *Bishop* Shalfoon, but now is an appropriate time for you to take your leave. We will be in touch,' Fujimoto said, his arms crossed.

Bishop Shalfoon looked ready to explode, but managed, through the grace of God, to rein in his anger. Instead he let his silence speak for him before striding from the shop leaving only a hint of expensive aftershave behind.

Nicole Pilcher broke the mood by packing away the paper she'd prepared for wrapping the statue.

'I'll still need that statue, Miss Pilcher,' Fujimoto said, running his hands through his hair. 'Miss Lester,' he sighed, 'I have an exorbitant number of questions for you, so the sooner you're ready, the faster we can get this over with.'

'I will come with you,' Brooke said.

'No, you won't,' Sarah said. 'Nicole, this is my friend Warren Brooke, and I know this puts you on the spot but can you look after him?' Sarah asked, her eyes pleading with Brooke to understand.

'Sure, but there's an auction—'

'I do not need looking after, I will come too,' Brooke said, grabbing Sarah's hand.

'You don't understand. I need you to stay here,' she pleaded.

'No, I need to be by your side, to protect you.'

'Sorry folks, but it's just Miss Lester who's coming to the station with us,' Fujimoto interrupted, checking the battered watch on his wrist.

'I'm ready, let's go,' Sarah said, pushing past Fujimoto and ignoring the anger on Brooke's face.

Flanked by Fiona Duodu and Inspector Fujimoto, Sarah Lester walked out of *The Old Curiosity Shop*, hands in her pockets, resisting the urge to run back into Brooke's arms. Fiona opened the door to the unmarked police car, slamming it shut after Sarah slipped into the plastic-coated back seat. Fiona and Fujimoto climbed in the front, and the car pulled away from the curb.

Swirling around in Sarah's head was the utter fear that Brooke too may disappear. It burrowed its way deep into her, gnawing at her until she shook uncontrollably and tears ran down her face.

Fujimoto glanced in his mirror.

'It's only questioning, you aren't under arrest,' he said, placating the sobbing woman in his car.

'Not yet, anyway,' Fiona said, calmly jotting notes into her hardcover notebook.

'Not helpful, Fiona,' Fuji snapped back.

∾

With the police gone, Nicole stood behind the counter fiddling with the statue which, unbelievably, they'd forgotten to take, and examined the barefoot man in front of her — his vintage uniform trousers and shirt not as out of place as they would have been in most other shops. Pulling her eyes from the man she was babysitting, she addressed the two other people standing in the aisle.

'How can I help?'

'We're here about the Roman statue online—' Ryan Francis began, until Nicole's laughing shamed him into silence.

'Join the queue,' Nicole said. 'This little guy isn't going anywhere, other than back to where I found him. They're causing far too many problems.'

'They?' asked Gemma Dance, the tiny battle-axe from the Art Loss Register.

Gemma was gripping Ryan's arm so hard, he winced as he prised her talons from his arm.

'Are there more like this one? More Roman statues?'

'I think this is a conversation I should have with the police sorry, not you,' Nicole said, placing the statue on the shelf behind her, tucking it between a bag of broken ivory chess pieces, stained red, and a carton of damaged mother-of-pearl card cases, potential replacement fragments rattling around in the bottom — a puzzle of a thousand shattered shards.

Gemma's face turned white. 'You can't just leave it there,' she protested.

'I can, and I am. And now I need to ask you both to leave. The shop won't be open today, for obvious reasons. I'll lock up behind you.'

Nicole stood firm, refusing to engage when Gemma tried arguing with her.

'The lady asked you to go,' Brooke said, the officer in his voice unmistakable.

'Come on, Gem. We'll find out direct from the police. You're flogging a dead Roman here,' Ryan said.

Gemma sniffed, facing off against Nicole's frank stare. It wasn't that she wanted the insufferable bishop to have the Roman statue, it was more that she couldn't stomach the idea that she'd been so close to finalising a case, mere feet away from unravelling a mystery. Success was so close, that walking away felt like defeat. And Gemma Dance hated that feeling more than anything.

'Fine, whatever,' Gemma tossed out as she sailed from the shop.

'Sorry, she gets…'

'Obsessive?' Nicole offered.

'That works,' Ryan replied. 'Here's my card, if you… well, if you want to tell us anything about the statues.'

'*Statue*,' Nicole corrected.

'Right, well thanks,' said Ryan, before following Gemma's disappearing act, leaving only Brooke and Nicole in the shop, and an uneasy silence.

'Do you want a coffee?' Nicole asked.

Brooke stared at Nicole. 'They've taken Sarah away and you offer me coffee?'

Nicole shrugged, aimlessly rearranging stock, moving a heavy brass stag ornament to a more prominent position.

'Why is this statue so important?'

'I've got no idea,' Nicole replied.

'Seems I have plenty of time, tell me what you know about it and maybe we can work it out,' Brooke said, his tone more conciliatory.

Nicole sighed. 'Lock the door and I'll make us a coffee, although we might need something stronger than that.'

With the door locked, and two steaming mugs on the counter, Nicole filled in the gaps as best she could. The statue's origins as much a mystery to her as they were to Sarah, and Nicole suspected that even Sarah's father — Albert Lester, wouldn't have known the true sources of the box of statues in his basement.

'Albert Lester?' Brooke asked.

'Sarah's father, he's been missing for years though. Her mother too but I can't remember her name. Anna or Isabelle? No, that's not right, it's Annabel. A huge mystery but I presume Sarah has told you all about that?'

Brooke nodded, Albert's name echoing around in his mind. Albert Lester, the Viceroy's chief advisor, his right-hand man, with no family and no past. The mysterious man who lived on the periphery of the army, always there, quietly in the Viceroy's ear with an omniscient opinion on the best course of action. Advice so logical, so correct, it was as if he knew what parliament would decree before the orders ever made it to India. Albert Lester was Sarah's father? The idea was too fantastical, but every fantasy has a basis in fact, and yet here he was in a time not of his own. He hadn't just crossed an ocean, he'd travelled through time and reality fell like dominos as every strange utterance, every peculiar word, all Albert and Sarah's odd mannerisms suddenly made sense.

'Albert Lester?' he asked again.

Nicole reached behind her and pulled a framed newspaper article from the shelf where she'd filed it during one of her innumerable tidy-ups. The headline heralded the up-and-coming young *Steptoe*, and highlighted the changing tastes of 1970s England, and detailed some of Albert Lester's more interesting antiques — a mounted shark jaw and a narwhal tusk — the unicorn of the sea. A taxidermy kiwi from New Zealand, complete with an absurdly large egg, and a pair of solid sterling silver stirrups, clearly made as a folly for the original owner. The man photographed for the article was young, younger than Brooke was now, and showed a face full of excitement for the future, a face identical to that of Albert Lester, confidant of the Viceroy of India.

THE AUCTION

'Next up, three wooden tea chests full of fabric swatches and late nineteenth century fashion sketches. Removed from the Crawford Market in Mumbai before its recent restoration, we are honoured to present this unique glimpse into Mumbai's past. Sadly, we've lost the name of the designer to time, but most of the sketches are in excellent condition making them a valuable resource for any costume designers or historical researchers. We start the bidding at three hundred pounds. Do we have any advances on three hundred pounds?'

And so the bidding carried on, hands raised, paddles lifting a fraction of an inch, fingers tapped, and the auctioneer magically tracking the various bidder's unique signals, whilst also incorporating bids from the telephone and over the internet. A good auctioneer is like the conductor of an orchestra, using an extraordinary skill set to keep the whole performance from descending into a toneless disaster. The hammer fell a smudge over eight thousand pounds, plus the buyer and seller's premium. A price far exceeding the guide of one thousand pounds in the auction catalogue.

There were no surprises that the successful bidder was the venerable Victoria and Albert Museum, although the American museums had done their best to buy the treasure trove of fashion history.

'And next up is a *carte de visite* photograph album, and assorted ephemera, featuring hereto-unknown images of the Viceroy of India, his officers and unnamed associates and correspondence from the same period. There has been considerable interest in this item, also unearthed in the basement of *Crawford Market* at the time of their recent restoration work, and entrusted to us to auction. Do I have any starting bids?... Yes, sir, two hundred pounds? I'll take your bid. Do I have a... three hundred pounds, thank you, madam. Four hundred, do I have... three hundred and twenty pounds, yes Madam, I will accept your bid. These funds will go towards the upkeep of the historic *Crawford Market* in Mumbai, established by Arthur Crawford, the Municipal Commissioner of Bombay, now Mumbai, in 1868, although these photographs predate that by eight or so years. It will probably always be a mystery how they ended up in his basement. Do I hear any advances on three hundred and twenty pounds? Going once, twice... the bid is with you, madam, paddle number 772... and a new bidder. Yes, madam, three hundred and fifty pounds, thank you. Any advances on three hundred and fifty pounds?'

The previous bidder shook her head as the auctioneer tried his best to cajole more profit from the crowd.

'Sold, for three hundred and fifty pounds to paddle number 405. Thank you, madam.'

Nicole Pilcher, the holder of paddle number 772, made a small notation in her catalogue before turning the page to await the next lot she was interested in — a collection of cabinet cards from a Victorian photographer in Liverpool.

She hoped that these two lots would swell her collection at *The Old Curiosity Shop*, keeping her regular collectors sated for a few weeks. It was disappointing to lose the first lot, but even at three hundred and twenty pounds she'd exceeded her own budget, so couldn't stretch the extra thirty quid. It was so hard finding good stock these days, that it was a miracle she'd caught wind of these lots. There'd been an increase of interest in old cabinet cards, although most people mixed up cabinet cards and *cartes de visite*, it didn't worry her too much, there was money in both of them, which was the point.

Meanwhile, the owner of paddle number 405, Eliza Broadbent, was fanning herself with an antique ivory and silk fan, overjoyed with her purchase. The price she'd paid was of no concern. Bidding was easy when the money wasn't your own.

Despite Sarah expecting Nicole to babysit him, Brooke had refused to attend the auction with Nicole, preferring instead to wait outside where he cut a peculiar figure, dressed in his uniform, leaning against the brick building watching the modern world pass.

The world had changed. It wasn't the roaring vehicles belching black smoke, or the flashing street lights and shop windows lit up like the sun that surprised him the most. It was the way the people carried themselves in their revealing clothing and public displays of affection. But the casualness of life astonished him the most. The future world was one of bare legs and electrical light, of an abundance of vehicles and almost a complete absence of joyful life on the streets.

During the two hours of the auction, Brooke decided he couldn't bear to live a life in this time. Pacing outside the auction house, he deliberated on the best way to tell Sarah. He assumed she'd be happy to leave, to be back with her father, safe. They could marry and live their lives together away from this madness.

By the time Nicole found him outside, he'd almost worn a path he'd spent so much time pacing, mulling over his decision.

'We need to get back,' he said.

'Don't you want something to eat first, I'm starving?'

'Sarah will have returned, we should go back.'

Nicole checked her watch. 'There's no guarantee she's back yet. I'll ring the shop and check.' She dialled the shop phone hanging on until the answerphone kicked in. 'She's not back yet.'

'There must be something wrong. Try again,' Brooke ordered.

Nicole dialled again. No one answered. 'We'll go for a cup of tea and something to eat. No doubt she'll be back then. Come on.'

Brooke trailed after Nicole, his vintage uniform drawing second glances from everyone they passed but Brooke didn't notice. Nicole sat him at a table in the nearest cafe and went to order their drinks. Seated at the table, he tapped his foot against the floor, and drummed his fingers on the table top. He wanted to return to Sarah. Although he knew she was with the police, he felt uncomfortable, unable to shake the feeling that something was coming to threaten them.

'They're bringing it over,' Nicole announced, slipping into her chair with a contented sigh. 'Just bought the most amazing collection of photos from India at the auction. It'll be fascinating to go through them. I only had the chance to look at the top ones,' she said. 'Are you okay?'

'There's something wrong with Miss Lester. We should return,' Brooke said standing.

Nicole sighed. Babysitting a grown man was not what she'd been expecting to do today. 'We'll go straight back after our tea. Can you sit down, everyone is staring.'

Brooke lowered himself back into his seat, his jaw set firm against Nicole's words.

Nicole stared at Brooke, 'Your uniform?'

'Excuse me?'

'The uniform you're wearing, where's it from?'

Brooke checked himself. 'My uniform is that of my unit. Why?'

Nicole had her auction programme open to the centre illustrated page, and her finger hovered above the picture of the lot she'd just won. She pushed the glossy brochure towards Brooke. 'It's the same as the one in these pictures, isn't it?'

Brooke took the book from Nicole, his heart beating faster. He'd accepted he was in a time not of his own; that he was in the future, but now he held in his hands a direct link to his past — a photograph of the Viceroy together with Albert Lester, Captain James Doulton, and standing to the left of the trio in partial shadow a familiar face, his own.

'Do you have this photograph with you?'

'I can pick it up tomorrow, with the rest of the lot. There are more photos in the album and knowing more about the uniforms would help sell them.'

Brooke closed the auction catalogue and handed it back. 'I can't help you,' he said. 'Can we go now?' He needed to get back to India, his India, with Sarah.

Nicole sipped her drink, the look on her face discouraging any further comment from Brooke. He toyed with his own cup, his unease rising with every minute they remained in the cafe, and when Nicole finished her tea, he leapt to his feet.

'Come on then,' Nicole said.

THE INTERVIEW

'offee?' Inspector Fujimoto asked Sarah Lester.

'Please.'

'Fiona, can you get the coffee?'

'So much for gender equality,' Fiona muttered, scraping back her chair and stalking from the interview room.

'She does that a lot, doesn't she?' Sarah commented.

'You get used to it and most of the time she means no harm,' Fujimoto replied. 'We'll wait till she gets back. Are you sure you don't want a lawyer with you?'

'Can't think why I'd need one,' Sarah said.

With coffee in hand, Fujimoto flicked the switch on the decades-old video interview equipment, fiddled with the dials and flinched when a screeching alarm sounded.

'Sorry, it's old and temperamental. We're waiting for a new machine. Are you ready?'

Sarah nodded, and the interview began.

As the interrogation progressed, it was clear the various threads of the investigation were far from interwoven.

'We need to return to your answer regarding your whereabouts for the past several months. You said you were in India?'

'That's right.'

'There is no record of you having left England, by plane, boat or train, nor of you returning.'

Sarah shrugged. So far she'd told the truth, not the whole truth, but enough to sustain her inquisitors.

'We're not getting everything from you, Miss Lester. Which can only mean that you are hiding something from us, so I'll ask again, do you want a lawyer here with you in this interview?'

'Look, I'm fine. We returned from India last night and I'm tired and hungry and I know nothing about the statue. My father was a hoarder who loved buying things. He loved selling things too, but he couldn't help himself — if there was a bargain, he'd buy it and store it away for a rainy day. You know more than I do. I haven't even talked to Nicole about the shop, or anything. It's not my fault your system hasn't recorded my travel.'

Fujimoto looked at Fiona scribbling in her notebook. They would make a complete transcript of the interview for the file, but it was Fiona's nature to record a whole interview in her peculiar shorthand. She often picked up on subtleties a written transcript missed.

'Fiona? Any further questions?'

Fiona looked up in mock surprise — they had their interview technique refined to a fine art.

'I have a couple,' she said, flicking back through her notes. 'The first one is about the *"we"*?'

'Pardon?' Sarah asked, looking to Fujimoto for clarification.

'You said, *"We only got back from India"* and I was wondering who *"we"* was?'

'Warren Brooke.'

Fiona scrawled in the margins, underlining the name twice. 'And your relationship with Warren Brooke?'

'What does that have to do with the *katar* or the statue?'

'It's not just the statue, Miss Lester. Someone murdered a man with your knife.'

'*Katar.*'

'A weapon you sent to auction. Another item whose ownership is in question, like the statue...'

Sarah toyed with the gold bangle on her wrist, a twenty-first present from her father. She twisted it round and round her wrist. It wasn't the most expensive piece of jewellery she owned, not by a long shot, but it was reassuringly solid and unbroken around her wrist. She'd always considered it symbolic of her relationship with her father. A father who hadn't wanted her to stay and who didn't want to come home.

Crushed by the realisation that he loved history more than her, she tugged the bangle off, leaving it spinning on the scarred table between her and the police officers. It spun loudly until it felt flat against the table.

Fiona sighed, turning the page in her notebook and trying again, 'And Patricia Bolton?' she asked, underlining more words in the hardcover book.

'What about Patricia?'

'Where is she?'

Sarah stumbled over her reply. Should she tell them that she'd left Patricia in 1860s India, cosseted in taffeta and silk? The truth was usually the best answer. 'She's in India,' Sarah said, spinning the bangle with a finger.

'India?'

'Yes.'

'Is that where you both fled after murdering the guard at the Foundling Museum?' Fiona asked, an expectant grin on her face as she delivered the question.

'Excuse me?'

'You heard me. The murdered night guard, Ravi Narayan, an aspiring actor, a husband and a cat owner. Bludgeoned to death. You and Miss Bolton were the only ones on the CCTV.'

'Do you want to reconsider your lawyer?' Fujimoto asked.

'We murdered no one. He helped carry in the boxes and then he went back to his office, or to do his rounds. Trish and I unpacked things and then we unrolled the tiger-skin rug.' Sarah paused. 'And I don't remember what happened after that.'

'Come on. Do you really expect us to believe that?' Fiona snapped.

'I don't know what else to tell you. Trish is in India. I came back with Major Brooke, and I've got no idea what happened while I was away.'

Fiona started to ask another question, but Fujimoto interrupted before she could get the words out, waving her quiet.

'Miss Lester, I'm advising you now to get a lawyer. And we'll recommence this interview once you have representation. This is best for all of us. I'm terminating this interview at 1045 hours,' said Fujimoto, and he flicked a switch, extinguishing the lights on the equipment.

Fiona opened the large cardboard file box on the chair next to her, shoving in the notebooks and folders she'd referenced during the interview.

'Hang on, Fiona,' Fujimoto said. 'Can you pass me those evidence bags?'

Fiona fished out two small see-through bags, and all but flung them at her supervisor.

Sarah's eyes widened. 'Where did you get those?'

'From your apartment, while you were *in India,*' Fiona mumbled, slamming shut the file box.

Fujimoto glared at his counterpart. 'Given its value, I thought it prudent that we looked after it in your absence. Normal people don't usually leave things like large gold nuggets on their bedside tables.'

'You've never met my father then,' Sarah said, taking the bag from Fujimoto's outstretched hand.

'I bet you're going to say your father is in India too,' Fiona quipped.

'Yes,' said Sarah, 'that's exactly where he is.'

The police officers sat together in stunned silence, as Sarah's words sank in.

'Can I go now?' Sarah asked.

'I'll give you a lift,' Fujimoto said, swiping his card to open the door, surreptitiously gesturing to Fiona to keep quiet.

The London traffic made for a slow, silent drive back to *The Old Curiosity Shop*, as Fujimoto mulled over Sarah's revelation about her father, a man missing for the past five or so years. Sarah sat beside him, fiddling with the bangle, the bracelet she'd nearly forgotten in the interview suite — he'd had to remind her to grab it as they left. The evidence bags lay unopened in her lap, which gave him a conversation starter, one which wouldn't get him in any trouble with any legal watchdog.

'How much is the gold nugget worth?' he asked, a much safer question than asking about her father.

'This one? I don't know. A couple of thousand pounds, somewhere around there. It's not mine, I'm meant to be delivering it to the family of a friend who died.'

'In Wales?'

'That's right, how did you know?'

'From the note under the gold nugget. I can help you track down the family if you like?'

'I don't rate your chances, they've probably moved by now,' Sarah laughed, her humour not making its way to her eyes.

'Tracking people is my job,' he joked, trying to establish some rapport with the strange woman next to him.

Sarah shook her head, 'Not this family.'

'Will you let me try?'

'It'll be impossible, but sure.'

'I didn't record the address so I need to get that from you,' he said, satisfied with how things were panning out. There were several ways to skin a cat.

Fujimoto pulled up outside *The Old Curiosity Shop*, noting the *closed* sign facing the disinterested foot traffic walking by. How the shop had survived this long was a mystery to him, and only enforced his belief that, if not Sarah herself, then her father must have been trading in goods with a darker than usual history to them.

Sarah had opened the car door, stepping onto the footpath before he remembered the nugget. He called out, 'The address?'

Without turning back, Sarah replied over her shoulder, 'I'll email you.'

Fishing her keys from her purse, she unlocked the door. After entering the shop, she tore open the exhibit bag and reached in for the scrap of paper with Isaac's mother's address, and disappeared.

THE MUSEUM

*E*liza Broadhead, the head curator of Textiles and Fashion at the V & A Museum, clapped her hands, strands of jet beads jiggling between her ample breasts. It wasn't every day she got to unpack tea chests filled to the brim with sketches and swatches from an era long gone. Her excitement was infectious.

The tea chests had been in the deep freeze in the bowels of the V & A Museum, killing off any nasties still inhabiting the dusty old chests. She hadn't thought it necessary, but the museum had its own rules, and *blah, blah, blah,* she had to obey them. Ridiculous waste of time in her opinion.

She pushed the porter out; she wanted to be alone when she opened the chests. It was as if it was Christmas, albeit a Christmas in a temperature-controlled climate in an office with windows instead of walls. But now she was in her own world, ensconced in the moment, oblivious to the gaggle of onlookers pouring into her little room until one of them spoke.

'Come on, open them. Let's have a look.'

For a woman the size she was, Eliza turned faster than a cheetah changing direction, to find the eager faces of her coworkers, who'd all heard about the V & A's latest acquisition.

'I... what are you doing in here?'

'We want to see them,' Steph Chinneck said, the latest intern in the Textiles department of the museum.

Eliza had no time for interns, they came and went, and knew very little about anything. This one was undoubtedly the same.

'It should only be full-time staff allowed in here,' Eliza muttered, loud enough for Steph to hear, but not quite loud enough to cause a stir amongst the other staff members, who were all quite taken with the Australian intern.

'Hurry, we want to see them. Comms have asked for some photos for the museum blog,' called out another voice.

The large woman harrumphed, turning her back on Steph whilst laboriously donning a clean pair of white cotton gloves. This was her moment to shine, and she didn't need a fly-by-night intern cluttering up her space.

Eliza had cleared her desk, ready for her newest acquisition. And one-by-one, Eliza removed the fragile fabric swatches, cradling the attached sketches so none of them came adrift from their fabric companions.

'Those colours,' whispered Steph.

'Do we know who the designer is yet?' asked someone else.

'No, *we* do not,' replied Eliza, her chest heaving as she tried to control her temper. Idiots surrounded her. How on earth was she meant to have discovered who the designer was when she hadn't even emptied the first chest, let alone the other ones?

The room filled with a chorus of *oohs* and *ah's* as Eliza laid out the contents of the box. Some sketches had faded, and two fabric swatches had disintegrated in Eliza's bejewelled hands, but what remained on the table was a remarkable snapshot of the fashion and style of the British Empire, circa 1870 to 1890, or even 1900.

The crowd shared their own theories about the designer, and took a thousand photographs — both official, and unofficial; the unofficial photos flooding Instagram with a hundred different filtered artistic shots, before the onlookers thinned as almost everyone returned to their work.

Eliza sank into her chair, exhausted by the exertion. She dabbed at her temples with a handkerchief extraordinarily delicate for a woman of her robust size.

'I can help,' Steph offered.

'No, no you can't,' Eliza replied, stuffing the hanky into her cleavage and struggling to her feet.

'Yes, she can,' replied Jasmine from the open door, the younger woman walking over to examine the sketches herself.

Eliza's chest tightened at the sight of the management trollop, sticking her nose in where it shouldn't belong. Why wasn't she out for lunch somewhere posh, wooing the wealthy donors? Wasn't that her job? Instead of tottering around on ridiculous heels as if she knew something about the important work the collections staff did here.

'Steph is here to learn, and who better to learn from than you, Eliza?'

Eliza sniffed, fiddling with the beads at her neck as she considered her reply. She wasn't stupid, she realised Jasmine, for whatever reason, held an influential position with management. It paid to keep abreast of whoever was the flavour of the month at the top, given it changed more often than the prime minister did, and Jasmine, with her overt floral perfume and manicured nails was the current *wunderkind*.

'I just needed a moment to gather my thoughts on how we'll manage this collection, it quite overwhelmed me,' Eliza lied.

Jasmine Gupta nodded, her face unreadable.

'Steph has plenty of experience from her time with the Australian Museum, so she'll be a real asset to you in preparing these for our exhibition during London Fashion Week this year.'

Steph grinned, but Eliza looked distraught.

'That's impossible,' she said.

Jasmine smiled. 'That's why you need Steph's help to ensure they're ready for September,' she said, winking at Steph, and leaving them to it.

'It's not enough time,' Eliza pouted, pouring herself back into her chair and fanning herself with the nearest auction catalogue.

'Where do you want to start?' Jasmine asked.

'Start?' Eliza exclaimed. 'Start? By photographing everything and then entering it into the register. That's where we start. And don't imagine you'll be handling these things, they are terribly fragile. You can do the data entry,' she said. 'That's all I trust interns to do.'

'I'll get my laptop then,' Steph said.

'No, there's no space for your machine. It would probably infect us with a virus, anyway. Use my machine,' Eliza said, opening the in-house system. The enlarged clock icon flashed in the screen's corner. 'Oh my goodness, is that the time? Well past morning tea, and I'm dying for a drink. You set up the camera and tripod — they're in that cupboard, and I'll be back soon,' Eliza said. 'Can't believe the conditions we are expected to work in,' she complained, waddling off to the lunchroom, leaving the incredulous intern alone in the office.

It took Steph a moment to realise that the older woman really had left for morning tea, abandoning her with a table full of unprotected exhibits, artefacts at risk of disintegrating if someone as much as sneezed anywhere near them.

It was all very well telling her to set up the camera, but shouldn't protecting the exhibits be her priority? There was no one around to ask. All she could see through the glass windows were empty offices or heads bent over other fragile pieces of clothing. Steph was certain they'd help her if she asked, but she had half a Bachelor's degree under her belt, and plenty of work experience, so trusted herself to figure it out on her own.

She'd heard rumours about Eliza Broadhead and her wanton spending of the department's budget on items *she* deemed important, rather than on things to complement or enhance the museum's collection. These sketches and fabric samples fell into that category, and with her heart in her mouth, Steph donned her own pair of white gloves, the ones with butterflies embroidered on the back so she never got them confused with anyone else's, and moved the first fragile sheet of paper and attached fabric square over to the microscope and light.

The swatch was a supple brown leather, but already showing signs of red rot, which wasn't really rot despite its name but something which caused the leather to take on a red crumbly appearance. She had to treat it with a consolidator before anything else. Steph looked around the room — it mirrored most other labs she was familiar with, except for the old pattern-making desk Eliza used — not the most sterile of environments to work on.

Steph opened cupboards and drawers until she found the chemicals she needed. First she'd need to separate the sketch from the leather, which meant finding a tool to tease out the rusted staple from the upper left corner.

With a mask over her face, and her cotton gloves replaced with blue latex gloves, and a scalpel in her hand, Steph more resembled a surgeon than a museum studies student. With the staple bagged up and out of the way, and the leather moved to the more sterile lab bench, Steph took a moment to examine the sketch under the powerful magnifying glass. The original artist had a good eye, and the proportions were amazing for a sketch done in freehand and not via a state-of-the-art computer programme.

Steph moved the magnifying glass around the sketch. She didn't know what she was looking for, but found the whole experience surreal, knowing that the last time someone had been this close to this piece of paper, was when the artist prepared the sketch, well over a hundred years ago. She moved the magnifying glass to the bottom right of the picture of a man in uniform and paused. Under his heel were two tiny stylised letters, both in lowercase — *pb*. The artist's initials.

Without hurrying, Steph moved the sketch to one side, leaving it next to the leather sample, and the bagged staple, and selected a second picture. She knew she shouldn't move on without properly dealing with the first sample, but there was a frisson of excitement running through her, she needed to check... And yes, more initials, identical to the first pair, underneath the heel of the right foot, two stylised lowercase letters, "*pb*".

The initials were familiar, and Steph wracked her brain gazing off into the distance as she trawled through her memory. After work experience in countless museums and galleries, three years of full-time classes and innumerable research papers, sometimes it seemed like everything she knew blurred together, merging seamlessly until her brain couldn't differentiate between a Roman hobnail boot and one of Vivienne Westwood's fantastical creations. But she knew those initials, they were on the tip of her tongue, shimmering on the periphery of her past.

Just as Steph felt the pieces of her memory finally slotting in space, a shriek jolted the threads from her mind.

'What are you doing?' Eliza screamed.

Steph explained, words rushing out over the top of each other, tangling themselves on her lips.

'Stupid girl. Get out, get out now.'

Steph protested, but Eliza cut her off.

'Don't touch a thing. I have never... What do you think you are doing? You young girls are all the same. Swan in here playing at being a curator or conservator. You only signed up for a *museum* internship because your daddy probably threatened to cut off your trust fund unless you did something worthwhile with your time. I've seen it all before and none of you last. You catch yourself some rich donor at one of the posh fundraising dinners, get a ring on your finger, and then you're out of here as fast as your Manolo's will take you, leaving nothing but a mess behind you. You're all the same. Stuck up little snobs. You'd be better off working for those criminals at the auction houses, they like pretty, useless things.' Eliza paused, cheeks flushing a dangerous shade of red. The pause gave way to a hacking cough, and Eliza pulled her hanky from her bra, coughing into the tiny square of fabric before once again wiping the sweat from her brow and the spittle from the corners of her mouth. She tugged at her open collar, pulling it further away from her fleshy neck.

'Are you okay?' asked Steph.

'No, I'm not okay, you, you little...,' Eliza faltered, grabbing the edge of the nearest tea chest, the sharp metal edges slicing into her palms.

Steph stepped forward, but Eliza shoved her out of the way, leaving a bloody smear across Steph's chest.

'I said get out,' Eliza wheezed, the redness in her face replaced by a clammy pallor.

Steph rushed out of the room. She'd worked with some hellish people before, most interns did, but this woman was the worst of the bunch. And to top things off, the blood would ruin her shirt if she didn't sponge it out straight away.

Steph headed for the toilets, thankful that they hadn't quite finished converting them all to unisex ones yet, whipping off her shirt as the door closed behind her. Blood and white silk weren't a match made in heaven. Running the patch under the tap, Steph rubbed a dash of foaming soap into the stain, massaging it until the blood vanished. The best stain remover is time. The earlier you can treat it, the better. She turned to the hand dryer, one of those tricky 'dunk your hands in' types. She awkwardly wrapped the shirt round her arm, so only the wet patch was in the heat and began the drawn out task of drying it so she'd look half respectable when she left the bathroom.

As a child, she'd read everything around her — the cereal packet at breakfast, the back of the air fresher when she was in the toilet, random advertising signs when she was in a queue. If she didn't have a book in her bag, she made do with what was around her. And it was no different in the staff bathroom at the V & A, except this time she was reading the label of her shirt. A shirt made by a London designer. One Steph had bought at a designer clearance warehouse sale. She had taken little notice of the designer's name when she'd bought the shirt — choosing it more for its Victorian flavour, but now she knew where she'd seen those initials before, the initials from the Indian sketches. They were the identical stylised *pb* as the designer's label in her shirt. A designer called Patricia Bolton.

THE EXHIBITION

*T*he *British Raj* exhibition kicked off with all the pomp and circumstance associated with the V&A's impeccable design aesthetics, including the wait staff decked out in replica uniforms made from the detailed sketches for uniforms for staff at *Watson's Esplanade Hotel*, a nineteenth century hotel in former Bombay, India.

The research team had conjured up a series of photographs from *Watson's*, and giant copies adorned the walls of the exhibition hall. And in a coup d'état, they'd discovered one sketch for a ceremonial costume made for the 9th Earl of Elgin when he was the Viceroy of India. A costume hidden deep in the bowels of the V&A, and acquired by the museum in 1971 after the death of the Earl's second, much younger, wife.

That discovery set the framework for the entire exhibition, and half a dozen researchers had donned their amateur sleuthing hats to try matching up the sketches with similar historical pieces held by the V&A. And they'd struck gold in the miles of storage — locating four outfits worn by a Naomi Abbott in Simla, India. They found her name in old cast lists of productions at the *Gaiety Theatre* in Simla, and the four costumes, along with hundreds of others from theatres around the world collected by Talbot Hughes, who had meticulously recorded their provenance. Harrods of London later purchased Hughes' collection, donating it to the V&A in 1913.

An inspired guest list floated around the hallowed halls, quaffing champagne and sampling canapés prepared by the in-house caterers. Photographers snapped shots of fashionistas chatting with the curators and new-money benefactors. Striking Instagram-worthy poses, with perfected pouts, the attendees angled for the perfect shot for the tabloid magazines, securing them yet another week of *celebrity* status. The old-money benefactors didn't need to court the media. Those who needed to know who they were and why they were there, knew. And the people who didn't know who they were or why they were there, were too unimportant to educate otherwise.

Andrew Harvard fell into neither category. He wasn't rich, nor famous. He was here tonight representing Christie's, the auction house. Despite Eliza Broadhead's protestations against Andrew's invitation, there still remained a delicate and symbiotic relationship between the two organisations. Over the years Christie's had, on many occasions, alerted the V&A to items of interest which might have otherwise passed unnoticed as a small entry in a full catalogue. Christie's had also thwarted several attempted sales of goods stolen from the V&A. Neither institution advertised that little nugget though.

Andrew wandered alone through the exhibition, his mind elsewhere. Normally he would have been the first to appreciate the ingenious presentation of the exhibit, but tonight he felt he was missing one half of himself. It had been months since Patricia had disappeared alongside Sarah Lester. He'd done his best to hold the fort in her absence, but he couldn't pay the lease on her shop or follow through on any of the orders for her designs. And not being a family member, he'd had to allow her family to close the shop to defray the mounting costs.

There were days when he could go hours without thinking about her, but then he'd catch a whiff of perfume, a scent identical to the fragrance Patrica had been partial to, and it would catapult him back to the moment the police rang about Patrica's disappearance, and his life had never been the same.

He banged into another guest and apologised for knocking the drink in their hand. She gave him a withering stare before returning to her companion. Everywhere Andrew looked, there were couples, or clusters of interesting people, but he had no one.

'They told me you were coming, but I didn't think you'd show up,' a voice said over Andrew's shoulder.

Eliza Broadhead's perspiring face loomed in front of him, forcing Andrew to take a step back, where he bumped into the same woman from only moments ago. This time she stalked off with her friend, high heels clicking on the marble floor.

'You have a habit of knocking people over,' Eliza wheezed, pulling at the bodice of her clingy burgundy cocktail dress, which was almost a relic itself.

Andrew apologised again, but realised nothing would redeem him, but he could be polite.

'Good crowd here tonight. Lots of donors,' Eliza said, her eyes scanning the room.

Andrew murmured a short *hmm*.

'Now there's someone interesting,' Eliza said, pointing towards a tall blonde woman standing next to a shorter man sporting a ruined nose and cauliflower ears.

'The woman?' Andrew asked, shrugging. He often saw mismatched couples at big auctions. It didn't matter how ugly you were, if you had money, you could always catch the prettiest butterfly in the garden.

'You don't recognise her?'

Andrew didn't have the foggiest idea who she was.

'She's our latest *benefactor*, American. Throws her cash around like confetti.'

THE DESIGNER

*A*ndrew watched the woman tottering on heels a thousand inches too high for comfort. Lagging behind was a dour-faced man sipping a glass of champagne, boredom splashed on his face.

'Who's the fellow with her?'

Eliza shrugged, her bosom bouncing beneath her strings of jet beads. 'Just following the money, although he doesn't look her type.'

Andrew backed away, trying to put as much room between him and the volatile Eliza as possible.

'Bet you wish you'd got your hands on this lot then?' Eliza said, sweeping her bare arm around the space.

'Not really, it's better that it's all together. Gives a complete picture, instead of a piecemeal Clayton's exhibition.'

Eliza peered at him, suspicion painted on her face.

'It's true. I'd rather see a cohesive collection exhibited with a story behind it. And whoever put together this one has done a masterful job.'

Eliza sniffed, the pink flush to her cheeks evidence that she approved of Andrew's comments.

'Have you seen the photo display yet?' she asked.

'No.' He'd spent most of his time examining the costumes,

dreaming of touching the fabrics and examining the stitching. But he could only gaze on the exhibits from the outside of the velvet ropes.

'My pride and joy since we matched some sketches to photographs of English ladies and gentlemen who are wearing the designs in India. The whole thing was a giant scavenger hunt. Hours of work,' she said, 'painstaking work. Mind you they gave me an intern to help, but you know what they're like, more trouble than they're worth sometimes. The poor thing thought she'd identified the designer straight off the bat, on her first day. Young girls have such *lofty* ideas. Everyone tells them the world's their oyster instead of the truth, that life isn't fair; that the only way to succeed is through hard work. Well, I put her straight. You can't compare the exquisite work of a nineteenth century fashion designer in India, with that of an unknown modern designer just because they share initials. I mean, for goodness' sake, how many people in the world share the initials *P* and *B*? Thousands? Tens of thousands?'

Eliza waddled off after a fast moving waiter, the allure of a free glass of bubbles too much to ignore. Andrew started to follow her, but checked his response. On second thoughts, the last thing he wanted to do was to spend any more time in Eliza's company, just in case he ruined the temporary repair job he'd done tonight.

Changing direction, he veered down another aisle of the exhibition, his experienced eye taking in every detail of the costumes.

Andrew paused at a tableau of polo playing mannequins decked out in sunny yellows and strawberry red. The clean lines of the uniforms and the relationship of the colours as pleasing to his eye as the opulent costumes on display elsewhere at the exhibition, making the uniforms almost modern in their cut, although he presumed modern designers had taken inspiration from designs similar to these.

The descriptive panel described the triumphant team who'd worn this very uniform, and how the club who was still operating today, had stayed true to the original design, making no substantial changes for over one hundred years. With the designer's name given only as "*PB*".

As Andrew meandered through the crowds, time and time again, the initials "*PB*" stared at him from the white descriptive cards. *Why didn't they know the designer?* He swallowed a mouthful of his champagne, ignoring the obvious answer screaming at him from the panels.

Onto the pièce de résistance, the costumes worn by Mrs Naomi Abbott and donated to the V&A after the death of the 2nd wife of the 9th Earl of Elgin. One costume featured layers and layers of white lace, as if to portray an elegant swan in a pantomime production of *Swan Lake*, which the framed, tattered programme suggested.

Fitted on a mannequin next to the frothy white vision stood an altogether different creation, that of a Māori princess, complete with a feathered cloak and a jade pendant hung on a strip of leather. No programme sat next to this one, so Andrew couldn't imagine which production could have called for such a unique outfit.

The third costume was that of a buxom farm maiden, with a crisp white apron and bonnet, blue silk stockings and three-quarter length sleeves trimmed with lace. The programme advertised a late 19th century production of *Jack and the Beanstalk*. A framed black-and-white print of the costumed cast took pride of place next to the mannequin. Although the costumes were recognisable, the actor's faces were indistinct.

Andrew carried on to the last display, making his move as a group carried on towards the exit. The last costume on display was a pair of costumes, that of Apollo and Eurydice from the play *Orpheus and Eurydice*. An enlarged photograph of the actors in the costumes accompanied the mannikins. One was the formidable Naomi Abbott, but her companion had no known name; her costume presenting her as a dark haired, slender woman, her waist encircled with a belt, utilising a large cameo brooch as a buckle. Her dress stopped at her knees, the red pattern on the hem almost reminiscent of the edging on a Roman toga. It wasn't the cascading sleeves, or the elaborate hairdo, or the nod to Roman history which captured Andrew's attention; it was the face, Patricia's face. He stopped breathing, quite forgetting where he was as he stepped closer to the image.

'Excuse me, sir, behind the ropes please,' a guard hissed, gesturing towards the velvet barrier Andrew had bypassed.

Andrew bumbled backwards, stammering out an apology. Racing to the group photo on the previous display, he scanned the faces. And there she was again. The distance made the people hard to recognise, but he would have picked Patricia's face out of a cast of thousands.

Like a madman, he retraced his steps around the exhibition, sending champagne sloshing, and causing more than one or two patrons to tut. Oblivious, Andrew careened around the hall, examining every photo. Patricia's face was everywhere. But it was a changing face. It was as if he were watching her age in front of his eyes. Her smile never changed but her face had morphed into middle age in the space of five minutes. A cruel trick of time.

Andrew returned to the first photograph of Patricia dressed as *Apollo* in an old *cartes de visite*. Tears fell as he stared at the photograph.

'It's quite moving, I agree,' Eliza said from behind Andrew, a glass in one hand, a programme in the other and a smirk on her face.

Andrew wiped his eyes with the back of his hand. There was nothing to say. How could he explain that he'd just found his girlfriend? He couldn't.

'It was a clever seamstress who made these costumes. Probably a local Indian woman,' Naomi went on, gesturing towards the display. 'Shame we don't know who it was. Lost to time.'

How right she was, Andrew thought as he watched her sail off yet again, probably to torment the other patrons with her clanking beads and rasping breath.

'I'd say the designer's name was Patrica Bolton,' came an accented voice from behind him.

Andrew spun around. Facing him was a young woman, her shirt hinting towards Victoriana contrasting with her rainbow-hued hair — pale pinks jostling with tender lavender and minty green.

'Who did you say?' he asked, the words sticking to his tongue.

'Patricia Bolton, not that anyone has ever heard of her, but records show she designed plenty of the polo uniforms. Eliza doesn't believe me, but...' and here she shrugged.

'Patricia Bolton?'

'I think so. It was the label inside this very shirt which

helped connect the dots. Not that it's really a connection, but it gave me something to work with and that's why I'm here I guess.'

'Sorry, who are you?' Andrew asked, a thousand different thoughts bouncing around in his head.

'Steph, the intern, I helped put the exhibition together, when they let me actually touch anything... Mostly Eliza left me to my own devices, so I snuck in some research on the pieces she didn't include for display, like the polo uniform sketches which had the same signature as the designer who made this shirt. I guess the modern Patricia Bolton didn't want to reinvent the wheel and just copied the Indian designer.'

Andrew turned back to the display, gathering his thoughts.

'Do you know what happened to the designer? The one from India?' he asked, unable to look at the young intern.

'I do. I can show you, it's on one of the end panels. Slipped it past Eliza's net, a copy of an old obituary. Silly bat never even noticed it. Shall I show you?'

Andrew swallowed. He turned on his heel and strode off, unable to see where he was going through the tears coursing down his face. The words *old obituary* replaying in his head.

THE MURDERER

*R*ichard Grey placed the phone in the centre of the desk, his hands palm down either side. How he'd ever conducted his affairs before mobile telephones was beyond him. Now information was instantaneous, and for him, information was power.

The call from his lawyer informing him that Sarah Lester had returned from wherever she'd been hiding and was now being interviewed by the police. How his lawyer knew was of no concern. Now Sarah had reappeared, Grey could settle things. The potential murder charge hanging over his head didn't bother him one iota. The court would dismiss those charges, of that he was sure. Dismissed in the same way Sarah Lester would be, once he'd had her questioned to his personal satisfaction. There was no doubt in his mind that Sarah had more treasures hidden away which rightfully belonged to the Grey family.

Grey straightened the phone until it was perfectly perpendicular with the sides of his desk. It would require another call to set things in motion, but not from this phone, but instead from a disposable one he kept locked away for this very purpose.

Pushing back, he poured a glass of red wine, the early hour of the day no deterrent. At the full-length window he sipped his drink and watched the Thames snake through the city below, imagining what life would have been like if they hadn't robbed his family of its wealth. He'd spent his life rebuilding it, buying back the antiques his ancestors had foolishly sold. And every time he'd uncapped his pen to write out a cheque to buy something he should have owned in the first place, the ink blackened his soul a little further until he'd simply stopped writing cheques, choosing to recover his goods through other means. The treasures were his and he was merely righting a historic wrong.

THE REVENGE

*F*ujimoto didn't see Sarah disappear as she stepped across the shop's threshold; he was checking his mirrors for traffic before pulling out. In the smallest fraction of a second, not more than a blink, he missed her vanishing act, keeping Sarah's secret safe, for now. But Fujimoto wasn't the only one interested in Sarah, and that person had nothing more to do with their time than to await Sarah's return from the station. And he saw everything.

Grey rubbed his eyes and wiped the inside of the window with his pristine shirt cuff. He knew what he'd seen, which didn't mean he believed it, but Sarah Lester had vanished from sight.

He waited for the undercover car to pull away. Grey didn't trust that the policeman would give him a fair hearing if he saw him loitering outside Sarah's shop, hence the hire vehicle he found himself in — a nondescript hatchback, popular with tourists on a budget. Although small and easy to park, it cramped his long legs and made him feel poor. The risk of prison didn't weigh on his mind, but the threat of poverty kept him awake at night.

With the detective gone, Grey eased himself out of his car and peered into *The Old Curiosity Shop*. He was aware the assistant and her male companion were out. He'd hired an associate to report on their whereabouts, and knew they were at an auction at Christie's; an auction he would normally have attended, plied with champagne and slavishly served by the minions who worked there. But since the unfortunate *incident* at Christie's, his social calendar was as empty as a pauper's pantry. Grey a persona non grata — no parties, no launches, no interviews. It was galling, but soon this would all be an unfortunate dream. His lawyers would earn their keep and have the ridiculous charges thrown out, proving he wasn't accountable for a clerk impaling himself on a knife.

Satisfied that the store was empty, he pushed through the half-open door, taking care to close it behind him. He wanted no surprise visitors.

Richard Grey wasn't as perturbed by Sarah's disappearance as he'd expected. The world was full of mysteries. It wasn't for him to question *how*, but more for him to profit from the knowledge.

To Grey, the place was filthy, the dust an affront to his particular dislike of dirt. Old photographs lay strewn across the countertop, as if someone had tried sorting the collection, giving up before they'd finished. What he was looking for wouldn't be on the counter. Now the stories he'd heard about Sarah disappearing started to make sense. He didn't try analysing it more than required. Somehow she had an advantage, which meant he needed it. Was this how she'd sourced the *katar* and candelabra? And his family's embroidered sampler? What other treasures did she have concealed? That the police had searched the premises didn't phase him, they couldn't tell the difference between *Lalique* and *Lladro,* so an air of calmness suffused him as he cast an appraising eye over the haphazard stock stacked around the room.

Grey continued his hurried exploration of *The Old Curiosity Shop*, his phone on silent awaiting a text from his associates warning him of Nicole's return. Grey checked his phone again, nothing. He could search this cesspit for a month and still not find what he needed. The problem was he had no idea what he was searching for. Only Sarah Lester knew.

Cursing under his breath, he accidentally kicked a box behind the counter, making him swear a second time, the ill-placed kick radiating pain up through his bespoke shoes, breaking a tiny bone in his toe. The carton he'd kicked was full of ugly hunks of carved green stone.

Grey lowered himself onto the foetid stool, easing his shoe off, and wincing as he peeled away his sock, the swelling instantaneous.

'Damn it to hell,' Grey muttered just as his phone started vibrating in his pocket. But it wasn't the message he was expecting.

He didn't normally stop to consider the whereabouts of his associates. His network was vast, each man or woman possessing a unique skill set Grey only called upon when he had need. He'd tasked Stokes with dealing to that neanderthal who'd failed to acquire the *katar* from this very store. Grey had assumed Stokes had completed the job and had carried on doing whatever it was Stokes did when he wasn't working for Grey. The last thing he'd expected to hear was that Stokes' putrid decaying body was now in the coroner's chiller, with the police investigating his murder.

'Damn it, Stokes.'

Grey didn't expect the police to link him to the dead man, but a small chance existed. There could only be one culprit, the ruffian with his own vendetta against Sarah Lester. *What had he called her? Bell, Sarah Bell?* Now Grey needed to decide whether to send good after bad; whether punishing Sinclair for what he'd done to Stokes was worth Grey's time and energy.

INDIA

THE ORDERS

*A*lbert Lester lay in bed staring up at the ceiling. Would today be when they questioned him about the whereabouts of Major Warren Brooke and Sarah Williams? He'd not slept well, as evidenced by the tangle of bedclothes around him. He'd lost his daughter, again. But this time she wasn't alone. Wherever she was, the thoroughly competent Major Warren Brooke of the British Army was with her. A grimace distorted his face as he imaged Brooke in modern day London — a London so far removed from what Brooke would have known, what he could have imagined, that a breakdown could be the only outcome. Albert also knew that it was entirely possible that his daughter might not even be home, in her own time, that she could be anywhere.

His mind going in impossible circles, Albert Lester stared up at the pressed ceiling panels, ignoring the sounds of life outside his room at the Viceregal Lodge. If asked about Brooke's disappearance, and that of Sarah, he had a story prepared. They'd believe him, so far he'd proven himself invaluable to the Governor General. Although he tried not interfering with what he knew would become history, he did his best to guide the Viceroy, and those around him, to avoid some smaller mistakes he knew they'd make. Of the consequences of his meddling, he tried not to think too hard about. He was doing the best he could in an unfathomable situation. A storm was about to hit the British, and he was more than thankful his daughter had left.

A knocking interrupted him looping over every potential scenario. *What ifs* could drive you crazy given half a chance.

'Come in.'

A uniformed servant opened the door, allowing another through with a sterling silver tray laden with coffee and cream and toast and jam.

'Good morning, Sir,' said the man in the doorway.

'Good morning, Sanjay. Naveen. Any news today?'

The men exchanged a glance.

'Nothing too much, Sir,' Sanjay replied, closing the door and twitching the curtains open.

The view from the window was as impressive as always and Albert momentarily forgot about the firestorm on the horizon, breathing in the magnificence of the distant visage of the Himalayas as Sanjay opened the windows.

Naveen poured the thick black liquid into the china cup, adding a dash of milk with his own peculiar flourish, as if performing for an audience. The tinkling of the silver teaspoon drew Albert's attention back to the present.

'Nothing too much?' Albert asked, his eyebrows lifting.

'Thank you, Naveen,' Sanjay said, opening the door once again, ushering the younger man out. He closed it behind the boy, shutting off the noise of the waking household, limiting the potential for others to overhear his words.

'There are rumours, Sir, bad ones, but they are true. There are things being said about the English. Bad things I think. It's like your coffee, Sir. You like it piping hot, so it takes longer to prepare it, to get the water as hot as you like it and to keep it hot all the way upstairs. It's a long way up here and sometimes that water spills, so we have to start again, annoyed by such a little thing as spilt water. We then have to boil the water again, to get it the right temperature. Every time the water spills, we get more annoyed. At ourselves, at you, at the idea that you will only drink very hot coffee. What's wrong with warm water? Why does it have to be boiling? And the resentment builds, and it builds, until one day, the spilt water becomes a coffee pot flung into the face of the man ordering the coffee...' Sanjay stopped, aghast at the direction his homily was taking. He turned for the door, eyes downcast.

'Where do you live, Sanjay?' Albert asked unexpectedly. 'Wherever it is, go home. I'm more than capable of making coffee.' Sanjay tried interrupting but Albert held up his hand. 'I'm not dismissing you, Sanjay. But I can't ignore the rumours. and I know what it is you are referring to. I'd hoped to have more time to prepare, but we don't. Go home and look after your family. They'll need you more than we will. I'll send your pay on, and you can come back when the troubles are over.'

Sanjay's face clouded with confusion before nodding. He had a family — two sons and a wife he adored. He hadn't told Albert everything, but he didn't need to. The staff whispered that Albert Lester was a *Maharishi* — a great seer. It never occurred to them that he was from the future. If Lester said trouble was coming, that was enough for him. Sanjay bowed his head and left the room.

Alone again, Albert knocked back his lukewarm coffee. Pouring a fresh cup from the pot, he swung his legs out of bed and padded over to the window. From this height he could see the manoeuvres of the detachment stationed at the Viceregal Lodge; men standing at attention, every inch of their uniforms gleaming in light diffused by the mountain air and the early autumnal fog. How many of these soldiers would still be alive after the fight that was coming their way?

After dressing, Albert made his way downstairs, sniffing the fragrant spices infusing the previously staid English breakfast now served at the Governor General's residence. A chatter of voices greeted him as he entered the dining room. As usual the table was full of an eclectic mixture of guests — visiting civil servants, favoured foreign emissaries, and a handful of relations of various sorts. The guests changed with great regularity, but they all knew who he was as he took his place to the right of where the Governor General sat if he joined them.

If Albert noticed any difference in the staffs' demeanour, he chose not to acknowledge it. He expected a level of circumspection from Sanjay, but it wouldn't have surprised him if his manservant had shared his forebodings. Bad news spread like a disease, before it infected them all, reaching its tentacles deep into the heart of the Empire.

'Porridge, Sir?' asked a servant in an impossibly white turban.

Albert waved, his mind already focussing on the day ahead, plans the foolish military commanders who suggest which he'd try to alter. History had taught him that the British Empire was awash with leaders appointed through bloodlines alone, and not through knowledge or skill.

A female laugh travelled the length of the grand table as he took a mouthful of porridge, a laugh no true Victorian lady would ever have uttered in front of so many men. His head spun round, *Patricia*. Sarah's friend. She'd be the first one to ask him where Sarah was, but she'd also understand if he told her the truth. Did he dare tell her though? She seemed happy holding court, her own plate piled high with kippers and eggs, and what looked like thick slices of cucumber. With sweat already forming between his shoulder blades, he motioned towards the cucumber. Only watermelon was better for cooling the insides of a person, but cucumber was a close second. It hadn't taken him long to become accustomed to having slices of the liquid-filled vegetable with every meal.

Patricia didn't seem interested in catching his attention, or querying Sarah's whereabouts, so Albert finished his breakfast and excused himself. The Governor General had not appeared, so either he was on the tennis courts or something had happened which was more important than breakfast. Albert hoped it was the former but expected it was the latter, and that scared him.

The Governor General's office was a wood panelled ode to masculinity, and a thick fug of cigar smoke obscured the worried representative of Queen Victoria sitting behind the large desk, his head in his hands.

'Bad news?' Albert asked, taking a seat opposite.

The other man took his hands from his face, revealing eyes which hadn't slept and a face which never expected the troubles now facing the British Army.

'You predicted this, Albert. I should have listened to you,' the Governor General sighed.

'There's still time to minimise the casualties, both ours and theirs,' Albert replied.

The Viceroy considered Albert's words, shuffling the papers on his leather-topped desk, the deep red reminiscent of the blood they would spill on the summer parched Indian landscape.

'They've issued the orders. London is firm on what our response to the uprising will be. Now we wait.'

Albert's face portrayed everything he felt. The horror at what was coming because of decisions made by those with no true knowledge of the region and its people. He opened his mouth to respond but closed it, the damage done. He'd thought he had more time. He was wrong.

THE FATHER

*A*lbert glanced around him as he unlocked the dilapidated warehouse. Compared to the day he'd been here with Sarah and Brooke, the place was empty save for one Indian lad watching him from beneath the shade of a tree, whittling away at a wooden trinket.

Concentrating on the task at hand, Albert ignored him and slipped into the dim warehouse. As tempting as it was to close the door behind him, Albert needed the light.

Small scurrying sounds greeted his entrance. Rodents, or insects the size of rodents had claimed this space as their own. As long as they didn't cause too much damage, he could tolerate their company.

The light didn't penetrate to the back of the warehouse but that didn't hinder Albert's activities as he moved with the easy comfort of a man who knew his way around the shrouded shapes and scattered boxes. His methodology in India was no different to how he'd operated back home — he was a collector who found joy in acquiring treasure, often more content in the knowledge of owning something exquisite than the profit gained from selling it.

Albert's grand plan had always been to stockpile enough fine furniture and valuable antiquities to provide a safety net for Sarah in a future he'd never see. He had enough money to acquire a building in

London, in an area untouched by the WWII bombs. And it was there he'd arranged to ship the contents of the warehouse. He'd considered every contingency; insurance, council tax, maintenance. There were enough companies still operating in London who had their genesis in the 1800s for him to prepay a century's worth of expenses. And banks who would hold a letter, only forwarding it to Sarah on a certain date. His plan was foolproof although Sarah's reappearance (and disappearance) had brought forward the shipping date. The carters were coming tomorrow with their teams of bullocks to haul his future priceless antiques to the nearest port and onwards to England.

He ran his hand over the heavy cloths protecting the pieces he'd spent the last few years collecting. Mahogany sideboards with delicate inlay. Gilt edged occasional tables with ebony highlights. Ornate towers of carved ivory — as common as pennies in a beggar's hand now, but which would one day only exist as museum pieces. The profit from the ivory alone enough to keep Sarah comfortable for the rest of her life.

He'd planned to travel to London with the shipment, to confirm the arrangements face-to-face, but the troubles made that impossible. The Viceroy needed him. He had to try his best to temper the outrage of the English and dampen the flames of discontent from the locals. The dark circles under his eyes evidence of the struggle between his loyalty to the Queen and his love for his daughter. He'd chosen the lives of the many over the life of his daughter, confident that wherever she was, Warren Brooke was with her, and that he would keep her safe. The missing link was Annabel, his wife. There hadn't been a single night he hadn't thought of her, where he'd wished things were different, that she was with him on this adventure, this journey. Gone so long now, that the edges of her memory were hazy, as though someone had taken an eraser to her memory and was slowly rubbing her out.

'Hey, mister, you want a carving?'

The young man from outside stood in the doorway, basket in hand.

Albert wiped the moisture from his eyes, interrupted from his reverie.

'They're good carvings, better than the things in here,' the carver added, taking two steps inside.

'I don't need a carving, thank you,' Albert replied.

'Be worth lots in the future,' the carver said, swinging his basket in a mesmerising pattern, the sun catching a horrific scar running through his cheek and ending at his jaw.

'What did you say?'

'The future, people pay a lot for these in the future.'

Albert stepped towards the young Indian man, who was still swinging his basket as he looked around.

'Be easy to add a statue to this lot.'

Albert decided the man's turn of phrase was just that, a turn of phrase. He was seeing shadows and ghosts where there was only flesh and blood. But his skin prickled at the man's words. *There was something…*

'I've no money on me today,' Albert dodged.

'You need one for your collection,' the man insisted, his free hand caressing his scar, an unconscious move to hide the vicious mark but which only drew Albert's attention.

'I've no money now. Off you go, I'm working. Come back tomorrow.' Albert shooed the man out, flapping his hands the way you would at an insistent seagull. The scar eliciting a modicum of pity.

'Tomorrow then. The perfect gift for your daughter,' he threw over his shoulder before vanishing down the road.

By the time Albert registered the man's choice of words, he'd disappeared, leaving only fine shavings of wood beneath the tree.

How in heaven's name did he know about his daughter? Lucky word choice, that was all. He didn't know the man from Adam. Still, the encounter left him unsettled, as he hurried around closing chests he'd left open ready for any final treasures. There'd be no more treasures until after the troubles ended, if he survived. His history was hazy, but he knew things were about to end badly for thousands of people. Now he'd have to return to buy a mediocre statue he didn't need nor want. Sarah would call him a pushover.

THE TROUBLES

'You will have heard the news then?' the Viceroy said to Albert Lester as he materialised at the polished desk.

Albert's face said more than words ever could.

Two hundred English women and children, butchered at what would become known as the Bibighar Massacre. The man who they'd gone to for aid, turning traitor and joining the mutiny, imprisoning the women and leaving them to their fate at the hands of other more brutal players.

'How did it come to this, Albert? How, damn it?'

Albert didn't have any answers. He'd tried warning the army about the potential problems associated with the grease the soldiers were using for their guns. Grease made from animal fats — beef or pork, prohibited by the Hindu religion. His pleas considered preposterous by those higher up the chain of command. Now they were reaping what they had sown.

Staying behind had been in vain. Nothing he'd done had changed the course of history. How many people would still die in this mutinous and unnecessary war?

'We must deal with them by the harshest means. The deaths cannot go unpunished,' the Viceroy said.

Albert almost spoke, to warn against inflaming the tensions, but held his tongue. There was nothing he could do now. He'd been unable to change any events leading to the mutiny in Cawnpore and the subsequent atrocities. Are the affairs of yesterday set in stone, meaning no one can alter history? If all he'd achieved was saving the lives of a handful of men, was that more significant than his family? More important than the life he'd abandoned?

'I'm sorry, Sir, but I need to go out for a short while? I have a personal issue.'

The Viceroy stared at him.

'A personal issue, Lester? After mutineers murdered hundreds of our women and children, throwing them into a well to rot? Where is your head at?'

'My head is with my wife and child, Sir. An hour, that's all I need.'

The atrocities had wounded the Viceroy, and he sighed. 'You've waited till now to tell me about a family, Lester? You are a dark horse. An hour, then I need you here.'

Albert hurried from the room with one thought, *was it too late to go home?*

THE CARVING

*A*lbert Lester hailed a palanquin and hurried back to the storage sheds. Leaping from his seat he searched for the mysterious carver. Something told him that the carver was more than a whittler of wood. Albert couldn't have been any more specific if anyone had asked him, but he *knew* the carver was more.

'Hello?'

No answer. The yard was empty, the workmen as absent as the summer rains. It wasn't only the courtyard which stood vacant, the doors to the warehouses gaped open, as if screaming in shock at the atrocities committed in India.

Albert took half a dozen steps towards the unlocked door. Was it only yesterday he'd been here, preparing a final inventory for shipment? An inventory as worthless as the paper he'd written it on. The ink wasted.

Beyond the open door the rats still scuttled into dim corners, and beetles scurried from sight, but the mahogany furniture and the ivory sculptures and the silverware and the eclectic pieces he'd collected over several years had vanished. Packing straw littered the floor where cartons had once stood. Nothing remained.

Backing out, he checked the rest of the warehouses. All empty. It would have taken a huge number of men, and a concerted effort to clear every shed of its contents. He couldn't recall what had been inside the other warehouses, but they had been hives of activity — a pottery production line in one, basket weaving in another, a spice trader at the far end, with similar small family run businesses in the others.

Albert wandered around the hand-packed earth, his thoughts in disarray. A tuneless whistling reached his ears, and he turned to see the carver sitting cross-legged under the tree, whittling away at a piece of wood.

'What happened here?' Albert asked.

The carver shrugged, his scarred face showing no sign of subterfuge.

'Did the carter take everything?' Albert suggested, the idea popping into his mind. It was a possibility that the carters had misunderstood his instructions. It wouldn't have been the first time a courier had got it wrong.

With a possible solution under his belt, Lester shifted his focus, his heart rate returning to normal. The carter must have taken everything.

'Yesterday you mentioned my daughter. How did you know about her?'

The carver ignored him, concentrating on his wood in his hands, whistling a peculiarly familiar harmony, but one which sat tantalisingly on the periphery of Albert's memory.

'My daughter?' he persisted, raising his voice.

The carver paused, laying the half completed piece on the ground before rummaging through the basket at his side. He laid an assortment of ornaments at Albert's feet.

'Choose the one you think she'd appreciate the most.'

Albert stared at the carvings, taking in the detail of a carved horse complete with bridle and ornate saddle, a pair of decorated recumbent elephants, a sleeping tiger, a coiled cobra just lifting its hooded head, and a peacock fanning its feathered tail.

'I asked you a question.'

'History won't change while you choose,' the carver replied, his hand caressing his cheek. 'Most people pick the horse, especially for a daughter.'

'She's not that sort of daughter,' Albert replied.

The carver lifted the cobra, examining the miniature lifelike creature, before returning it to the basket. Likewise, he packed away the elephants and the horse, leaving only the tiger and the peacock.

'Which one is your daughter then? Pick one. But choose the right one. Time is not on our side.'

In turmoil, Albert started stuttering a response, a retort to the effrontery of the Indian carver, but his words faded away, like a mirage across the parched desert. And his shoulders slumped forward. He had no daughter, not anymore. His daughter was a grown woman, forging her own path now. Buying a carved toy was akin to giving a rattle for an eighteenth birthday present, too little, too late.

'Pick one, Mister Lester. Quickly, the troubles are coming.'

The troubles. Rape, murder, mutiny and misunderstandings, the precursor to the end of British rule in India.

'The tiger, Sarah is more a tiger. She's never been a peacock.'

'The right choice,' the carver replied, packing away the peacock, leaving the sleeping wooden tiger. 'Time to go, there's nothing more you can do here. You are a good man, Mister Lester. Sarah is lucky to have you as her father. Keep the tiger with you, and you will always be able to find India should you need her.'

Before Albert could register the use of Sarah's name, the carver ambled away, his basket swinging from one arm, once again whistling the maddening familiar tune as he vanished around a sharp twist in the road.

'Sarah, he said Sarah,' Albert muttered. He almost went after the man, but there wasn't time. The Viceroy needed him back. They had a mutiny to quell, and Albert had to be there to make sure more lives weren't being lost through stupidity and egocentric decision making.

As Albert bent to retrieve the carved tiger, he hummed the same tune. A song he hadn't heard for many years, the title coming to him as he plucked the tiny tiger from the ground — *Time of the Season* by English rock band *The Zombies*. And it was that song he was humming the moment he disappeared. Vanishing from sight, from India.

LIVERPOOL

~

THE OFFICER

*C*lifford Meredith wiped at the watery windows and peered out. The snow had finally stopped, coating everything with a beautiful white mantle, not that the bitter Customs man recognised the beauty in that. He only saw a freezing world outside which would disrupt his journey home. Turning his back, he lumbered over to the fireplace. This wasn't his office, his was a grimy hole on the other side of the warehouse where the stench from the wharves pervaded every nook and cranny even in the cold weather. This office belonged to his superior, to the man who had the role Meredith thought was his by right. His supervisor was an imbecile who hadn't bothered coming in to work today. That wasn't how you ran one of the country's busiest ports.

Clifford Meredith didn't view the sideways shift to Liverpool Port as a demotion, he lacked that level of awareness. In his warped self-obsessed mind, he'd viewed it as an alternative track to the rank he believed he was due. He was cognisant they'd shifted him because of his investigation into the business dealings of Williams and Kurdi, but his being in Liverpool instead of London didn't mean he'd forget about the investigation and how those two men were defrauding the

Crown of its rightful revenue. He'd see justice, he still had his fat fingers in all sorts of pies, and had favours he could call in.

Meredith rubbed his hands in front of the flames and surveyed the room. This office would suit him well. He'd change a few things, but for the most part the government issue desk was suitably intimidating, the rug large enough to cover most of the floorboards and the framed visages of the former Port Collectors added a level of import to the room. Those he'd keep. The bookcase held shipping ledgers and copies of the legislation they operated under. It had been years since he'd opened one; he didn't need to because he knew the law like the back of his hand. Meredith knew what was right and what was wrong. Just as he knew Williams and Kurdi were having a laugh with the concessions they were claiming on the rubbish they were importing from India. He spent almost every waking moment imagining their faces as they locked them up for fraud, or treason, or the hundred other offences he suspected them of committing. It was his favourite daydream. A knock on the door of the office interrupted his reverie.

'Come in.'

A clerk with a shiny polished head and a Rumpelstiltskin beard entered the office, a pile of manilla folders under his arm.

'Put them there,' Meredith barked as the clerk started towards the fireplace.

With hands blue with cold, the clerk placed the folders on the desk, mouthing his feelings towards Meredith's back.

'Off you go, the dirty buggers won't declare their shipments on their own,' Meredith said, waving him away before returning to the lovely enveloping heat of the fireplace. He shook his head at the laziness of the staff here. Imagine the cheek of the clerk, wanting to laze away by the fire? He tried to remember the man's name. When he was finally in charge, the lazy git with the foreign name would be the first one fired. God knows how he was ever let into Britain. What was it? Skaky? Satkey? No, he remembered now, Shaskey, Paul Shaskey. Polish maybe or something foreign, anyway. Only good English men should work for Her Majesty's Customs. The man was probably a spy or else he was letting all his foreign cronies in. He looked shady. Shady Shaskey, yes, that's how he'd remember him. And Clifford Meredith laughed, ignoring the files waiting for his attention. It wasn't his desk after all, so someone else could deal with them.

THE WAREHOUSE

*C*lifford Meredith stopped in the doorway of the cavernous warehouse, clipboard under his arm, picking at his teeth with his free hand. The man beside him rattled off the items on the manifest attached to his own wooden board.

'And it's all from India then?' Meredith asked, wiping his fingers on his black uniform pants, adding to the pattern of unidentifiable stains already there.

'Yes, sir. All of it. It shows the consignor as Williams and Ye Ltd.'

'Ye? That's not an English name. That's a heathen name. I want every nook and cranny searched. Every drawer, unroll every bolt of cloth. And if you find even one stick of furniture not listed on the manifest, you come tell me,' Meredith said, his face a picture of glee.

Here he was, at the arse end of England, and like a gift from God himself, he'd stumbled across another company owned by those thieving, underhanded conmen — Williams and Kurdi. Although they now seemed in cahoots with the Chinese. Meredith was certain there'd be evidence of smuggling this time, irrefutable evidence. Maybe even collusion with a foreign power? Could Williams and Kurdi, and this mysterious Ye, be part of a plot against their glorious Queen? Meredith got quite carried away with his fanciful dreams and the litany of potential offences the traders could have committed, so didn't notice the look of contempt on the clerk as he sauntered out in high spirits.

Meredith's glee warmed the cockles of his heart. A good day's work done, so now he could reward himself with some afternoon delight. Being sent to Liverpool had been a blow, but it wasn't all bad. Liverpool had its attractions, attractions which were much more affordable than they had been in London. It was just as well, as he had a healthy appetite. Given what he'd achieved today, a long lunch, followed by some slap and tickle was more than well deserved.

The ladies at the *Cheshire Cheese* in Newton Lane were his personal favourites. He'd come to this decision after trying dozens of the local establishments. Some he'd never deign to step foot in again, after some lacklustre experiences, whilst others wouldn't have him back again, not that he gave them much thought—it was their loss. But the fare at the *Cheshire Cheese* far surpassed the other brothels around town. What he liked best was being shown into the front parlour adorned with framed photographs of the girls on offer. He had his favourites but still examined the portraits in case there were any new offerings. For two shillings, he had a room to himself for half an hour, and it even included a glass of gin.

Meredith made his selection and lounged with his gin on the couch for someone to summon the girl from wherever they waited. A newspaper abandoned on the table lay open on an essay decrying brothels. Meredith smirked. The newspapers were full of do-gooders trying to have prostitution and brothels abolished, claiming that they were dens of inequity, frequented by sadists, and populated with girls of disrepute. He'd never come across any sadists, neither in London nor Liverpool. He'd seen plenty of acquaintances coming and going from pleasure houses, more so in London than here, but then he was new to the city. No, he believed that the reformers wouldn't get very far in their protests on this issue.

'Welcome back, Mr Meredith,' came a sweet voice from the doorway. 'The usual?'

'A little extra today, Josephine, as I have cause to celebrate,'

Meredith said, tossing a handful of coins to the woman, where they disappeared from view.

'You're my first customer since we done up the room,' Josephine replied, her hips swaying more than what was natural as she encouraged him up the Georgian staircase.

Meredith wondered how the *Cheshire Cheese* could improve upon the erotic plaster tiles which graced the surround of the fireplaces in the brothel. He delighted in examining the different tiles in each of the rooms, more for entertainment than for motivation, although the tiles had provided some inspiration in the past.

Upon entering Josephine's room, Meredith felt a punch in the gut, such was his visceral reaction to the sight in front of him.

Josephine clapped her hands, mistaking Meredith's stunned silence and his gaping mouth as wonderment.

'Isn't it glorious? Closest I'm likely to get to India,' she exclaimed, blonde curls bobbing in time to her petticoats.

The room was an ode to the colourful chaos of India, with exotic sari's hung on the walls, the old English furniture replaced with hideous carved monstrosities, and gilt and brass everywhere. Someone had even painstakingly painted the ceiling in reds and greens and a gold leaf pattern, complete with peacocks in corners. To Meredith it was as if rioting mob of Indians were let loose in the room, vomiting colour everywhere.

'How... where... the brass? Is this Indian?'

'How did you guess? How smart to know that this was from India! Imagine what it must be like there. I follow the magazines, and I know everything about it, all the girls do. Have you been there?'

'Where did you get it from?' Meredith asked, trying to run the numbers in his head. His two shillings didn't seem like such a bargain if this was what they spent it on.

He ripped a red sari from the wall, eliciting a scream from Josephine, which she stifled as he shot her a furious look.

'If you don't like it, we can move to another room? I'll find an empty room. It's a quiet time of the day. You've already paid... it seems a waste to—'

'Is this filth what you've spent my money on?' Meredith screamed, the irony lost on him that he'd paid for a service and what the brothel then did with that coin was of no concern of his. 'Where did it come from, this… foreign rubbish?'

Josephine inched closer to the door. 'I don't know. There was a catalogue, and we all chose something.'

'Bring me the catalogue,' Meredith snarled, ripping down another sari, before bundling it up and tossing it into the fireplace, now sans its decorative erotic tiles. The flames licked at the gold ribbon edging the red silk before devouring the fabric.

Josephine vanished from the room, hiking her petticoats up as she ran, but hate clouded Meredith's eyes so much, that her tiny little ankles and shapely legs held no attraction, and rage fuelled him as he ripped the Indian sari's from the walls as though he was ripping the clothes from the bodies of the men who'd forced him from London and had ruined his life — Robert Williams and Samer Kurdi, the filthy traders bringing in heathen rubbish from India.

Running footsteps echoed down the hall, it wasn't just Josephine coming towards the room. A cluster of painted faces crowded the doorway, accompanied by gasps of shock. The burly handyman-cum-security guard barged through the twittering girls, before grabbing Meredith by the scruff of his neck.

They manhandled Meredith from the ruined room, and marched past the onlookers, and before he knew it someone threw him down the front stoop. From his ignominious position on the ground, he looked at Josephine.

'Here's your catalogue. I'll keep your coin as payment for the damage you've caused. Don't come back,' and she slammed the door.

Meredith reached into the gutter for the grubby pages. After wiping away the dirt, the words *Williams and Kurdi* emerged, the blackness of the ink fuelling his rage. They would pay for this.

THE BOX

*M*eredith returned to his lodgings, barging past all and sundry, oblivious to the frigid pall over Liverpool. The revenge in his heart kept him warm. The grubby catalogue thrust deep in his pocket burned through his coat, scorching his skin, tainting him by its proximity. But he was nothing if not efficient. He planned to comb through the catalogue the harlot Josephine had given him, comparing it to the manifests he had filed away for Williams and Kurdi, the files for the shipments he knew about, before they'd deviously changed their importing name. He'd have to pull the records for Williams and Ye now and compare those too. Oh, what a merry dance he would lead them on. And after that, he may just lend his name to the side of the reformers. It was about time someone taught those sneaky whores a lesson or two. They shouldn't go unpunished for stealing from men like him. He'd heard the rumours that the girls worked in pairs, one distracting while the other did the thieving, and it aggrieved him. Yes, he'd write to the papers, support the cause. Religious righteousness overcame him, soothing him as he considered his course of action. But first a nap, snuffing out the dark underbelly of Liverpool was most taxing.

Clifford Meredith paid no heed to Christmas being one week away.

There was no winding down of activity, no joyful imbibing of rum in the office. Criminals didn't take holidays, and he didn't expect his colleagues to either. The port was no place for Christmas festivities, bar the obligatory Christmas Day service. The American's had the right idea, slaves. In Meredith's mind, the Slavery Abolition Act of 1833 was an utter tragedy, and if he was in parliament he'd have it repealed faster than the harlots downed their knickers.

His poky office awash with paperwork, he ignored the mutinous glances of his colleagues and scribbled away in his notebook, building a watertight case against Williams and Kurdi. They couldn't escape from the full weight of the law this time.

He painstakingly cross-referenced everything in the catalogue against the items listed in all the manifests he'd been able to find, item after item after item. Screeds of figures and calculations marched down the pages of his notebook. The catalogue was almost indecipherable now with Meredith's scratchings all over it.

'Aha! Got them,' Meredith yelled.

No one bothered enquiring what he'd got, they didn't care. His colleagues were sick to death of his obsession with some random importer. There was enough going on at the Liverpool docks to keep them busy without also engaging in a witch hunt. They'd had word that a smuggling ring was operating out of the Prince's Dock, and involved the dock-masters, which was of more concern than a furniture importer bringing in two or three more chairs than they declared on the manifest.

Nothing annoyed Meredith more than being ignored. He was protecting the revenue of the Crown, so why didn't they appreciate his efforts? That they tasked him with rolling out the Merchant Shipping Act, and not to examine the manifests for one importer, didn't bother him.

Meredith's colleagues ignored his obsession, having decided it was better staying well away from it. And it was easier having Meredith occupied elsewhere, leaving them to get on with real customs work, unimpeded.

'I'm going to the Salthouse Dock,' Meredith called out.

No one acknowledged his announcement, a raucous game of cards was underway, with a bottle of rum rapidly consumed by the players. Meredith snorted in disgust. They must all be on the take. Once his promotion came through, he'd toss them all out.

With his trusty notebook under his arm, he trudged down the narrow wooden staircase, the temperature dropping with every step. At the bottom of the stairwell the beginnings of a snow flurry, and the outstretched hand of a young boy begging greeted him.

'Get away with you,' Meredith grumbled, brushing by the boy, immune to his pleas.

The snow never lasted long, becoming more of an inconvenience. Still, the people of Liverpool would complain and the poor would die, not that he cared. If people like that infernal beggar were too lazy to provide a roof over their own heads through hard, honest work, then they were better off dead. Looking after them was not his concern. He was not a charity.

It took every ounce of concentration to walk along the icy paths. He would not be one of those idiots who went arse over tail by rushing. You gained nothing by rushing something. His government issue boots provided excellent protection against the inclement weather as he trudged the seven hundred yards from the office to a warehouse on the Salthouse Dock. Usually a bustling hive of activity, filled with square-rigged sailing ships servicing China and India, but today it was eerily quiet — the stevedores and dockers given leave to travel home for the Christmas season. Tall red brick warehouses brooded on the water's edge, locked up tight awaiting Her Majesty's Customs and Excise men to sign off the goods being landed or exported, depending on the paperwork. The paperwork was Meredith's secret weapon.

Clutched in his hand was the key for warehouse #5, the bonded warehouse shown on the Williams and Ye manifests.

Opening the door unleashed an overpowering stench of exotic woods and spices, curdling in his nasal passages, clogging up his sinuses. Meredith's eyes watered and he clamped a dirty handkerchief over his nose. Stealing his nerves, he entered the cavernous space, closing the door. After striking a match to the lamp on the wall, he lifted it from its hook and waved it around.

Everywhere he looked there were towering crates and barrels and boxes. The scuttling of rats the only other sound he could hear. He checked his notes, and made his way up to the next floor, where he was sure he was about to find evidence of smuggling, irrefutable evidence.

The wooden floors echoed under his boots, the lamplight casting grotesque mockeries on the walls. Although the warehouse was new, industry had covered the windows in grime, further diffusing the winter light, turning them into shadows haunting every corner. In the middle of the space was an undulating mass, giant white sheets obscuring what could only have been a full consignment of furniture, of every type imaginable.

Meredith struggled with the tarpaulin, the scraping of wood against wood ungodly loud in his ears. And there in the kerosene lantern's light was the latest shipment brought in from India by Williams and Ye. Every stick represented in the prostitute's catalogue by exceptional lifelike drawings. The stink of corruption filled Meredith's lungs.

After lighting a second lamp and bringing it closer to the goods, Meredith got to work. There was only one item he was after — a writing box clearly illustrated in the Williams catalogue, but missing from any of the manifests. Not a single manifest mentioned anything resembling a writing box, or slope. So like a demon collecting souls from a cemetery, he fired through the shipment, hauling out tables and shifting sideboards, stacking delicate mother-of-pearl tables on top of rosewood occasional tables, with no care whether he inflicted any damage, such was his single-minded attention to his goal. Soon the warehouse looked like a gang of thieves had forced their way through. Night had fallen whilst Meredith worked, and unusually for Liverpool, the snow had stuck, blanketing the empty quays, layers of white crystalline snow shimmering under the hissing gas lamps of the city.

Then he uncovered four tea chests standing against the wall and

Meredith stood back, wiping the sweat from his brow, a smile spreading across his face. Still nailed shut, they had to be where Williams and Kurdi had hidden the writing boxes, the boxes which weren't on any manifest but which their catalogue gloriously depicted. Boxes inlaid with silver and ivory, boxes which were the among the most expensive items in the catalogue.

Abandoning his search for want of a tool to open the sealed chests, Meredith moved to a row of small offices along the far wall. Unkempt and half stuffed with confiscated goods, the offices were an exercise in how not to conduct the Queen's business. If Meredith had been a better customs and excise man, he'd have realised this was the area he should focus on if he wanted to ascend the ranks. Once Meredith spied a crowbar in the corner, he lost all logic.

Almost hollering in glee, he was so intent on his endeavours that he didn't hear the downstairs door open and close, and was oblivious to the gust of cool air which whipped up the wooden stairs.

With the heavy crow bar over his shoulder, Meredith skipped back to the chests taunting him with their secrets. The screech of nails pulled from their homes assaulted the frigid air. Sweat beaded on Meredith's face with the effort of using muscles which hadn't done more than lift a pint of beer to his lips for the past twenty years.

Finally the lid flew off, crashing against a brass topped table, toppling it over. The noise didn't worry Meredith, no one was around to hear it. By now everyone had finished for the day, and was home beside their fireplaces, with their wives in their laps. Dropping the crowbar, he moved his lantern closer to the tea chest.

Meredith pulled out handfuls of brittle straw from the open chest making the warehouse floor look like the abandoned nesting site of a flock of cormorants. As he sat on his heels, Meredith savoured the moment, overwhelmed by success as he uncovered a mirror image of the catalogue's writing box.

'I've got you,' he said, frightening a small rodent at the top of the stairs, who scuttled into the darkest corner behind a wall of packing crates.

Meredith could see the brass corner of a second box under the first. If this chest contained writing boxes then there must be more in the others. In his mind, he already had Williams and Kurdi tried, found guilty, hanged, drawn and quartered, despite that punishment being reserved for treason. His quest for vengeance had no room for mercy.

Moving onto the second chest, Meredith stabbed the crowbar into the lid, using his body weight as leverage, sending it careering into the darkness. Oblivious to his surroundings, and digging through the straw packaging like a madman, Meredith threw handfuls behind him until he revealed another writing box. He ran his hands over the smooth inlaid wood, which was almost warm under his skin. He lifted the lid. The box wasn't empty.

A sickly sweet scent filled the space as Meredith gazed upon row after row of packed rolls of fabric, oily to the touch. He didn't bother pulling them out because he knew what they were — rolls of raw opium. This put a delightful spin on things.

Meredith decided to bring back one of the town's photographers to take irrefutable photographic evidence of the smuggling — something far more useful than the criminal's photograph in the rogues gallery of the local constabulary. He removed one roll, for evidential purposes, shoving it into his coat pocket. He'd take it to someone he knew for them to value it, evidence for the file. Evidence was key.

By the time Meredith had removed the lid of the last tea chest, nothing could have dampened his pleasure at a job well done. He'd left the writing boxes in situ for the photographer tomorrow. There was no risk to them going missing from the Customs bonded warehouse that he held the key for, and the power to deny entry. Oh, tomorrow would be a glorious day.

Only after Meredith had swaggered down the dock, back towards his office, did the shadow emerge from the bowels of the warehouse — the beggar looking for shelter for the night.

Begging had never been his life plan, he was barely old enough to have imagined any life for himself at all. His only goals were to survive each day, with enough food in his belly to see him survive. Tonight was another all-too-common night where he'd be going to bed hungry, but because of the distracted customs man, he had a dry place to sleep.

Meredith had left a lantern burning in the office during his hunt for the crowbar, and the beggar used the lantern to help collect up the straw and tarpaulins for his bed.

As the boy wrapped himself in the heavy cotton throw, snuggling into his makeshift bed, ignoring his rumbling stomach, he counselled himself to wake before the men arrived for work. They'd be filthy if they found him, and would blame him for the mess the other man had made.

As the beggar drifted off to sleep, his world-weary eyes watched the little flames of the fire he'd built on the upturned brass table-top using handfuls of straw, and pieces of tea chests he'd broken into smaller pieces. The fire made it warm and dry, and Christmas was coming and there was always something to eat at Christmas. Maybe he'd go to that new Muslim church which was opening. He'd heard there would be plenty of food for all the children there.

A hungry belly makes for a fitful sleep, and regardless of the night's haven, the boy tossed and turned. His thrashing sending swirls of straw into the air, where it danced and weaved its way through the night, touching on the wooden floors before moving its impressionist dance on the warm currents above the boy's makeshift fireplace.

The flames were just as hungry as the sleeping vagrant, welcoming the dry fuel into its sweet embrace, before another puff of wind whipped the smouldering straw from the warmth, sending it dancing into a corner filled with dusty straw and cotton fibres. And from the smoulder, another fire grew, one unconfined by the circumference of a table-top, one who would eat well tonight as it tasted the exquisite furniture and licked the floors and window frames, before finally consuming the young lad dreaming of Christmas dinner, his tired head nestled on a bed of Indian straw.

THE PHOTOGRAPHER

$\mathcal{M}$eredith slept the sleep of the virtuous, the inclement weather no dampener to his dreams of glory. Before going into the office, he stopped by the rooms of a photographer whose work he'd admired over the past few months. The photographer was more used to framing half-naked women than smuggled furniture, but Meredith had reasoned that the man would be more than competent to take photographs of static furniture as there was no temptation there, unlike the women he shot in provocative *come hither* poses. Meredith thought that there may even be an opportunity to collect a few images for his personal collection.

The snow had partially melted, icing the streets with a filthy slime, waiting to catch an unwary footfall. The ice didn't delay Meredith as he hurried to the photographer's studio. Retribution for his ungainly fall from grace in London would soon be his.

Roused from his bed by Meredith's incessant knocking, Garth Moodie, the photographer, reluctantly showed Meredith through to his studio. A gilt daybed sat in front of a painted backdrop featuring the white columns and urns full of pale green ivy. The hooded camera took centre stage, with a modesty screen positioned to one side, which

Meredith thought was a joke given that the photographer photographed the women nude.

'So explain to me again what you want me to do?' Garth Moodie asked, sinking into a tasselled armchair which served as a prop.

Meredith examined the framed photographs on the walls—elegant couples, or ladies posing with parasols. He stopped to fiddle with a nasty looking piece of equipment.

'Neck clamp stops them from moving while I take the photo.'

'Hmm, well you won't need that for what I want today. I need you to photograph some freight from India. It's stored in a warehouse at the port. An easy job for a professional like you,' Meredith said, paging through an album full of half-nude women, all posed on the daybed, or draped over the armchair. Meredith's eye paused as he located a picture of Josephine, and he slammed the album shut.

'They don't mind you taking photos of them then?' Meredith asked.

The photographer shook his head, confusion still plastered across his sleepy face.

'How do you control yourself around them then? You're a young man, how does payment work? Perk of the job?'

Moodie stood up, his earlier confusion replaced with a simmering anger at the interruption to his sleep, and the intrusion into his affairs.

'Look, mister, I don't know who you are, but this is a legitimate business. If you want to hire me to take photographs for you, then yes, I can do that. But if you're only here to make trouble, then I'll show you the door.'

'You don't want to go making me an enemy. This could be a lucrative market for you, you'd be the first of your kind in Liverpool. Crime photographers are big in London, mainly for bodies though... but you're well versed in taking photographs of bodies, aren't you? I only want you to take photos of the evidence,' Meredith explained.

Moodie slumped. His shoulders folded in on themselves as he trudged over to the monstrous tripod.

'Oh, and I think it prudent to take my photograph, for the file. It is a very important case I am working on, and the papers would consider it a coup to have a shot ready for their late editions, I'm sure,' Meredith declared.

'Fine. Give me half an hour to pack up my gear, and I'll take your photographs.'

'Good man, I'll just wait here and peruse your work, you have an excellent eye for detail,' Meredith said, stretching out on the bed with the heavy leather-bound album in his lap.

The men hailed a carriage, the bulky camera equipment taking up most of the back seat, making it an uncomfortable ride for the pair. As they approached the port, excited voices reached their ears, and they came to an abrupt stop.

'Can't get you any closer, there's trouble on the wharves,' shouted the driver.

Meredith peered out. There wasn't much more that he could see other than a crowd of onlookers blocking the road ahead.

'Drive on,' Meredith said.

'No bloody way, there are children there and I ain't driving my carriage through them. This is as far as I go. You don't like it? Tough, you're getting out either way,' the driver replied.

Meredith and the photographer climbed out. Meredith paid no attention to the struggle the photographer had with his gear, and marched off through the crowd, intent on finding out what was happening.

'It's a fire, mister,' said the first person Meredith interrogated.

'At the port,' chimed another.

'Don't know how many men have died. Story is that it's dozens at least,' said a third, although from the smell of him, he'd been toasting the deceased since the early hours of the morning, the fug of rum keeping him upright.

Meredith fought through to the iron gates at the entrance, with the photographer trailing in his wake. It was only at the gate that Meredith stopped, frozen in place with shock. He didn't even blink when Moodie pushed past and assembled his equipment, the enormity of the scene too good to ignore.

One of Meredith's colleagues approached him.

'Nice of you to join us this morning, Meredith,' the customs officer said, his lips curling around Meredith's name.

'What happened?' Meredith asked, counting the warehouses alongside the wharf, trying to figure which of them was on fire.

'Now that's the question isn't it? No one knows what happened, but we know there's a fire, and a damn big one at that. All hands on deck it was, except not all the hands were here, were they?'

'I was working on an important file, hence why I brought a photographer with me,' Meredith replied.

'At least we'll have pretty photographs of our burning wharves to remember them by, won't we?'

'Your mouth will get you into trouble, so I suggest you mind how you speak,' Meredith snarled. 'You've been lax in your duties, so it's a good thing I'm here to tighten things up. One of my first tasks is addressing the staffing—'

'Ho, that's rich coming from you. Rumour is the higher ups want a word with you about the fire. Seems you were the last man in there yesterday. Something to do with… now what was it they said? Oh yes, that's right, being on a *wild goose chase*. I hope you like your poultry well-cooked Londoner, because that's what's about to happen.'

Meredith's lips flattened as the officer's word hit him. He counted the warehouses again, but there was no mistake, warehouse #5 was aflame, the one filled with the Indian furniture and handicrafts imported by Williams and Kurdi. Meredith didn't know whether to laugh or cry. Laugh because the fire must have destroyed the shipment. Or cry because he'd lost the smuggling evidence to the flames.

As the fire finished its ravenous meal, the crowd dispersed from boredom, leaving only the stragglers and hand-wringing importers waiting to learn the fate of their goods. Meredith abandoned the photographer, now engrossed in documenting the destruction, and made his way into work sinking into the chair behind his desk. His notebooks and files stared at him, challenging him to open them, to finish the job he started, but he couldn't summon the energy. There were too many thoughts swirling around in his head to function on any level, the least of all being how the fire had started. The key to warehouse #5 was burning a hole in his pocket. He should have thrown it into the water when he had a chance, thereby claiming no knowledge of the fire's origins. As it stood now, they could hold him accountable, which was ridiculous, he was the hardest working man in the whole port. *Ridiculous.*

'Meredith?' came a voice outside his poky cupboard.

'Come in,' Meredith called from his wooden swivel chair, shuffling the files on his desk.

The door opened and in walked Mervyn Bulford, the Collector of Customs, the highest ranked revenue man in Liverpool.

Meredith leapt to his feet. 'Terrible business this fire, terrible. Any ideas on who started it?'

'Sit down, Meredith,' Bulford commanded, clearing off a chair before closing the door behind him and taking a seat. 'Instead of summoning you to my office to discuss this further, I find myself here. Do you know how that makes me feel?'

'No, Sir,' Meredith replied, his face conveying utter confusion at Bulford's attitude.

'I'm informed that you were in warehouse #5 last night, so one assumes you are the reason for the position we find ourselves in.'

Meredith's face paled. 'You must be mistaken, Sir.'

'Mistaken? You dare accuse me of being mistaken? They saw you. By god someone saw you entering the warehouse and leaving the port itself some hours later. And you sure as hell weren't working in the office. From what I hear, and from my own observations, work has been the least of your achievements. Cavorting with whores and wasting her Majesty's resources seem to be activities you excel in. I'm only here because I didn't want your taint in my office, an office you'll never attain while I draw breath.'

Meredith spluttered, but Bulford carried on.

'Pack your things, Meredith. Your services are no longer required. I have to face the importers who have lost everything, with a head on a plate, and it's your head I've chosen... without difficulty.'

'But Williams and Kurdi, there was evidence-'

'Evidence? You want to talk evidence with me? Shall we discuss the evidence of the body of your *liaison* that you left behind? You disgust me. As a good Christian man, it disgusts me that you cavort with prostitutes, but to use a bonded warehouse to entertain your less salubrious proclivities? Now get out before the papers learn your name. And when I say, 'get out', I don't just mean the port, I mean town. We don't want your type here.'

Bulford left the room, leaving Meredith in full sight of half a dozen of his colleagues loitering in the hallway who heard every word.

Meredith got up and scowled at them before slamming the door. *Vermin.* Blocking it with his bulk, he drew the strength to go on, although that seemed an impossible task at present. Wiping his sweaty palms on his trousers, he puzzled over the words of the Collector. He'd never once brought a girl onto the port, which was no place for women. He even resented having them in the workplace. The Collector must have been giving the wrong information. That someone had died in the fire was of no interest to Meredith. He didn't know who they were, and nor did he care. Williams and Kurdi would pay for this development. They hadn't ceased trying to ruin his career, even here in Liverpool. They must have people on their payroll who'd tipped them off to his discovery. Had to be. They must have lit the damn fire themselves, sacrificing the inside man. It was the most likely scenario. That he'd left a lantern alight amidst a nighttime tsunami of tinder dry straw never entered his mind.

And so it was with revenge in his heart that he stuffed his files and notebooks into his leather case. The blotter and ink pot went in too. He'd need those in the coming weeks. He'd prove to the Collector that he was innocent of any wrongdoing, just as he would prove who the guilty parties were.

With his chin up, he sauntered out of his office, his bag tucked under his arm, nodding at the staring faces.

'See you after Christmas,' he called out, as if he was taking a short break instead of the ignominious termination of twenty-odd years of service.

No one shed any tears or showed any surprise at Meredith's exit, it was like a parasitic tumour being purged from the workplace. With Meredith gone, the mood lifted, and those required to work with him could breathe again.

THE CAMPAIGN

A hammering outside woke Meredith from dreams filled with fragments of half-remembered moments and imagined slights, and he stumbled from his bed in a sour mood. He struggled into a robe, before wrenching the door open to find his landlady, a perpetual smoker whose only redeeming qualities were that she served a good fish pie and kept a clean house, if you ignored the deposits of ash left in her wake.

'Mr Meredith,' she said through a cigarette clamped between her thin lips. 'An interesting read in the morning papers today...' she said.

'Pardon? And?'

'The papers downstairs, in the dining room. Part of my morning routine, reading them...' she tapped the ash off the end of the cigarette, watching it float down to the bare wooden floorboards.

'Get on with it. I have a busy day,' Meredith snapped.

'Oh, I don't think your day will be all that full,' the landlady said, fixing Meredith with her wandering eye. 'Papers say Her Majesty doesn't want you working for her anymore. So, I must ask... how'll you pay your rent?'

'The papers have made a mistake-'

'There was a photo of you in front of the fire, at the port. You've a very distinctive profile, Mr Meredith. I'll not be too worried if you can't make your board next week. You understand it might harm my reputation harbouring someone who lights fires, that it could upset my other boarders? The stories were crystal clear about how that poor boy died. Mentioned you by name, and everything.'

'That's ridiculous—'

'You've got till Friday, then I want you out. I have to think of my other tenants,' she said, before tottering back downstairs, her message delivered.

Meredith shut the door, his jaw slack. The whole thing was preposterous, it had to be a huge misunderstanding. He never posed for any photographs, and now his landlady was accusing him of murdering a boy. The papers were printing lies.

Still in his robe, he pulled his curtains to check the street below, half expecting to see the police outside waiting. The window framed the usual daily activities — delivery boys, nurses with prams, prattling women travelling in pairs, a stray mongrel foraging in the gutter, and Meredith's stomach relaxed. There were no policemen waiting for him, no crowd gathered to witness his downfall. The landlady must have been drinking.

Meredith dressed. If journalists were spreading lies about him, he needed to clear his name and time was running out. It was already the morning of Christmas Eve, and the people who needed persuading of his innocence, of the injustice, would be travelling home for Christmas, and there'd be no one to present his evidence to until the new year, and by then, the press would have finished vilifying him.

He raced downstairs to the dining room, snatching the newspapers from the table. There was no mistaking the identity of the person photographed against the backdrop of the warehouse fire. The realisation that he'd brought the photographer to the port hit him like a tonne of bricks and he slammed his hand against the table, rattling the crockery laid out for breakfast. *That conniving reprobate.* Garth Moodie would rue the day he crossed him. Meredith would ruin him; have him prosecuted for taking lewd photographs, or engaging in unnatural sex, or something. There was plenty of evidence in the photographers studio. But Moodie was the least of his concerns, he'd keep. It was Williams and Kurdi who required immediate attention. And once breakfast was over, he'd deal to them, permanently.

His stomach full, he retired to his room to gather everything he needed for his investigations to continue, there were other ways to skin a cat. He'd taken the papers from breakfast so his fellow boarders couldn't read the printed lies about him.

Meredith slipped a small pistol into his bag, together with his gun licence. Since the Cornermen had used guns in their terrorisation of the Liverpool population, anyone with a pistol outside of their house needed a licence, not that the gangs paid any heed to that. He didn't want to give the press any more ammunition.

His notebooks and files went into the bag. He'd spent hours last night pouring over the finer details of what he considered one of the most complex smuggling operations ever conducted on Her Majesty's soil. He just needed a confession to tie everything together. *A confession* had such a delicious ring to it.

Meredith checked his room, ensuring everything was in its place, his valuables hidden from temptation, and the fire damped down for the day. Thanks to the newspapers he'd devoured, cover-to-cover, he'd formulated a plan. An Englishman turned Muslim was opening a Mosque in Liverpool, tomorrow, on Christmas Day, the holiest of days. And Meredith had a good idea of who might be there — his favourite smuggler, Mr Samer Kurdi himself.

THE FIRST TELEGRAM

For Samer Kurdi, Liverpool would be the turning point in his life. Raised a trader, by a trader, living an entrepreneurial life from the moment he could walk. Although he was a successful entrepreneur in business with Robert Williams, a Christian Englishman, Samer's Muslim faith guided his work and life. And with no family in England, and Robert on urgent business in India, he'd travelled to Liverpool not only to oversee the arrival of their latest shipment from India, but also to witness England's first functioning mosque opening on Christmas Day.

Samer Kurdi reached for the folded newspaper when a diminutive uniformed bellboy appeared.

'Mr Kurdi? There's a telegram for you,' said the bellboy, slipping a slim envelope onto the plate at Samer's elbow.

Samer tipped the boy and took a sip of his tea, making no hurry to open the missive waiting for him. Telegrams never delivered good news, so whatever it had to say could wait until he was ready.

Breakfast at the North Western Hotel was a busy affair since the 330 room hotel servicing the Lime Street Railway station had become a key venue for business conducted over breakfast. Men whispered over toast and marmalade, steaming pots of tea and coffee at their elbows. The blackness of their suits the dominant colour of the room, as if shadows of the men who'd been before had remained in the seats, until there was layer-upon-layer of residue left behind, building into one homogenous bespectacled man, who thought himself too busy and important to breakfast with his family.

Samer wiped his mouth clean and lay the linen napkin next to the china plate. His hand hesitated above the telegram. On the other side lay the unopened newspaper, also waiting for his attention, but curiously he had no interest. He enjoyed living in the bubble of travel and the anonymity it brought with it. No one knew him, therefore cast no suspicious glances his way. The court case in London had impacted both him and Robert Williams. Associates looked at them askance, communications had dwindled. Imperceptible changes but Samer felt them. And as much as he tried to ignore them, their whispers wriggled into the darkest corners of his mind, taunting him, questioning his choices.

The pull of the telegram beat out the beckoning newspaper, and he opened the crisp monogrammed envelope.

Addressed to him, it was from their shipping agent in Liverpool, the man he was to meet after the Christmas festivities.

Fire at port. Warehouse destroyed. Everything lost. Meet me at the shipping office 2pm.

Samer's stomach threatened to disgorge his breakfast and the other diners shimmered in his narrowing vision as he struggled to maintain his composure. The words *everything lost* seared into his heart. The money he and Robert had invested in that shipment far surpassed anything they'd done before. Shipping furniture and homeware was riskier than the usual shipments of cloth and tea and required a much greater investment. Although it wasn't only furniture they'd imported this time. The last shipment contained a quantity of opium. They'd argued about continuing to import it, and despite the importation of opium being legal, Samer considered it a fool's errand. The writing was on the wall, and his entrepreneurial spirit warned him that opium was on the way out. The Chinese were increasingly vocal about their distaste for the trade, and yet the English carried on as though the harm the drug caused was pure imagination.

Samer didn't know what to do. If the fire had destroyed their shipment, he should return to London to meet with their insurance agent. At least they'd be able to salvage some funds from the loss. But that didn't address the loss of revenue from the goods they'd sold through their catalogues - Robert's most recent business improvement. It worked well for their American competitors, so Robert had sunk thousands of pounds into printing and distributing catalogues for customers to preorder their goods, all handled by staff based in Liverpool, where the rents and labour were cheaper. How they would reimburse those customers was a headache he didn't want to handle alone, but Robert had sailed to India to source new products and to secure a better deal on the opium they'd had such a profitable run with, despite Samer's protestations.

He folded the telegram into quarters, slipping it into his waistcoat pocket. The only way to handle disappointment was to know it was the will of Allah, and that a reason would become clear as time passed. He could not change history. They'd lost the shipment but life must go on.

Samer signalled to a hovering waiter and ordered another tea with honey and shook open the newspaper. Emblazoned on the front page was an image of an all-too-familiar warehouse engulfed in fire. But it wasn't the fire which drew his eye, it was the profile of a man on the left of the shot, someone he knew far too well - Clifford Meredith. This changed everything.

THE PORT

*S*amer abandoned the newspaper on the table, sweeping past the waiter returning with his fragrant tea and honey. His shipping agent had requested a meeting this afternoon, but Clifford Meredith's involvement created an added complication. Samer's guts twisted, lending an English pallor to his middle eastern complexion.

The bellboy hailed a cab for him. Although the telegram arrived still sealed, the staff at the hotel knew the contents intimately — there were no secrets in a hotel, no matter what the guests thought.

Samer's ride to the port was equal measures too short and too long, and he could smell it before he saw the shell of warehouse #5, the acrid smoke hung over the port, fine ash clinging to the red bricks of the remaining warehouses; warehouses miraculously untouched by the fire, either through sheer luck, but more likely through the efforts of the firemen from Liverpool's new auxiliary fire station at Langton Dock.

Samer shoved a handful of coins into the driver's waiting hand and stepped down from the cab. Macabre sightseers loitered at the gates, each vocal in their thoughts on the tragedy.

The shipping agent's office was a riot of noise, for it wasn't only Samer's cargo lost in the fire. Warehouse #5 housed goods belonging to countless importers, both small shipments and shipments much larger than his own. The anguish on every importer's face was identical, regardless of the value of their freight. Most businessmen lived life on a finely balanced set of scales. To lose one's investment could send a man's family to the workhouse in the matter of weeks. His own financial position was not so precarious, but he was yet to communicate the loss to the insurance company. He still had that to do.

'You have to wait your turn,' yelled a voice from the counter.

Samer stood back, pushing to the front would achieve nothing. His time would come. Clamouring for attention within an angry crowd wouldn't bring his goods back and he didn't need to attract any attention. When a crowd was angry, anyone out of place could find themselves a target for that anger, and in a matter of seconds the crowd could morph into a hysterical mob, their anger and fear fuelling the situation.

The time of the appointment the agent had suggested in his telegram now seemed sensible. The crowd in the shipping office never grew any smaller, and Samer's back ached from the hard wooden bench he'd occupied for the better part of two hours. His ears hurt from the snarls of angry men around him, the tobacco smoke as vile as the heavy scent of fire each man had tramped into the room. Anger has its own scent, which mingled with the sweat, the ash and the tobacco, turning Samer's queasy stomach. He'd almost given up, the desire for fresh air overwhelming, when a space appeared to the side of him and the familiar face of his agent beckoned him forward.

Samer wasted no time, springing from his seat, he slipped through the partially opened door into the sweet confines of a long corridor.

'Thank you,' said Samer, pumping the hand of the weary agent.

'Don't know if I can add anything else to what's in the papers,' his agent said, sliding into a chair behind a desk obscured by folders.

Samer took a seat opposite and waited.

'It has destroyed everything of yours, and those of the poor souls out there,' the agent said, pulling Samer's manifest from the pile and leafing through the stapled pages.

'There is no blame on your shoulders,' Samer reassured the man, who looked on the brink of a breakdown. 'There is nothing I can do, and I only came because I have a question I need answered.'

'Just one?' laughed the agent, running his fingers through his hair, making it stand up in ruins, like the warehouse outside.

'The paper had a photograph on the front-'

'Peculiar timing the photographer being there then wouldn't you say?'

'Well... I hadn't considered that aspect, but it's more the man in the photograph—'

'Meredith,' spat the agent. 'Rumour has it they've fired him, because of the poor sod who died in the fire.'

'Someone died?'

'Yeah, they don't know who yet. Still going through the employment lists. No one should have been inside. But Meredith was in there... Investigating a smuggling case...'

Samer stood up and moved to the window. There wasn't much to see, the port carried on, cargo still needed loading and unloading. Life went on.

'I don't know anything about smuggling. Will they question him?'

'They'd rather let him go than invite any scandal to taint the port, that's the talk.'

Samer swore under his breath, which said far more than actual words.

'Some of us heard about his vendetta towards you and Mr Williams. And I'm not suggesting that he burnt the place down in retaliation, but others have suggested it. I mention it to warn you in case the papers ask questions. You know how they are, demons from hell some of them.'

'They can be, but that can also work on our behalf,' Samer replied, pleased that there was no reference to the smuggling accusation, replaced instead by a far more salacious rumour.

'So you want the papers involved then?' the agent asked, eyebrows raised.

'I think the photographer is the best place to start, don't you?

Perhaps invite him to take photographs, for insurance purposes. Williams and Kurdi will pay his fee.'

'Right, right, I'll send a boy to track him down, excellent idea. But what of Williams and Ye, do I mention your business partner?'

'No need to quibble over names, we are the same company. Send any bills to my hotel for settlement. I am here for the duration of the Christmas season. And send word of any more you hear about Meredith.'

The agent scratched notes in his file and escorted Samer back through the throng to the waiting room. No one paid them any heed, a foreigner and a clerk, nobody of any importance.

Samer stood by the gates to wait for a cab and gazed at the destructive force wrought by the fire. He whispered a short prayer for the poor innocent who had lost his life, before relinquishing his mind to the fear that someone had discovered their smuggling, and Meredith of all people. Samer had warned Robert. Like the opium, it was something they'd fought over, and it was the reason Robert was so insistent about going to India to secure new revenue streams. Their business relationship was unravelling, and perhaps their personal one too.

THE MOSQUE

*S*amer spent no more time thinking about Meredith and his interest in him. There was a mountain of work to do to recover the costs of the lost cargo, and everything associated with that. So he retired to his rooms at the North Western Hotel and fired off telegrams to the London office, to Robert in India, and to their insurance company. He drafted letters and checked manifests, several times over, and despite the burden on his shoulders, all he could think about was that this could wait — he had an important social engagement to attend.

Samer had no trouble making his way through the crowd milling outside the white-marbled walls of the building. The bundled-up onlookers making space for the exotic-looking man — strangers on London's streets were common, but less so in Liverpool, despite its bustling industry and shipping movements.

Samer knocked on the door, conscious of the throng watching his every move. A harried face peered out.

'*As-salamu alaykum.* I'm Samer Kurdi,' he said before the face at the door could brush him off.

'We're not ready yet, but soon, soon.'

'Can I help?'

The door opened a fraction further, the man appraising Samer. With no further words he ushered Samer inside, where the chorus of a well known Christian hymn washed over him and added to his confusion as he took in the Christmas decorations adorning the interior of the building and the puzzling mashup of the two faiths.

'Welcome, I am Abdullah Quilliam. You have come at an auspicious time, we are preparing our first Christmas breakfast. The doors will soon open to the city's poor, and we will feed them on this special day. You are welcome to help.'

Samer stared at his host, an Englishman through and through, albeit sporting an impressive beard and wearing a *taqiyah*, an Islamic hat. The name Abdullah was not one he would have associated with the man.

'Thank you for allowing me in. I am Samer Kurdi, here from London on business, and out of curiosity.'

'Curiosity is a fine trait, Mr. Kurdi. You will find a warm welcome at Brougham Terrace. Come through to the warmth. The food is almost ready.'

Samer followed Quilliam through an ornate plaster archway decorated in the Moroccan style into a room warmed by a roaring fire in a cast iron fireplace. Ladies bustled about, slicing slabs of seed loaf and straightening plates of sandwiches and good sized hunks of meat. A young woman, her head covered, pushed a mug of tea into his hands before hurrying away. A small choir closed their hymn books as their rehearsal ended. The organist turned to address the choristers — one of whom was her spitting image, except the organ player wasn't wearing a wedding ring. For a moment his mind flicked back to *The Crescent* article, England's only Islamic newspaper. Were they the sisters from the article he'd read? Englishwomen who had converted to Islam?

Samer sipped his tea. Coffee was his preference, strong Arabic coffee served with honey, but it was almost impossible to source the stuff, so had become accustomed to the insipid tea the English preferred. Just as he found the courage to approach the woman at the organ, the doors opened and the Brougham Terrace house surged with the poor and underprivileged. Before he knew what had happened, he was pouring hot drinks for the visitors and asking hungry orphans if they wanted sugar with their tea. The stream of humanity seemed endless and yet the tea never ran out. Huge industrial copper teapots, filled with boiling water, appeared magically at his elbow. And he plopped teaspoon after teaspoon of gritty sugar into the mugs. The whole experience was even more surreal as the choir raised its collective voice and sang Christmas themed hymns to entertain the guests. And around him, the wretched and the destitute, eyes wide with wonder, stood talking to other Muslims and among each other, in easy comfort. This simple act of charity, with no strings attached, carried more weight than any efforts to convert or persecute. Compassion and philanthropy, or rather, faith, hope, and love.

'The children like you,' said a quiet voice at his shoulder.

Samer tuned to see the organist, now wearing an apron, taking her turn to serve the orphans who would soon live at the Brougham Terrace, in an orphanage attached to the mosque, and funded by Quilliam and his supporters.

The scarf covering her hair highlighted her dark eyes and flawless skin, and Samer blushed like a schoolboy in her presence.

'They are the least judgemental,' Samer replied. 'You played beautifully before. But the choice of hymns…'

'We chose them to make our guests more at ease. We want to be part of the community and it would be impossible to break down prejudices if no one bent a little to fit,' she replied.

'Wise words,' Samer said.

'Were you bothered by the music?'

'No, I wasn't. Music speaks a thousand different languages, and yet everyone understands it, regardless of their faith. These people,' he said, gesturing to the strangers filling the room, 'They are here out of curiosity, and you have made their transition through your doors an easy one. Maybe they'll come back, perhaps they won't. But they will carry this joyous occasion in their hearts. There isn't enough gold in the world to replicate this moment.'

She looked at him and smiled, before returning to the copper pot of tea and refilling the mugs.

Samer lost track of time, measuring his day in increments of smiles and stolen glances. He played parlour games with children ravenous for attention, and a raucous game of Blind-man Buff entertained both the watching adults and the delighted children, with Samer careering into furniture and the audience.

The melodic strains of the hymn *There's A Friend For Little Children* emerged from the organ, and the children's pure voices took up the song as they gathered around the organ. The adults laid down their mugs and plates, their physical hunger sated and their faith assured, and they too gathered behind the children, lending their voices to the praise of a familiar god. And when they reached the line *'There's a home for little children,'* everyone smiled at Abdullah Quilliam, the selfless benefactor, and a saviour of sorts to Liverpool's orphans.

The crowd began to disperse but Samer stayed behind hoping there'd be a moment to talk further with the organist, but there was no sign of her. So it was with some reluctance he found himself pressed into washing a never ending supply of used crockery. How this transpired was beyond him, but the mindless scrubbing of cake crumbs and smears of grease was cathartic, allowing his mind to wander.

'I didn't expect to meet you at the sink, Mr Kurdi,' came a familiar voice.

Samer found Abdullah Quilliam grinning at him from behind a gigantic black beard.

'It was the least I could do to repay you for your hospitality.'

'Come, leave that to the ladies. There are some gentlemen wanting to meet you,' Quilliam said, proffering a hand towel.

Perplexed, Samer dried his hands and retrieved his jacket from the back of a kitchen chair, before following Quilliam upstairs to a well appointed study, the lingering fresh paint smell overpowering.

Four men filled the chairs in the study, none of them familiar to Samer. Quilliam made the introductions and cigars were lit, disguising the paint odour but accentuating the stench of business.

That they were conducting business on Christmas Day was a surprise, but he was a businessman at heart, and business was why he was in Liverpool.

'Gentlemen, thank you for coming to Brougham Terrace today, the most auspicious of days. Today marks the start of a wonderful relationship between men of faith and the people of Liverpool. We meet here as brothers, and as loyal subjects to the Queen. Mr Kurdi, it is with great joy that we receive you under our roof. We had received word that you had come to Liverpool in response to our advertisement in my paper, *The Crescent-*'

Samer started to interject.

'We understand the confusion, but trust that you are not here under any false pretences, although I must make it clear from the outset, my role in this endeavour is only one of guidance in all things legal, I have no other part to play. These gentlemen will enlighten you as to our lofty aims and your hopeful involvement. And with that, I'll leave you to discuss the finer details. I need to return to the remaining guests downstairs.'

'I feel that I am at a disadvantage,' Samer announced, pouring himself a coffee, uncomfortable under the gaze of the four strangers, in a room full of pungent cigar smoke. 'You know who I am, but I do not know any of you, nor why you'd want to meet with me?'

'Not at all, you are looking for a business opportunity, and we are seeking an established business partner. The perfect confluence of wants and needs,' said the man in the gold-rimmed glasses opposite him.

'We require a legitimate importer,' elaborated a lanky gentleman seated to Samer's right.

'Williams and Kurdi Limited have been trading for twenty years now. We are importers of goods from around the world, but I guess you knew that, or I wouldn't be here today?' Samer surmised.

'Correct,' replied the portly gentleman with a beard as rotund as his stomach.

The fourth man nodded, his attention more on his pipe than the conversation.

'We heard of your loss at the port-'

'A terrible affair-'

'And to think they suspect one of Her Majesty's employees of having started it-'

'It could have spread to the other warehouses, affecting any one of us.'

The gentlemen went to great pains to commiserate with Samer, sending tiny alarm bells ringing, although the reason for his unease was unclear.

'I don't know how the fire started, but yes, we lost the cargo from our last shipment. Our insurance company will recompense us for our loss, but the damage to our business is frustrating,' Samer responded, holding his cards close to his chest. He didn't know these people, or what they wanted from him. With everything in life, there was a catch.

'You have other shipments arriving soon though, yes?' asked the bespectacled man, removing his glasses and polishing them with a handkerchief.

Samer had a vague idea that there were two more shipments arriving in Liverpool in January, and at least two others coming into London. How these men knew, was a worry.

'We have some goods we need shipped to England-'

'Goods which need to come in quietly,' interrupted the lanky man, his face as long as his body, his fingers steepled under his pronounced chin.

Samer's body stilled, and he fancied he could hear his heartbeat above the red flush infusing his cheeks. This happens once you bend the law — one lie leads to another, and another, until the web becomes so tangled that other spiders, bigger spiders, step out of the shadows to devour you.

'I think you are asking the wrong man,' Samer said.

'Oh, we have it on good authority that you are the perfect company. It isn't much that we ask, one shipment, brought here into Liverpool, unlisted on your manifest, but stored in a new warehouse we will make available for your sole use, although we will have a key.'

'Our relationship will be discreet.'

Samer stood up, shrugging off his cloak of civility, 'You have the wrong man. I'm sorry I can't be of more assistance. Good night, gentlemen.'

'We'll be in touch,' called out the lanky gentleman, his false smile as skinny as his frame and his blue eyes just as narrow.

Samer stumbled down the stairs, desperate to leave the taint of their indecent proposal behind him, and careened into the woman in the headscarf.

Ooompf

'Oh, excuse me,' Samer said, clutching his head where he'd knocked it against hers.

The woman, who'd sunk to the ground holding her own head, laughed, her headscarf askew, sitting amongst the tray of leftovers littering the tiled floor.

Samer forgot his own pain as he reached down to help her stand. And together they gathered up the ruined cakes and sandwiches, laughing at the absurdity of their clash, apologies falling from his lips.

'I will forgive you if you take me to tea,' she replied.

'It's an honour, but how can I take you to tea when I don't even know your name?'

'My name is Sally Glynn.'

'Miss Glynn, I shall collect you tomorrow for afternoon tea,' Samer said, his earlier misgivings about the gentlemen upstairs smothered by the look in Sally's eyes.

'You will escort both my sister and I,' Sally replied smiling.

'Till tomorrow,' said Samer.

The crowd had dispersed and Samer wasted no time hailing a cab to ferry him back to his hotel, unaware that he was being watched from the windows above, and from the blackest of shadows across the street. Even if he had noticed his audience, he would have been hard pressed to state which one of them concerned him more.

THE LUNCH

'Oi, where's the fire?' a vagabond laughed as Meredith scuttled from his lodgings, his bag clasped to his chest.

Meredith ignored him. Let him have his fun, the man was a nobody. But still his laughs haunted Meredith as he hurried down the freezing street, chilling him more than the arctic wind sweeping through the city.

Still a relative newcomer to the city, Meredith turned himself around more than once as he tried to find the mosque on Brougham Terrace.

As Meredith rounded the corner, he staggered to a stop, his way obstructed by a crowd forming outside the ornate building. His jaw hung open. Were all these people desirous of converting to a different faith?

The crowd surged forward, jostling Meredith and his heavy bag. Ahead of him the doors had opened to admit a dark-haired man. A man Meredith recognised in a heartbeat; Kurdi.

Meredith let the crowd flow around him, his feet rooted to the spot as he struggled to decide a course of action. His first instinct was to barge into the building, but to what end? No, he needed more circumspection. He had time on his side, and the element of surprise.

No one expected anything to happen at Christmas. Kurdi and Williams would expect to carry on with their nefarious smuggling activities with the utmost impunity. But they hadn't countered on Clifford Meredith. He'd feed every thing they imported into the ravenous Queen's Pipes — the giant chimneys used to destroy smuggled goods, then he'd see them hang for their crimes.

'Going to hell, the lot of them,' a voice said behind him, 'although at least they'll have full bellies.'

Meredith turned to find a nondescript man, small and weedy, wrapped up in a giant overcoat, his hat pulled low over an acne-scarred face.

'What did you say?'

'I know who you are, and why you're here. Who you're here to see. I'm right aren't I? The name's Noel Glynn and you and I have got a lot in common.'

'You're delusional, we've got nothing in common and I've no idea what you're talking about,' Meredith spluttered.

'Kurdi's just gone into that building, and I bet you a badger's tail that they're not discussing Christmas pudding in there. He's not alone inside—'

'I'm not blind, I can very well see other people are in there with him,' Meredith snapped, annoyed at the interruption to his quest.

'Never said you were. But you're barking up the wrong tree. Mark my words,' the man said, tugging his scarf tighter around his skinny neck, 'you should look at who he's keeping company with. That'll get you your job back.'

'What do you know...' Meredith started, but broke off, his mind racing in a hundred different directions. 'How do you know this? Where's your evidence?'

'You shout me a pint somewhere warm, and we can talk more,' the man offered, rubbing his hands together.

Meredith snorted in disgust. The leech was conning him.

'Clear off, I'm working.'

'But you're not, are you, Mister Meredith? They let you go. Showed you the door because of your obsession with Kurdi and Mister

Williams. Word is you started the fire which burnt up that poor lad looking for a dry place to sleep. You don't want to ignore my offer Mister Meredith, I've got my own reasons for sharing this information with you. Up to you whether you do anything with it. Come on, let's go for that pint. Surely I've piqued your interest, eh?'

With the crowd disbursing, Meredith realised he was an island of conspicuousness amidst an emptying street.

'Be quick about it. But if you're playing games, let me warn you it doesn't pay to cross Clifford Meredith.'

The men turned away from Liverpool's first mosque and hurried against the icy wind towards the nearest tavern where the fire-warmed interior embraced them like a lover.

Meredith reluctantly dumped a handful of coins on the counter and joined his companion with two handles of ale, the liquid spilling over as he slammed them onto the table.

'Good cheers to you,' Meredith's newest confidant toasted, and he swallowed half his drink without pausing for breath.

Meredith sipped his pint, no point in dulling his wits. He wanted this over and done with so he could return to Brougham Terrace before Kurdi left.

'Right, Glynn, you've got your drink. You're in a warm place. You've got what you wanted, so now it's time to spill. What is it you wanted to tell me about Kurdi and Williams?'

'Oh, nothing about Williams. He's not involved in this—'

'So you've wasted my time, and my coin.'

'Hang on there. I only said it didn't involve Mister Williams. I bet by now Mister Kurdi is sitting in a pile of his own shit, wondering where his paddle is,' Noel Glynn said

Meredith's hands curled into fists, a vein pulsing in his temple, years of frustration threatening to boil over.

'Stop speaking in riddles, man.'

'Guns.'

'I beg your pardon?'

'Guns, that's what they want him to bring in. Guns for their holy war. And he's not the only one they've asked, there are others. Some said yes, some said no, but those that said no aren't celebrating Christmas this year, not when they're buried six feet under. Another pint?'

In a daze Meredith motioned for another round, his dwindling supply of coins exchanged for two more pints even though he'd hardly touched his first drink. He couldn't wrap his head around the information. Guns? They'd give him a medal if he destroyed a gun smuggling network.

'A holy war you say?'

'Yip. Stole my sisters away whilst they were at it. That killed my poor Ma. At least my father didn't live to see the day his baby married one of them.'

Revenge was the best motivator, as Meredith himself well knew.

'Now I'm not saying that Quilliam knows anything about it. He's one of the good ones, doing grand deeds for the poor. Hell, he even offered to take me in when my sisters turned tail. No, don't you focus on him, but it's his acquaintances ye see, they're the ones who're speaking to our mutual friend today. Asking Kurdi to make a fast decision. They like quick decisions — a yes or a no. And if he's still alive come Boxing Day, then them guns aren't far behind. Now that's worth a pint, ain't it?'

Meredith stared into the ale, his watery reflection gazing back at him. He was imagining Queen Victoria herself pinning the medal to his jacket, and a promotion to Collector of Customs in London. *Guns.* He still couldn't believe it. His ample stomach rumbled, the thrill of the chase generating a sudden hunger.

'Lunch?' Meredith asked, a fervent brightness to his eyes. The day was improving.

Over lunch, they prepared a plan of action guaranteed to cause maximum disruption to the gun smugglers. Meredith suggested bringing in some support, but the protestations of his companion knocked that on the head. It was to be the two of them, dependent on which way Kurdi went.

'When will you find out his decision?' Meredith asked, trying to fathom the logistics. He'd never been very good at big picture thinking, preferring the rip, shit and bust approach to life. Using threats and intimidation to get what he wanted.

'We have eyes and ears in his hotel. Since he'll want his partner's approval first, he'll write. That's how they operate, and how we'll find out.'

Meredith eyed his companion. As much as he was distasteful, Glynn knew more about Kurdi and Williams than he did.

'Did your sister tell you about the guns?'

The acne-scarred Glynn tapped the side of his nose.

'It don't matter how I found out. And my sisters are dead to me now, so you leave them out of it. They picked their side and God will punish them.'

Meredith toyed with the remains of his lunch, his appetite not as ravenous as it had been, uncomfortable with the gaps in the man's story. But the glorious vision of his lofty promotion stirred again, and he shrugged off the unease. England didn't need more guns in circulation, especially if someone planned on using them against the Queen's men. This was why they'd destroyed the established arms manufacturers in India. Didn't pay to let your subjects arm themselves. He squared away his concerns, attacking his lamb shank with renewed vigour. He fancied they were eating the last supper before retribution rained down upon the heads of the sinners among them. And nothing made him happier.

'You'll be in contact, then, after you hear from your eyes at Kurdi's hotel?'

'I will. You sit tight in your rooms and wait for my word. Once we hear, you'll know what to do.'

Meredith lay his cutlery on his plate. This was the best Christmas ever. Either way, it'd ruin Williams and Kurdi. They'd either be dead, or locked away awaiting the imminent pleasure of death at the end of the hangman's noose. He'd sleep well tonight.

THE LETTER

*S*amer struggled over his letter to Robert. It would take weeks to hear from Robert in any robust form. Potentially they could exchange telegrams, but that was akin to telling the world, and he needed to be more circumspect. He didn't know if he could bring himself to become embroiled with the plans of the men from Brougham Terrace.

Frustrated, Samer slammed his fist against the desk, sending the ink bottle toppling over. For the smallest of moments he watched the dark ink inch across the heavy wood, the whorls of the grain making the ink appear wavelike in its encroachment. With a sudden start he rushed to clean up the spill, mopping the tacky liquid with his handkerchief. Ruined, he threw it into the rubbish bin, where it joined several discarded drafts of his report to Robert. How did one compose a message asking another to agree to a deal which could be viewed as treasonous? The worst part was that he suspected Robert wouldn't be against the idea. Profit came first.

Samer sat with his back to the window, he didn't want to see people carrying about their business when he had such a heavy load on his own shoulders. He allowed himself a moment to drift towards Sally Glynn. Discreet enquiries had established that the Glynn family were a reasonably large household, with Sally one of the younger siblings, he wondered if her conversion to the Muslim faith had caused any friction within the family. Their outing this afternoon would be interesting.

'Damn it, Robert,' Samer said to the room. With a flourish he signed off the latest draft of his letter, sealing it with a finality which felt all too significant. 'Where to from here, Robert? Where to?'

THE INTERCEPT

*I*n the morning light of Meredith's rooms, the avalanche of blackheads on Noel Glynn's bulbous nose did nothing to improve his looks — the protrusion out of proportion to the rest of him — fat and pudgy whereas everywhere else he was skinny, underfed. Meredith tried focussing his thoughts elsewhere, but with every word that came out from between Glynn's non-existent lips drew Meredith's eyes to Glynn's nose.

'Yer not listening to me,' Glynn said.

Meredith's mind had wandered. The landlady had made another unwelcome appearance at his door that morning pestering him for his overdue rent, and it had taken every fibre in his body to stop shaking sense into her. He was the saviour of Britain, a modern day Crusader. The papers would proclaim him a hero and then how would she feel? Glynn clicked his filthy fingers in front of Meredith's eyes, and his halcyon daydreams evaporated.

'Yer not thinking of backing out now, Meredith? Are yer?'

'Just running through the permutations,' Meredith replied, taking perverse enjoyment from Glynn's perplexed look — the man clearly lacked any formal education. It amused Meredith to use complex words with his underlings. Put them in their place.

'Yeah, whatever. So… I have here in my hot little hand a copy of the letter our mutual friend sent to India—'

'A draft isn't evidence,' Meredith retorted. It wasn't good enough, he needed to catch Kurdi with the guns, although that would take time and time wasn't an ally. He'd never been a canny saver, preferring to spend his discretionary income on his personal pursuits. So what he had left was running out making it imperative he got his job reinstated.

'It's enough when you read what it says.'

Without his hat, scarf and the bulky overcoat, Noel Glynn looked like someone had tried inflating his nose with a bicycle pump, and as he talked, he wheezed, as if that air was trying its hardest to escape. And despite the seriousness of their conversation, Meredith giggled as Glynn blew his nose into a snot-encrusted handkerchief.

'Yer think this is funny do you that they will use those guns on good people, who don't deserve it. And it's up to us to stop them, you and me, and show the world what they are monsters who steal away good women whilst planning to murder us all in our beds,' Glynn said, eyes wide, spittle forming at the edges of his mouth. 'We have to kill them before they kill us.'

Meredith threw up his hands. 'Arrest them you mean?'

Glynn shook his head. 'I said nothing about arresting anyone. They don't deserve justice. That there is all the evidence you need to nab them at their next meeting; to take them by surprise. Then Sally will realise and come home where she should be.'

'Sally?'

'My sister, the one they stole away. But we're not talking about Sally, we're talking about the plan. Read the letter.'

Meredith looked at the crumpled sheet of paper he hadn't realised he was holding, the edges smudged with ink. All his life he'd obeyed the laws, enforced them. He'd never turned a blind eye or gone soft on an importer. The rules were the rules. The law was as black and white as the zebra he'd once seen at London Zoo. If you broke the law, you risked the consequences, which ranged from a fine, to imprisonment, and transportation to the colonies in the old days. That was justice.

What Glynn wanted to do wasn't justice, it was murder. It was against the law.

'Read the letter,' Glynn yelled.

The paper remained crumpled in Meredith's hand. If he opened it and read it, what would that mean? It meant he had in his possession evidence, evidence the relevant authorities should have, either Scotland Yard or Customs and Excise. And if he acted on it, what would that make him? Glynn wanted him to break the law. To do the very thing he'd been fighting for thirty years. Who was he fooling, there would be no medal from the Queen.

He shoved the paper into his pocket.

'What are you doing?'

'I'm taking it to the authorities. Thank you for your help but—'

'No, no, we're going now, to sort them. To save my Sally.' Glynn pleaded.

'This isn't about Sally—'

'It is. We need her at home but they stole her—'

'It's about the guns, and so we're handing it over to the authorities. I am not a vigilante,' Meredith said, the words hollow on his tongue. He'd almost abandoned his moral compass to kill a man he hated with every fibre of his being, but that wasn't who he was.

'You said you'd take him down, you swore to me,' Glynn screamed, his pale skin marred by a tide of red indignation flowing upwards from his neck.

'And I will, through the courts,' Meredith answered, still shocked at how close he'd been to breaking the law. Kurdi and Williams would face justice, but not at the hands of a madman with a pistol.

Glynn glared at Meredith before turning tail and disappearing down the stairs of Meredith's rooms, startling the landlady who'd been eavesdropping.

Alone in his room, Meredith smoothed the sheet of paper, the smudged ink barely legible. If Kurdi's letter was about the illegal shipment of guns, then he'd written it in code. From what Meredith could decipher it was more a plea to remove themselves from the opium trade, a brief discussion detailing future business opportunities and a final blurred paragraph, where he could only read every fifth or sixth word, including the words *holy war*.

Meredith stood next to the meagre fire in his room; the landlady extra parsimonious with firewood since his ability to pay his board would soon cease. His hand wavered above the flames. There was nothing he wanted more than to destroy Williams and Kurdi, but not in the way Glynn suggested. Justice through the courts was the right course of action, and this letter wasn't enough evidence for a constable to even question the men. It was nothing.

Screwing into a ball, Meredith tossed it into the flames, the fire devouring the fresh fuel with a flash of light, before simmering down to an emaciated flickering.

He would catch them, his way, one day soon. Glynn still had his part to play in assisting him. But they needed a new plan, one of Meredith's special plans.

THE AUTHORITIES

*M*eredith rubbed his hands in front of the flames, confident he'd made the right choice. It was out of his control now. He could relax and reap the acclaim from unmasking a threat to the nation. Perhaps that medal would be his.

'You sit tight, Meredith,' the officer instructed, adjusting his hat and tweaking his leather gloves.

'Eh? No way, I'm coming too,' Meredith said, jumping up from his seat.

'No civilians allowed.'

'I am hardly a civilian.'

'But you are now. If your information is correct, we'll have the buggers by dinner time.'

There was no point in arguing, the other men's faces set in stone with sombre moustaches and hooded eyes, shifty hands holding wicked batons. Meredith decided it was better to let them get themselves shot than putting himself in harm's way, and he returned to the fireplace.

The policemen filed from the room. Heads would roll today, including Kurdi's if everything went to plan. It wasn't only the heat which made Meredith rub his hands together.

His ample stomach rumbling, Meredith waited until the sounds of action disappeared before rummaging through the Chief Inspector's desk. Just as he thought, the requisite bottle of rum lay ready for him in the bottom drawer. People should learn to lock their drawers. You never knew who was about.

Pouring himself a generous measure, he nursed his drink by the fire, loading another two logs into the grate, the sap spitting in the heat. Contentment was a wonderful thing. So was revenge. Oh how they'd fete him afterwards.

A second tot of rum warmed him right through as he imagined what was happening at a nondescript warehouse near the port. He envisioned armed officers hammering down doors, surrounding bearded men unpacking crates of rifles and ammunition. He went as far as painting a picture of a gun fight, like on the frontiers of California. And what a glorious battle it was.

Meredith was dozing off with a third shot of rum in his glass when the glass door slammed open.

'What a load of poppycock. It was a wild goose chase you sent us on. Do you have no morals? Has your conscience become so corrupt that you're still hounding the poor man to an early grave?'

'Kurdi is dead?'

'What? No, but no thanks to you and your machinations. Get out before you're thrown out. You've wasted precious time and resources. It's no wonder you were let go. You are an embarrassment to the crown.'

'I don't understand—'

'That's obvious.'

'But the guns?'

'There were no guns.'

'There must have been. Crates and crates of them.'

'No guns, no conspiracy. Just a group of very confused men holding a religious meeting in an old warehouse. There were dozens of crates, so your information was correct.'

Incredulous, Meredith shook his head, fuzzy from the rum.

'Did you open the boxes?'

'We did.'

'And?'

'Books. Filled with books, not guns. Foreign bibles. And since we're not living in Tudor England anymore, there's nothing I can do about importing religious texts.'

'Bibles?'

The officer sighed. 'Korans, the bible of the Muslims. The Holy War you accused them of planning doesn't involve guns, but distributing their holy book to convert more followers. Hardly a cause for panic. You embarrassed us, and yourself. You're free to go. Have a good day, *sir*.'

Meredith stumbled from the building, his illusions of grandeur shattered and the beginnings of a migraine wrapping itself around his head. How could he have got it so wrong? How could the police ignore the threat at the end of their noses? *Idiots*. Everyone was an idiot except him. Now Kurdi, and by extension Williams, had got away with it *again*.

With no real plan other than a pint and a bit of fun with one of the lesser girls on call, Meredith took the well-worn path back to his flat to change into something more suitable for the afternoon's activities. A pile of furniture lay stacked against the side of the building, a new tenant moving in Meredith predicted. That might keep the old bat off his case for a few more weeks if she was getting more cash coming in. He tried to think which of the rooms were vacant, but his rum-addled brain wouldn't cooperate.

A fine gentleman's cane poked out of a crate. It was criminal leaving that lying around for a vagrant to steal. It reminded him of his own cane, one he'd *acquired* on the job several years ago — a splendid piece of ivory ringed with a simple band of sterling silver. He'd had it engraved with his initials C.F.M., just like this...

The penny dropped.

These were his belongings. The landlady had emptied his flat of everything he owned, stacking it on the footpath for beggars and freeloaders to help themselves. Evicting him without notice.

Meredith sank to the stoop. No job, no home, no revenge. His pistol sat heavily in his pocket, but he ignored it. A pistol was the weak man's option, and he wasn't feeble. He needed to regroup; figure out where to from here. The best place for that was from home.

His elderly parents had a farm in Corbridge, a tiny town he couldn't wait to escape from as a young teen, ill-equipped to become a stone-mason like his brothers. He could return home and plot his revenge from there. He still had friends within Customs and Excise who would keep him updated about the activities of Williams and Kurdi until he could destroy them. Yes, that was the plan. It would delight his parents to see him again given it was several years since he'd been home. He could dress it up as an early retirement and they'd believe him — their son — their golden boy.

INDIA

~

THE ORIENTAL

*A*fter his long journey to Bombay from England, the trader Robert Williams thought only of the bed in the Great Western Hotel he'd arranged via telegram, weeks earlier. He was travelling alone, with only business on his mind. This wasn't his first trip to India, but it never got easier. The scents, the sights, the abject poverty everywhere you looked. Such a preposterous kaleidoscope of colours. But now there was just one colour surrounding him, red — red. The rich maroon of an apple fallen from a tree, the crimson of fresh blood.

The *dhoti* driver had delivered him to a Chinese enclave, and had all but thrown Robert's luggage from the carriage, before vaulting back into his seat and urging his horse away as if his life depended upon it. And it may well have.

Suspicious eyes narrowed at the English gentleman standing in the middle of the road, his hat in one hand, and his other resting protectively on his watch chain.

'Come, mister, come,' beckoned a boy to Robert, the boy's black hair snaking down his back in a simple plait, swinging as he turned and ran towards the nearest establishment.

Robert nudged his trunk with his foot. Too heavy to lift, he was loath to leave it in the street, but the boy had disappeared inside, and the surrounding eyes had become no more welcoming.

His indecision vanished as two men stepped from behind a cart hawking red bolts of cloth, and between them heaved his trunk onto their shoulders, ushering Robert towards the house which had swallowed the child.

The awkward threesome crossed the road, and the men disappeared around the corner, leaving Robert at the base of the staircase, all rational thought disappearing with his trunk.

'Come, please!' the lad implored from the doorway. 'Madame Ye waits.'

Robert turned to survey the street before taking the stairs, his heart as heavy as his footfall.

Once inside, the door shut behind him.

'Why am I here?' Robert asked, gazing at his surroundings. He was a well travelled and educated man, yet hadn't been anywhere like this. It was as if they'd plucked him from this world, transporting him to the imaginary realm of a warrior battling contortionist dragons. Never in his life had he seen such intricate carvings on everything. On door frames and cornices, on every inch of the heavy furniture in the entrance way, and on the leather robes hanging on the walls.

And the smell; unidentifiable but sickly sweet with tangy overtones. Not unpleasant, but nothing he recognised, and it set him on edge.

A pair of carved wooden doors opened, the brass hinges silent.

'Come,' the boy said, gesturing to Robert.

The peculiar scent enveloped them both as they stepped forward and the room beyond revealed itself.

A piece of the orient had nestled itself into the heart of Bombay. Fierce dragons curled their way up the legs of the card tables and brass vases squatted on every surface, with leaping fish cast as handles on their pregnant sides. Enormous goldfish adorned the *Ming dynasty* urns which sat on either side of a hearth filled with a roaring fire, making the room lava hot.

Opposite the doorway, seated behind a frail desk, was an

equally frail Chinese woman, her age indeterminate, her hair secured in a stylish bun. Each of her tiny wrists encircled with jade bangles and matching teardrop-shaped earrings fell from her earlobes.

'Mr Williams, you honour us with your presence,' said the woman.

'I had no choice,' Robert replied.

'That is a matter of interpretation,' she said, motioning towards a high-backed settle.

Robert squared his shoulders and strode over to the couch, his English body seemed too robust for the delicate piece of furniture, but it held his weight as he lowered himself down.

'Well, I'm here now, so why is it that you've drawn me into your web?'

'Tea first, then we talk,' Madam Ye replied.

With an imperceptible flick of her wrist, the waiting boy vanished through another door, almost invisible in the patterned wall.

Silence hung, allowing Robert a moment to acclimatise to his surroundings. The silence didn't bother him, he understood using it as a weapon, as a means of manipulation, so left the woman to her game playing. He was wary but not concerned, he was certain no harm would befall him here.

The boy reappeared, unseen hands holding open the concealed door allowing him through whilst carrying a bronze tray laden with a steaming pot of tea and two almost translucent, handleless cups.

'You pour, Mr Williams,' Madam Ye directed. 'I find even lifting a teapot too difficult these days.'

Robert moved to the table and swirled the teapot in the English fashion, before pouring the contents into the cups. Another foreign odour replaced the sickly sweet scent, but one which was fresh. Mottled brown leaves settled to the bottom of each cup, marring the cream of their glaze. Robert's hands dwarfed the cup of tea as he carried it over to the woman, the heat penetrating the delicate porcelain burning his hands. Placing it on Madam Ye's desk, he glanced over the paperwork covering every inch, but the writing on the pages was indecipherable, written in a strange language, making no sense.

'Can you read my papers, Mr Williams?'

Robert flushed at the exposure and returned to the teapot to disguise his embarrassment.

'I'll explain them to you, and your involvement, after our refreshments,' she said, closing her eyes to sip the fragrant liquid.

Time stilled while she sipped her drink. Robert knew no one who took so long to sip their tea. Somewhere a clock chimed the hour. The green tea was a curious mix of fig and lemon and woody vanilla, if there were even such a thing. He left half in his cup, the peculiar freshness too foreign for his palate. And he waited.

'I can hear your impatience, Mr Williams. You didn't enjoy your tea?'

'There's nothing wrong with it, I'd just prefer to know the reason I'm not relaxing in my hotel with a whisky and a cigar, unpacked, and ready to conduct some real business.'

'But we are. Although ink doesn't stain my fingers, this is the correct way of things. Time is always on our side, Mr Williams. No one prospers from hurrying through time.'

Robert pulled his pocket-watch from his pocket. Frowning, he tapped at its frozen hands.

'See? Time has no place here,' said Madam Ye, leveraging herself up from her chair, her tiny frame almost doubled over giving her a hunched appearance. The boy sprung forward with an ivory cane, placing it into her hands, his own small hands strong under her elbows, supporting her to the opposite settle where he helped lower her down. She sank into the corner, a sigh escaping from her lips, the only sign of her discomfort. The boy spirited away the cane once he had settled her, and only then did she reopen her eyes, eyes which showed none of the pain coursing through her body.

'It is time to discuss the black smoke you are buying,' she said.

Robert's head jerked back.

'I'm sorry?'

'The black smoke, the opium. Secrets are my trade, Mr Williams. And I know yours.'

Robert's mind raced. Smuggling opium into England had been a business decision he and Samer had agreed. Despite its legality, not declaring it had been both a financial decision, and one of pride. The papers were full of reformists trying to have the drug outlawed because of some perceived harm, and his company was a reputable firm, with a long established import licence he didn't want tainted when the bell finally tolled for opium being declared as illegal as slave labour.

'My supplier is renowned, they also supply Ah Sing's in London, a fine establishment, well regarded and run by a Chinese gentleman.'

Madam Ye's nostrils flared.

'One opium den in London is much like any other. I do not know Ah Sing, and his practices are of no concern. It is your business choices which we are here to discuss, Mr Williams.'

'I'm not here to discuss my business, Madam Ye. I'm here because you have brought me here, to this place not of my choosing. You speak in riddles of time and of smoke, but *my* time is valuable and you are wasting it,' Robert replied, pushing off the settle, his bulk towering over the diminutive woman.

She laughed at him, the sound raspy, as if rough stones jumbled her voice as it rattled up through her throat.

'Sit down, Mr Williams. Some food perhaps?'

'No thank you, I want to go to my hotel. But before I go I want you to tell me how you know about my business.'

'You want me to tell you? What if I told you the tea leaves foretold it, from the leaves in your cup?'

'Then I'd say you've been on the pipe too long. That's what's in the air isn't it? This is an opium den?'

'How perceptible, Mr Williams. We cater for all desires here. But again, that is not why you are here. Think of our meeting as a warning; a premonition of what may be, to you or your children.'

Robert stood open-mouthed, the mention of Grace and his young son chilling him to the core. His daughter, his beautiful, feisty daughter. No one threatened his family.

'You dare threaten my family?'

'As I said before, Mr Williams, that is a matter of interpretation.

I'm not so hungry now, and so I will retire. I look forward to continuing this conversation when you are more congenial,' Madam Ye said, and in a heartbeat the boy returned to her side with her cane.

Before Robert could even react, another man was at his side, the larger man who'd carried his trunk. His body blocking any attempt by Robert to remonstrate with the woman, who'd disappeared through the hidden door, only the *tap tap tap* of her cane any indication that she'd ever been there.

Robert shook him off and stormed over to the veiled door, but found no handle or latch or any depression. Only a fingernail width gap showed there was a door there at all. Defeated, Robert turned back. It felt to Robert like he was walking into the jaws of a dragon as he crossed the threshold.

A *dhoti* stood outside, Robert's trunk already strapped to the back, and lurched off as soon as Robert climbed in. He turned to check his surroundings, promising himself he'd remember the location, and that he'd be back. No one threatened his family.

THE TRADER

*R*obert Williams paced the floor of his hotel room, back and
forth, counting his steps as a mechanism to stop himself
losing control.

His Grace, that woman had all but threatened his girl; his impulsive
and inappropriate Grace. Which made it even more important to get
her married and out of harm's way. And as for his son? He barely
knew him. A late addition to the family through an ill-timed dalliance.
He'd reluctantly accepted him as his responsibility, allowing the boy to
take his surname, but he had sent him away to boarding school,
refusing any other communication until the boy was of a suitable age
for conversation. How did the woman even know of his existence? It
was a dark secret that even some of his closest friends had no
knowledge of.

And the opium? He couldn't understand why their small enterprise
shipping opium from India to England concerned anyone? No one was
being hurt, the drug was legal. Admittedly, they were avoiding any
Customs duties, but everyone did that, and the Excise men knew it.

All he could do was wait. He had a months' worth of meetings
scheduled with manufacturers in town and out in the wild. You had to
stretch yourself to get the quality their clients now expected from

them. The easiest option wasn't necessarily the best one. But should he make those appointments? What if he missed Madam Ye summoning him whilst he was gadding about the countryside and out of touch for days on end?

Sweat beaded on his brow. He couldn't erase the memory of the sickly sweet smell of Madam Ye's rooms and fancied that it had somehow followed him back to his hotel. He needed a bath and would have to have his clothes laundered to wash the woman out of his life. *Blast this country*, Robert thought, for the hundredth time.

A knock outside interrupted his inner monologue, but before he could open it, an envelope appeared underneath the door.

The little white rectangle sat there, waiting for him to pick it up, to read it. Why was he being such a victim? This mentality he'd adopted was tearing him apart, he should be on the hunt, knocking heads together, not wasting away waiting for the sky to fall.

Robert ripped open the envelope. One of the hotel's monogrammed telegrams fell out — a telegram from his business partner Samer Kurdi. The news was bad.

'Damn it,' Robert yelled.

A fire at the port had destroyed everything, including the smuggled opium. The enormity hit him like a sucker punch to the stomach. They'd pre-sold so much of that shipment through his fancy catalogues, both to retailers and to private customers. Insurance wouldn't cover the goodwill they would lose by not delivering, as Samer pointed out in his telegram. Nothing would recover that. Some other hustler would step forward to fill the void and Robert imagined the ships in the port were being loaded with pallet after pallet of almost identical stock, going to exactly the same place, Liverpool.

He had to do something fast to recoup the money and goodwill they'd lose. Thankfully they had insurance to support them in the short term, but it was his customers and their future goodwill he needed. And as much as it turned his stomach, there was only one solution - Madam Ye.

Depending on how quickly she could supply what he needed, he could have a part shipment on the water to England within the week which might placate the opium dens he'd agreed to supply. He'd kept Samer in the dark about that side of things, for good reason. Samer hadn't wanted to bring in opium at all, it being against his faith, but Robert had strong armed him, promising it was just the one shipment, to fund the initial costs of the catalogue business, expenses which had ballooned out of control. It wouldn't be too long before he wouldn't be able to hide their perilous financial position for too much longer, which was why they needed the opium money, to tide them over. It made sense to him and he prayed Samer would agree. Oh he had plenty of assets to sell if required, but those were assets he'd built up for Grace's future, and she needed the legitimacy of those to bolster her chances of a decent marriage. This was the only way.

Robert penned a short telegram to Madam Ye and rang for the bellboy to come deliver it. He kept it suitably vague, trying to use words the woman herself spoke. He didn't trust anyone anymore, not when his livelihood and the life of his daughter were at stake.

Looking forward to tea. Smoky this week.
Black pudding is on the menu.

With the telegram on its way to Madam Ye's, Robert stripped off and sank into the bath he'd drawn, the scalding water stripping the stench of opium smoke from his body but doing little about the insidious thoughts butterflying around his brain.

THE GAME

*W*aiting for a reply was worse than torture and sent Robert back to his pacing. He'd refused to leave the hotel for fear of missing any word from Madam Ye, so when the bellboy delivered another monogrammed envelope, he snatched it from his hand.

Heart beating, he ripped open the envelope, but it wasn't a telegram and bore no news of a fire nor any threats. It was an invitation to a polo game, from the Indian Polo Association.

Robert knew polo, he'd even dabbled in the old ball and stick back at his club when he was younger, but he lacked the passion for it. He propped the invitation above the unlit hearth and considered the embossed card. Given his company's reputation, maybe someone in the Association was trying to curry a favour? He could think of no other reason to invite him, although as he regarded social occasions useful for fostering new business and contacts, he would go.

He made a note of the date; the game was in two days and didn't impact on any of the meetings his agent had lined up for him. The only ball in the air was Madam Ye and her demands. He just had to trust that she'd interpret his telegram and be in contact. He didn't have to wait long.

On Robert's return from his evening meal in the dining room of the Great Western Hotel, a curious mix of a saddle of mutton and veal sweetbreads, with artichokes and asparagus in a creamy sauce. He was full and feeling somnolent when he spied the third monogrammed envelope under his door in as many days.

His dinner threatened to come up as he opened the envelope. Robert's blue eyes scanned the short missive, and he released the breath he hadn't realised he was holding. A reply from Madam Ye, offering to send a boy to bring him to tea at the end of the week. Another line on the page urged him to enjoy the upcoming polo match. *There were no secrets in this city.*

The day of the game mirrored the day before and the one before that, the temperature climbing no higher than 27 degrees; hot but bearable compared to other parts of India Robert had visited. The sky was an unimaginable blue, as if Rembrandt himself had painted it, and the city teemed underneath it as Robert travelled to the polo field. A newer club than the more established polo grounds in India. Today teams from Alwar, Bhopal, Jaipur, Jodhpur and Kashmir were competing. The hotel staff urging him to support one or the other of the teams, depending on their origins. Robert had no intention of placing any bets unless he saw other gentlemen such as himself betting on the games. He was there to connect and to establish new trading partners, and where possible, arrange more favourable terms with whichever minor royalty was in attendance, that was the way of things here in India.

After a few enquiries, it transpired that Robert's shipping agent was sponsoring a game, hence his invitation. And it made sense for him to be there, a valuable client. It may even be fertile ground to find Grace a husband, as Indian polo grounds were the preferred haunt of English Army Officers, where they could show off their horsemanship and ball skills for the glory of their corps.

Every officer desired membership to the Bombay Polo Club. There was a narrow window for applications, so attendance for someone such as Robert, as the guest of a sponsor, was the only way he could enter the club, otherwise he'd be relegated to the 'B' enclosure, and as an Englishman, that just wasn't acceptable.

Bombay was a thriving metropolis, and although Robert had stayed many times, it never ceased to amaze him that the view from his carriage rivalled most other European cities. Surrounded by soaring majestic buildings such as the Tata mansion, Crawford Market, Watson's Hotel, and the iconic Victoria Railway Station, if you ignored the incessant clamouring, the inescapable noise, and the heat, you could just as easily be in Paris or Rome or Prague, or even London.

After checking his pocket for his invitation, Robert exited his carriage and entered the polo grounds, surrounded by uniforms and men of business. A fair number of the attendees were women with parasols and ribboned sun hats, tittering amongst themselves, angling for attention — part of the *Fishing Fleet* - third daughter of the pastor type women, sent to India to secure suitable husbands. Most succeeded. The ratio of eligible bachelors skewed in the women's favour, although the women knew far too much about military ranks now to settle for a minor notary posted to a backwater town. No, they were clever little things the Fishing Fleet girls.

'Robert!'

Robert Williams turned at the sound of a familiar voice.

'Winston! What the devil are you doing here?'

'Competing with the 4th Queen's Own Hussars, how did you wangle an invitation? Those are worth more than gold, every man and his dog wants one,' Winston motioned towards the invitation in Robert's hand.

'Business, Winston, it's always business. I've no time to prance around on ponies like you army chaps,' Robert replied, a twinkle in his eye.

He'd met Winston at a cram school years ago, when he had a half-baked ambition to join the civil service. He'd dropped out, but Winston had stayed. They'd kept in contact for a brief while before going their separate ways, Winston into the army and Robert into trade.

'Come on, Winston, hop to it, team talk,' shouted out another officer, resplendent in his uniform, white jodhpurs pressed within an inch of their lives.

'We'll talk afterwards,' Winston called back, as he dashed away.

Robert made his way into the club rooms, fielding greetings from various fellows — both acquaintances and old friends in equal measures. It was akin to being in his club in London, although adding women into the mix was a novelty. They didn't admit women to his club. Allowing them entrée was a hideous thought — they'd stamp out the gambling, and the cigars and agitate to gussy up the place with floral print cushions and lace at the windows. A club was a place for men, but he couldn't deny that here they provided a level of delicate refinement.

Robert had been single for so long that he was unpractised with interacting with the fairer sex. The only women he socialised with were his daughter Grace, and his sister Jessica, the rest he didn't bother with. So it shocked him to end up standing by the trophy cabinet conversing with an all-too-frank dark haired woman who knew more about polo than the staff at the hotel.

'And what's that trophy?' Robert asked, pointing to one of the less ostentatious trophies on display, distinctive because of its lack of horse-type embellishment most traditional polo trophies exhibited.

'With the jade handles?'

Robert nodded.

'The Ye Family donated that. The Association couldn't say no to such a magnificent piece, especially as the family are a significant financial supporter of the club,' Miss Bolton said.

Robert turned to scan the room. The game had begun outside, meaning the club rooms had emptied somewhat, leaving a smattering of couples sitting at the tables, avoiding the stifling dust churned up by the ponies. There were European faces and Indian faces, but not a single Chinese face.

'Are they here?' Robert asked.

His companion laughed. 'Here? Heavens no, they frequent the 'B' enclosure. They have their own pavilion, you can see it if you come this way,' she said, pulling him by his hand.

So taken aback by the unfamiliar touch, Robert allowed her to lead him to the windows where she pointed with her gloved hand to the opposite side of the grounds. You couldn't miss it, the redness of the silk drew the eye as much as fire attracted moths to its naked flames. Robert couldn't see the people sitting beneath the roomy tent, but in his mind he imagined Madam Ye on a golden throne watching him, waiting. He turned his back on the tent, back to his companion.

'Where should we watch the match from?' he asked, steering her deeper inside, ostensibly towards the bar, but more to shield himself from any curious eyes.

'From the centre of the stand of course,' she said. 'But drinks first, an excellent idea. I'll have a gin and tonic.'

Robert ordered them both drinks, and they made their way out onto the stands decorated with a sea of white parasols, as if someone had lowered a sky full of clouds from heaven to hover above the crowds.

She muscled her way to some empty seats, and without spilling a drop of her drink, pulled a pair of binoculars from the bag looped over her wrist, bringing them up to her eyes in a practised motion.

'Just look at that form, *ooh* offside. That's Buckmaster, no idea how he made the team, he is always offside. Here hold this,' she answered, passing him her gin and removing a small pocketbook and silver propelling pencil from her bag before jotting off a quick note.

'What do you think of old Winston?' Robert chanced, catching sight of his friend cantering past as the umpires and referee decided on the penalty.

'He's improving but his handicap is still average. The officers improve the longer they are out here, so hope exists. Seems a shame that he'll go back to England soon, but that's for the best given... never mind that. I've read that the polo scene is picking up at home,' she said, flicking through her notes.

Robert ignored the hint of scandal which slipped from her lips. 'How is it that you know so much about this sport?'

'Mr Williams, only two sports exist in India — polo and gossip. I'm not overly fond of gossip so I'm left with polo. If they allowed me to play, I'd be giving those boys a run for their money. None of them can follow the line of the ball, although the Indians are better than the English, at least *they* know how to ride off another fellow without being called for a foul. Makes the play so much faster and far more interesting.'

Robert stared at her in fascination, quite forgetting that he had her drink, and she had to ask him for it. Moments later, she thrust it back into his hand, bringing the tiny binoculars up to her large brown eyes.

'Ooh, now that is fascinating. See over there?' she said, passing the sterling and mother-of-pearl glasses to Robert and pointing to another tent erected behind the opposing teams goalposts.

Robert adjusted the focus and the luxurious pavilion of an Indian noble came into view, with a phalanx of attendees in immaculate uniforms fussing over an elderly gentleman draped in pearl necklaces and gold braid, a ceremonial sword at his side. A common sight in India, where there were more Indian royal families than there were states, and all as rich as Croesus.

'We rarely see him out anymore,' Patricia said.

'Who is he?'

'The Raja of Nahan. He was a real man about town back in the day but he doesn't get out much. Odd that he's here today with his whole entourage. Can you imagine the secrets he knows? Everyone has heard the rumours about him...'

Robert shrugged, he had no time for gossip regarding people he couldn't use.

'Didn't sit well with his family. Afterwards there were big fallings out over their business dealings, and it got carved into pieces. He kept the largest portion. Still a catch for someone, even at his age, so I'm surprised there isn't a flock of peacocks around him vying for his attention today. Money always brings out the vultures.'

Her words piqued Robert's interest.

'What businesses does he own?'

'Almost everything, but I don't know for sure. You should ask the officers, they'll tell you,' Patricia Bolton said.

'Come now, Miss Bolton. You profess to avoiding gossip, but from the little I have observed of you today, I'd wager that you have a sharp head on those shoulders, and that not much gets past you. Am I correct?'

'Mr Williams, you've made a shocking assumption. Here I am, risking my reputation, talking to you unchaperoned, sharing my binoculars, and you suspect me of knowing a gentleman's business? I am but a mere woman, which is obvious-'

A huge roar went up as the home team scored a resounding goal, and Robert and Miss Bolton paused their repartee to applaud.

'Hardly a *mere woman...*'

'I confess, Mr Williams, I know little about the Raja's cotton, indigo and opium businesses these days but I can find someone who understands his shipping methodologies and who his preferred agents are, if that suits? But if it's his charitable works you are more interested in — funding of schools alongside the Christian missionaries, then that'd be harder.'

Why was it that every woman he'd met in India spoke in riddles? How hard was it to get a straightforward answer to a question? He needed another drink.

'Another drink, Miss Bolton?'

'Lovely, thank you. I'll come and peruse the offerings at the bar. The gin has left me feeling rather light headed in the sun.'

Once at the bar, Patricia ordered a Pimm's Cup. The waiter looked to Robert for guidance — women ordering drinks wasn't the done thing. Patricia muttered something under her breath, and stalked off to a table, leaving Robert to placate the distressed wait staff.

Robert joined her, a second gin and tonic for him, and a Pimm's for her. They'd advised him to drink gin and tonic in India - the quinine in the tonic thought to combat the threat of malaria.

'You're not like the other girls here,' he said.

'I'm not a girl,' Patricia snorted.

Robert cleared his throat. He didn't want to comment on her age, which he guessed was somewhere in her fifties, maybe, he was no good at judging a woman's age.

'You're wondering why I'm still in India? Without a ring on my finger?'

'Well, I...'

'Don't worry, I'm used to it. Did you notice the uniforms the boys are wearing out there?' Patricia asked. 'I designed most of those. Even teams in England and some American teams wear my uniforms. Would that have happened if I'd returned to England? Highly doubtful, as I'm sure you'd agree. There isn't the scope for a single woman to be as successful as I have been here. There's plenty of money in uniforms, Mr Williams, if you have the right contacts and if you can read between the lines in the newspapers, which I'm sure you can do. Personally, I'm investing in military uniforms. And I recommend you give that some consideration,' Patricia said before sipping her drink. 'I love a good Pimm's, don't you?'

'Where did you get the money to finance it?' Robert asked, his own drink forgotten on the table.

'There was another woman who provided the initial capital, sadly she's long gone now, Naomi Abbott. She took me under her wing after someone abandoned me.'

'Abandoned? Who would do such a thing, was it an army officer?'

'No, no, perhaps I used the wrong word. Not so much abandoned, but... hell, it's too hard to explain. It's worked out for the best,' Patricia laughed. 'There's nothing left for me in England, so here I am, drinking Pimm's at a bar at a polo game in India. If I'd gone home, I'd just be drinking the same drink at Wimbledon but with only a tiny shop and not much else to show for a lifetime of hard work. So I chose this life, which has been a dash more life threatening than I thought, but much more enjoyable than what I had.'

Robert shook his head, lost, he'd never have been able to comprehend that Patricia was from the future. He was so focussed on Patricia's words about military uniforms, that he didn't hear her Wimbledon comment.

Another roar from the stands swung their heads around, and silence fell at the table. Robert contemplating everything on his plate and whether he should add something else, and Patricia allowing herself a moment of reflection for the life she'd given up once Sarah Lester disappeared.

The crowd swarmed inside, wreathed in smiles and drunk on joy. Patricia slipped an embossed card across the table before excusing herself and taking her glass over to another group where their infectious joy cured her of the melancholy on her face. Robert tucked the card into his waistcoat pocket. He'd call on her later, for they had much to discuss. The shipping agent then paraded Robert around the room, making introductions and arranging meetings. An excellent day overall, apart from the glimpses of red Robert caught sight of now and then, red flags fluttering across the field, blood red.

THE MERCHANT

*P*atricia fingered the delicate red cloth, the possibilities of the fabric filtering through her mind. It would never fly at home in England, it was too garish, too full of the joy of life. But in India, it was beyond perfect.

'I'll take two bolts of this,' she said to the merchant, whose bedraggled countenance was nothing like the exquisite fabrics he was hawking.

The fabric merchant wasn't the usual trader she dealt with, but he'd come highly recommended by someone's cousin's cousin, or something similarly complicated. That was the nature of business — you either went with the flow, or nothing got done. Everybody knew somebody who could help you, and you were honour bound to trust their judgement. So far, capitulating to the advice of her assistant had stood her in good stead.

Thoughts of home had petered away, but sometimes they nudged their way back in, like today. Dressing a populace obsessed with mourning was never something she'd had to consider in her previous life. But here, people dressed to the expectations of others, and woe betide if anyone strayed from those expectations.

The merchant presented a bolt of a dark blue pinstripe, eerily reminiscent of a suit Andrew Harvard used to wear. Andrew was the one thing she missed most about her old life. But she hadn't wasted away without him. There'd been plenty of men to escort her to the theatre, or to entertain her at dinner. There'd been no special companion like Andrew, but she had fantasised about a life with him, before she ended up in India. And now she wouldn't have it any different.

'No, not that one, have you got anything lighter? A cream or a caramel?'

He rummaged through his collection before pulling out a beautiful coffee-coloured linen, light and beautifully woven. Perfect.

Patricia's enthusiasm was infectious, clapping her hands in child-like wonder. Ideal for the most wonderful range of gentlemen's suits. She tried not to think 'safari suit' but couldn't help remembering the images of colonial Englishmen lounging about on lush Indian lawns from the history books. She strived to keep her designs unaffected by what she remembered of the past, wanting to create her own designs and not just recreating fashion she knew to be contemporary to the times. But the words 'safari suit' jangled around in her brain. She'd make it her own. It's not like the future fashion curators would be any the wiser.

'I'll take everything you've got of this one, and I want to put in an order for another four bolts of the same. Can you do that?'

The cloth merchant said yes. Whether it was or wasn't possible, he would agree. It was the way they operated. If four additional bolts arrived, she'd be a happy lady. If they didn't, it wouldn't be the merchant's fault, he'd blame it on the weavers or the roads or the weather or anyone other than himself. And she'd nod and smile and sympathise. That was life.

Patricia lifted the bolt of cloth and wrangled it upstairs to her workroom. The rest she left for her assistant to carry but she wanted to unroll this exquisite linen and imagine what she might create with it.

As she made her way upstairs, she paused to scratch an itch on the inside of her elbow. There was always something trying to bite you in

India. Big things, small things, slippery things, flying things. She spent half her life with a fly swat in one hand and applying calming lotion with the other. Patricia hated bugs with a passion and was happiest hidden under her mosquito net laughing at the stupid creatures fruitlessly trying to reach her.

Once upstairs, she rolled the fabric out over her giant cutting bench, checking for flaws. The merchant was a genius, and she could hug him. She was more excited about working with this than the red fabric Ajay was bringing upstairs. She'd given up designing dresses for lazy women sent out from England to fill in time before breeding. Fashion for men was far more interesting with more scope for clever detailing and pockets and hidden seams and layering.

She scratched at her arm again. She'd have to remember to put cream on it when she got home.

Her assistant Ajay Turilay arrived, panting with the effort of carrying the rest of the cloth, which Patricia waved into a corner, her mind focussed on her design.

"What do you think of this?" she asked, doodling a quick sketch.

She was lucky to have Ajay as her assistant. As one of the most brutally honest men in India he would tell her if he thought her designs a folly.

Ajay agreed enthusiastically.

'Excellent.' Patricia's face deepened into well-worn smile lines. 'I'll keep working on this while you head off to find some suitable buttons and buckles for the jacket. I'm thinking brassy-gold or something similar. Your thoughts?'

'Too much,' Ajay said, thin eyebrows disappearing under his turban.

'You're right, too much for here. Silver?'

'A matching colour,' Ajay replied, cutting a sliver of fabric from the corner. 'I'll find the correct ones.'

'Knew I could trust you. See you when I see you,' she said, waving him off, her mind already elsewhere.

As Ajay disappeared downstairs, Patricia missed seeing him scratch at *his* arm, and at another spot under his collar.

146

THE MALADY

*P*atricia double-checked her figures. The measurements had to be right otherwise they would waste the cloth. It had been a steep learning curve mastering the old-fashioned fountain pen, but now she found it a thousand times more satisfying than using a computer. There were a million things she missed about living in the 21st century, but being bound to her laptop wasn't one.

She rubbed at the ache in her arm but no amount of rubbing shifted the pain. What she needed was a long soak and a holiday. Repetitive strain injury or occupational overuse syndrome wasn't just a modern affliction. She'd been working too hard.

'Ajay?' she called out, not even looking up from her figures. 'Can you see this goes in the post this afternoon?'

The young man got up to take the letter from Patricia's hand. Caught up in her work, Patricia never noticed his slow carriage as he hobbled over to her desk.

'And Ajay?'

'Yes, Miss Bolton?'

'After that, don't come back until Monday,' she suggested.

Conscientious about timekeeping, she expected him to argue with her, but to her surprise he agreed.

'Think of it as my gift to you. Go take your girl for a drive, and her mother and I'll see you Monday, not too early,' she said, a wave of exhaustion sweeping over her.

Ajay Turilay bobbed his head and left Patricia's large office on the first floor of the Crawford Market. From her vantage point, Patrica watched him walk off down the road, not bothering to hail a rickshaw. He was frugal with his money like that. He had dreams of moving to England, and for that he required every penny he could save.

At her desk, Patricia half-heartedly shuffled paperwork around, trying to decide what to do next. A breeze from the open window ruffled the papers she'd just tidied. Air conditioning was something else she missed. She'd never needed it in London, nor during the years she lived up in Simla, but it would be a welcome addition to her life here in Bombay, and she wondered how long it was until someone invented air conditioning units, probably long after she was decaying deep underground somewhere.

Patricia opened the top drawer of her desk and pulled out an album full of *cartes de visite*, an album she'd carried around with her for twenty-odd years. The album's first page revealed a much younger version of herself, clad in clothes of an era long passed. The next always made her eyes water as she wondered what had befallen her friend. A photograph of her and Sarah Lester, or Sarah Williams as she knew her then. A visiting photographer had been passing through Simla, and after the roaring success of Napoléon's own *carte de visite*, every man and his dog had lined up to have one themselves. The photographer was in such high demand, he'd stayed long enough for a *Fishing Fleet* girl to get her claws into him. Before he blinked, she had married him, and demanded that they return to London post haste, explaining that it was a far more suitable location for his photography business. Sarah and Patricia had scoffed that the silly cow had never even considered that the India was the much bigger, and more poorly catered for, market. Even now it made Patricia smile remembering the man's shellshocked demeanour in the few short weeks he'd stayed in Simla. He never knew what hit him.

It was during the photographer's Simla stay that Patricia and Sarah had several sittings, varying their outfits and their positions, quite perturbing the poor man, although there'd been a great deal of mirth at those sessions, until the wife had a ring on her finger, and then they'd come to an abrupt halt. What was it with women and jealousy?

Patricia's finger strayed across the sepia-coloured face of her friend. She could only hope that Sarah and Major Brooke were in a safe place. Every birthday, and on every shiny new star, she wished she knew where Sarah was, and if she'd found happiness. There were hundreds of rumours, every year new ones poured out of the woodwork, some so fanciful that they put the truth to shame. But the consensus was that Major Brooke had gone AWOL, taking Sarah with him. There was to have been a search for the pair, but the uprising had quashed their plans, and after the troubles were over, they'd assumed Sarah and Brooke were two of the unfortunate casualties, recording their suspected deaths at the hands of the Indian mutineers.

Patricia gazed around her workroom, still marvelling at her workspace in this magnificent building. She'd first met Arthur Crawford, the Municipal Commissioner of Bombay, at a dinner in Simla — any one of importance found their way to Simla — you were no one if you didn't. Although entranced with each other, nothing developed between them. Mainly because she had no family behind her to impress him, and she refused to become a plaything, discarded when something better came along. But their friendship had evolved to where he'd asked her to design the uniforms for the municipal employees in Bombay, and in exchange he'd provide space for her burgeoning seamstress business in his new building. Patricia had hesitated, moving to Bombay meant she wouldn't be in Simla if Sarah returned, but it had been years and the winds of change were tugging at her hems. She needed to live her own life. After coercing Albert Lester into promising to send word if Sarah materialised, she'd packed up what little she had, and moved to the elegant city of Bombay, and never looked back.

'Silly girl,' she remonstrated with herself, slamming the album shut. In a fit of industry, Patricia packed the photographs away in a chest half filled with fabric remnants. She kept offcuts from all the fabrics she used in her designs, an album of sorts to remind her of what she'd done and how far she'd come. Stapled to each remnant was a sketch of the design. There were already two tea chests in the basement full of her designs which she'd made Ajay cart down earlier to get them out of the office. He could move this one too, it was ridiculous clinging to the past. She only had a limited amount of future left to her and damn it, she wanted to live it. Patricia sealed up the last tea chest, severing her final link to Sarah and her life in London.

Patricia left the office early. Tonight she'd throw her past behind her. It was twenty years too late, but she'd give life a chance without the baggage of the past. Drinks and dinner at Watson's Esplanade Hotel would be an excellent way of cheering herself up, dragging herself out of the malaise she felt, with the potential likelihood of running into the enigmatic Mr Williams high — everyone ate at Watson's on a Friday night in Bombay, it was the done thing.

She locked the workroom, tugging her sleeve over the angry red rash which had developed around the bite. Bloody bugs. Not for the first time, she wished for a nice ozone-depleting, industrial-sized can of fly spray.

Patricia's bath did little to soothe her painful arm, and the nasty red welt meant she had to change her planned attire. No one wanted to talk with someone who looked like they'd been ravaged by a zombie high on meth. Tonight she'd have to wear something long-sleeved, which she hated. The Indian climate was no more suited to long sleeves than Antarctica suited bikinis.

Doing her hair proved to add more drama to her night. Even trying to lift her arm to brush her hair was painful. *Perhaps it was time for a proper holiday?*

She called for her ladies maid to pin it properly, which wasn't as restful as one thought. Pins jabbing in at her scalp from every angle, terrifying tugs and twists threatened to wrench her head right off her shoulders, started an almighty headache which went from one side of her forehead to the other.

But dinner and the prospect of talking with Robert Williams made her push through. She'd plaster on her lipstick, dredge up a smile, and play the part of a society lady. She'd been playing a part her whole time in India, it was a second skin to her now, which rarely slipped.

But by god, if the itching on her arm didn't go away soon, she'd scream. After lathering it in every potion she had in the house, it was still unbearable. She'd even allowed the cook to apply some pungent natural remedy, which she'd suffered through for ten minutes before wiping the foul concoction off. There was only one solution, and it was something she almost never partook of knowing the consequences through innumerable episodes of *China Beach* and *Tour of Duty*, back in the day.

The first sweet puff of the long tapered opium pipe did the trick as she felt the headache melting away. Slipping her sleeve up to check, she smiled with satisfaction as the speckled crimson lines vanished under her gaze. One more puff might help keep the aches and pains away for the night.

On an opium haze, Patricia climbed into her open-topped carriage, and stared into the skies, remembering a past in London where she never saw a single star let alone a whole galaxy. This too would change, in time. Electricity becoming commonplace, fast-food outlets littering every street. And they would lose the stars.

The carriage ride jolted the bones in her body, sending pain through every joint. A torment even the opium couldn't dull.

Pulling her gloves off, she wiped her clammy forehead. Now was not the time to come down with the flu. She'd been so lucky. Food and personal hygiene had been a big deal since she'd landed here with Sarah all those years ago. The dreaded *Delhi Belly* visited her occasionally, but she was still one of the healthiest people she knew. It was Murphy's Law that tonight of all nights, when she was planning to captivate an interesting man with her wit and charm, she fell sick. She couldn't entertain any defeatist thoughts. A strong gin once she arrived, on top of the opium, and she'd be right.

As expected, Watson's Esplanade Hotel was a hive of activity. Officers with medals, ladies in elegant dresses, waiters in pristine uniforms, uniforms Patricia herself had designed. Greeted like an old friend at the door, the maître d' escorted Patricia into Watson's, where she ordered a large gin and tonic. A large shot of quinine would keep the bugs away tonight. The bar was full of friends, old and new, and the whole environment was a huge carousel of laughter of hijinks. She spied Robert Williams as soon as he entered the premises and prepared for a night of flirtatious fun. She was behaving like one of those young girls sent out to India to find a suitable husband.

Patricia stayed by the bar, leaning on it for moral and physical support. The gin must have affected her more than usual. Smiling, she allowed Williams to kiss her on the cheek, frowning as he pulled away.

'Your cheeks...'

Patricia raised a hand, surprised to find that she'd abandoned her gloves at some point. She examined her naked fingers. Age made them puffy tonight. It was just as well she hadn't put her rings on, because in this state she'd never be able to take them off.

'My cheeks?' she asked, pressing her fingers into her flesh, recoiling in pain. Of all the things to happen, now she had a toothache?

'They're quite...' Williams couldn't finish the sentence, his own cheeks flushing red.

Patricia felt the flush of heat in her cheeks, pulling a face as she predicted a trip to the dentist in her future. She added proper dental care to this comprehensive list of 21st century inventions she missed, like microwaves, the internet, dependable hot water, air conditioning, and shorts and singlets, and bikinis by the pool.

'I think it's a touch of the flu,' she explained. She couldn't tell him she had a toothache, highly unladylike.

'Should I escort you home?'

Patricia laughed off his concern, explaining that after another gin and tonic she'd be fine.

Robert ordered her a drink, and they commandeered a table.

Waiters came and went and Patricia regaled Williams with the background to the designs of their uniforms and her plans for the coming season. She probed him about his reasons for being in India, but found her own thoughts getting tangled as he discussed the various business ventures under way.

'Sorry, you lost me there for a minute,' she said. 'I'm so silly sometimes, head in the clouds and all that. Can you rewind and run that past me again?'

'Rewind?'

'You know, rewind the tape, start from the beginning? Not that we wind tapes anymore, not with DVDs anyway. Or with streaming, you watch from where you left off,' Patricia explained. *Why was he staring at her? Rewind was such an obvious term to use. Why were men so obtuse?*

'I think you should let me take you home,' Robert said, pushing back his chair.

'Home? Of course. Call me an Uber, I'll be fine,' Patrica lurched to her feet where the room rocked underneath her. She hadn't felt a proper earthquake for ages. 'Ooh, an earthquake, quick under the table,' she said, dropping to the ground.

Patrons at the neighbouring tables tittered at her deliciously unbecoming behaviour.

'There's no earthquake,' Robert said, scooping Patricia up from the floor, his face a mask.

'No earthquake?'

'No, you're drunk.'

'Me, drunk? Not bloody likely, not after two drinks. Was it two? I think I lost count. Maybe three, but it's hot in here, and my tooth is killing me.'

Patricia babbled as Robert and the maître d' carried her into a waiting taxi.

'What's your address?' Williams asked.

'Portsmouth Street, can't miss it. There's an entrance round the back,' she mumbled, slumped in the corner.

Williams looked to the others for confirmation. They both shook their heads. There was no such street.

'She can't come in here,' the maître d' said. Not good for business,' he added, scurrying inside.

The driver waited for Robert to give him his instructions.

Williams gave the man the name of his hotel. He'd pay for a room, and when she'd sobered up in the morning, she could reimburse him. But what an appalling situation to put him in, highly irregular. He prayed there weren't any press lurking. The last thing he needed was word getting out linking him romantically with this woman. At the races she'd seemed so interesting, so fresh compared to the vacuous strumpets he'd known — women after him for financial certainty and a place in society. Patricia Bolton was nothing like those other women. She was a drunk though, and he didn't need that complication in his life.

THE BREAKFAST

*T*he young lad set the breakfast tray down and knocked softly at the polished door. The gossip in the kitchen was that she'd arrived drunk, carried to her room by the porter. There'd been a scuffle between the various waiters and bellboys before chef had decreed that he'd be the one to deliver her breakfast, by dint of him being related to the wife of the night manager.

The lady resident didn't answer his quiet knocking, so he pulled an ornate key from his pocket, and twisted it in the lock, pushing the door open.

As he bent to retrieve the breakfast tray, trying not to spill the tea or disturb the arranged plate of eggs, he almost gagged at the stench emanating from the room. The tray rattled as he checked his grip and took a tentative step into the darkened room.

'Breakfast service, ma'am,' he announced.

The odour inside was pungent, like that of a rotting carcass.

The boy dropped the tray on the table and tried not to breathe through his mouth, his eyes watering at the foul stench. He raced to the windows, desperate for fresh air.

Wrenching open the heavy blinds, fumbling with the latch on the balcony doors in his haste, he threw open the windows and fell onto

155

the small balcony taking in lungfuls of fresh air. He almost collapsed when a voice came from behind.

'Close the curtains, the light hurts my eyes.'

The woman in the bed was alive, speaking to him. But even from his position on the balcony, he could see there was something wrong, even if the smell hadn't given it away.

'The curtains,' she moaned, lifting a bare arm to cover her face... a face of nightmares.

The boy expected no one would discipline him for upsetting a customer this time as he fled from the room. Flying from the balcony, past the bed and out the door, his skinny arm held over his nose to avoid the reek of death. He was several feet away from the door, before he retraced his steps and quickly shut the door, locking it behind him. Running back down the corridor, he released his breath, taking several gulps of the untainted air at this end of the hallway, his whole body shaking.

As he made his way back to the kitchens, he considered what he'd tell the others. They were all eagerly awaiting his report, the trade in gossip the lifeblood of the hotel employees. Hotels didn't have secrets. But this was one secret he wanted no part of. He could claim she was still asleep when he delivered the tray, embellishing it by saying that she asked him to open the balcony door when she woke up. Yes, yes, that was what he'd say. That way they'd absolve him from any blame, and he would never go back in there. They could send someone else to clear the breakfast tray and they'd find her and then it would be on their heads, not his.

THE TRAIN

*R*obert Williams stretched out in bed and greeted the bellboy as he laid out the breakfast tray. Conscious that the lad was casting his enquiring glances he kept his tone polite with a supercilious overtone. Stories about his late arrival with Patricia would run through the hotel like water. Who knew what the boy was thinking? He tried not to let it bother him, but the kid kept staring at him every time he thought Robert wasn't paying attention.

He finally threw off the covers, shouting at the boy to get out.

Satisfied, he watched the uniform-clad waiter scurry from the room, bowing as he went.

A starched envelope sat propped up against the china sugar bowl, his name written in blood-red ink. This didn't bode well.

Ignoring the envelope, he poured his tea, the familiar motions soothing his troubled mind. Tea first, then business, no point ruining the day anymore than it already had been. Hopefully, the woman had the good sense to go straight home after her appalling behaviour the night before, although he was loath to ask any of the staff if that had happened.

Overnight he'd persuaded himself he'd had a lucky escape, identifying her fatal flaws so early in the piece. Heaven forbid if he'd got tangled up in such an unsuitable match. Grace would never forgive him.

Thinking about Grace gave him pause. His daughter was the love of his life and he should have brought her with him. She had a brain in her head, of that he was certain. He couldn't say whether he would have talked through his issues with Madame Ye, and what to do about the arrangement she'd proposed, but he might have. He needed someone to discuss it with. All this palaver in the papers about banning the trade in opium. For goodness' sake, it was such a small fragment of society who abused it. Like alcohol, he'd met many men unable to hold their liquor, and now a woman too.

Robert shivered and took a sip of the cooling tea. There was no point in imagining *what if* or *if only?* Grace wasn't with him. Samer had gone on a wild goose chase up to the north of England, heavens knew what he was up to, he'd not received any telegrams updating him. No, as usual, he was on his own and had to decide based on the figures, and his gut feeling.

He scrolled through the letter from Madame Ye, postponing their meeting because of ill health. He threw it down, a headache forming behind his frown. Robert couldn't abide business associates using delaying tactics. He had business to attend to elsewhere in the country, a contract to negotiate for indigo dye, and treading water in his hotel room wasn't part of his plan.

Robert paced the room, like a lion in a cage. Travelling inland was always tedious and took longer than one expected. He could send a telegram advising of his delayed arrival, but what if other traders were sniffing around the indigo? No, there was only one thing to do, and that was to pen a reply to Madame Ye wishing her a *speedy recovery*, whilst keeping his train booking.

With a decision made, he ran off a quick reply, and called for the bellboy to deliver it, stretching the aching muscles in his neck. By god he hated hotel beds and travel. If he negotiated the contact for the indigo, and came to a satisfactory arrangement with the Chinese, then odds were he wouldn't have to leave England again. Samer could do it, he had no ties, no dependents. Then he could relax and concentrate on finding Grace a suitable husband, one which met his sister's strict quality measures. Then he'd spend his time playing the congenial grandfather, taking his grandsons around his country estate, teach them to hunt and the practical side of land management, perhaps even take up a role in local government. Yes, that would suit him quite well.

With his case sent on ahead to the luggage car, Robert ignored the grasping hands of the beggars littering the station and climbed into his first-class carriage, a newspaper tucked under his arm, and a folder of paperwork under the other.

Sinking into his seat, he tipped his hat to the two other occupants of his carriage, ignorant of the dozen other carriages filled several times over their rated capacity. The three first-class passengers cared not one whit for the poor beggars on the carriage roof, or those hanging from the doorways of carriages teeming with humanity, the cloying stink of body odour partnered with the fragrant spices spilling from hundreds of tiffin tins.

The strangers ignored each other in a way only the English can achieve, each rustling the pages of their papers, trying to ignore the humidity and the ridiculousness of wearing woollen suits and socks in a climate more suited to light cotton and leather sandals.

Robert pondered who his fellow passengers were but their existence was of no consequence, and tiring of his own thoughts and a newspaper full of pessimistic predictions about the state of India, Robert folded his paper away, choosing to read over the draft contract for the indigo deal.

He coughed once, as he skimmed the first few pages, laying the papers on the empty seat next to him. He coughed a second time, exacerbating the headache he'd been cultivating since the morning.

No one had said anything about the peculiar activities of the previous night, and he had to admit that he'd all but scurried from the hotel, lest she was lurking in the lobby. The stress of the subterfuge adding to his aches and pains. He hoped the hotel he was staying in tonight was better equipped given how bad his neck was.

'Indigo, eh?' commented the gentleman opposite him.

Robert, in the midst of massaging his neck, slapped the folder shut. The effrontery of the man, reading his file.

'We're headed to the same place,' the man carried on saying, stroking his well-oiled moustache.

'No idea what you're talking about,' Robert said.

'The indigo business, plenty of money in that, although the American's are here too. It's a big contract they're offering. Easy to split between several interested parties I'd say. Wouldn't you agree?'

Robert stared at him. He'd travelled across oceans, suffered threats, endured an unconscionable embarrassment at his hotel, meaning he'd never be able to stay there again, only to find out that the contract he'd hoped to sign might not be his. That he had to share it with a man with more oil in his hair than there was in the ground, was especially galling.

'I can't comment,' Robert blustered. 'I'm a long-time trader in India, our business spans many sectors—'

'Oh I know who you are, Mr Williams,' the man interrupted. 'And why you're on this train today. I'm here to ensure your deal includes provision for our mutual friend,' he said, leaning towards Robert as he whispered the last part.

Robert Williams was used to success and deference, and unfamiliar with threats and intimidation. And he wasn't going to submit to an oily squirrel.

'You, sir, are out of line,' Robert said, taking to his feet. 'I'll have the conductor see you on your way.'

'You don't want to be doing that, Mr Williams. It would disappoint Madame Ye. We know how much Grace is looking forward to seeing you on your return. Didn't she ask you to bring her back a small keepsake? You wouldn't want that to be your heart, in a box?'

'How dare you bring my daughter into this?'

'You're mistaken, sir. Did you hear me threaten our companion?' the moustached man asked the third man in the carriage.

In the far corner, the quiet gentleman lowered his newspaper, his face inscrutable. With long fingers devoid of adornment, he removed his pocket-watch to check the time. Only then did he reply.

'I heard nothing,' he said, replacing his watch. 'We've arrived,' he said, peering out the window.

Open-mouthed, Robert watched the men gather up their belongings, walking to the front of the carriage as they pulled into the station. A uniformed conductor blew his whistle as the train stopped, and more attendants rushed to escort the passengers from the train.

Left alone, a lethargy took hold of Robert's limbs as he repacked his bag. Needing a moment to catch his breath, he retook his seat, closing his eyes. They flew open again, after what felt like only a few seconds, but which must have been longer because the train was pulling out of the station, great plumes of steam rushing past the window.

'Stop this train, stop the train,' he yelled, hammering on the glass.

But the carriage was empty, and his cries went unheeded. The station disappeared into the distance, the teeming mass of humanity obscuring the faces of the two men who'd expected Robert to alight the train with them.

Robert sank into the corner, his head on fire. In ordinary circumstances, missing his stop would be a complete disaster, something to rant and rave about, to demand that the train stop and that they take him back to his stop by any means necessary. But this was no ordinary circumstance. He could get off at the next station to telegram the indigo supplier, and Samer. He could still resurrect a deal from the delay. Losing his unwanted companions was a silver lining.

Robert nursed his headache, resting his aching arms. First, he'd find a decent hotel at the next stop, to rest before this malaise got any worse. Stations were the worst place to pick something up, full of coughing and sneezing people, with no respect for cleanliness and personal hygiene. Once he completed his business here, he'd retire to the country. He wanted nothing more to do with the shenanigans of protracted negotiations for a slice of some international pie. He had more than enough put away for several lifetimes, Grace's lifetime too. Her wellbeing was of more concern to him than his own. He'd send her a telegram too, letting her know where he was, and that he'd come down with a chill. He couldn't help worrying her, but he felt it prudent to let someone know he was unwell. You couldn't trust the doctors here.

When the train pulled in to the next station, any thoughts Robert had of sending a telegram, had fled his mind. He wasn't in his right mind. By the time the conductor appeared, Robert was a gibbering mess, with a fever shy high and two bright red circles on his pasty English cheeks.

The conductor brought his handkerchief to his mouth as he ran from the carriage. With a brother training to be a doctor, he knew what was happening. The late morning editions of the newspapers were full of the news — the plague had arrived in India, and people were dying. Local doctors were preparing for it, and the English had finally accepted it as a fact, with the Governor of Bombay sending a telegram to Lord Elgin, the Governor General of India notifying him of the outbreak of bubonic plague.

The British establishment moved quickly to segregate and hospitalise the infected, but the horse had bolted, and it would be years before the outbreak came under control, as people fled the cities, pulling their loved ones from hospitals, desperate to find a cure elsewhere.

Robert may have been the first casualty the conductor had stumbled across, but he would not be the last. And the conductor did everything in his power to prevent the spread of the disease via *his* station, in *his* town. An unsung hero.

They conveyed Robert by bullock cart to the nearest hospital. And the conductor, by dint of his important role, instructed that they burn the Englishman's clothes, along with his luggage. One impoverished porter tried ferreting the quality case away, but got a slap around the head for his troubles.

'Do you have a death wish?' the conductor barked.

The chastised man scuffed at the ground, refusing to meet the conductor's eye.

'Wash out that carriage, with hot water,' he commanded. The lackey scuttled away.

The conductor refused to allow the train's departure until they had scrubbed the carriage. He'd doused his own hands with scalding water after transporting the Englishman to hospital. His brother was an assistant surgeon there, almost a full doctor, and he would treat the man, but the conductor didn't want to give him any other patients. Even one was too many.

THE SURVIVOR

*W*hen the next bellboy retrieved the memsahib's breakfast tray, he did so with no warning from the first, who'd claimed a terrible headache, before escaping the disease-ridden hotel, his secret stashed away, festering inside him.

That first bellboy had scuttled away like a cockroach in the sun, his feet barely touching the ground as he ran through the teeming streets, unaware that in rooms all over Bombay, more people were succumbing to the plague. Struck down by fevers and racing pulses and bubo — angry, red shiny bumps and lumps in their necks and armpits and groin, sometimes pulsing black with infection.

As the first bellboy slid through his doorway and greeted his beloved mother, the furthest thing from his mind was the safety of his colleagues. He was looking out for himself, for number one. Already he'd decided a trip home to their village might be a plan. His dear mother had begged him to take her home, and he would do anything to make her happy. Going home would wipe out his savings, but it would remove them from the necrotising abomination he'd witnessed today, one which he'd never forget.

As the second turbaned bellboy opened the door, a pungent smell leaked from the room, wending its way into his nostrils, past the abundance of starch used on his uniform and the perfumed oil in his coiled hair.

He tried ignoring the stench as he called out to the memsahib, but it caught in his throat. The open windows washing the foul odour through the silent room.

The midday sun gave all the illumination he needed to see that the woman on the bed wasn't a woman, but more a monster.

Motionless by her untouched breakfast, he hesitantly took a step forward, then another, poking at her swollen black hand with his finger. Stone cold. Panicking, he wiped his hands on his tunic as he backed into the tray, sending the teapot crashing to the ground, along with the congealing eggs and fly-blown fruit.

By the time he reached the kitchens, he was incoherent and Patricia Bolton was dead.

The fabric merchant, who'd sold the delicious linen to Patricia, died hours before she did, in much less salubrious surroundings. Laid out in a prostitute's bed, his blackened tongue hanging from his head, the buboes in his exposed groin as grotesque as the bubo adorning the neck of the prostitute he'd spent the night with.

The unchecked spread of the disease tore apart families and businesses. Officials blamed the outbreak on fabric from Hong Kong, along with overflowing drains, and damp homes. Some even cast blame on rotting grains. Although the biggest problem was the rampant urbanisation and overcrowding, which encouraged the abundant rat population.

For all his faults and foibles, Patricia Bolton's assistant, Ajay Turilay, was one of the lucky survivors. He lay ill in his room for weeks, tended by his mother, who for whatever reason, did not contract the disease. She had burnt his clothes and boiled her own, on the advice of a local doctor who'd passed through on his bicycle, dispensing aid where possible. She'd lime washed the inside and the outside of their two-roomed house and allowed no one across the stoop, save a visit by the Sanitary Commissioner who was more than satisfied that they harboured no festering illness.

It took several days before the death of Patricia Bolton made the papers. By then, her passing was one of many and she only rated three paragraphs in the newspaper, where the editor praised her designs and her insistence on safe work practices for the local ladies who made her uniforms.

Ajay's mother brought the article to her convalescing son. Well educated for a woman, she read the paper every day, always had, sharing the salient points with her son. She'd wanted her youngest son to go into government service, but she'd been soft, allowing him to follow his dream of becoming a tailor like his father. And he'd surprised them all by being taken on by the clever memsahib, and now she was the proud mother who crowed about her son's achievements amongst the other women — who he'd met, who he'd dressed. She still dined off the story of Ajay meeting the Governor of Bombay, when fitting him for a new uniform. Who would run the business now? What would become of her son, and her?

Patricia Bolton's contribution to the couture of the Indian civil service, the English army, the expat community in Bombay and the lily-white ladies swanning about in hill country stations like Simla, would have faded away to dust, if it had not been for Ajay Turilay.

Upon recovering, and against his mother's protestations, Ajay returned to work, expecting to see deserted streets and empty markets, but life went on, even when people were dropping like flies.

His commute had changed, after the English ordered the demolition of the areas of Bombay most affected by the plague, citing public health reasons. Reactions had been mixed, but Ajay supported the measures. Already the city felt cleaner, more open — a huge improvement.

Ajay walked up the stairs, his heart heavy with the loss of Patricia and her incredible visionary approach to fashion and design. Despite his physical weakness, Ajay knew he had to sort things out before an over-zealous official closed them down and burnt their store of fabrics.

His mother had warned him that the Sanitary Commissioners had been ordering tailors all over the city to destroy any cloth imported from Hong Kong, and he was acutely aware of the rolls of caramel linen they'd carried upstairs before they'd both got sick. His arm still ached where something had bitten him that same day.

Musty with neglect, Ajay threw open the windows of the workroom, and a warm breeze washed through the room, ruffling paperwork and fabric swatches. As usual, Patricia's desk was a study in chaos and Ajay didn't know where to start. Should he pack everything away or carry on as normal? They had orders to fill and workers to pay, if any of their workers were still alive.

Ajay drew up a plan of action. He'd keep the business running until someone told him not to. Familiar with the state of the financial accounts, he could manage things as long as they had seamstresses to churn out the garments. Could he recreate the magic of Patricia? He thought it unlikely, but he'd do his best. And hopefully their clients would continue doing business with him.

After almost a day of procrastination, Ajay knew he'd have to pack Patricia's personal things. She'd never once mentioned her family, in India, or in England, so he didn't know what he'd do with her things other than to pack them away, hoping her family might one day enquire about her whereabouts. As for her home in Bombay, he'd never been there. Despite Patricia's more progressive ideas about workplace safety and pay, he'd never visited her there, and never expected to. He'd leave that to whatever staff she had; it wasn't his concern. Only the business was his to sustain, for the sake of both him and his mother, and the ladies who worked for them. No, not them, the ladies who worked for him.

Ajay operated under the auspices that it was easier not to look at Patricia's things as he packed them up. Unless they looked business related, he stored everything in a sturdy tea chest. Photo albums, old invitations, menus. He cast a quick eye over half finished sketches of abandoned designs before also packing those away.

Once the desk was clear, and the drawers emptied, Ajay sat in Patricia's chair, the view far superior to the one from his desk. There was always a silver lining. He caught a glimpse of the harbour bristling with ships masts and sails which looked like white-capped waves. His plan of moving to London had faded. From this desk, he was the captain of his own destiny. The man in charge of a profitable business supplying the British. Giving it all up and moving to England didn't seem so inviting now. As sad as he was about Patricia's passing, she'd left him a life he'd never imagined possible.

The bolts of linen taunted him from the corner of the room. Patricia had such wonderful plans for that fabric, it would be a crime to destroy it. He'd spend some time working on her initial sketches, before finalising the pattern and then he'd send the fabric out to the ladies for them to work. If he took his time, the panic in the city would die down, and hopefully the manic knee-jerk reaction of the British would dissipate, and they'd all move on. Life had to go on.

THE BUSINESS

The earlier dusting of snow on Liverpool's streets had turned into a sooty slush on the side of the road. The pristine snow giving way to a putrid grey mush which leaked into boots and infiltrated doorways — the bane of every housewife and tradesman alike.

As men stood in doorways reading the daily papers, their feet as cold as ice in their hardy boots, the headlines screamed of a very different ailment, the plague.

Samer Kurdi sipped his honeyed tea, eyes skimming the paper. The tea did nothing to assuage the twisting in his gut as he read about the casualties in India, both native and foreign, the plague relentless in its pursuit of victims.

He'd heard nothing from Robert, and was even now fielding queries from Robert's sister and daughter, asking after Robert's wellbeing.

He had sent telegram after to Robert's hotel in India, and onwards to his other known stops. It was conceivable that Robert had holed up somewhere safe to wait out the contagion. Robert was a lucky man in all areas of his life, both business and personal. He would have landed on his feet in a delightful town, being entertained by a local dignitary whilst they both waited out the disruption to travel caused by the Special Plague Committees. Or perhaps Robert was being held in one of the isolation camps. But as the weeks passed, Samer had lost hope. Perhaps Robert was dead?

'A telegram for you, sir,' said a waiter, presenting a crisp white envelope.

Samer tipped the lad and opened the envelope. It took but a moment to read the one line of text. One line which simultaneously broke his heart and opened his horizons.

Regret to inform you Robert Williams deceased.

The worst news.

Samer stared into the distance. There were lawyers he'd need to instruct to settle Robert's affairs and dissolve the partnership. His family to tell... Samer's heart pounded as he considered Robert's daughter Grace and her reaction to the news. He should tell her face-to-face, not through the impersonal coarseness of a telegram or letter.

He'd almost forgotten about the lovely Grace Williams and the dreams he'd once harboured about asking for her hand in marriage. Sally Glynn had consumed him since he'd arrived in Liverpool, and more than once he'd delayed his return to London to spend more time with her and in the company of the incredible Abdullah Quilliam, a most fascinating man.

It hadn't surprised him when the police had raided their meeting at the warehouse, as they discussed plans to distribute copies of Koran using his network of retailers. He'd half expected it. The police hadn't been shy in throwing Meredith's name out as the man responsible.

Whilst he treasured his friendship with Robert, and valued their lucrative business relationship, he was now free to follow his heart and the teachings of Allah. No more shipments of opium, no more smuggling of contraband or wiggling within the rules of HM Customs and Excise. He could run the business the way he wanted. And with Sally Glynn at his side.

There wasn't the time for tears, those would come later in the privacy of his room. Now he had letters to write, telegrams to send, and a train journey to arrange. His priority was to Miss Glynn, to beg her to wait for him until he returned from London.

NEW ZEALAND

~

THE MOTHER

*A*nnabel Lester had never ridden a horse before. The closest she'd been were the years she'd stroked the flea-bitten donkeys littering the English seaside beach resorts she visited as a child. Even then her father had refused to pay the daylight robbery prices he accused the donkey operators of charging to ride the poor beasts, so patting their velvety noses was her lot. She'd never once imagined she'd be galloping across the rugged hills of colonial New Zealand, hands around the waist of a man she'd only just met. A man who wasn't her husband and had asked no questions when she'd appeared at his doorway, clasping her worldly possessions.

When Annabel Lester was first married, and later when she was raising her only daughter, life caught her in its spiral of consumerism — a larger car, another pair of diamond earrings, the next seasons boots and coat. Holidays in Spain, replacing her crockery with the latest offerings by the celebrity chef of the day, and now she was clinging to the back of a man charging across a frothy windswept beach.

This seashore was a different beast to the shoreline of her childhood. This sea hurled itself at the shore with a fury only matched by the wind, a bitter gale which pummelled at the surging sea, whipping it into even angrier crests which crashed upon the shore. The ocean held a special place in her heart, going to the seaside had been a rare and relished treat seen through rose-coloured glasses and ice creams in a cone, but Mother Nature's display today was one to remember. Devoid of a human cast, the only actors in this production were the lonely trees standing sentinel over what had once been forests, now plundered by mankind.

'We'll stop soon,' the man in front of her called out, shouting over the wind and the vicious waves at their side.

Annabel squeezed her arms around his middle in response. She wasn't sure she cared how much longer the ride was. If it wasn't for the bitterly cold air flinging needles of sand into her face, she'd have said this was the most memorable moments of her life. But like all exquisite moments, this one ended far too soon, with the cloud saturated sky giving way to a darkness which didn't so much sneak up on them, but more darted behind them, forcing them from their to horse to shelter from the coastal storm which now threatened them.

Warden William Price made quick work of building a fire in a copse of spindly trees left untouched by the woodsman's axe. Annabel offered to help, but he'd rebuffed her, so instead sat propped against an ancient tree, knees pulled to her chest, her long skirts tidied away beneath her. She watched him coax flames from the dry undergrowth he'd piled atop of some salt laden logs.

'Tea?' he asked.

Her husband used to make her tea in the mornings, bringing it to her bedside before leaving for work. The difference between that past and this present had never been more acute, and the grief and disbelief that she'd quashed over the years, overcame her.

Warden Price had stiffened at Annabel's sobbing but made no move towards her, focussing instead on the billy boiling over the fire. His mind flew in a million different directions, like the dance of the flames, except the fire didn't have to worry about anyone else; it didn't care if plans fell aside or tilted off course. Fire didn't give one toss if you gave up hunting the woman you thought you loved. Fire loved no one.

He cast another glance at Annabel, unsure of his own feelings and that didn't rest easily on his shoulders or in his heart. In the fire dappled dark, it was easier to recall the precious few memories he had of Sarah Bell, but increasingly those images were being overlaid with newer forms, fresher feelings, tinged with the likeness of Annabel Lester, and not of Sarah Bell. It tore at him. The decision which had seemed so solid in Dunedin, so right, wavered like the flames he'd coaxed into life.

Price poured the boiling water onto the loose tea he'd measured out. His supplies wouldn't last them long. If they reached the next settlement by the end of the week they'd be fine, otherwise the woman he'd become responsible for would go hungry. Although there were worse things than hunger on the road they now travelled.

An icy breeze rubbed itself against his face, forcing its way beneath his heavy coat, burrowing into his skin, sending shivers into his soul.

'Come closer, Mrs Lester,' he said, doubting her garments were at all suitable for the West Coast winter threatening to arrive early. He watched Annabel shimmy closer to the fire, her eyes closing as she absorbed the flickering heat.

'Warmer?'

'Yes, thank you,' Annabel replied.

'Have you packed anything... warmer?' he asked. He'd been about to ask if she'd packed anything more sensible before realising that was a ridiculous question.

Annabel shook her head, cursing her own stupidity. She didn't have much, but she'd left her winter weight clothes behind, not imagining a long trek on horseback through the New Zealand countryside was in her future. There was no *popping out to the high street*. It was all make do and mend, but her sewing was atrocious and hadn't improved during her time in this crazy reality.

Price had replied with little more than a *hrumpf*, before magicking up a light supper over the flames to accompany the tea. There was no chance she'd be able to survive out here without him, she'd barely survived the streets of Dunedin before the Reverend had rescued her.

For the millionth time she allowed her mind to wander to a different time, to a family she had no hope of ever seeing again.

Annabel had tried suppressing her memories of before, of before she'd ended up here, in this time, but now and then they overtook her. Price's fire reminded her of the fireplace at *The Old Curiosity Shop*, and how in winter they had a roaring open fire, at work, and the customers loved it. Even the grubbiness of Price's trousers were reminiscent of her husband's jeans after a long day of carting dusty cobwebby furniture in and out of the van. She didn't miss those days. She'd always been more a dress for the antique fairs type wife, using them as an excuse to pull her fine jewellery out of the safe, wearing a new outfit to impress the other dealers and customers. But now she didn't miss her jewellery. She considered it a currency she could have used here, which would have solved several issues.

Price placed an enamel bowl of stew into her hands and Annabel looked up in amazement. 'How did you prepare this so quickly?' She'd been in a world of her own and had missed his machinations over the fire. Her stomach grumbled, anticipating the hunks of rough cut potato and thick pieces of succulent pork in a fragrant broth. She took a bite. No, it wasn't a potato, it was something different, sweeter. She considered the unusual buttery taste but couldn't place it.

'Is it potato?'

Price looked up from his own plate, his eyes lit by the fire. 'It's *kumara*,' he replied before returning to his meal.

'*Kumara*?' Annabel parroted the foreign word. '*Kumara*,' she repeated, taking another bite of the root vegetable.

The sound of birdsong interspersed their companionable silence. Since being in New Zealand, she'd become used to the cacophony of the native wildlife. There was no such music in the London of her past life. She'd never spent a night in the New Zealand bush though, and the variety of bird calls were akin to a complete orchestral performance. In the darkness it was impossible to spot the performers but beautiful song surrounded them.

A crack opened in the sky and the foreshore lit up like a field on Bonfire Night. A majestic sound and light show to accompany the birdsong surrounding them. Thunder followed, drowning out the birds and the waves and the wind, and their conversation. In the flashing lightning and the flickering fire, Annabel felt she was in a nightclub with fluorescent strobe lights highlighting the frenetic movements of Price as he gathered up their belongings, pushing further into the undergrowth, and rigging up a refuge for them both. His voice lost to the elements as he hauled Annabel from her perch, the two of them pelted with bullets of rain.

Huddling under the makeshift shelter, Annabel ducked into the protective bulk of the man next to her. She threw her arm over her face, shivering as the icy wind forced its way through the branches dipping and diving under the onslaught of the weather. Warden Price wrapped his jacket around her shoulders. The sudden warmth in her cheeks was nothing to do with the jacket protecting her from the violent storm.

Annabel tucked her chin into Price's chest and closed her eyes. If she could hold onto this moment forever, she'd forgo hot showers and fresh coffee and diamond rings to be here, in the middle of a storm in the arms of a stranger where she felt safer than she ever had in England. Her life in England, with her husband and her daughter, wasn't bad, but here she felt complete. Having nothing and being no one of any great import made her safe and free and whole. And she wouldn't change it for all the diamonds in the world.

THE JOURNEY

*A*roha's innate sense of direction had no trouble sending her south, but she hadn't factored in the seventeen hundred men the Governor of New Zealand had building a road to link Auckland to the mighty Waikato River. At almost every point on her journey, gangs were sawing through the magnificent native forests, determinedly clearing scoria whilst itching to go to war. Rifle shots rang out through the countryside, causing Aroha to stumble, as if someone had shot her. Her mind fumbled with geography. She'd been living in Auckland far too long, and the landscape she'd travelled through years ago bore no resemblance to the scarred world she walked through now.

Her soul ached for her husband Wiremu, killed at the behest of the Jowl brothers, but life itself was fleeting, and Wiremu's spirit would live on through his daughter. Now it was the flayed flesh of her home tearing at her heart. Tree trunks lay rotting on the edges of the desecration, the limbs of mother earth torn from her soil, left to decay. And all around her were the sounds of the oppressors — the English soldiers.

Aroha travelled on old traditional paths, skirting the more obvious signs of *progress* by the English, but the babe was fussing and she needed to find somewhere more settled to rest and take stock of her situation. Tiredness threatened to overwhelm her, and that's when mistakes happened, potentially leading to her death, or worse. Aroha shifted the woven basket, relieving the chaffing on her shoulders. The baby whimpered and Aroha shushed it using her finger as a makeshift pacifier. The baby sucked greedily on her slender finger. It would only distract her daughter for a moment, she had to feed the poor thing, but with the two of them huddled deep in the undergrowth, hiding from the men carousing only steps away from them on the new road slashed from the land of her ancestors, they had to hide. She whispered in her daughter's tiny ears, smothering her face with maternal kisses. The sound of the soldier's revelry grew fainter. She couldn't be sure what they'd do with her if they found her in their alcohol fuelled state and she didn't want to know. To them she was nothing — a pest in their house and they wouldn't think twice of disposing of her the way you would a rat, stomping it underfoot and discarding it for the dogs to devour.

Aroha travelled under cover of darkness, spending her days cloistered in dank grottos of storm-tossed trees and knotty undergrowth. The land provided both food and shelter if you knew where to look. There'd been times she hadn't walked alone, joining other Māori making the pilgrimage south for whatever reason. No one shared their stories, they merely travelled in the same direction. History wouldn't remember well those who fought for the other side. It was better to keep to oneself, taking sides was a dangerous position.

Her daughter cried again, Aroha's finger losing its effectiveness. Adrenaline leaked from her pores and the wind snuck through the branches of the trees, encircling them with their icy embrace as the soldiers drifted away, their noisy jocularity now just a shadow further down Great South Road. It wasn't a *great* road; it was a scar marring the backbone of New Zealand. A weeping sore delivering white men and their rifles and their illnesses to every corner of her country. But soon she'd be home, and from there, with the support of her tribe, her people, she'd seek retribution for the great harm done to her family.

With the threat of the drunkards gone, Aroha eased the flaxen sling from her shoulders and pressed the baby to her breast, sighing as her perfect daughter suckled greedily. With her free hand, she probed at the raw graze on her shoulder. Her daughter was getting heavier with every passing day and unless she was eating or sleeping, she constantly squirmed to be free. Aroha swallowed back the tears forming as she remembered how only a fortnight ago she and Wiremu had watched their tiny daughter discover her own feet and hands as she lay in their bed, safe from what the future was about to fire at them.

The night hummed with the snuffles and calls of the native wildlife. Aroha feared nothing from the bush, only the two legged men on the road who killed for fun. Wild creatures who slaughtered others, not for need but for pleasure. Aroha wrapped a blanket around them both. She was so tired, and the baby was sleeping, and the risk of being found in this hollow was low, she'd doze... just for a minute.

The stillness of the air vanished as voices cast dangerous shadows in the night, waking her. Only a foot away, Aroha shrank into the bushes.

'How many have we got then?'

'Enough to pay our way home, that's for sure,' replied a deeper voice.

'You certain the Jowl's will pay for them?' whined the first voice.

'They're good for it. Don't you worry, they've been doing it for years, I'm told.'

'Don't you think about them using the guns on us?'

'There ain't no *us* anymore, is there? These rifles are our ticket back to England, where no one is trying to kill us. Where it's not likely someone will try slitting your throat as you sleep.'

'But it'll be English soldiers who'll get shot...'

'But not these two soldiers, eh? Don't worry about them, mate. They're nothing to us. We've got a few days up our sleeves before they notice we didn't come back, and that's time enough to get these guns up to Auckland and sell them to the Jowl's, then we'll be no one the army has ever heard of. They'll be looking for Amos Wood and Jack Antony, but those fellas won't exist anymore except on paper. We'll be someone else. I always fancied the name Matthew, very biblical, honest-like,' he laughed. 'Matthew bloody Canterbury, can't get more Christian than that, can you? Who are you going to be then, Amos?'

'Still don't feel right,' Amos whined again. 'Them selling these rifles to the natives. What if they use them to kill—'

'Shush,' Jack hissed. 'Thought I heard something?'

Aroha held her breath, afraid it was her heartbeat the man was talking about. Her broken heart pounding so loudly within her chest it sounded like a horse thundering down a racetrack. The baby snuffled in her arms, a sure sign she was about to wake. Aroha's heart beat faster. *Keep sleeping, for just a few minutes more,* she prayed to the baby girl.

'Grab that bag, I'm already carrying these. Better we get as much distance between us and camp while we can. And quit your whining. We're in this together now, you and me. Let's go.'

And the deserters stomped off, passing within a breath of Aroha and her baby, their thrashing through the virgin undergrowth masking the whimpers of the baby woken from its slumber.

As her baby fed again, Aroha considered the conversation she'd overheard. Of all the names they could have said, why was it fated that it connected her to the Jowl brothers? The men responsible for the vicious beating which killed her husband? And now these soldiers were selling their own guns to the Jowl's. A thousand thoughts ran through her head. Her heart told her to carry on south, to the safety of her family, her *whanau*, in the Waikato. But revenge was a powerful motivator, and she looked at the babe on her breast. This wasn't a battle for her daughter — she deserved safety and stability. Her daughter came first, but then came revenge.

Loosening her cramped limbs she stood up, wincing as the fibrous straps bit into her shoulders again. After emerging from her hiding place, she picked her way towards the soulless road, her pace faster than before. Revenge providing the fuel she needed to continue her journey south.

THE CHASE

'He had a wife.'

'What?'

'The miller had a wife, and she's skipped town, gone down country,' said Joe Jowl.

Jimmy Jowl scowled. 'What're we going to do?'

'We'll find her, and that other slut who got away. I'll warrant she's running back to her family, taking our money with her. I want that back, to reimburse us for our losses,' Joe said.

The brothers sat at the scrubbed kitchen table, the windows shut against the elements outside and the gossiping ears of any passersby. Each man reminiscing about the woman they'd found in their cellar, and her subsequent escape from their weatherboard home in Auckland, followed by the fracas with the native man on the road, trying to protect the harlot. The fight, in front of all their neighbours and clientele and the embarrassment, couldn't have gone unpunished, their reputation was at stake. So they had punished the Māori man. And now they had two women to track down. Women always caused the most problems.

'We'll go tomorrow after I make some arrangements at the bar. No doubt the thieving bastards will try to fleece us while we're not looking, but if they do, we'll deal with them upon our return. You know what to do,' Joe instructed his brother. Jimmy could follow instructions — he was the perfect tool if used right.

Jimmy flexed his meaty paws, already scarred from carrying out years of Joe's directives, and some of his own personal entertainment behind closed doors. He didn't care about the native woman, she wasn't worth any thought at all. But Sarah was a different story. Her disappearance gnawed at him, making his skin itch. Even in church, the slightest feminine scent, the merest brush of a woman as she skirted his giant girth, was enough to send his pulse quickening, his breath laboured. The church women were respectable, according to his brother, so he didn't play with them. But God had sent the Sarah woman to release the demons within him. Joe told him that too. But sometimes the demons were nigh on impossible to placate, and occasionally the numbers of women in their congregation dropped by one or two, quieting the demons a little longer. At heart, all women were instruments of the devil, Joe had said. They used their magic to steal your money, corral your life , and then they pressed you into the soil until you were nothing more than an earthworm. He was looking forward to this chase.

'Remember, Jimmy. Family business is for behind family doors. Don't you be telling anyone why we're going away. You make your deliveries like normal, say nothing, and we leave tomorrow afternoon. You understand?'

Jimmy's cheeks flushed at the thought of Sarah's neck between his hands. He'd do whatever Joe said to do. As the eldest, Joe was always right.

With their liquor operations under temporary management, the Jowl brothers headed south, rifles slung over their shoulders, their identical faces set like stone atop of their matching horses. As the Jowls made their way south down the ever lengthening Great South Road, they stopped to talk with the soldiers and the roading gangs, and travellers worthy of their time. You never knew when someone might have seen or heard something of value. And on the odd night, travellers who looked like they were carrying something more valuable than information, joined the long list of people missing in the prosperous new world. The indigenous population blamed, fuelling the simmering tension which sat like a mirage upon the lush land, and clung to the boots and the rifles of men plucked from the confines of a Victorian England, free from the shackles of societal expectations.

'No one's seen them, Joe,' Jimmy complained.

Joe ignored him, he was counting the coins in his purse, although he already knew how much he carried, but nevertheless, he liked to check.

'Joe?' Jimmy interrupted again, his simple face reflected in the fire.

'I'm counting, Jimmy. Leave it.'

Jimmy stirred the contents of the pot over the fire. Joe never made the supper, that was Jimmy's job, always was, but tonight was different, a frisson of resentment for his older brother simmered with the stew. Joe was much cleverer than him — his mother had told him enough times, until he'd told her to shut up the best way he knew how — in the cellar with his hands around her throat. But tonight he felt differently. Maybe it was a sign they were getting closer to Sarah, but still he stirred the pot harder than required.

'Careful, Jimmy, don't go spilling the stuff. I wanna eat tonight not tomorrow,' Joe chastised, tucking his pocketbook deep inside his jacket. He moved closer to the fire, peering into his brother's pot. Joe Jowl was oblivious to Jimmy's tortured face, casting him as a hideous stone gargoyle in the firelight.

Jimmy ladled their supper into a pair of blue rimmed enamel bowls, settling on his haunches to spoon it into his mouth as fast as possible. Growing up, they'd often had their food whipped away from underneath them by their mother, for whatever imagined infraction they'd committed, so both men ate like it could vanish without warning. With no small talk between them, the only sound in night air were the voices of the nearby soldiers, settling down into camp for the night, ready for another day extending the fingers of civilisation into the untamed land.

'How long till we find them?' Jimmy tried again, picking at his teeth.

Joe ignored his brother, intent on finishing his meal. Besides, he had no answer for his twin. Joe himself couldn't shake the suspicion that there was some magic afoot, although he'd never voice those concerns to his brother. Jimmy operated on the delicate edge of a knife as it was. Joe kept his leash short, and strong.

Joe laid his empty bowl on the ground, 'We'll find them. There'll be word at a hotel down the line, I'm sure. Patience is a virtue, and we've got the whole country on our side. They're just common whores, with their legs in the air and a man between their thighs.'

Jimmy's features rearranged themselves into their more familiar form — that of a compliant younger brother. He collected the bowls, rinsing them clean with water from the billy. His world was back on track. If Joe said they'd find them soon, then that was the truth. He could still feel the itch, inching its way down his body, licking at his thighs, tightening his hands, and his cock.

THE BOY

*C*olin Lloyd waited in Dunedin for what seemed like weeks, months even, but Warden Price never returned, despite promising he would. Once they discharged Colin from hospital, he'd tried calling at the Manse to ask after the woman Price had mentioned, but a man at the door had sent him away using language which burnt Colin's ears. He was in a town where he knew no one and had nothing. The only thing he had was the knowledge that his older brother Isaac was in Bruce Bay. So, with the resilience of youth, he set off into the great unknown, heading for the gold mining mecca of Bruce Bay on the West Coast of New Zealand. Price had told him that gold mining was for fools, but Bruce Bay was where his brother was, so that was where he needed to go.

With no money behind him, and his belongings on the silty bottom of Port Chalmers, Colin was at a distinct disadvantage, but the road north promised adventures for those freshly arrived with ample to spare for the skinny lad from Wales who reminded them of their own brothers back home. And so it wasn't long before Colin was firm friends with a fresh-eyed group of men venturing north.

The prospective miners cared nothing about news of worsening relations between the settlers and the Māori, instead mesmerised by reports of fountain-like gold gushing from the rivers and streams of the West Coast, and their dreams of incredible wealth buoyed them through rain storms and scurvy, hunger and cold.

With little to distract them, they turned to sport for entertainment.

'All right lads, let's have a wager then, on whether James here can best old Milne,' John Regan announced, throwing a handful of pennies into his empty gold pan.

Colin wiped his mouth. Someone had caught two fat pigeons, and for the first time in days, he was full to the brim. The cooking fire kept them warm, as did the stories told by Bob Milne, a somewhat experienced miner heading north with them to take up a new claim. What Colin didn't see was the alcoholic glint in John's eye. John Regan and James Allen had been sharing slugs from a bottle of illicit gin. Nobody cared about the drinking, so Colin hadn't paid much notice to the quantity they'd consumed. Perhaps he should have.

With hollers and hoots, the men threw coins into Regan's pan as they placed their wagers. Bob Milne was older but built like a brick shit-house, whereas James Allen was as skinny as a beanpole but a good ten years younger, so the odds were pretty even.

The miners formed a rough ring, scuffing at the tussock to give the fighters a flatter surface. Filthy comments describing the size of the men's tackle and their ability to use it filled the air, giving Colin an education to mortify his mother.

Regan held up his hand, a hand which had already seen the inside of a gaol over in Victoria in Australia, not that anyone else knew that. New Zealand was about starting afresh, reinventing himself to be a better man, if Regan had a different nature.

'Come on then boys, nothing below the belt and no rabbit punches. Understood?' Regan said.

The two fighters grinned and Regan dropped his hand and it was on.

'Bet you he fades,' said a miner.

'Nah, he's got form, look at him feeling out the beanpole. My money's on Milne, for sure,' replied another.

The men shouted at the fighters, working themselves up on the blood and the ready availability of strong drink. It wasn't just Regan and Allen knocking back the cheap gin, most had bottles of grog stashed in their bags. Booze, half empty stomachs, moody firelight, and inequitable gambling was never going to end well for a group of men in the wild. Especially when they weren't on an even keel to start with.

Milne threw the first real punch, a liver shot, sending Allen to his knees. Someone rushed in to pull Milne away from Allen who struggled to get to his feet.

'Get off,' Milne shouted, an early victory within his grasp. And he shook off the other man.

Allen stood unsteadily, his arms up protecting his face. He feigned a left hook, before delivering an uppercut with his right, sending Milne into the crowd.

The miners parted, allowing Milne to sprawl to the ground. He bounced up, shaking off the punch, and launched straight into Allen, jabbing like a woodpecker at a tree.

Allen retaliated with a cross. Milne ducked to the side and delivered his own powerful punch to Allen's torso. Punch after punch followed, almost all of them finding their mark. There were jeers from the crowd, and more money flew Regan's way as allegiances shifted. Advice came from every corner. If it had been in a ring, any referee worth his salt would have halted the fight, given the blood which bathed the faces of both fighters, and the audience.

Regan called a timeout, and huddled with Allen, whilst Milne took a mug of water from Colin's eager hands, slugging half of it and tipping the rest over his head. The older man bounced back into the circle invigorated, bouncing on his toes waiting for Allen.

Allen entered the circle, dancing round till his back was to the fire, darting in and delivering a quick right-handed jabs then darting back again, well away from Milne's reach.

'Quit your dancing.'

'Are you bloody girls?'

'Get in there!'

'Kill him!'

In the bloodlust surrounding the fight, nobody had noticed Allen taking something from Regan's hand, no one except Colin, who wasn't certain what he'd just seen. Perhaps it was a cloth to stem the blood?

Then Allen was on Milne, gripping him as Milne delivered short jabs to the taller man's stomach, then Allen got a punch away with his left fist, and Milne fell to the ground, stunned.

In the jeers of the crowd, something landed at Colin's feet. He bent to pick it up, only to find a heavy boot crushing his hand into the broken tussock.

'Leave it, boy,' said Regan, scooping up the object, before removing his foot from Colin's hand.

Colin rubbed his hand, tall enough to stare into the eyes of Regan.

'Be a man and keep your mouth shut,' Regan said, slipping the chunk of metal into his pocket.

It didn't matter, Colin had seen what it was — a crudely fashioned knuckleduster, brass knuckles, guaranteed to knock an opponent out.

Regan turned away, rattling the pennies in the pan, and allocated the winnings, pocketing the leftovers.

No one bothered with Milne on the ground, barely coherent and making no effort to get up.

Colin wanted to join the crowd carousing around the fire, the grog flowing freely. He wasn't a stranger to drink, but his mam had beaten the joy out of it once when she'd caught him swigging from his brother's leftovers, well before Isaac had come to New Zealand, which seemed a lifetime ago, and didn't bear thinking about too much. But his decent morality won out over the booze.

'You okay, Mister Milne?' Colin asked, kneeling beside the bleeding man.

Milne's face looked funny in the firelight, like he'd had too much to drink himself, his mouth floppy.

'Are you drunk?' Colin asked, incredulous that a man that drunk could have fought as he did.

Milne tried to speak but slurred his words while blood dribbled down his chin.

'Here, sit up,' Colin said, tugging on Milne's shoulders, heaving him into a lopsided sitting position.

Again, Milne tried speaking but nothing but gibberish came out.

'You need to sleep it off,' Colin said, echoing the words he'd heard his mam say time and time again.

Milne's strong right arm lay useless in his lap and when Colin walked off, he tried grabbing for him with his left arm. Unbalanced, he toppled over. Unable to right himself, Milne lay crying into the earth, the tussock grass tickling his ears and scratching his face, and there was nothing he could do about it.

THE LICENCE

$\mathcal{T}$he next morning dawned with clear skies and birdsong, and no other noise.

Something woke him, and Colin stirred under his blanket, shivering in the dawn chill and looked around for his companions. Most of the miners lay fast asleep, their alcohol soaked brains requiring a few more hours to recover. But not all of them were asleep. Colin watched through half-closed eyes as Allen and Regan, moving like ballerinas, rifled through the bags of their sleeping companions extracting handfuls of coins or anything else small and portable. When they got to the immobile form of Milne still lying where he fell the night before, the men conversed in close quarters, whispering so softly that Colin couldn't hear a word they exchanged.

Colin saw Allen kneel at Milne's side, his hand on Milne's shoulder. Milne moaned as Allen pushed him onto his back. Half of Milne's face looked as if a fire had melted it, drooping in a grotesque caricature of what it had once been. Milne reached up with one hand, his words indistinct. Regan leapt forward, placing his palm over Milne's mouth.

'Just find it,' Regan whispered.

Allen rifled through Milne's pockets, the older man trying to push

Allen's hands away, but there was no strength behind his struggles.

Allen pulled a piece of paper from Milne's pocket, Milne's *Miner's Right*, his legitimate licence to prospect at Bruce Bay. An official licence, one which neither Allen nor Regan had bothered paying for.

Allen pocketed the licence and Regan moved his hand to cover both Milne's drooping mouth, and his nose.

Colin stuffed the blanket into his mouth to stop from crying out as he watched Milne's weakened body struggle briefly before falling still. Regan held his hand over Milne's face for a moment longer, before finally stripping the man of his thin wedding band and rolling him back onto his side and covering him up with a blanket from Milne's own bag.

With the licence in hand, Regan and Allen vanished across the tussock covered hills. Whether killing Milne had always been their intention, Colin couldn't be sure, but it was in that moment that he finished doing his growing up, and the moment he realised there was no one he could trust, no one other than his family.

Apart from when they were under the influence of greed or cheap grog, the miners were a friendly group. When they discovered that Milne had passed away they buried the man and divvied up his belongings according to need amongst the remaining men. Wisely, Colin kept silent on the cause of death, and thus found himself the uncomfortable owner of a canvas bag containing a blanket, a gold pan, an enamel bowl and a too-big waistcoat. He kept the waistcoat despite its size as it added an extra layer of warmth to his meagre wardrobe.

Surprised murmurs filled the campsite as the diggers noticed Regan and Allen's absence, but that was the way of things and after a few minutes no one thought any more of it. Miners were notoriously flighty, and men with horses were prone to leaving at first light, eager to get to the gold fields as fast as possible — and there was no time to waste developing friendships. And unless you were travelling with a friend, the momentary friendships you made on the rough road were fleeting and ethereal.

The rest of the men followed in their wake, knowing that by nightfall, their campsite would contain a whole new set of miners —

men and, if they were lucky, some small number of hardy female miners. Enthusiastic miners were making their way to the West Coast from all over New Zealand, and from further afield, from Australia, America, England, even China.

Colin plodded along the barren landscape, the unfamiliar pack chafing at his shoulders. He didn't know the way, so followed the backs of the men in front of him. He'd been walking for days and still couldn't get the image of Regan's hand over Milne's face out of his mind. It was the one thing which made him grateful he didn't have a horse to carry him to Bruce Bay and faster. The last thing he wanted was to see them again.

Milne wasn't the only dead body Colin saw on his travels, men were dropping faster than flies. Ill health, old age, poor nutrition, untreated infections, the list was endless. They stripped the corpses of anything valuable or useful, divvying the goods up amongst those who stopped to help give the poor sod a Christian burial. Which was how, by the time Colin made it to Bruce Bay, he looked like every other miner there, albeit a younger version, but one just as world weary.

Bruce Bay wasn't what Colin expected. He'd imagined a place more like Dunedin, with shops and hotels and, well, buildings. More buildings than those he could see from the ridge. And he expected more people. There were a few people in the streets — older men for the most part, but none of the younger men he'd encountered on the way.

Colin limped over the last ridge and made his way down the hill, passing a church with its simple cross on its apex. A graveyard dwarfed the tiny building, and Colin tried to ignore the number of people buried in a place which boasted only a handful of buildings, and a flattened field with a few dozen tents and lopsided shacks. Gold mining seemed to walk hand-in-hand with death.

He'd jarred his ankle after catching it in a hole in the ground. One miner telling him it was the burrow of a *kiwi* bird. He didn't know what a *kiwi* bird was, or why it burrowed underground like a mole. He'd never seen so many strange-looking birds as he had since landing in New Zealand. Birds should be in trees, instead of walking the earth and making holes in the ground.

Because of the fall, his ankle was the size of an apple, and tender to the touch. He'd loosened his boot, but that only made him walk like a drunk on a trapeze. Colin stopped to lean against the porch railings of one of the better looking buildings lining the main street, when he spied a woman emerge from a building further down the road. He spied her just as he saw Regan sauntering up the road towards the very same building. Colin tried tucking himself into the railings to avoid catching the eye of the other man. *Why wasn't Regan out digging his claim?*

But it wasn't Colin the other man had his eye on, it was the girl. And the set of her shoulders and the tilt of her head made it obvious Regan's presence bothered her.

'Hey there,' Regan said.

The girl changed the angle of her journey.

'Oi, I'm talking to you, pretty lady,' Regan said, shuffling his feet, mirroring her new direction.

'Sorry,' she said.

She kept walking, her disinterest obvious even to Colin who had had little experience with any girl apart from his mother, and his brief flirtation with the girl rescued from the harbour with him. Their dalliance cut short when her family found out he was Welsh with nothing to his name. He wasn't someone they wanted for their daughter, and so there'd been no further communication.

Colin pushed off from the painted railings and hobbled after the pair. She was heading towards the jetty he could see pushing out into the waves of the bay. Regan had matched his pace to hers, and even Colin could hear him becoming increasingly vocal in his complaints that she wasn't answering him.

Other eyes watched the proceedings, men crushed by failure, who could hardly lift a finger to save themselves, let alone save anyone else. They watched Regan with empty eyes and even emptier pockets.

'Please, leave me alone,' said the girl, stopping in the street to face Regan.

'Give me a kiss, and I'll leave you alone, I promise,' Regan replied, insincerity oozing from his lips.

The girl turned to head back towards the beach, and Regan grabbed her.

'I said, give us a kiss.'

The girl pulled away from him.

'What? You think you're too high and mighty to give a man a kiss? You're a bloody girl in a mining town, you've probably had every man here between your legs, and all before breakfast. I'm only asking for a kiss. Now be a good girl and give me what I asked for.'

Regan puckered up, his thin lips looking more like the arse of a monkey than the mouth of a potential lover.

And in wonderment, Colin watched her hurl her basket into Regan's head, before turning tail and running back up the hill.

'You little slut, I'll kill you,' Regan shouted, grabbing for the girl.

The girl was fast, but Regan was faster as he jerked her off her feet and onto the ground, dragging her towards the very building Colin had stopped at. A building more ramshackle than the last — the glass in the front window as splintered as the railings on the porch, but enough to conceal him.

The girl struggled, twisted like an eel, but Regan's strength overpowered her, his filthy hand clamped tightly against the lips she refused to kiss him with.

'I only wanted a kiss. Should have kissed me you little tart, because now I'll be taking more than a kiss from you. You owe me,' Regan said, pinning her to the wooden floorboards of the abandoned mining cottage.

It wasn't just the cottage which had been abandoned, the former occupant had left a long handled shovel standing sentinel in the corner. Absently forgotten perhaps in the shadow of their departure.

Colin remembered only too well Regan killing Milne, and his viciousness at the mining camp, but the girl wasn't another miner. Dressed well, and armed only with her shopping basket, she was someone's daughter, well cared for and in clean clothes. There was no way she was a prostitute, and even if she were, no one deserved the fate Regan had in mind.

Shuffling silently from his hidden doorway, Colin reached for the spade. Only one chance existed to get this right. If he missed, Regan would kill him. Colin had no skills to defend himself from Regan's violence.

The battle continued on the porch, with the girl bucking and twisting to avoid Regan's hands. Then Regan swore as she found purchase against the skin of his palm, and he pulled his hand away to slap her.

In that instance, she rolled to the side and Colin swung downwards with the shovel, the sharp metal edge connecting with the soft skin of Regan's temple. The wiry miner slumped to the ground, pinning the girl under his weight. Silence descended. Colin lifted the shovel to prepare for a second strike, not trusting his luck, adrenaline masking the pain in his ankle.

The girl shrugged Regan's inert body from her own and scrambled to her feet, pulling down her skirt. She paused as she caught Colin's eye, before hightailing it back up the hill and into a much larger building. From this angle Colin could only just read the professional sign on the building which had swallowed the girl — Sweeney's Bar.

No one emerged from the bar to investigate the attack and the miners loitering in the street had returned to their previous activities, the entertainment over. Colin nudged Regan's body with the shovel, and the man rolled over, his eyes open but unseeing. He'd just killed a man. Not with his bare hands, but he may as well have. This wasn't the adventure he'd imagined when he'd first left Wales. But curiously he felt no guilt. He'd done the right thing, and in an obscure way, he'd avenged the death of Milne, as well as saving the girl.

Satisfied the coast was clear, he adjusted the pack on his back and limped to the tavern, twitching, as if he expected the dead man to leer up behind him at any stage.

Colin stepped into the darkened interior, dumping his pack on the nearest table, stretching his shoulders as he approached the bar. The room was empty, with no sight of the girl, although he could hear a heated discussion coming from the other side of the door behind the bar.

Not wanting to interrupt the discussion, Colin surveyed the bar which looked no different to the one he'd lived above in Wales with his mam and brothers. Bottles of booze lined the shelves behind the bar, and an assortment of mismatched glassware. There were suggestions of a woman's touch everywhere, with artwork on the walls and a vase of flowers positioned under a gilt-framed mirror.

The door swung open, and the man blustered in surprise when he saw Colin standing at the bar.

'Sorry, didn't hear you come in,' the man said.

Colin shrugged. He wasn't sure why he came in, just looking at the booze unsettled him. He'd seen too many drunkards on the road that he'd decided that being a teetotaller was a far more sensible decision, at least until he found his brother Isaac.

'You got permission from your parents to be here?' the publican laughed. 'Unless you're here to make a delivery get along with you,' Frederick Sweeney said, a smile on his face.

'No, sir, I'm not here to drink. Thought this might be the best place to ask if you might know where my brother is?' Colin said.

'There's too many men gone through this town for me to keep track of them. He's long gone, like the rest of them have, as you can see for yourself,' Sweeney said, sweeping his arm around the empty bar.

It was then that Colin noticed the film of undisturbed dust on the floor, unmarred by any boots save his own and a small set of footprints which must belong to the girl.

Colin tried a different tack, 'And I thought I'd see if the lady was okay after what happened outside. Might be that I broke my ankle otherwise I would have got to her in time to stop the attack,' he fibbed, stretching the truth a dash.

'You saw what happened out there?' Sweeney asked. 'You're the one who killed the man who attacked Felicity? Friends are you?'

'No, sir. Truth is that I shared a campsite with him a few days out of Dunedin and had hoped not to bump into him again.'

'So not a great loss. I'm surprised anyone bothers coming here at all, you included. There's no more gold, boy, not here anyway—'

'But everyone in Dunedin says Bruce Bay is where the gold is, the motherlode,' Colin interrupted.

'Last week's news. Everyone's gone north, your brother too I expect. Everyone except those who arrived too late and those old hatters who don't have the cash to buy their way out. They don't even have enough money to drink in here anymore. Your brother is long gone.'

'But maybe you remember him?' Colin pleaded, eyes wide with hope.

'Hundreds of men have been through here. If he's not gone north, and isn't sucking on an opium pipe down in the Chinese camp, check the graveyard by the church.'

'You stop that talk, Fred,' said Margaret Sweeney, emerging from the back room, with Felicity in tow.

'Sit down and let me look at your ankle,' Margaret said, escorting Colin to the nearest chair.

'Fred remembers them all, we all do. Because half of them probably still owe us money,' Margaret laughed, her easy nature an exact mirror of her husband's. 'He's too generous by far. Go on then, what's your brother's name?'

'My brother is Isaac Lloyd. I'm Colin Lloyd. And we've not heard from him for a long time… so I came to look for him.'

The room had fallen silent, the two women looking to Fred for guidance, who shook his head.

'Do you know who he was travelling with? Was he on his own or with a friend?' Fred asked, delaying the inevitable.

Colin wracked his memory. Mam had only read out the letters and there were parts he had paid little attention to given that Isaac was prone to harping on about the fantastical sea creatures surrounding New Zealand, which didn't really interest Colin. At the time he'd been more interested in hearing about the gold and whether there were cannibals there or not.

'I can't remember sorry, I think he'd made a friend. Simon? Or Stewart? It began with an 's'.'

'Maybe *Seth*?' Margaret asked softly.

Colin rolled the name over his tongue, giving it due consideration.

'That's it, I think I remember Mam reading that name. She probably muttered something about hoping Isaac was careful about who he hung out with. Mam always said Isaac was a real follower, and it'd get him into trouble if he wasn't careful. Half the time I didn't know whether that was what she said she'd read in Isaac's letters or whether she was adding her own words in. She worries.'

Margaret had Colin's boot off and Felicity had produced a roll of bandages which between them they were wrapping around Colin's sprained ankle. They'd both stopped when it became clear Colin's brother was the same Isaac Lloyd who'd died during the riots the previous year. The lad who'd been with Seth, but had redeemed himself by saving Sarah Bell from Seth, before she'd mysteriously disappeared with Bryce Sinclair. The mystery of her disappearance fascinated the remaining townsfolk and there wasn't a week which went by when some miner claimed he'd seen her ghostly figure in the bush. It was usually the illicit alcohol talking, but it only grew the legend.

Margaret stood up, placing her hand on Colin's shoulder. 'You poor thing, we remember your brother, and the man he worked the fields with. Your mam was right to worry, wasn't she, Fred?'

Fred nodded. He'd poured a nip of rum out and brought it over to the table, placing the glass into Colin's hands.

'What's this for... oh,' Colin said, turning to face Margaret, then Felicity, before looking back at Fred Sweeney. 'He's dead?' Colin asked.

'Sorry, lad,' Fred said. 'Drink up, it'll take the sting out.'

Colin examined the liquid in the bottom of the cloudy glass, the fumes stinging his weepy eyes, swallowing it in one go, where it burnt a trail through his broken heart.

'Finish fixing up his ankle, then you and Felicity take him to see

Reverend Young, he'll show you where Isaac is now. Best I can do lad,' Fred said.

With his ankle strapped, and Margaret on one side, and Felicity on the other carrying his pack, the trio made their way up the hill towards Reverend Greg Young's house, the house he shared with his wife Christine, and their ward Samuel. Here there were signs of a well-loved garden, and an oft-visited house. The women didn't bother knocking, entering the house calling for Christine, who did as much ministering to the woes of the township as the Reverend himself did for their souls.

'You found another stray for me to feed?' asked Christine Young, her hands on her hips standing silhouetted in the kitchen doorway, Cook beavering away behind her, trying to catch glimpses of the latest arrival.

'This is Colin Lloyd, just arrived in town. Cleaned up some rubbish on the way in, which we'll need the Reverend for later. But he's here searching for his brother—'

'Probably gone north with the rest,' Christine interrupted.

'Looking for his brother, Isaac Lloyd...' Margaret finished, tilting her head.

'I, oh,' Christine replied, bustling forward to gather the boy in her arms despite him towering over her. 'You poor boy, to come all this way, and to find out he's in heaven now. Let's get a cup of tea into you, and then we'll... well, then we'll get the Reverend himself to take you to see poor Isaac. Such a shame that he went when he did, but Sarah was with him when he died, so he wasn't alone. You'll get some comfort out of that I'm sure. Just wish she was here to tell you herself,' Christine prattled on, in between calling for tea and ushering everyone into the front room.

The room contained the trappings of a traditional English parlour, apart from the exotic weapons hanging on the walls. Made of greenstone, they gleamed with an almost supernatural light, their edges super sharp. There was an incredible beauty in their lines. Some featured intricate carving, the likes of which Colin had never seen before. Isaac's death weighed heavily upon his shoulders but it was also surreal. He hadn't seen his brother for years, and thus had built him up to be something Isaac probably wasn't. Colin had imagined Isaac as a successful prospector, saving his earnings to build a large home for them and their mam, away from the squalor and poverty of Wales. And with a few simple sentences, no matter how delicately delivered, these strangers had shattered his dreams.

With the tea delivered, and after Christine had dispatched Samuel to fetch the Reverend, she quizzed Colin about his family, his travels, who he'd seen, what he'd done, so that by the time Reverend Young arrived, Colin's head was spinning.

Reverend Young, his wild hair in disarray and mud up the back of his legs, greeted Christine with a kiss on the cheek and dropped into an armchair, his sock-clad feet stretched out towards the fire his wife had just lit.

"Welcome, dear boy, sorry for your loss. Samuel filled me in on the way here. A terrible tragedy and a dark time in Bruce Bay's history. It's settled down now that most of the men have moved on, but this is the final resting place for so many, your brother included."

"Thank you," Colin said, his eyes prickling. He wasn't the same boy who'd nearly drowned in Port Chalmers, so he shouldered the pain, brushing it away.

"It's callous to ask so soon, but have you given any thought to what you might do?" Reverend Young asked.

Colin shrugged. He'd only ever planned on mining gold alongside Isaac. He didn't have the foggiest idea what he'd do now that he had no brother and that the gold had run out.

'Stay here for a few days, till you sort yourself out,' Christine suggested. 'You can share a room with Samuel, we've got the space and you can help us pack as a way of earning your keep,' she said, looking to her husband for approval.

'Excellent idea, Christine always knows best.'

'You're leaving Bruce Bay?' Colin asked.

'We're going to Dunedin as soon as it's arranged, except the Chinese. I've just been over to their camp and they're staying. They don't come to church, so apart from the Sweeneys and the Toomers, and a few of the old hatters — the washed-up miners, there's not much of a congregation. It's back to Otago for us. You're more than welcome to join us. It's still safer to travel as a group. Things have calmed down since last year's troubles, but the papers are full of idiots advocating war with the Māori.'

'I've just come from Dunedin,' Colin said, frustrated. This wasn't how he'd imagined life working out. It had seemed so simple back in Wales, and now he'd have to go home with his tail between his legs like a mongrel beaten by its master.

'You're welcome to come with us, or stay in town, or work your way north with the others. Hardly any boats call now that there's no need for supplies, so you'll have to go north or south on foot unless you want to wait for the next boat who bothers coming in,' the Reverend said.

'We're staying,' Felicity added. 'Father thinks it'll pick up again, that the Chinese will strike it lucky after everyone goes, and he wants to be here for that.'

'He's lost his mind. And after what happened to you today,' Christine said, stabbing at the fire with the poker, sending sparks flying out of the grate, hammering her point home. 'Come to Dunedin. You can't stay here, not now.'

'Or go with the Sweeney's, they'll take you on as a nanny, for the short term. Won't you Margaret?' Reverend Young suggested, fiddling with his grubby shirt sleeves

'Of course we would have you, Felicity. Fred is almost ready to pack it in, and we've been talking about going to Christchurch — plenty of decent opportunities in a bigger town. Following the gold has paid off, but Fred wants something more stable now because of the baby.'

The room fell silent as the occupants contemplated the inevitability of parting ways. This wasn't the first time they'd held this discussion. There'd been plenty of dinners where Toomer pontificated that staying was the best thing to do, to *show the Māori who was boss*. Fred Sweeney maintained he'd stay as long as his bar was profitable, and not a minute longer. A congregation bound its reverend the same way a crime confined a prisoner to his chains. But there was no congregation anymore and the little church which opened with such joyous festivities only a year ago had emptied pew-by-pew until it made more sense for those who remained to meet in the Reverend's front room, which was warmer and had the extra benefit of hot cups of tea no matter the weather.

'I could go north, to the gold mines up there,' Colin said, breaking the silence, although the chorus of dissent which greeted him made him regret his words.

'That's the most ridiculous thing—'

'They'll eat you alive up there, besides, war is coming—'

'Yes, war is inevitable now the Governor has ordered hundreds of troops. The last thing you want is to get involved there—'

'Come to Dunedin, they're crying out for sensible lads. You could be a clerk, or an apprentice.'

'Or join the church,' the Reverend finished for them. 'But I expect anyone brave enough to cross the oceans to find their big brother is old enough to make their own decisions. Christine and I will pray for you.'

'Silly idea going to the gold fields,' Christine muttered.

'As I was saying, before I was interrupted, stay here until you figure things out, and whatever you decide, well, we'll be here to help. Now, are you ready to see your brother?'

The room stood as one, but the Reverend waved them back down.

'It'll just be me and the lad. Come on then, Colin.'

With Colin leaning on the Reverend's arm, the men left the house and limped up the muddied street to the church.

Standing by the simple wooden cross bearing Isaac's name and the date of his death, with the Reverend's hand on his shoulder, Colin let himself cry, his tears mixing with the drizzle falling.

The following weeks passed in a blur. As news of the gold up north increased, Bruce Bay had emptied fast, with even the poorest of miners finding the means to pack up and leave. Colin hadn't decided which direction he'd go but until his ankle healed he had to stay in a town filled with ghosts.

THE PIPE

*T*he body in the ditch wavered as the water tried navigating the obstacle in its path. His glassy eyes crying with the relentless West Coast rain falling into them.

Reverend Young stood with his head bowed, oblivious to the weather. A new soul was in heaven today. Another unexplained death to add to the growing list he kept tucked away inside his bible. The number of deaths at Bruce Bay should have been decreasing at the same rate as the residents were flooding out of Bruce Bay in search of golden pastures elsewhere. But that wasn't the case. The deaths had been increasing — mostly those society wouldn't miss, but they were all God's children.

A group of Chinese miners stared at the minister, the language barrier making the moment even more awkward. They usually dealt with their own but this wasn't any ordinary death. The strangled man had angry finger marks around his neck, with his long handled opium pipe hammered down his throat until only the black lacquer bowl protruded from his mouth.

Fred Sweeney and a few his regulars stood behind Reverend Young, co-opted to help give the man a Christian burial in the overflowing graveyard.

'Ready?' Reverend Young asked, bending down beside the corpse. And he tugged on the long wooden pipe until it slipped from its ghastly home. He wrapped it in his handkerchief and passed it to the nearest miner, a man more wrinkled than alive. The package disappeared within the folds of the man's voluminous sleeves.

'Help me,' Young said, climbing into the ditch, reaching under the dead man's slight shoulders.

Sweeney and his men waded into the mud and grabbed the man by his skinny legs, and on the count of three they heaved him out of his resting place and onto a canvas tarpaulin from Toomer's store.

Toomer didn't seem to care that people were dying in town, he profited whether they lived or died and had added the charge for the tarpaulin to Reverend Young's account. Sweeney would miss Toomer about as much as he'd miss the driving rain of Bruce Bay.

THE CART

*P*acking took place haphazardly, with Christine Young changing her mind about what she was and wasn't taking with her to Otago with great regularity. They'd packed Cook off to Dunedin on the last scheduled ferry, and from hereon any boats calling at the Bruce Bay wharf were an unexpected bonus.

The Sweeney's cart and horses were ready to go. They were heading to the city of Nelson. To everyone's surprise, John Toomer had bought the Sweeney's bar, with grand plans to turn it into a proper hotel. Whilst everyone thought he'd lost his mind, the Sweeney's hadn't given him a chance to back out of the deal, wasting no time in packing up, leaving behind most of the bar's fixtures and fittings.

Today they all stood in Reverend Young's parlour, listening to him reading from his well-worn bible. The parlour's walls and floor empty of everything except the dining room chairs, moved in for the final service.

John Toomer stood smirking on the edge, his fat gut hanging over his trousers, his own bible unopened on his chair. He jiggled from one foot to another, his disdain for religion obvious as he sighed overly loud when Young announced it was time to pray.

'Amen,' Toomer said a little loudly when the prayers were over and the small crowd milled around saying their final goodbyes. 'Come on, Felicity, let's go,' Toomer instructed once it was clear there was no food on offer.

Everyone fell silent except for Samuel dragging the chairs into the hallway, oblivious to the sudden tension.

'I'm going with the Sweeneys,' Felicity said, looking at her boots.

Toomer's jaw slackened.

'Like hell you are,' he said, forgetting where he was, with Reverend Young only three feet away.

'They've engaged me as a nanny for the babe. It's a good job, Papa,' she said, not daring to meet his eyes.

'Better than working behind a bar,' Christine added, placing her arm around Felicity's shoulders.

'She'll be in safe hands,' Fred Sweeney said.

They'd all colluded about what to do with the girl, knowing that to leave her under her father's thumb, in a failing town full of drunkards and opium addicts was a recipe for disaster. Leaving it to the last minute had been the best idea the group had come up with.

'You can't steal my daughter from me,' Toomer blustered, the cords on his neck pulsing.

'I'm old enough to work, Papa. I'll be learning a skill in the city, with good people,' Felicity added, darting a look towards her father.

'You'll stay here and help me. That's your place.'

Colin stayed out of the argument raging around him, it wasn't his battle. He would travel part of the way with the Sweeney's, but would leave them to travel further north, to the goldfields in the Coromandel. The others weren't pleased, but he'd decided that as Isaac wasn't here to send money home to their mam, it was up to him.

'And I suppose you're taking the boy, whoring my daughter out?' Toomer spat towards Sweeney.

'That's enough,' Reverend Young commanded.

'If you go, you're no daughter of mine. Soiled goods is what they'll call you, you cheap whore. Get out of my sight,' Toomer said.

'You go, the door is right there,' Christine said.

Toomer spat at Christine's feet before storming out, the door almost wrenched from its hinges.

Felicity collapsed where she stood, finally released from the abusive shackles of her father. Colin leapt forward to catch her, relief surging through him. At last the adventure could continue. He'd nearly left on his own half a dozen times, frustrated with the delays. But now they were truly leaving.

'Up you get, gotta go before he changes his mind,' Colin joked, lifting Felicity to her feet.

She looked as pale as churned butter and whilst Colin was conscious of the needs of others, he didn't think he could survive another delay. They had to leave today.

'You sure you're up to travelling today?' asked Margaret Sweeney.

'She's fine, just needs a cup of tea,' Christine interrupted, as business-like as usual. 'Best to take advantage of the good weather while it's here, too changeable for my liking. Come on love, into the kitchen with you, a cup of tea then it's goodbye Bruce Bay.'

The road to Nelson felt longer without the comforting humour of the Reverend and Mrs Young. Toomer he didn't miss, but Colin had leaned on the Reverend, soaking up his humorous pearls of wisdom. He'd had a brief taste of how good men could be during his time with Warden Price in Dunedin, but in Bruce Bay he'd left the horrors of the past behind and had relaxed into this new life. Although the Sweeney's were a lovely family, Fred Sweeney was too preoccupied with his wife and child to spend any quality time raising a teenage boy.

They'd been on the road for days, when a passing comment by Felicity Toomer sent Colin tumbling from his seat by the fire.

'Do you think Warden Price ever found Sarah?'

'Warden Price?' Colin asked, brushing damp earth from his trousers.

'Do you know him?' Felicity asked, eyes wide in the firelight.

'He saved me from drowning.'

'That sounds like him,' Fred said.

'How do *you* know him?' Colin asked.

'He was the law in Bruce Bay, until he left to hunt down Sinclair, Samuel's father,' Fred replied for her. 'The Reverend won't have us speak about it anymore, but we all agreed—'

'Not all of us,' Margaret interrupted.

'Most of us believe something must have happened. Price was too good not to have tracked down Sinclair, and Mrs Bell. So probably…'

'There was a lot of confusion that day, Fred, but nothing *unnatural*. Sinclair took Sarah, and Price couldn't find them. Sinclair probably went to Australia and sadly Sarah is most likely dead. Don't go scaring the boy with ghost stories.'

'But that's why Price couldn't find them. They vanished.'

'But Mister Price ran away with Mrs Lester.'

The group gawped at Colin, supper cooling on their plates.

'Mrs Lester?'

'The lady at the manse. I never met her, but they told me Mister Price had taken Mrs Lester north to his new posting. At least, that's what I think happened.' Colin shook his head. 'It's all hazy now. Seems like years ago.'

'Christine sent Sarah's bible onto a woman in Dunedin. Her name was Lester, wasn't it?' Margaret asked Felicity.

Felicity nodded, recalling how perturbed Christine Young had been that the woman she'd sent the bible to hadn't bothered responding. *The height of rudeness* Christine had been fond of saying. They'd all quite forgotten about it, Sarah and her disappearance fading into folklore. They even brushed Samuel's parentage under the carpet, with Reverend Young and his wife quietly taking him in as their own, and no one new to town knew any different.

'Did they say where he went?' Fred asked.

'Not that I remember,' Colin said, trying to think if Greene had mentioned Price's new posting. 'He helped me send a letter to my mam, but I never had time to say thank you,' Colin added. What he didn't say was how slighted he still felt and wasn't sure whether he even wanted to see Price again if he bumped into him.

THE GOODBYE

*T*he impending boat trip across the Cook Strait to the northern island of New Zealand nearly persuaded him to stay. But his duty to his family stamped down his newfound fear of the open water, and he'd boarded the vessel, waving a resolute goodbye to his companions, promising to send word of his safe arrival at the Coromandel goldfields.

Once Colin parted ways with Felicity and the Sweeneys, things didn't pan out as expected.

Without the Sweeney's company, and coin, Colin soon found himself hungry, lonely and at the mercy of ruthless fellow travellers — the road north a boiling cesspit of thievery.

His kit wasn't worth much, and consisted mostly of scraps scavenged for him back in Bruce Bay. Despite his obvious poverty, there'd been plenty of nights he'd woken to find thieves rummaging through his meagre belongings looking for anything of value. He tried reminding himself there was always someone worse off when he woke to their furtive fumbles. Usually a choice curse was enough to see off most of the beggars, but he'd received several beatings from the more forthright thieves.

One such beating was how he found himself, without his pack or boots, coughing and shivering in the doorway of a random township he'd stumbled into late that night. His damaged lungs struggling to cope with the cold.

Booming thunder woke him from his uneasy slumber and he huddled into the doorframe and fat rain globules hurled themselves at the earth, splashing up towards him. He was invisible to everyone in the rain except for the butcher across the road, throwing open his door.

'Oi! Get away with you, boy,' yelled the heavyset man in a bloodstained apron.

No one heard his bellowing or took any notice of his agitation, the thunder drowning out everything other than Colin's racing heartbeat and laboured breathing. Colin ran, the man with the knife clearly not in the mood for polite discourse.

All around him were men in uniform, carrying rifles, jogging through the rain with important business plastered on their faces. And they looked scared, almost as scared as he was. The town smelt unusual — a heady scent of decay and life, of earth and man, foretelling the carnage mankind would inflict upon each other in the coming days, weeks, years and decades.

Colin tripped and stumbled as he ran from the butcher. The road chopped into pieces by the ghosts of feet marching past, the imprints of their boots a telling clue as to the vast numbers of men unleashed on the native population. These were the soldiers he'd considered joining, to further the glory of the Crown, but for some reason he ran into the forest, far beyond the imagined scent of destruction. He didn't understand his decision. He'd come north for work, and if he wasn't going to work in the gold mines, he could enlist as a soldier. Soldiering was an admirable profession, one which would make his mother proud. But the prospect of killing someone choked him.

After an hour of ducking and weaving through the trees, the impossibility of the situation overtook him and he sank to the ground beneath a giant *Kauri* tree. Here the earth was almost dry, the thick canopy shielding the undergrowth from the weather, which had moved further south as he'd fled the encampment by the mouth of Waikato River.

Tearing the fronds from a leafy fern, Colin made himself a bed of sorts at the foot of the tree, and pulled the remaining fronds over him. It wasn't warm, but it was warmer than he'd been, and safer. He was so tired, '*bone tired*' his mother was fond of saying. He wasn't afraid of the dark, but if God saw fit to send a beast to devour him now, he would accept his fate.

The soft snuffles of something creeping nearby woke him. Colin lay still, eyes closed. When you were the prey, it was better to pretend not to notice the predator chasing you. As his eyes adjusted to the gloom of the forest floor, he had a unique view from the base of the tree. His jumbled dreams had been more real than he knew, for there in front of him was the most peculiar creature. At first glance it was a bird, but dull and indistinct in the filtered light, a bird armed with a terrible spear for a beak, with feet almost as large as his palms. It wasn't interested in him, digging in the disturbed earth from when he'd made his bed of ferns. Colin knew it knew he was there, but it showed no fear of him.

A screaming echoed through the trees, and Colin scrambled up, ready to run from whatever madness approached, but then the mad bird thing lifted its head and screamed back. A girlish high-pitched scream caterwauled through the forest, answered by another, then another.

Expecting the camouflaged bird to take flight towards its mate, Colin had to jump back to avoid the bird running into the bush, hurdling fallen logs and skinny saplings struggling to thrive beneath the giants above them. In the blink of an eye the bird vanished, and the undergrowth resumed its silent form.

The autumn breeze snaked around Colin's naked shoulders, making the chill a more immediate threat than his hunger. Nothing was familiar, but he ventured forward, following the erratic zig-zag path of the flightless bird.

Colin's imagination played childish games with him with the darkening forest, summoning forth a bird standing as tall as a man, peering at him from deep within the gloom but then it vanished, crashing through the undergrowth, the sound making the dream more realistic. Then another bird, dressed as an English missionary, sang to him from the branch above, its clerical collar a stark white against its black feathery coat. Colin knew he was dreaming when he heard a baby cry, followed by a woman's voice shushing it.

The surrounding forest grew blacker as his breathing became shallower, as he struggled to contend with the worsening cold, the exertion and the hunger. Colin staggered to a stop, resting his clammy forehead against the rough bark of the closest tree. The baby crying reminded him of his baby brother. He'd see him soon, him and Isaac and Mam. And what tales he could tell — stories of sea monsters and beautiful girls, wild beasts and flightless birds with swords instead of beaks. And then Colin Lloyd collapsed, his fall cushioned by old leaves and rotting logs, his body giving in to total fatigue.

Aroha Kepa shushed the babe tucked beneath her arm. The foul weather forcing them from the path to shelter from the needle-like hail, making it impossible for them to continue. She'd lost one child to illness born on the winter winds, and cursed herself for risking another, but she had no choice. To protect her baby, she'd spent hours hunched under the branches of a sturdy tree, sheltering her daughter with her body. Every inch of her ached from the unnatural position she'd maintained, her own comfort of no concern.

The babe cared nothing for the wind or the rain or the circumstances which lead them to shelter in the forest. The baby wanted feeding now, and was making it known, louder and louder. No amount of offering a knuckle to suckle satisfied her greedy cheeks, so Aroha unfurled herself from the cocoon of mother and child and offered the baby girl her breast, fearful that their days on the road had ended her milk supply. The baby fussed, refusing to latch on, frustrated at the delay and unnerved by the cold. Aroha offered her nipple again, and the babe latched on. She held her breath, only releasing it when she felt the milk let down within her breast.

Aroha readjusted her position at the base of a tree, her own stress melting away under the protection of Tāne — god of the forest. Soon she'd be with her *iwi* — her tribe, and the danger threatening them would diminish to nothing. Wiremu's murder had left a void in her heart, but within the bosom of her *iwi*, the void's sharp edges would soften, blurring until only a dull ache remained.

The forest sounds were as welcome and familiar as the sound of her daughter's tiny heartbeat. The crying call of the *kiwi* and the lyrical song of the *tūī* complemented the first moment of peace she'd felt since Wiremu's death at the hand of the Jowl brothers in Auckland. She knew they'd be coming after her for the money which had been in Wiremu's pocket, money which she now had.

A great squawking crescendoed around them, as birds took to the air, interrupted from their own forest feasting. Aroha's small knife was instantly in her hand, knowing that only man could disturb the birds of Tāne's forest like that. She peered through the dark for any sign of threat, praying the babe would stay silent.

A laboured coughing reached her ears, as though whoever was out there was trying to be as quiet as she herself was. Aroha waited, her knuckles tightening around the horn hilt of the knife.

The undergrowth crackled, flushing another kiwi from the bush, but what followed next was not what Aroha was expecting. A young man materialised, his whole frame shivering as he rested against an immature tree, his eyes closed, dragging lungfuls of air into his wheezing chest, before sinking to his knees, and then onto his side, corpse-like in the gloom.

Aroha lowered the knife, still holding it loosely around the hilt, because it wasn't just herself she was protecting.

The baby had fallen into a milk-drunk sleep, and with a practised hand she readjusted her daughter, pulling her top closed, her eyes never leaving the body in front of her.

Aroha nudged the man with her toe, his eyes flickering, his pale lips the colour of the sky on a summer day. Even in the shadows, she could see how cold he was, how ill-equipped.

The moonlight made Aroha appear almost ethereal as she pulled a blanket from her bag and covered the boy, eliciting an incoherent mumble, deeper than she'd expected. Perhaps he was older than he seemed?

Undecided on what to do now, she settled down to wait for the boy to wake, busying herself by lighting a meagre fire, one which was more smoke than fire in the damp undergrowth.

Although the fire was not her best work, its warmth still spread to the unconscious boy, quieting his unintelligible moaning. His shivering gradually stilled until he looked no different to any other man asleep in his bed at night. And when he woke, Aroha was ready for him.

"It's okay, I won't hurt you. How did you get here?" she asked, standing up with her knife in her hand.

His eyes followed the knife as she moved away, her movements slow and measured. He didn't answer, so she tried again. Still nothing. Aroha could hear his teeth chattering and her heart softened. In the darkness, he looked no older than a child.

Colin's eyes flicked from her face towards the fire and back again, and Aroha nodded, her fingers still holding the knife as he shuffled closer, holding his long-fingered hands out towards the flames until he was close enough for the heat to wrap itself around his frame.

Aroha sank onto her heels, her leather boots and thick woollen skirt protecting her legs from the damp of the ground. The bird life resumed its nocturnal activities, ignoring the interlopers. A rumble from the boy's stomach startled both Aroha and an inquisitive *weka* — who'd crept closer to see what was going on before it went careering back into the bush in fright. Aroha smiled and rummaged in her bag again, leaving the dagger in her lap. She pulled out a cloth-wrapped package and laid it on the ground, revealing two mutton chops, and a cooked *kumara* — a sweet potato, the last of Aroha's provisions. Just visible inside the top of the bag was the bundle of notes Aroha had rescued from her husband's suit, the money from the sale of their flour mill. Tucking it into her pocket, Aroha never noticed the boy's eyes widening as he spied the money.

Aroha offered the mutton chop to the boy who tore into it faster than a dog with a bone.

She leaned against the tree, the knife heavy in her lap and assessed her guest. Dried blood in his hairline and a half-swollen eye showed he'd been roughed up, and apart from being cold and hungry something must have happened for him to be in the bush alone. Aroha didn't need any more complications than she already had, but this was someone's child, scared and alone. He wouldn't last long without her she thought, watching him devour the meat chop and eye up the remaining one. Aroha offered the sweet potato to the boy, rewrapping the remaining chop for herself. She was okay for now but she'd need it tomorrow, and whilst she felt some measure of concern for the boy, she needed her strength for the baby.

'Thank you,' the boy said, reaching for the potato, his unusual accent curling the words.

Aroha's guard slipped. 'Where are your family?'

The boy shook his head, his mouth full of potato.

'No family?' she tried again.

He shrugged, his eyes on the ground.

'Are you on your own?'

At that, he nodded, tightening the blanket around his shoulders.

Although trees protected the trio, icy tentacles of rain slipped through as the heavens opened again. A crack of thunder above them made them jump, and the babe wailed. The forest lit up like a gypsy fairground.

'Quick, under here with us,' Aroha shouted above the thunder, backing into the thicker shrubs behind her.

The boy didn't need a second invitation. He shot over to Aroha's side, and together they rode out the clamouring noise and the apocalyptic lightning sending wave after wave of electrical power crashing to the earth, filling the air with a metallic scent washed clean by lashings of rain.

They slept as a curious trio, waking to the dawn chorus of a thousand different birds and an impressionist sky filled with every shade of pink and red and the palest of yellows.

The morning light proved that the boy was far from the youth Aroha had mistaken him to be. He was all but a man, taking his tentative first steps into adulthood. But his face was so different from what she'd imagined that all she could do was stare.

'Sorry about last night—' Colin began but Aroha held her finger to her lips as the birds launched themselves upwards, their calls piercing the dawn light.

Indistinct voices filtered through the foliage, branches cracked and muffled curses uttered.

Aroha adjusted the blanket, its mottled woollen fibres an effective camouflage in the undergrowth. She held her fingers to her lips again, long enough to ensure that Colin understood that he needed to be silent.

Sweat and leather overpowered the stagnating leaf rot as the soldiers scrambled through the bush.

'How the hell are we meant to know when they were last seen?' muttered one soldier to another, close enough for Colin to grab his ankle.

By pure chance, the question made his colleague fractionally change direction, keeping Aroha, Colin and the baby safe from discovery. As the man passed, he tripped over a rotting log.

'Argh, Jesus Christ,' he screamed as he tumbled over the tree trunk. It splintered under his weight. 'Shit, shit, holy shit, look at these things. They're on me. Get me up. Shit, hurry, get them off me, quick before they burrow into my skin.'

They did a ridiculous hopping dance, brushing the writhing white worms from the fallen soldier's trousers.

'Jesus, what do you think those are?'

'No idea, but this...' he said, crushing a fat grub under his heel, 'is what those guys will get when they do them for treason,' commented his friend.

'They can't hide for long.'

'Bet they've gone bush.'

'Nah, they've got those rifles to sell. They'll have gone north to Auckland. There's no one to sell them to here.'

And as their voices faded away, Colin and Aroha held their breath a moment longer, until the only sound was of the men crashing through the bush far, far away.

'I know where those rifles are,' Aroha whispered into Colin's ear.

He stared at her — the woman who'd fed and sheltered him, and couldn't help shuddering as he remembered the knife she'd held on him before.

Aroha tried smiling as she interpreted his thoughts. 'I don't have them, but I overheard the men who took them, and I know where they're taking them,' she explained.

'I don't know about any rifles,' Colin said. 'But then I also never imagined myself hiding in forests. I should have stayed in Dunedin. Only God knows what I was thinking because I don't. It's been a hellish trip this far, and the last thing I want anything to do with is rifles or soldiers.'

'Too late for that,' Aroha replied. 'There will be a war soon. And you won't want to be anywhere near here then.'

'I didn't come here for a war, just for my brother, and the gold.'

Aroha laughed a long feminine laugh, one at odds with their situation.

'War finds everyone. Where is your brother now?'

Colin shrugged. He was so close to the gold fields, the ones he'd heard stories about the whole road here. Tales of chunks of gold laying on the river bed. Men wearing nuggets round their necks and golden baubles on their knuckles as if they were nothing more than tin tokens from home. And he wanted part of that. Isaac never made it.

'He was going to the goldfields. I'm going there.' He didn't need to share his life story with this stranger, his grief still too raw.

Hunger gnawed at Aroha. She needed to move on, despite the daylight. They'd dallied too long waiting for the sound of soldiers to disappear. 'We've wasted too much time here, we should leave before they do a proper search.'

Colin jumped up, dusting dirt from his trousers, toes poking through the holes in his stockinged feet. 'I'm ready, hungry, but ready.'

Aroha, in the middle of loading the baby into the woven basket, froze. She hadn't factored in this added complication and a thousand thoughts ran through her mind. Despite his skinny frame, he was a man, an Englishman, so he'd provide a level of security, and comfort. She couldn't discount his cheery outlook and how he'd made her laugh, but knew nothing about him. He was barefoot and without a pack, or anything beneficial to them. She threw the basket onto her shoulders, wincing at the pain as the weight of the baby settled onto the raw wounds festering there.

Colin rushed over, 'And I can help carry the baby,' he said, trying to lift the basket from her.

'I'm fine,' Aroha said, pulling away.

'No, you're not. Look, I'll carry the little one for a while. You lead the way, and when we're further away from the soldiers, you can leave me on the side of the road. It's not like I can be much worse off than I am now, but I don't fancy my chances in this forest. There's nothing to eat to start with and I'd starve to death in the first couple of days.'

Aroha weighed his words but when Colin took the basket, it was as if he'd extinguished the bands of fire across her shoulders, which decided for her and she didn't protest as he slung it over his own skinny back. She could let him travel a little way with them, she'd welcome the company, but that meant feeding him too.

She left him standing with the baby on his back, as she scooped up a handful of the squirming white grubs from the rotting log disturbed by the soldiers. Selecting a plump specimen, she popped the creature into her mouth and swallowed it. Then she held one out to Colin.

'Bolt it down, and you won't even taste it. They're tasty cooked but we can't light a fire now. Something is better than nothing, right?'

Colin had paled as soon as she'd bitten into the first one but took the slug-like creature from her, and without thinking too much about what he was about to do, threw it into his mouth, clamping his fingers on his nose, and chewing faster than he'd ever chewed before. His body threatened to expel the foreign object, and he had to swallow it back down a second time after. Colin tried not imagining that the grub was inching its way back up from his stomach. So when Aroha offered him another, he couldn't say no fast enough. Hungry was better than living with worms inside him, eating their way out.

'It's okay. That one did the job. Thanks.'

Aroha laughed, shoving the remaining grubs into her mouth and chewed, all with a smile on her face — one which transformed the sadness living in her eyes, into something magical. And in that moment, she was the most beautiful woman in the world. And Colin lost his heart to her.

The soldiers carried on, leaving an empty road churned into a muddy morass, pockmarked with pools of rain. Winter flexed its fingers as the trio walked along the road's edge. They weren't the only ones on the road, but the other travellers gave them no bother.

Colin couldn't stop thinking about the white worm she'd fed him, replaying the moment it had been in his mouth, worrying whether he'd chewed it enough to make sure it was dead, or had he swallowed it, leaving it alive enough to crawl back out. His stomach heaved, and he coughed in response, his damaged lungs refusing to let in the frigid air. He stopped to catch his breath whilst trying not to disturb the sleeping child in the basket on his back.

It was all Aroha could do to not seize the baby from him and run. She'd forgotten about his coughing the night before. Had she exposed her child to death once again? Was this boy sick with the white man's disease? Would he pass his sickness onto her child, killing another one of her babies, leaving her with nothing?

'Are you sick?' she asked, forcing the words out.

'It's just a problem I have with my lungs from when I swallowed too much water after our boat sank. I really am lucky to be alive… although sometimes it's hard to remember that,' he laughed. 'I should be a clerk, sitting in a nice cosy office in Dunedin, by a roaring fire, shuffling paperwork for a fat lawyer or banker. Warden Price offered to help me find a job, and I should have listened to him. This cold isn't helping any.'

Aroha released the breath she hadn't realised she was holding.

'I'll take you as far as the nearest marae, they'll be able to point you towards the gold fields, and from there I go south to my people,' she said, wondering all the time if that was the right choice. Or whether carrying on was a foolhardy decision. Her heart was telling her to go home, that it wasn't safe here, for anyone. Her brain told her it wasn't safe anywhere.

THE TRIBE

*A*s they walked, Colin quizzed Aroha about herself and her family. She struggled with her answers — her emotions so raw he didn't need a translation. Love and loss transcend the language barrier. In comparison, his life was as bland as the tasteless bread he'd been eating on this journey. If he never ate another mouthful of damper, it would be too soon.

Colin tried to ignore the hunger in his belly and shook his head when Aroha offered him a bite of the remaining mutton chop she'd held back the night before. Even he recognised that the mother needed the food more than he did, given she was eating for two. At this point in time he'd probably eat a handful of the hideous white grubs she'd forced him to swallow that morning, a lifetime ago. His feet screamed at the cold, a cold which tore at the rest of his body. He imagined surviving a winter in this cruel country would be beyond him.

'You need something for those,' Aroha announced, during a break as he sank to the ground, poking at his hobbled feet, his socks reduced to woollen decorations for his ankles.

Colin watched in fascination as Aroha settled the dozing baby before stripping the fronds from a cabbage plant tree next to them and began plaiting sections of the strips.

'What are you making?'

'*Paraerae*,' she said, not bothering to provide the English translation.

Colin rolled the word about on his tongue, but the tricky vowels shed no further light on what she was making.

'Sandals,' Aroha clucked, like exasperated mothers the world over when faced with a foolish child.

'You're making me sandals?' he asked incredulously.

Aroha rolled her eyes, and stripped more fronds from the now half-naked cabbage tree, tearing the fronds into thinner strips to weave a double-plaited sole. Every so often she'd cast a glance over the baby before returning her attention to sandals emerging between her hands.

The dizzying movement of Aroha's slender fingers was almost too much to watch, so Colin let his gaze wander over the landscape. The thousand shades of green and brown embraced him — colours as unfamiliar to his life in Wales as the feelings were which threatened to overwhelm him every time he caught Aroha's eye.

After what only seemed like minutes, Aroha passed him a pair of woven sandals, just as the baby woke from her nap. So while he pulled on the sturdy footwear she fed the child, angling her body away from him.

He stretched out his legs to admire the workmanship of the sandals, and after standing, he jumped for joy given the relief they provided from the rough ground — his soft Welsh feet unsuited to running around the countryside barefoot.

'How are they?' Aroha asked.

'They are amazing. Thank you. Not sure I'd go back to wearing boots after this,' he joked, bringing a smile to Aroha's sad eyes.

'Good, let's go, I want to be off the road as soon as possible. Can you hear that?' Aroha said, looking off into the distance.

Colin cocked his head. He heard nothing but birdcall and the icy wind punishing the high branches above them.

'Soldiers, lots of them. We'll have to go back into the bush to skirt around them. Trust me,' she said, patting his hand, her touch sending shivers up his arm.

With his feet encased in Aroha's handmade sandals, he agreed. He didn't know where they were going, but as long as it wasn't near the soldiers Aroha feared so much, he'd follow her anywhere.

Colin jumped at every shadow in the rich Waikato forest, his nerves fraught. He was hungry and cold and tired, but at least his feet weren't being ripped to shreds anymore which was the only high point in the punishing trek Aroha lead them on. Under pain of torture, there was no way he would have been able to find his way out of this labyrinth and he'd probably die of starvation trying. There was food available — an abundance of bird life followed their trail through the trees, chasing the bugs and beetles they disturbed, but Aroha had forbidden any form of fire for fear of being caught by the soldiers, or the *others*, although she refused to elaborate on who the others were. Her face as dark as the falling light when he pressed her. She'd stopped talking then, her silence as disquieting as the path she was following.

At one point, Aroha paused beside a giant tree, its girth more than double the width of his arms. The bark slashed with horizontal scores, all the way up and around the back. He watched as the girl ran her fingers over the mutilated bark. The marks confused him. If someone had been trying to cut down the giant tree, they'd been going about it the wrong way. And he couldn't fathom how anyone could have made the cuts so high up.

'What happened to the tree?'

'Gum-diggers,' Aroha replied. 'Stupid men who know nothing, including where to find *Kauri* gum.'

'For what?'

'For this,' Aroha said, scuffing the leaf rot away with her foot and scrabbling around in the dirt. She presented Colin with a palm-sized lump of gum. Not the beautiful, polished *Kauri* gum you'd see set in jewellery or for sale in an antiques shop, but a dirty, crusty yellow rock, far lighter than it looked, and New Zealand's largest export earner, thousands of tonnes shipped overseas for use as resin.

Colin examined the rock, and the light caught a fragment of its smooth, golden surface, allowing a glimpse of its true beauty to emerge.

'You can carve it,' Aroha suggested. 'That's what Wiremu did, my husband.'

Colin nodded. He'd heard about Wiremu's death at the hands of the Jowls. One reason never to go to Auckland. Colin pocketed the gum, an idea bubbling away. He'd carve it as a gift for Aroha, he used to whittle wood back home. She'd said that the name Aroha meant *love* in English, so he'd make the piece into a heart — an easy shape to start with.

Aroha navigated their way through the oppressive forest, disentangling themselves from monster trees and spiky shrubs, flightless birds and the bulging eyes of prehistoric lizards which would haunt Colin's nightmares.

'Step where I step,' she'd said.

And he had, recognising the unmistakable odour of waterlogged ground, not quite the peat bogs of home, but something just as dangerous — impossible ground for an army to cross. And in the last pink blush of dusk they arrived at a Māori settlement.

Cautious eyes watched them as they stepped through the fortified entrance of the settlement — entrenched parapets with deep ditches on either side, Roman-like in their construction. Aroha held her chin high, to conceal the quivering inside. Here she was, not of the tribe whose land she walked, hoping to throw herself upon their mercy, but with no claim to their help, no history. She only had hope.

Warriors stood on the parapets, weapons in their hands, assessing whether the unlikely trio posed any threat. Hidden from view were three ancient ships guns, traded years before the troubles started. Also now lost, was the body of the former East India gunner forced to train the warriors in using the guns. The lack of ammunition no obstacle — before their arrival, the women of the village were preparing improvised shells from iron chains and nails and old pound weights they'd collected. Their industriousness hastily concealed from the visitors.

'*Kia ora*,' came the voice of an older woman stepping forward, her chin adorned with the traditional *moko* — a facial tattoo of the Māori.

Relief washed over Aroha at the sound of the woman's voice, and she all but fell at her feet, leaving Colin standing awkwardly behind with the baby.

Moments later, eager hands plucked the babe from the basket, ignoring Colin's protestations, whilst still more hands helped Aroha up before guiding her to the meeting house, ignoring Colin.

In her heavy English clothes, Aroha looked more like an interloper than someone who belonged. The other women wore an uneasy mixture of native and English clothing, making them an unusual sight to behold.

'You travel alone?' they asked.

Aroha nodded, the weight of her journey falling from her shoulders, and the memory of Colin's company conveniently forgotten.

'You take a big risk,' the woman replied.

'I know, but I'm returning to my family.'

The group murmured their understanding.

'How far do you go?'

'To Taranaki,' Aroha replied.

'You're welcome to stay, but trouble comes this way. More soldiers come every day, on land and the river. It would be safer for you to move on as soon as you can, before... before we tire of their demands.'

Aroha had no knowledge of what the woman spoke of. Wiremu had told her of the warmongering filling the papers — the inflammatory proclamations of the Governor planning the fall of the *Kīngitanga*. But she had no idea that the soldiers on the edges of the settlement were manning the Queen's Redoubt, preparing for the army's attack of inland New Zealand. None of them knew.

One woman tossed her head towards Colin, who was shuffling his feet in the gathering dark.

'Your husband?' she asked, her contempt unmistakable.

'A companion,' Aroha replied, embarrassed that she'd forgotten about the boy. No, a man — a man who'd made her laugh and who had, for the short time they'd been together, made her feel safe.

'He sleeps with you?'

'No, just a companion. We haven't... my husband died,' she faltered, blushing as she considered what could have been. 'He's searching for his brother.'

'A soldier?' The woman spat.

'No, not a soldier, a miner.'

'Just as bad, the yellow fever infects them all. Turns them feral as they burrow into the earth. We've nowhere for him to sleep, he should move on,' she said, before adding 'Unless he's prepared to fight.'

'Please? For one night? Then he just needs directions to the new gold mine, the one the men are travelling to. That's where his brother will be.'

The woman beckoned to Colin. Although he couldn't understand their language, it hadn't been hard to pick up the general tone.

'We can stay tonight and eat with them. Tomorrow they'll show you the way to the nearest mine, and your brother,' Aroha translated, nodding at the older woman as she spoke, checking that she'd interpreted the woman's answers correctly.

Colin almost corrected Aroha then, about his brother, but the moment wasn't right. He should have just told her in the beginning, that Isaac had died, but he didn't want it to seem like he was looking for sympathy when she had her own grief to bear. The word *mine* made him frown; he'd expected to work outside, panning for gold like his brother had, in Bruce Bay. He hadn't escaped from the prospect of spending a very short life working in the Welsh coal mines only to work down a shaft in New Zealand.

Despite Colin's misgivings about the terminology the Māori had used, the heavy atmosphere changed, and other members of the tribe joined them to eat and share tales of their travels around the most welcome of fires. Colin's sandals were much admired, with Aroha's fine weaving praised. Someone handed a warm jacket to Colin, who sighed with relief as he donned the jacket, too grateful for its added warmth to wonder how an English overcoat came to be in the tribe's possession.

Colin felt his skin prickle, as if someone was staring at him from the darkness. It was more than that, there was a vibe coursing through the women gathered by the fire, and the men who'd joined them. They seemed on edge, as if they too felt the eyes of someone watching them from the dark.

He tried to shake the feeling off, because for the first time in weeks, he had a full stomach. It wasn't a bed he slept in, but on woven mats on the floor. Sated and warm, pushing away the niggling doubt that something was wrong, he slept like a king, trusting that the hospitality he'd enjoyed that evening would continue through the night.

And on the other side of the room, Aroha was experiencing the same relief of a full stomach, a warm bed and a happy baby. But it wasn't just the food and the warmth which filled her heart, it was the people who surrounded her. Her people. As she drifted off into her first full night sleep since the death of her husband, little did she know that this would be the last such sleep she'd experience.

THE SOLDIER

*T*he experience of Warden William Price and Annabel Lester on the road was as far removed from that of Colin Lloyd as a pampered house cat was away from an African lion.

Price had received his orders to travel north to the Waikato. Almost every available soldier called to bolster the defences of the army, ready for an expected attack on Auckland.

As they moved north, men mustered to his side, and provisions obtained. As with any army, there were enough women travelling on their coattails for Annabel to merge seamlessly with the crowd. Nobody ever asked what had happened in Dunedin between Annabel and the Bishop; she was just one more woman to help with cooking and mending and tending.

Although they hadn't journeyed as a couple, Annabel hadn't attracted any trouble from the men they collected on the way. Price making it explicit to the men that Annabel was off limits.

The worst of the weather was behind them, but inland the nights were bitterly cold. The roads were not city roads but dirt tracks forged by heavy carts pulled by beasts. They'd eaten more dinners made from the flanks of fallen bullocks than Annabel would care to remember.

Hot showers, television, libraries and coffee shops were distant memories, ones she tried not to think about. But at night she pined for the ease and simplicity of just ordering a curry — butter chicken with garlic *naan*, poppadoms and onion *bhaji*. She'd never bothered learning the recipe for a chicken curry so couldn't try replicating it. Spices were a foreign word here. She hadn't been the best of cooks before she'd arrived in New Zealand, and not much had changed.

And here she found herself again, stirring a cast-iron pot hung over an open fire, wishing for a phone and a home delivery menu. She was so lost in her thoughts she screamed when Price loomed up behind her, checking on supper.

'Hey, it's okay, it's me,' he said, taking her by the shoulders.

Her heart racing, Annabel couldn't smile. The further north they'd travelled, the more uncomfortable and withdrawn she'd become. Not with Price's company, that was the one thing which kept her from going mad. But there was an overwhelming sense something was coming, something no one could control.

The school curriculum in England hadn't covered New Zealand's history, so she hadn't heard of the land wars which would tear the young country apart. But even if she had known what was coming, she couldn't have said it was that which was bothering her. It was more indefinable, as if her time here was ending.

'Come sit with me awhile, we need to talk,' Price said, patting the space next to him on a fallen log, another giant of the forest felled by the tsunami of development flooding the country.

Around the camp, low voices murmured over their own fires and pots of stew. One more day's trek and they would be at their destination, and from there who knew what would happen?

Annabel slipped the heavy lid onto the pot before joining Price on the log, tucking her long skirts around her ankles to keep out the chill now she was further away from their little fire. Spread above them was a blanket of stars, more than she'd ever seen. She'd trade all the electricity in the world to have this every night. The universe so vast, so unending that it made her problems infinitesimal, small annoyances inconsequential. As long as you had food in your stomach, it didn't matter if there were no spices. And if there was a fire, it didn't matter that you didn't own the latest designer down-filled jacket. And if you were safe, you didn't care that you'd missed the final episode of *Lost*. The stars kept her grounded, placing her problems in perspective.

'Annabel,' Price began, 'the Governor has decreed that we go to war.'

'I know.'

'And you can't be with us then.'

'Women can be soldiers too.'

Price shook his head. 'I don't think so.'

'You'd be surprised.'

'I don't like surprises,' he said, his voice turning to stone. 'This has been hard enough.'

'Hard?' Annabel snapped back. 'How do you think I feel? I left everything behind in Dunedin to ride behind you and to sail across harbours on boats not fit for their purpose. I've walked for miles and miles in boots as heavy as lead, with no idea of how long till our next hot meal or soft bed. So how hard do you think it has been for me? And all this time, you've kept your distance from me like you've just woken up in a leper colony.'

'I... ah.'

'See, you can't even bloody well comment, because you're a man who's not in touch with their *feelings*. Maybe that's because of your age, or your inexperience, but you need to know that I have feelings, and you've ignored them. And now you're going to ride off into the sunset to fight in a stupid war, leaving me, what, here? In the middle of nowhere? With a tent and a cooking pot like some neanderthal's wife waiting for you to drag a woolly mammoth home for dinner?'

Price stared at her, and she bit her lip. *Did he know what a woolly mammoth was*, she chided herself, her emotions threatening to overwhelm her. Running off with a handsome young stranger was all very well in books, but in reality it was pretty grim. Shitting in the woods, no toilet paper, no proper bed most nights, sideways looks from men armed with rifles and women armed with knives, no electricity, no real friends, no changes of clothes, no makeup. And no clean underwear. The list was endless. And she couldn't complain about any of those things because she'd chosen this life. She'd flung herself at the man, begging him to take him with her. She couldn't explain her past, her strange turn of a phrase or knowledge of geology and astronomy, history and physiology. And she couldn't describe her feelings for Price, or how she felt about the husband she hadn't seen for more years than she dared to remember. Lost to her now, but still she fiddled with the gold band on her finger, the one she'd been wearing long enough to leave a permanent dent at the base of her ring finger.

'I'm not planning on leaving you here,' Price said. 'The men will make their way to Queens Redoubt. We'll find the nearest, and safest, town. I'm not sure what a neanderthal is, but I don't think I am one. And if you want to eat a woolly mammoth, we can ask the first butcher we find...'

Annabel erupted into laughter. She couldn't help but imagine what her local butcher would have said if she'd waltzed in asking for a haunch of mammoth.

'I'm sorry,' she said, wiping her eyes, her good mood restored. There was nothing she could do about her situation, so there was no point reminiscing. This was her reality, and she had to make the best of it, for it was the only reality she had.

'If you've finished, I was going to say that tomorrow the men will carry on without us. I'll join them later, after I've deposited you in town.'

'Deposited? You make it sound like I'm a bank cheque.'

'We'll find respectable lodgings for you, where you won't have to worry that the bishop...' he left the rest unsaid.

Annabel had taken nothing from Bishop Dascent's home, but that hadn't stopped him from accusing her of theft, which had made the papers, the report revelling in her flight, and all but consigning her to the gallows.

'He wouldn't have any reason to travel here,' she said, persuading herself more than Price.

'True, but the lodgings must be suitable for a woman on her own.

Miners and gum diggers and loggers and militia fill the towns, and to be honest, I'd probably trust the bishop more than any of them,' Price said. 'At least the bishop doesn't drink.'

'True, but that's because his insides are rotten from the evil in his soul,' Annabel quipped, refusing to let her mood evaporate.

'Let's eat and get a good night's sleep. We should leave before the others tomorrow, we don't want to be travelling in their wake. The roads are bad enough.'

'That's no different to a man choking to death on his own vomit... but sure, we can leave early. A proper bed is more exciting than seeing stupid men shoot each other.'

Price ignored the barb and moved to stir the contents of the pot. He'd never seemed to care too much about what she served for supper and always thanked her for whatever it was she made, regardless of what it tasted like. But stirring the pot was as much of the cooking he did since they joined the army. And Annabel struggled to stay positive as she remembered her place in the hierarchy of life in the 1800s.

Annabel settled down to another sleep, alone. Not once during their journey had there been anything more than a chaste peck on the cheek, a gentle squeeze or a guiding hand on the hip. Scared that if she made the first move, he'd view her the same way she'd seen him look at the working girls — with a mixture of pity and horror. In a way, her time was easier. Living with a man without marrying him was fine, living with a woman before marriage was also fine. Not getting married was cool. Having a dozen children without being married was also acceptable. But not here, no. Even when she was first playing the role of a widowed woman in Dunedin, the married women cast sideway glances at her in church, as if they expected her to throw herself across the stark wooden pews at their buttoned-up husbands. No, she had far better things to do with her time than conduct illicit affairs with other women's husbands.

Camp filled with sounds of the night — the snores of men and the snuffles of beasts. The stomping of hooves and the crackle and pop of fires left to die. The calls of the birds and the other creatures who hunted in the dark. Familiar sounds, safe sounds.

But tonight something different filtered its way through, a sinister creeping sound, a tight shuffle, a leaf flutter. Not loud enough to wake the men nor strange enough to disturb the horses or bullock teams who'd stopped with the camp overnight. Annabel lay in her tent, eyes wide in the dark. With the moon only a sliver of its circular self, the stars barely lit the sky. And with the dying campfires reduced to hot embers, there was no bright burning light to scare away the horrors of the night. Horrors which crept closer.

There was a rustle outside. Annabel slipped from her blanket onto her knees, a knife in her hand — the blade more suited for fruit than for anything else, but it was all she had.

With the ties undone, the tent flap opened, and Annabel's nightmares came true. Her scream froze in her throat and her heart pulsed faster than she thought possible as an unidentifiable figure, waddled inside, pulling the waxy linen flap shut behind him.

A thousand plans flashed like a kaleidoscope across her brain, each one more impossible than the first. Her body refused to obey a single order she tried to give.

The man loomed closer, reaching for her. Annabel struck, launching herself from her knees towards her otherworldly attacker, knife in hand.

The man deflected her knife with the ease of experience, before grabbing her wrist and slapping a hand over her still silent mouth. 'Be quiet, or you'll get us both killed.'

THE AMBUSH

*T*ime stopped until Annabel realised whose hand was over her mouth. Price's. She relaxed, folding into Price's body, his scent as familiar as her own. She didn't miss men drowning themselves in expensive aftershave. A real man didn't need designer perfume to be attractive.

'Wha—'

'Shh, put your boots on, grab your coat, and follow me,' he whispered in her ear.

He turned to peer through the tent flap, and to give her some privacy. Although given the blackness of the night, she could have pranced around naked and he wouldn't have seen a thing.

Annabel slipped on her outer clothes, shaking as she tried doing up her laces. He must have realised, as he put his hands over hers and finished the job before giving her fingers a gentle squeeze.

Part of Annabel wished he'd come into her tent for other reasons, that he was undoing her laces, her buttons. She'd dreamt of that almost every night they'd been together, but the insufferable man was a paragon of virtue, and now it was too late for anything more exciting than holding hands as they waited for death.

'What's going on?'

'Not now, please trust me and do what I say.'

Annabel bristled. She wasn't a child — incapable of understanding the complexities of life. She was a grown woman, older than Price. This was the unspoken obstacle between them — he treated her as a second-class citizen. She supposed he couldn't help it, society ingrained it in the men of the time. But the Reverend Cummings, the man who'd first saved her from the streets in Dunedin, hadn't been that way, and she'd met other men on the road who treated their partners as equals. So why couldn't Price treat her as an equal?

'Not until you tell me what's happening,' she whispered back.

'We don't have time for this,' Price said, grabbing her by the wrist. 'We have to go now.' He pulled her from the tent and set off at a low run with Annabel stumbling behind.

To Annabel, the night sounded the same. There were no shouts of alarm nor the clinking of harnesses. But the birds had fallen silent, and it was then she knew something wasn't right. And instead of hindering their flight from camp, Annabel picked up her pace until she was running alongside Price instead of being dragged behind him. He let go of her wrist, nudging her when they needed to change direction or slow down or speed up. Then she heard the first cries.

Chaos erupted in camp, accompanied by a chorus of accents from around the world. Guttural tones of the Cornish miners, en route to the gold-filled hills of the Coromandel; stoic Scots who'd followed their more adventurous family out for a better life; the short but hardy West Coast miners — their heavy accents almost indecipherable to anyone other than their own countrymen. A handful of Americans, distinguishable not only by their drawling vowels, but by their height and their hats, everything about them oversized compared to the English. There'd been a handful of Australians in their camp too, drafted into the militia; and volunteers — who'd decided an army pay was better than dying down a mine shaft.

But in the still night air, they screamed in the same language — that of utter terror and despair.

'Shouldn't we help?' Annabel asked.

Price ignored her, picking up the pace before suddenly changing direction as they came to an impassable load of giant *Kauri* logs blocking their path.

Zigzagging around the trees, stumbling over unseen obstacles, the screams behind them, the giant hills lost in the pregnant cloud cloaking the stars she'd admired only hours earlier. And then the ground was pulling at her boots, their flight hampered by the soft ground. Price turned back towards her, tugging her through the swampy ground.

'My boot,' she cried, turning to retrieve the boot sucked from her foot by the mud.

'No time, leave it.'

And still the screams of men being butchered followed them. Shots rang out, echoing off the surrounding hills stripped naked for profit.

Annabel stumbled again in the boggy ground. Price scooped her up, her muddied skirts adding to her weight.

'Hold on,' he said, navigating the ground churned up by gum diggers, cart wheels, pack horses and the boots of thousands of men.

Annabel held on, survival the only thought in her head. She clamped her thighs around Price's waist and hung on round his neck. So much for being a strong woman, capable of holding her own. If it took being carried like a toddler to survive, then that's what she'd do.

The ground hardened and Price moved faster, his breathing heavy.

'I can manage from here.'

Price slowed, sweat pouring from his face,

The sun had risen over the hills as surreptitiously as the attack on their campsite. It wasn't just sweat Annabel could see on Price, it was the complete exhaustion of a man who'd given everything of himself. A man who had abandoned the many to save her. The weight on his conscience as visible as the sun on the horizon.

Annabel stretched out her hands to hold Price's face.

'Thank you,' she said.

She leaned in and kissed him. Not a quick kiss at the door after a first date, but a torrential outpouring of pent up love. And he returned her kiss.

THE RIFLES

*E*ntwined like a vine against the rough bark of an ancient tree, they stood for hours, centuries even. Hands snaked around each other's waists, connected at the hip, the chest, the thigh. Two people in their own world, the rest of the universe as ethereal as a morning mist over low-lying fields.

A musket fired.

Annabel screamed.

Price fell.

'Run,' Price said. 'Go.'

Annabel ran blindly with no idea of where she was going And what she'd do once she got there. She thought only of what she was leaving.

Scrappy trees tore at her legs and the undulating ground took every opportunity to trip her. Her bootless foot screamed as concealed obstacles in the earth pierced her skin, but she carried on, limping towards an unknown destination. Until pain, and fear and hopelessness pulled her down, leaving her sobbing amongst the tatty ferns and fluffy *toi toi*.

If she'd looked through the leafy fern fronds, she might have seen the impressive wooden palisades of the Māori pā, the fort, but grief overwhelmed what little energy she left. And so she lay not caring whether she lived or died. Memories of her daughter Sarah ran through her mind. Sarah playing at the beach, her first day of school, having to stand on a stool to help behind the counter at *The Old Curiosity Shop*. When she thought of her husband Albert, his face kept morphing into Price's, her memory fragmented by history. It was time to give up, to die.

Two pairs of hands lifted her from the ground and Annabel's body a dead weight between them. They didn't carry her far — only twenty or thirty metres — she was too tired to check, keeping her eyes closed hoping if this was the end, it would be over quickly.

Her skin prickled as though there were a hundred pairs of eyes on her and she felt the temperature change as they carried her into a building, which confused her. They weren't near anything resembling civilisation. The people carrying her let her slump to the ground and Annabel chanced opening her eyes. She was lying on a woven mat on the wooden floor of a house, with a pitched roof and walls, but no dividing walls, just one large room with a front entrance way. With no other doors or windows, the dawn light struggled to enter the room.

Was this where she'd die? She had a moment of craziness worrying about her blood staining the woven mats on the floor.

A conversation ranged above her head, one she couldn't follow. A baby cried behind her. Strange words flowed around her, filling the cracks in her imagination. This was what *speaking in tongues* was like, she thought. People at the church were in awe of the phenomenon, she'd never seen it. The most exciting her church ever got, the one back in London, was some flag waving instigated by a visiting minister from America. He hadn't lasted. The English weren't fond of flags being waved in the aisles of their churches.

Annabel tried focusing on the voices from her position on the floor. Dark faces loomed around her, adorned by tribal tattoos with huge hunks of greenstone round their necks and hanging from their ears. Pieces of jewellery she'd seen in catalogues from the best auction houses — Christie's and Bonhams and Sotheby's, but never in the flesh. She rolled over, and the crowd stepped back.

'I recognise you,' said a young man, stepping forward with a baby in his arms.

Annabel looked up, confusion smothering her. *Did she know this boy?* His voice pulled at her memories, but memories from when? And where?

'You're the lady from Dunedin,' the boy said. 'I'm Colin Lloyd.'

His name elicited no recognition for Annabel and a flood of unintelligible language interrupted them. A woman stepped forward, relieving the boy of the baby, whilst replying to the unseen speaker. Annabel pushed herself to a sitting position. If they were talking about her, she wanted to see who it was.

Māori women and a handful of men surrounded Annabel, all of them armed.

'What's happening?'

The woman with the baby stepped forward. 'They found you in the bush after we heard rifle fire and they brought you back here. Are you with the English?' the girl asked.

'No, but... well I was travelling with them, sharing their camp, but I'm not... someone shot my companion...'

Again they talked above her, in a language she couldn't understand, and there was a quiet whispering between the girl and the man who claimed to know who she was.

'Not by them,' he translated.

'Pardon?' Annabel said.

'The Māori didn't shoot your friend. Someone else shot him,' Colin explained. 'Not the natives,' he reiterated.

'Who shot him? Why?'

'We don't know. But they were using the soldier's rifles because our warriors caught one,' Aroha said.

Annabel struggled to swallow her fear as she asked, 'Did you find my... is he dead?'

'They're dead,' Colin mumbled. 'There was no one alive at your campsite, only you, and only because you were so close to the fort's defences.'

'Everyone?' she repeated.

A sudden volley of rifle fire took everyone by surprise, followed by the shouts and screams of a hundred men. The room emptied, leaving just Annabel, Colin, and Aroha with the baby. The baby's cries competed with whatever was happening outside of the building.

'Get up,' yelled Aroha. 'Help me with her,' she said to Colin as she tried to fit the squirming, crying baby into a woven basket which she slung over her shoulders.

'What's happening?' Annabel asked. 'Are they attacking here now?'

'The English are,' Aroha replied.

'But we're English,' Annabel said, cringing at the rifle fire.

A massive booming filled the air, as the three old ships guns fired.

'We have to get out,' Colin said. 'To tell them to stop attacking.'

'They won't though,' Annabel said, vague historical knowledge floating to the surface. 'They'll attack until everyone is dead, that's what they always do.'

The group hesitated at the doorway, the central courtyard area was awash with men and women — the women reloading the muskets for the warriors to fire. They watched as an English scaling party appeared atop of the defensive palisades, the red of their uniforms like a matador's flag to a Spanish bull.

In seconds, the Māori warriors had the ladder down and the screams of the English soldiers drowned out the booming canons of the three ships guns wheeled into position. A bevy of women were passing the improvised shells to the men.

'They will die,' Colin cried.

'Or we will. We need to get out,' Annabel said. 'Which way?'

'I can't leave them, I have to help. Here, take the baby, go round the back and follow the line of the palisades,' Aroha said, sloughing the woven basket from her back and shoving it at Annabel.

Annabel hugged the screaming infant to her chest.

'There's nothing you can do to help them. You're outgunned and outnumbered,' Colin screamed, grabbing at the Māori girl's hand, but she wiggled from his grasp — an eel slithering free from a trap.

'I can't just leave them,' Aroha said. 'I'll find you afterwards,' and she raced over to the nearest group of women.

Colin went to go after her, but Annabel seized him by his jacket and pulled him after her. 'Leave her, there's nothing we can do. She doesn't want you being shot by accident. Come on.'

They ducked around the back of the building, avoiding the slop of carnage around them. Not stopping to help tore at Annabel, but it was them or her. She'd been so close to giving up the will to live that her sudden desire to survive surprised her. And her companions, keeping them alive was a priority. She turned back for one last look towards the girl who reminded her so much of her own daughter, they'd be about the same age but Annabel couldn't imagine her daughter having her own child, it was possible, but she'd never know.

'This way,' Colin said, the urgency in his voice unmistakable.

The human noise cascaded around them, but a dam of bodies stopped the tinkling flow of the stream. Annabel wanted to scream at them to stop. That fighting was futile, that the British Empire didn't need to flex its might to subdue a smaller country, a people ill-equipped against a better armed foe. She wanted to yell at them that *she* was English, to appeal to their chivalrous side — how could they endanger the lives of the women and children? Was nothing sacred?

The wooden palisades were so tightly packed that squeezing through them was impossible.

Colin got stuck halfway through, and wiggled backwards, 'We have to find another route,' he said looking behind them, but everyone was too busy fighting to worry that they were trying to leave.

'What if they try killing us too?' Annabel asked, panicking.

'We'll find another way out,' Colin said, shoving her further along the protective fence line.

The boy was almost half her age, yet she followed him without question. Had life conditioned her to follow a man? And like pebbles in a maelstrom, they tumbled together through an unfortified gap in the palisades, landing in an untidy heap at the bottom.

An angry shout turned them. A pair of tattooed warriors stood above, training their rifles trained on them.

Annabel froze despite Colin's desperate pleas to get up, which fell silent as he dropped his own hands in defeat. So many times she'd almost given up and now seemed the most opportune time to fall on the mercy of whoever held the guns. The two men tumbled down the ditch behind them, replaced by English soldiers — the morning sun reflecting off the polished brass buttons of the uniforms. The soldiers peered over the edge, sun spots distorting their vision.

'Play dead,' Colin hissed.

Annabel slumped to the ground, playing the role of her life in the dirt. The stench of gunpowder and death washing away their fear and replacing it with a fatalistic stance of *what will be, will be*. And they waited.

The soldiers vanished back into the fray, the murderous annihilation of a tribe who didn't want to part with their lands so the English could extract gold from the quartz underground. For the want of gold, the English had slaughtered the people who'd rescued Annabel. She still had no idea who they had rescued her from. If it wasn't the army, or the Māori who shot Price, who was it? And were they still out there?

'Go back into the bush, it's safer there,' Colin said, scrambling up, and they ran towards the scrubby bush beyond the pā. Annabel's lack of a boot no impediment to her ability to run.

'Stop or I'll shoot,' yelled a soldier.

Still they ran, the baby crying in Annabel's arms, the wailing adding to the thunderous noise coming at them from all angles.

'Stop,' said a closer voice. A soldier emerged from one of the defensive pits, dug to protect the fort, and trained his long barrelled rifle on the group.

'I've got them here, sir,' he yelled back.

'Keep them there,' came the answer.

Annabel looked at Colin, and at the soldier, and weighed up her options. She could run or give up. She was English, so she should be okay, and nobody would hurt a baby. Colin was nothing more than a boy, his accent identifying him as Welsh, so they wouldn't hurt him. There was no point challenging the army, it was best to surrender and let this nightmare be over.

'We should have stayed put, don't know why I was running. One of those soldiers could've been Warden Price. He'd have seen no harm come to us.'

Annabel stared at him incredulously. 'You know Warden Price?'

'He saved my life at Port Chalmers when my ship sank,' Colin said. 'That was you?'

'I guess so. He saved lots of other people too, but he swam out and dragged me back to shore. Visited me in the hospital too, until he disappeared. They told me he was trying to track down a girl abducted from Bruce Bay. Was that you?'

Annabel shook her head, what a peculiar conversation to have at the end of a rifle. Colin's name prickled at the back of her mind. There'd been a letter... but what had happened to it? That was a blur. Price had asked her to send it on but for the life of her she couldn't recollect whether she had. Water under the bridge now.

'Up you get,' the soldier said, prodding Colin with his rifle.

Colin helped Annabel up, who was limping now. 'Where are we going?' Colin asked.

'If I had my way, I'd be back in Australia, back to my cushy little number in Melbourne. But I got shipped here, conscripted to hunt down them cannibals you were with.'

'They aren't cannibals,' Annabel said.

'You would say that wouldn't you, lady. Living with the natives.'

'*They* rescued her from the bandits who attacked her camp. She'd only arrived moments before you unleashed your unholy hell,' Colin blustered. 'We're both friends of Warden William Price,' he tried.

A second soldier joined them, his uniform denoting him as an officer. The starched cuffs of his sleeves had started the day a brilliant white, but were now the colour of rust-tainted water.

The booming ships cannons had fallen silent, replaced with the occasional crack of musket fire, instead of the whole symphony which had played moments earlier. Now men were shouting orders to surrender in English, which provided some hope that the English hadn't slaughtered the whole tribe.

'He says they're friends of Warden Price,' the soldier relayed to the officer.

'Does he now? That's interesting because Warden Price never made it to the Queens Redoubt, where he was to muster with his men. His men never made it either. Perhaps you can enlighten us about that?'

'Now?' Annabel asked. 'When people are dying all around us?'

The officer tugged at his bloodied cuffs, examining them as if he was seeing them for the first time. 'Terrible business, completely unnecessary. We'd almost got them to agree access but Auckland gave us the hurry up. Damn the telegraph. If they'd delayed the connection a few more weeks... but orders are orders, so what could I do?' He swivelled his head between Annabel and Colin, driving home his point, before noticing the baby. 'What the devil is a baby doing out here? Harper, get them back to the Queens Redoubt and get that baby out of the cold. Plenty of time to find out who they are back at HQ.' And then he carried on, 'Orders are orders. Had to attack, no choice. *It's us or them*, the Governor said, and they still think an attack on Auckland is imminent. I was under orders.'

THE REUNION

*D*espite Colin begging to search for Aroha, Harper marched them around the damaged defences of the pā by Harper, his finger never far from the trigger of his rifle. The man's carrot-orange hair did nothing to enhance his tiny pig-like eyes set in his pasty face. The soldier was a jumbled up mishmash of anger and petulance and relief that he'd been let off the unsavoury task of sorting the living from the dead.

'Move it, you two. I ain't got all day. Should have shot you on the spot, bloody collaborators. The natives are moving to attack Auckland next. They'll slit our necks in bed, you mark my words,' Harper rambled.

Colin and Annabel paid no attention to him, concerned more about the lethargic baby in Annabel's grazed arms.

'She's hungry,' Colin said.

'I think it's more than that, she needs a doctor,' Annabel said.

'Who needs a doctor? That mongrel you've got in your arms?' Harper replied, squinting at the baby.

'What did you say?' Annabel asked, her face white.

'Me? I said nothing.'

'You called the baby a mongrel.'

'Only said the truth,' Harper replied.

Annabel's face changed from white to apocalyptic red, 'This is a child.'

'My child,' Colin said, plucking the baby from Annabel. 'And you murdered her mother. So who's the mongrel now?'

'Get a move on and shut up. No more talking from either of you,' Harper said.

By the time they reached the wagons, they were teeming with injured men and bodies, but they made room for the newcomers, and with Harper glaring at them the whole way, they travelled the bumpy road to the Queens Redoubt, the headquarters of the army's defence of the imagined invasion of Auckland.

Capable of housing four hundred and fifty men, the place was overflowing with the dead and dying, the conscripted and the volunteers, the professional soldier and his sadistic, opportunistic militia colleague — the sort of man who'd never make it in the real army, a man like Harper.

Faced with housing a woman, a baby, and a potential collaborator, the commander of the garrison, a man they'd already met, billeted them with the doctor, asking Annabel to help where possible. Annabel agreed, on the proviso that the doctor first examine the baby, whose lethargy was even more pronounced.

The doctor pronounced the baby dehydrated, directing Colin to dip a rag in a bowl of boiled water, for the baby to suck. So with Colin ensconced at the end of the doctor's cot, cooing and clucking to the infant, the harried doctor tasked Annabel with redressing wounds and seeing to the lesser injuries. No one asked if she knew what she was doing. Her mere existence as a woman was enough for them to assume she had a wealth of healing knowledge. Like all mothers, she could remove a splinter from a finger, or dress a graze. She wasn't much good at bandaging up broken fingers or plugging wounds caused by musket fire, but she did her best.

The pace was frenetic, providing no chance to dwell on her own problems. She gave no thought to the future — with no past, no present and no future, she was a ghost walking through time. She fell asleep across the doctor's bed, breathing in the sweet scent of the baby. Annabel's last thoughts before she slept, were of her own baby girl, Sarah.

A military camp is no place for a woman and a baby, so the commander decreed that they go to Auckland for questioning. The army transported Annabel, the baby, and Colin — who they'd accepted as the baby's father, up Great South Road, to a town preparing for invasion.

Deposited at the Albert Barracks, the soldiers didn't know what to do with them. Although Harper had volunteered to escort them, the commanding officer ordered him to stay at the Queens Redoubt, otherwise their fate might have been quite different given the way the arrogant red-haired soldier leered at Annabel whenever she went near him in the course of her duties.

The duty sergeant deduced that they were in the wrong place at the wrong time, and that they were lucky to escape with their lives. He reiterated that the army was preparing for the native invasion and no one wanted to waste any time on them. He all but shoved them outside.

The army had returned Annabel's belongings, together with Warden Prices', from the campsite after they gave the dead decent Christian burials. Rumours were rife about the culprits, but as far as Colin knew, only Aroha had any idea who they were. And she couldn't tell anyone. He prayed her death had been quick, that she'd died trying to save her people. Colin couldn't stop thinking about how he'd abandoned Aroha; how he'd failed to find his brother; how he'd run away from his mother and his other brothers. But he was adamant he wouldn't fail the baby. He didn't know what he needed to adopt her, but that was a problem for another day. For now their first task was to secure lodgings until they decided what to do next. He thought about them as a group, as an extended family. Annabel's husband died long ago, she'd said, leaving her no family in New Zealand, and Aroha had perished in the attack on the fort. He'd heard that there were few survivors, and those who hadn't perished, vanished into the bush. But first they needed a room — a bed, and a bath, and then they could plan. Fate had decided he shouldn't be a gold miner, that was clear.

~

He secured them both rooms at *Sheehan's Hotel*, using the cash from Warden Price's bags. Annabel assuring him it was fine to use the Warden's money, that he'd understand their need. After arranging for someone to bring a bath up to the room, he left Annabel to her ablutions and descended to the public bar.

The bar was awash with men — miners, gum-diggers, loggers, merchants. It was obvious who wasn't there — not a single native was on the premises, but the subject of the natives were on the tongue of every man there, a wave of festering discontent. Colin chose a quiet spot by the door to swallow his ale, already regretting his naïve decision to come downstairs. What did he think he would achieve? That luck would smile upon him and he'd find Warden Price sharing a drink with Aroha?

No, Colin kept his eyes downcast, content to listen to the babble of voices around him, the accents as familiar as the beat of his own heart.

'Room for us at this table?'

Colin looked up from his drink and blinked, convinced there was a problem with his eyesight. The image didn't change, there were two identical men standing in front of him, just as filthy and road-weary as he was, but older, and fit the narrative of the place better than he did.

'Well?'

'Yes sorry I...' but he didn't finish, a flash in the eyes of one twin giving him pause. 'Sorry, you surprised me,' he finished. 'Please join me.'

'You get the drinks,' the man said to his twin, and the giant brute lumbered off. It was clear to Colin that one wasn't as smart as the other. That was the way of things sometimes. Nature didn't always get everything right.

'You look lost, friend,' Colin's companion commented.

'It hasn't been the easiest of times,' Colin admitted. 'Colin Lloyd,' he said, sticking his hand out.

'Nice to share a table with you, Mr Lloyd. My name's Joe, and that's my brother, Jimmy, getting the drinks.'

Colin sipped his ale. There was something familiar about the man's name, but he'd met so many people on his journey, more people than he'd met in his lifetime in Wales, that it was probable he'd heard the names somewhere along the way.

The men made small talk about Auckland, the strengthening numbers of the army, general tittle-tattle from the road and before he knew it, Colin had finished his drink. He made to get up from the table, but Joe pulled him back down.

'We'll shout the next round. Jimmy, get us another round,' Joe directed. 'Besides, you need your money for your girl and baby.'

Jimmy hadn't uttered a single word, and Colin was even more convinced Jimmy must be a simpleton, capable only of following instructions.

'Thank you, but I've no coin to repay you,' Colin explained. 'I lost everything on the road here. Fat lot of help I've been to me Mam back home,' he said, and he tipped out his muddied pockets to prove his claim. A carved *Kauri* gum heart skipped across the table, coming to rest against Joe's glass.

'A nice piece of work,' Joe whistled. 'Did you carve this?'

Colin's heart sank. Would the payment for a round of drinks cost him Aroha's heart? Reluctantly he nodded.

'Incredible work. Are you a jeweller by trade?'

Colin checked Joe's face. The man wasn't joking, his face a picture of seriousness, his calculating blue eyes ice cold.

'No, it's just something I can do. I've always whittled away at whatever was at hand, and this was just the same.'

'Do you mind if I keep this, to show a friend?'

It was as he feared. 'Sorry, but I made it for my friend, Aroha. She told me Aroha means love. So love, heart, you know...'

'Aroha?' Joe said, turning the trinket over in his hand. 'Yes, I see. I just need to borrow it for a while, to show my friend in the city, He's a jeweller, and there's much call for someone of your talent. Might be a job opening at his business,' Joe explained.

That was the last thing Colin expected the big man to say, and he couldn't hide his excitement.

'Absolutely, yes, thank you. I'd be in your debt. A job, as a jeweller? My Mam won't believe it.'

'It's agreed then. I'll meet you here tomorrow to return your trinket and to let you know what my friend says to my proposal.'

The men drank, each toasting their good fortune — Colin celebrating a potential job, and Joe Jowl celebrating his luck that he'd located the man who rumour had it was cavorting with the miller's wife at the site of the army's latest battle. He and Jimmy had struck out on their enquiries down south, but now it seemed their prey had come to them.

The battle was the talk of the town, the stories growing on their travels north. Joe Jowl lived for gossip and rumours, and traded in them to run his business, he was also an expert in sorting the wheat from the chaff. And he knew without doubt that this man had been with Aroha Kepa, the wife of the miller. She had Joe Jowl's money, and he wanted it back, and this scrawny little man would help him find her.

As for the woman ensconced upstairs, Joe thought they'd found Sarah — the woman the miller helped escape. It was all he could do to keep Jimmy from barrelling upstairs and doing his thing with her. That wouldn't do. The bar was too close to home with too many witnesses. It was lucky he'd determined that the woman wasn't the one they were after, but it had been a close call. Too close. Jimmy was behaving like a wild animal, his impulses almost untameable. Joe did his best to cater to his brother's peculiarities but time would tell if Jimmy was a risk to the family name. Regardless of how Joe felt, *family business was for behind family doors*. Jimmy was his brother, and he'd deal with him.

THE JEWELLER

*J*ust as Joe Jowl suspected, the jeweller jumped at the chance to employ a skilled Kauri gum carver. The jeweller also didn't want to piss off the Jowl Brothers and would have accepted a braindead logger as a jeweller's apprentice if Joe Jowl wanted him to, so it was fortuitous that the man Joe Jowl had proposed possessed a skill set he desperately needed.

The demand for Kauri gum abroad was insatiable. It had started with the resin industry, but soon morphed into other industries — the jewellery business being one. The lustre of the gum, its versatility and abundance made it sought after as an alternative to the rarer amber of the northern hemisphere.

Henry Neumegen ran a successful pawnbroking business but recognised that there was value in selling the unclaimed items he held, which morphed into a successful jewellery store. The intricate detailing on the heart had impressed him, and he had a thousand ideas for other pieces his newest apprentice could make, including a lovely line of Kauri gum bibles, sure to be a popular choice for the newly wealthy miners to send home to their loved ones.

On Colin Lloyd's first day at work, the jeweller laid out his employment terms and conditions. Lloyd was to work five days a week in the shop, but could work one day a week at home, as long as he met his quota of carved gum. Colin had agreed to the terms without question. The money Annabel had found in Price's satchel wouldn't last them much longer, and he was itching to get his little family set up in their own home. From there he would start putting money aside for his family back home.

Colin tried not to think about his mother, and the news he needed to share. There was always a reason he never got round to writing to tell her about Isaac. Some other errand he had to make. Or the baby needed something. Colin tried asking old Neumegen for advice, but he'd refused to discuss it, so Colin assumed that Neumegen had himself lost someone to the 'yellow fever'.

Annabel had been ecstatic that he'd found himself a job, vowing to care for the baby whilst he was at work. This wasn't quite the life he'd imagined when he'd first stepped foot on the ship at home, but things were panning out. Aroha's loss pulled at him in his quieter moments. When the baby cried, he knew she was crying for her mother. Every night he dreamt of the heroic deeds he'd attempted to save Aroha, but they all ended the same way, with Aroha dead. Those nights he woke up sweating, knowing he'd cried out in his sleep but that Annabel was too considerate to raise it with him in the morning. He hoped that with a regular job and income, the bad dreams would drift away, leaving him to grieve in his own way.

He'd only been working for three days before Joe Jowl and Jimmy dropped into Neumegen's shop. Ostensibly, Jowl was checking on how well the job was working out for both Colin and Neumegen and to congratulate Colin on his good fortune, subtly reminding him not to forget that he owed the Jowl's for his luck, That part of the conversation didn't concern Colin, it was the next part which vexed him.

'Would she have liked this?' Joe asked, fingering a *Kauri* gum necklace, the beads uniform in shape and translucent in the sunshine streaming in through the window.

'She wasn't one for jewellery,' Colin replied.

'Did she not wear any jewellery?' Joe asked.

'Only a carved *tiki*.'

'A *tiki*? Anything special about it?'

Colin thought for a moment but shook his head. He'd noticed it but couldn't recall anything memorable about it. Every memory about Aroha made his eyes prickle.

'Can you remember if it had shell for eyes?'

Colin wiped his eyes. He couldn't remember what her necklace looked like. It had never interested him. 'No idea,' he said, scraping the gum in his hand so hard the piece splintered apart. 'Why?'

'No real reason, just the name is familiar and Auckland's such a small place I wondered whether I'd met her. The Aroha I knew wore a very distinctive *tiki* with *paua* shells for eyes. Unusual,' Joe mused, before beckoning to his brother who was loafing in the corner, eyes downcast, fists clenching and unclenching by his side. 'We'll be off, business to see to, but we'll drop by again in a week or two. It would be lovely to have a heart like the one you carved for your friend. I've taken quite a fancy to it. Good day.'

The Jowl's walked out of the shop, leaving behind an invisible scent of corruption.

Neumegen emerged from the shadows of the back room, his sombre suit a fitting epitaph to the Jowl's visit.

'You want to be careful of that man, and his brother,' Neumegen said, adjusting the plain gold tie pin at his neck. 'He wants something from you. Best you figure out what it is and make sure you either secret it away or give it to him, otherwise he'll never leave you alone.'

'I've no idea what he wants,' Colin said. 'I only met him at the bar the one time. This is the first time I've been to Auckland, the first visit for Mrs Lester too.'

Neumegen rearranged one of the jewellery displays in a wooden framed cabinet whilst Colin was talking. He pulled out a heart-shaped greenstone pendant and examined it with an eyepiece on a gold chain around his neck.

'Jowl's *Kauri* gum heart won't carve itself, boy,' Neumegen said. 'Think long and hard about the style of *tiki* your friend was wearing. If it's the girl I'm thinking of, the Jowls won't stop hounding you until they find her body.'

Colin stood open-mouthed in front of his employer, a thousand questions on his tongue. He'd been so sure Aroha must have died in the attack on the pā that he'd never thought to seek her out. The soldiers had treated the native survivors alongside the wounded soldiers, and Annabel hadn't seen her during her days of assisting the army's doctor. How did Neumegen know who she was, Colin had barely mentioned her?

'It's a small place, New Zealand,' Neumegen said, interpreting the look on Colin's face. 'She'll turn up, dead or alive. They'll find her, with or without your help, but things will be easier for you if you help them. Their fingers are in every pie in town, and more men, and women owe them favours than you could imagine.'

'But she's dead.'

'Dead doesn't always mean dead,' Neumegen said. 'You'll need a fresh kerosene rag for that one — better than using your palm to polish it,' he said, pointing at the piece of gum emerging from Colin's ministrations with his three-inch jack-knife. 'Finish that then work on Jowl's piece. It'll be better for both of us.'

THE ARRIVAL

*S*arah groaned and held her hands to her head, which was spinning out of control. There was no mistaking what had happened, she'd been flung back in time. This time she was alone, and too terrified to open her eyes, wishing the nightmare away.

As the pain ebbed away, Sarah's senses came into focus and the scents and sounds of her new location enveloped her — scents and sounds which were not native to modern-day England, or even bygone England. Sarah chanced squinting through her still painful eyes and shut them just as fast. Whilst she wasn't in someone's basement this time, the outlook wasn't that much better. One of her first thoughts was that at least she hadn't ended up in the Jurassic period or in the midst of the Black Plague. As she sorted through the long vowel sounds washing over her, she realised she was back in New Zealand. Not a progressive modern-day New Zealand with a female prime minister and a predilection for bike lanes. This was a version where a woman's place was in the kitchen or on her back.

As feeling returned to her limbs, and the tingling subsided, she opened her eyes to find the drooling mouth of a four-legged beast above her. Although the dog was more interested in licking her face with his long tongue, Sarah froze with fear. She'd been a child when an ugly whippet had jumped her from behind, sending her sprawling to the ground before sinking its teeth into her skinny leg. She maintained that she wasn't afraid of dogs, despite that early negative experience, but she'd kept a healthy distance from man's best friend for most of her life.

'Come away. Oi, come away,' yelled a voice.

The dog bounded off, its tail a fast moving pendulum of joy, and Sarah scrambled to her feet. The owner of the exuberant creature cast an incredulous look her way, but hurried away before she could call out for help.

Alone once again, she examined her situation. Dressed, with shoes, was a better start to the day than previous experiences. It wasn't raining although the air smelt heavy as though the clouds were battling to hold back a deluge. The street looked more established than the road in Bruce Bay or even the road leading from the Jowl's house on an Auckland hillside. Holding her head with one hand, she waited for the world to stop spinning. From where she was, it was clear she wasn't on a main road, but down a side street which explained the lack of foot traffic. Appearing in front of a hoard of midday shoppers required more explaining than she had the brain capacity for. What Inspector Fujimoto was thinking right now was a problem for another time.

At the end of the street was a steady stream of women in long skirts and waistcoated men, some carrying horn-handled umbrellas, others with brown paper packages tied up with string. Emerging wearing jeans and shirt might have gone unnoticed in the dark, but in the middle of the day she'd be the centre of attention, which was not what she wanted.

Sarah turned and walked away from the main street, reading the signs in the windows of the businesses she passed. Like any street in any town in any city, the road held an assortment of tenanted and empty shops, alternating between dust-coated windows and gleaming glass panes with gold lettering.

The wind picked up, sending the hanging signs swinging under the quaint awnings which protected the footpaths. A sign ahead caught her eye, *Henry Neumegen, Pawnbroker*. Sarah looked at Isaac's gold nugget still clasped in her hand, the plastic evidence bag decidedly out of place. It was as if the world was telling her what she needed to do.

Sarah entered the poky little premises, letting the door swing shut behind her. There was a glass door behind the counter which led to the proprietor's private office, and probably to his residence above the shop. Old fashioned wooden cabinets ran the width of the shop filled with pocket watches and watch chains, gold-rimmed glasses, and various gentlemanly trinkets, all unclaimed pawns. She couldn't help being drawn to the cabinet at the end of the room, the one by the window where the sun fell upon a choice of ladies accoutrements — simple engagement rings, delicate pendants, earrings fashioned from small gold nuggets, and a gleaming array of amber beads and jewellery. Sarah had never seen such a delightful assortment of amber. It was rare to come across anything more than a strand of beads or a pair of earrings, but to see so much in one place was unheard of.

'Can I help you?' asked a young man who'd materialised behind the counter.

Sarah started to speak but her words stuck in her throat, her mouth dry. The young man too, looked lost for words, as she stared at him open mouthed.

It couldn't be! She'd held him as he'd died. 'Isaac?' Sarah stammered.

'Isaac? No, ma'am, it's Colin,' he said, his tongue darting out to wet his lips.

'You aren't Isaac, I was... never mind, I—'

'I had a brother called Isaac,' he interrupted.

'A brother?'

'I came here to join him, make enough money to send home,' he added. 'You must have met him? Mam said we all look alike...'

'I'm sorry, I'm sure it wasn't your brother I met, probably just a trick of the light. Sadly, the Isaac I knew died on the West Coast.'

'That was my brother,' he said, his body deflating like a balloon caught on the thorn of a rose. Tears filled his eyes, piercing her with his little-boy-lost look.

'Oh,' she said, her hand halfway out of her pocket, the gold nugget heavy with grief. She shoved it back in. She'd sort that out later. 'Oh.'

The frosted glass door opened and a dark figure loomed behind the crying man.

'Off you go out back, Lloyd. Pick yourself up, I'll help the young lady.'

Sarah faced a serious looking man, dressed in black, an eye piece dangling from his neck, a caricature of a pawnbroker straight from the pages of Dickens.

'I would ask what you did to upset my apprentice, but I caught the tail-end of your conversation. There can be no mistake then, you knew his brother, Isaac Lloyd?'

'He died in my arms,' she said, 'protecting me.'

Neumegen sniffed as he processed the information. 'You've opened his wound all over again. So much loss for someone so young... you weren't to know.'

The pain of Isaac's death wrestled with her heart, and coupled with the trauma of travelling through time once again, Sarah couldn't keep her own tears at bay. At once the pawnbroker threw open the counter's access hatch and ushered her through to his private quarters.

Sarah sat opposite Colin on a sturdy dining chair, the boy's face a mirror of her own. She smiled at him, trying to portray her own loss, a loss so unimaginable that she'd never be able to explain it to anyone. Her mother, her father, her business, her best friend, her life, her lover. Every name on the list sending another wave of loss through her heart.

Neumegen bustled about making tea, unobtrusively, as was his way. He'd never been one to make a fuss or postulate. When operating as a pawnbroker, one learnt to be circumspect with the lives of others. Their business was their business, he merely offered a momentary service for a fraction of time, and for a fee.

The pawnbroker handed hot cups of tea to Sarah and his apprentice, trying not to stare at Sarah's clothing. If it weren't for her feminine features and attributes, she could easily pass as a man in her trousers and a shirt. Occasionally he pawned better quality clothes and considered offering his unexpected guest something more suitable. But after tea. He'd become well accustomed to the English tradition of taking tea, adopting it in his early years as he tried assimilating into a culture not of his own.

'Do you take sugar?' Neumegen asked, a silver teaspoon poised in the air.

'I think today I do, yes,' Sarah replied. 'Sorry about before. I should have been kinder with my words, more... I didn't know. Sorry,' she said clumsily.

Colin coughed into his sodden handkerchief, his lungs struggling with the effort, leaving him wheezing.

'Are you okay?' Sarah asked.

'I'm fine. Damaged my lungs. Good thing you don't need strong lungs to work in here. The lungs would've killed me if I'd joined Isaac on the gold fields. But I would have been with him when he died. Might have been better,' Colin brooded.

'Time heals all wounds, not just the physical ones,' Neumegen preached. 'Besides, you need your health now you have other people relying on you. You have the baby, and Mrs Lester. They both need you.'

'Mrs Lester?' Sarah said. 'Who's Mrs Lester?'

'The lady who looks after his baby,' Neumegen said, sipping his tea.

Colin made a noise of agreement. He hadn't been entirely truthful with Neumegen about his relationship with baby Sophia and Mrs Lester. Annabel had agreed it best that they pass themselves off as an extended family unit. Warden Price's money, and Colin's apprentice wage would cover their board at the hotel until they put aside enough for their own place. Annabel was earning her own small pittance by helping with the hotel's laundry, again because of the Jowl's largesse. Another reason to be in their debt.

Sarah wanted to ask more about Mrs Lester, she desperately wanted her to be her mother, but expected disappointment. She fought with herself, until the bell above the door chimed, and Neumegen and Colin disappeared to attend the counter.

Could this Mrs Lester be Annabel Lester, her mother? Sarah didn't dare let herself dream.

Raised voices outside wiped the thoughts of her mother from her mind, and Sarah moved to eavesdrop at the door.

'You call yourself a jeweller? You wouldn't know gold if it jumped up and bit you on the arse. Next you'll be saying that these aren't pearls. My late mother only ever wore the best quality pearls, straight from the Orient. And you can't even offer me enough for a new pair of boots, when this here strand of pearls is worth twenty pairs of the finest boots money can buy. A thief, that's what you are, a thief.'

Neumegen's voice too quiet for Annabel to hear his reply, but the customer's cursed response was enough to turn a sailor pale, as he blustered and threatened and swore until he'd used every foul word available. And still Neumegen kept calm, never once raising his voice. It was Colin who took the mantle of bad cop to Neumegen's good cop.

The added insult of Colin coming to the defence of Neumegen sent the disgruntled customer into a rage, forcing Sarah to jump back as he hurled something at the glass door, shattering it into a thousand pointed icicles. Sarah retreated behind the workbench, out of harm's way.

The smashing glass brought the neighbouring shopkeepers out onto the street, and the burlier men stepped into the fray, pulling the blustering man from the tangle of Neumegen and Colin's tiring arms. Cabinets lay smashed on the smart wooden floorboards, the light glinting off shards of glass caught in the gaps. The cabinet of pocket watches sat on a drunken angle, leaning against another whose glass now decorated an austere display of silver propelling pencils and double sovereign cases.

Sarah watched as Colin and Neumegen dusted themselves off, Neumegen wiping blood from a split lip, and Colin coughing into a handkerchief held over his own bleeding mouth. The blustering idiot appeared to be suffering from nothing more than cuts to his fists, his face disfigured from fights in both the near and distant past. He was lead away by two men resembling henchmen from an episode of *James Bond*. Sarah emerged from the workroom, glass crunching underfoot like a walk through autumn leaves.

'Well that escalated quickly,' she said, before noticing the eyes of the crowd staring at her through the open door.

Neumegen squeezed past the upturned counters to close the door. 'It'll give them something to talk about, but best we don't offer more fodder for their gossip,' he said, sliding home the lock on the latch.

'He never took his necklace,' Colin said, pointing to the strand of pearls half-concealed under a damaged cabinet.

Sarah bent to retrieve it, the pearls light in her hands. Instinctively she rubbed them against her teeth, the graininess of genuine pearls completely missing.

'They're not real,' Sarah said, looking back at Neumegen.

'Of course not. They rarely are.'

'How do you know?' Colin asked.

'That's why she was biting them, lad. If they're gritty, they come from the oyster. If they are smooth, then they're manufactured by man. And a clasp made from junk metal. It may fool someone on the goldfields, desperate for a gift for a sweetheart, but in this business, you take nothing at face value. Like our lady friend here...'

Both men stared at Sarah, shuffling under their gaze.

'I don't think she is your ordinary customer,' Neumegen said, dabbing at his lip. 'But we've time to dwell on that later. Colin, you go for the glazier, while we sort things out here. And find William Norrie, the cabinet maker on Shortland Street — he's done work for me before and may have something suitable in stock.'

Colin stared a moment longer at Sarah, before grabbing his hat from the hook, and slipping out the door, with Neumegen re-locking it behind him.

'First, you must change,' Neumegen said. 'Follow me.'

Sarah trailed behind the gaunt man, following him out through the workroom into a room filled with floor to ceiling shelves. A staircase at the back lead upstairs, but it was to the shelves that Neumegen guided her.

Without hesitating, he selected a hatbox which may have been mauve in the sun, but in the weak lantern light, it appeared a sickly beige.

'A hat,' he said, before pulling a small leather suitcase from another shelf. 'And in here a suitable skirt in your size. The jacket may be more problematic, unless you don't care for fashion, and then I have ample possibilities?'

Laden with options, he showed her upstairs to a spartan arrangement of very little furniture and evidence of quiet wealth far exceeding the value of the stock downstairs.

'Please use my room to change. Your shirt... will do, but I will dispose of your trousers. Please leave them by the hearth, and your shoes. I'll check for boots. What size should I look for?'

Sarah muttered her size, shockingly large for a lady in the 1860s she knew, but Neumegen didn't seem fazed, his stiff figure retreating downstairs giving her a birdseye view of the thinning crown on his head.

She let her eyes roam over the room — everything utilitarian but of the highest quality, and not a speck of dust anywhere. Sarah wondered who did his cleaning for him. Her mother used a Croatian couple to clean their house. She'd never been able to get her bathroom as clean as Lily and Pavao had. There'd been no funds for a cleaner after her parents had disappeared. She doubted Neumegen was the type to waste money on a cleaner either, or a maid. But there was no sign of any womanly things.

Once in Neumegen's bedroom — a single bed with a nightstand, a straight-backed wooden chair and an ornate upright travelling trunk-cum-wardrobe, she wasted no time in slipping out of her jeans and pulling on the voluminous skirt he'd handed her. Retrieving the nugget from her jeans pocket, she turned it over in her hands. By rights this should go to Colin. Isaac had asked her to send it to his mam, Colin's mam too, but fate had decreed otherwise. *What to do with it now?*

Neumegen called out to say he'd left a jacket and boots on the chair by the fireplace for her consideration, and so Sarah shoved the nugget and letter deep into the pocket concealed in the folds of her skirt, and emerged from Neumegen's bedroom. Neumegen had a defined sense of style and had paired her skirt with a fitted jacket in a contrasting yet complementary pattern; delicate green embroidery on the lapels the only nod to decoration. The first pair of boots she pulled on chafed at her ankles. Nothing in the 1800s would ever be as comfortable as *Converse* sneakers, but she couldn't wander the streets of Auckland wearing her *All Stars*. So, she tried on the second pair — a better fit but stiff and the laces cut into her fingers as she tied them up. As much as she hated to admit it, they'd do.

The walls held no mirror to check her reflection, but there was probably one inside the trunk, so returning to Neumegen's bedroom, she fiddled with the latch until the lock sprang open, and she opened up the doors. There was no way on earth, in this time or another, that she expected to see what she saw.

THE ARMOURY

Sarah stepped back from the wardrobe, her hands over her mouth, eyes wide. Her own father had kept an old police-baton under the bed for 'security'. People usually kept hockey sticks behind the door, or baseball bats in the hall cupboard, in case they ever needed to fend off a burglar. But no one stored a dozen or more rifles in their travelling trunks.

She closed the case up and rearranged her features into something less shocked when she heard the pawnbrokers boots on the stairs. Plastering on a smile, she returned to the front room, trying to put the rifles from her mind.

'Better,' Neumegen said. 'Your hair needs fixing, but I have no pins here, I'll send the lad out for a packet when he returns. But before that, time to talk, yes?'

'I'm not sure what you want me to say?' Sarah said. How could she tell him who she was and where she was from? It was too fantastical for anyone to understand.

'From the beginning, or how you could tell the pearls were paste, or from when the brother died. You choose.'

She considered her options for a moment. The beginning wasn't an option. The pearls? Well, that was an easy one. Isaac was too painful.

Going from having never seen a dead body to having a man die in her arms had sent her into a deep well of depression, that he'd died because of her was almost the end of her, so the pearls it was.

'My father was a jeweller,' she said. 'In England.'

'And he has passed now?'

'Not quite, but he lives in India now, so it's virtually the same thing.'

Neumegen laughing was not the reaction Sarah expected, but it lightened the mood, and she laughed in response.

'Family doesn't always work out the way you imagine,' Neumegen said, his fingers straying to the pin at his neck.

Sarah assumed the pin had some significance to the man, but let her eyes wander to the sole piece of art on the wall.

'Is that from home?' she asked.

Neumegen followed her gaze. The picture was from his hometown — a small oil painting of a Bavarian landscape, the old church at Ramsau prominent in the centre of the image.

'You recognise Ramsau?' he asked.

She'd had a childhood friend who'd invited her to winter with her family after Sarah's mother's disappearance. Her father had come too, and although the skiing was brilliant, their accommodation was lacklustre. She'd never forget the dreary countenance of *Haus Michael*, including the complete lack of toilet paper when they'd first arrived.

'The only part of home I brought with me,' he shared. 'All I have left,' he added, a faraway look in his eyes. 'So, you are familiar with jewellery then?' he asked, changing the subject abruptly.

'I do.'

'You know jewellery and you have been on the goldfields so you know miners, yes?'

'Yes.'

'Good.'

'That's good?'

'It is for me, and for you too, now you fit in. We must always fit in. I have spent a lifetime trying to fit in, you should do the same. If you can't, join your father, otherwise life will be hard here, especially now,' he said staring past Sarah towards the painting.

Sarah cast a glance towards Neumegen's bedroom, wondering what scared him so much that he had a personal armoury in his room.

'Business is good, and I can no longer do it on my own,' he said.

'But you have Colin,' Sarah said, eyebrows raised. This was not the development she'd expected. This man didn't know her from Adam, and yet he was offering her a job?

'He is my apprentice, for the *kauri* gum, not to sell trinkets to miners with nothing better to spend their money on. A girl is best for that,' he declared.

It wasn't home, but it far surpassed her last experience in Auckland being held captive by the Jowl's, forced to act as a servant and scullery maid.

'Good,' Neumegen said, despite Sarah having not uttered a single word. 'Have you found accommodation?'

She shook her head, her mind adrift at the sudden change in her circumstances — working as a shop assistant for this strange man. He seemed harmless enough, despite the arsenal next to his bed. She didn't know when she'd return to the future, if she'd return. But working alongside a pawnbroker seemed the most likely route home of all the options she'd considered both now and before.

'There might be room with the boy's companion, Mrs Lester. Otherwise I shall enquiry on your behalf. Enquiries on behalf of the daughter of my cousin… Do you understand what I am saying?'

Sarah nodded dumbly. This man had his secrets, and he recognised she had hers, and although he knew nothing about her, why would he pass her off as a member of his family? *For what gain?*

'Good, now we have a shop to clean. The boy should be back with the glazier soon. Come.'

They made their way down the narrow staircase, through the storeroom and into the workroom. Neumegen pointed to a dustpan and brush, while he himself took hold of a long-handled broom, and they worked in companionable silence.

Much of the damage looked worse than it was. By the time they cleared the glass away, and set the cabinets straight, Colin had reappeared with William Norrie, the cabinetmaker, in tow. Norrie had with him a tattered notebook and a well-used measuring tape in a leather case.

As Norrie and Neumegen discussed the damage, they decided one cabinet was beyond salvaging, and he ordered a replacement. Neumegen surprised everyone by asking Sarah her opinion on the design of the new cabinet.

'I think one with curved shelves, with narrower width shelves at the top, and full width lower down, better to display smaller pieces and highlight larger pieces of silverware, if that's something you might go for...' she tapered off, the men all gaping at her.

'Large silver pieces,' Neumegen muttered. 'Yes, perhaps that is an idea. Good. Can you do that then Mister Norrie?'

The cabinetmaker dashed off a quick sketch which under his artistic hand, looked as though he'd copied it straight from an auction catalogue, so beautifully rendered were the lines, right down to his customary eight-point star he'd added to the base of the cabinet. 'Like this?'

'Exactly like that,' Sarah said, her ideas perfectly replicated in William Norrie's notebook. She made a mental note to research him on Google on her return, if she returned.

They agreed a price and Norrie left the trio to their duties.

'The glazier, Colin?'

'He's delayed, but will be here within the hour,' Colin said, who kept casting sideways glances at Sarah every few seconds. 'There is something different.'

'Her case arrived,' Neumegen said, 'with her clothes.'

Colin pondered Neumegen's answer before a coughing fit took over and Neumegen manoeuvred the boy onto a high stool. A crystal carafe sat on the workbench and the jeweller poured Colin a drink, encouraging him to take small sips of the tepid water.

'Can I help?' Sarah asked, floating about in the background.

'He will be fine, too much excitement. Perhaps enough today for us all,' Neumegen pontificated. 'When he has recovered, walk with him to his rooms, and avail yourself of the accommodation there, with Mrs Lester if she is agreeable.'

Sarah couldn't breathe, this was fate, it had to be. She was certain she was about to see her mother again. Her excitement dimmed as she realised she had no money to pay for food, let alone board.

Again Neumegen surprised them both by pressing several coins into her palm. 'This is an advance on your wages. Come tomorrow with Colin at eight o'clock. We break for lunch at midday.'

Colin clambered off the stool, his face a pasty white. 'It would be my pleasure,' he wheezed, wiping his mouth with his handkerchief.

Sarah followed Colin out of the shop and turned to wave goodbye to the jeweller standing in the doorway. A curious look crossed his face, and he never saw the wave, he was facing the opposite direction, towards something she couldn't see. Perhaps only Neumegen himself could see it, something from his past, or perhaps his future.

THE WORKER

*A*nnabel Lester checked on the baby asleep in the drawer next to her, and couldn't help chuckling at the absurdity of her position. Here she was, mothering a child who wasn't hers, for a boy old enough to be her own son, in an inn she hadn't paid for, doing the laundry for a dozen men she didn't know.

With the dry edge of her apron, she wiped the perspiration from her face. She'd give her right eye, and her left, for an industrial washing machine at this point in time. Annabel assumed the men weren't too fussy about the cleanliness of their clothes, happy that she'd removed the mud stains and their sweaty stench. As for mending? She'd done her best, but wouldn't win any sewing badges.

With the washing hung on the line outside, Annabel rested for a moment. There was no point in complaining about her lot to young Colin, he was doing his best to care for her and baby Sophia. But she couldn't help feeling cheated out of happiness. She'd been so close to a new life, until they stole Warden Price from her after the violent attack on their camp.

To preserve the memory of Price, she wore a cotton shirt she'd found in his bag. Thicker than the ladies shirts she'd worn, and a looser fit, she revelled in its comfort. Annabel rolled up the sleeves, exposing her white arms to the bright sun. She'd left her jacket inside, there was no need for it this afternoon. The unseasonably warm day made even more pleasant without the jacket's restrictive collar threatening to strangle her.

Soon she'd have to help with the midday meal — steak, chops and potatoes, all washed down with ale. She ate for free, part of the deal Colin had negotiated with the proprietors. The customers paid a shilling for their meal, which included the grog. The menu never varied, but no one complained.

Baby Sophia woke from her nap and Annabel's moment of quiet contemplation popped like a bubble. Managing her day around the child's naps was a juggle until they had enough set aside to find their own accommodation. She'd not seen much of the Jowls, the proprietors of the tavern. They'd barely spoken to her, with Colin doing the talking for them both. She'd learnt the hard way to keep quiet in this time — to swallow her opinions, and to freeze her tongue.

The Jowl brothers were as identical as two pools of water, although she'd sensed an underlying current of something from one twin, as if danger lurked beneath the surface, a monster waiting to prey on the unwary. She'd tried to ignore the feeling but when Colin and Joe were talking in the kitchen, the quiet one kept clenching his fists, then flexing his fingers, over and over. Soundless words forming on his lips, without ever looking her in the eye, even though she knew he was staring at her.

Sophia's crying swept away those thoughts, and on autopilot she fed and changed her, *oh what she'd give for disposable nappies.* She propped the babe up in a homemade playpen in the corner. When you considered the hazards of the 1800s, it amazed her the world had the population it did. The absolute lack of attention to health and safety astounded her, and keeping the baby safe was a daily struggle, but like millions of mothers before her, she managed.

The stifling hot kitchen was no place for a jacket either, as lunch morphed into the supper service. She didn't need it as she gathered in the washing — ironing and folding it, before helping cook the supper, followed by more dishwashing, then feeding the baby and changing her again, before taking a moment to stuff food into her own hungry mouth.

Too exhausted to retrieve her jacket, she slunk up the creaky wooden stairs to her room, where she settled the baby, trying not to think how good a hot shower would be right now. Even as she slipped into bed and drifted off to sleep, she gave no thought to her jacket hanging on the kitchen door, nor to the crumpled letter in the pocket. A letter never sent.

THE FIRE

*A*nnabel was so used to the pungent smell of hops clinging to everything around her, that the smoky scent of fire woke her. Expecting to wait until her eyes had adjusted to the dark, tonight it looked like someone had taped a sheet of cellophane over her window, diffusing the moonlight with a rose-coloured filter.

Through sleep-encrusted eyes, the colour was pleasing and Annabel nestled further into a mattress which was neither soft nor hard, but like Baby Bear's bed in *Goldilocks*, it was just right. Warm and cosy, surrounded by a comforting light, with the baby sleeping, all was quiet, and someone had a comforting fire alight. She'd always loved the cosiness of a fire in the hearth. It was weird that she could smell the fire when she knew her windows were closed.

What Annabel couldn't see were the flames bursting through the wooden shutters of the building belonging to the firm of Morrin, and Co., and the fire spreading across the shingle roofs of the adjacent buildings. She slept on, oblivious to Mister Baker and his brother clambering from the window of the smouldering building and jumping for their lives. Annabel slept through Constable Hastie giving the alarm as amber flames licked the sides of the large wooden building. A frenzied hammering on her bedroom door finally woke her.

Stumbling from her bed, Annabel turned the iron key in the lock to find Colin pulling on his boots.

'Get Sophia and grab your things, we need to get out,' he yelled.

'What? Why?'

'There's a fire, and it's spreading. We have to leave.'

'A fire?' she said, sniffing the air. The tang of fire obliterating the usually pervasive scent of hops used to brew the gallons of ale which lubricated the new city.

Colin pushed past to pluck Sophia from her makeshift bassinet. The supernatural glow outside lit the room like a Las Vegas stage production, and orange lights danced over the spartan room.

Annabel shoved her feet into her boots, thrusting her few remaining belongings into her bag.

'Where's your jacket?' Colin asked, the fear in his voice as loud as the bells of the volunteer fire engines labouring their way towards the conflagration.

'I don't know,' she said, giving up her search of the room.

'Forget it, we have to go. This place will be next if the wind changes,' Colin directed.

Annabel grabbed the blanket from her bed, wrapping it over her shoulders. *Would she ever have any peace in this godforsaken country?*

By now the other residents of the inn had roused, either by Colin's yells or the peals of the alarms, and the stairways filled with people fleeing, their possessions in tow.

Colin shepherded Annabel through the dark corridors. The building was like a rabbit warren, with rooms and hallways added on haphazardly as the need arose. He'd thought it quaint when they'd first arrived, but in the darkness it was a potential death trap for anyone confused by the strange corners and sliced off hallways. It was fortunate that they'd been there long enough to know their way around, even in the dark.

The streets filled with refugees from the innumerable taverns and inns catering to the burgeoning population, and Colin stood with Annabel and dozens of other half-dressed residents clutching their earthly belongings. An air of inevitability cloaked the crowd as flames leapt from one building to another, the crackling and splitting of wood a peculiar symphony in the night air.

'It's got the Thistle Tavern,' yelled someone, pointing to a building further up the road. That building danced, dressed in layers of orange tulle, twirling like a ballerina in the wind. The tavern's windows shattered in the heat, sending glass missiles dozens of feet into the air.

Desperate men rallied the bystanders to help, cajoling the crowd to step forward to soak blankets or ferry buckets or to empty the buildings of their stock, to just do something, anything, to slow the path of the fire or to save what they could on behalf of their fellow citizens.

'Quick, there's a well behind Levy's building, get some water from there,' yelled a man, short of breath from sprinting up Queen Street, only half dressed.

'Where's the bloody army?' asked a man next to Colin.

Colin turned to reply but a cry from across the road swallowed his answer as the walls of the Thistle Tavern gave a great sigh and the building collapsed inwards on itself, sending spark-laden lumber spinning towards its neighbouring buildings.

The bells from two more fire engines joined the cacophony of screams and shouts and crashes and bangs and the smashing of glass and the buckling of timbers. A chain gang had formed nearby as countless people emptied the stock of McGuffie's Saddlery and the provisions from Prime's Grocery store, piling up in a place of relative safety.

'I should help,' wheezed Colin as the smoke wound its way into his damaged lungs. 'Take Sophia away from here and I'll find you afterwards. Take her to Neumegen's place, it's a brick building, it's safer than the others,' he said, kissing the baby on her uncovered head.

The insatiable fire devoured everything in its path, with no thought to the people left homeless by its hunger. Colin expected her to know her way to Neumegen's shop, but Annabel only had a vague idea of where it was, and in the crowds filling the streets, she had little hope of finding a direct route there.

'Come on, Sophia,' she said, turning away from the crowd.

A hand grabbed her on the shoulder, spinning her back. It was Colin, the fire's reflection twisting his face into an anguishing visage.

'I forgot about Sarah, oh my god I forgot,' he screamed.

Annabel shook her head. 'Who's Sarah?'

'The girl from Neumegen's. You'd gone to bed when we got back last night so I couldn't introduce you. She was in the room at the end of the hall,' he said, scanning the faces of the crowd milling in front of *Sheehan's Hotel*.

'Can you see her?' Annabel asked, checking the crowd herself even though she didn't know who she was looking for. Never once considering that the girl was her daughter.

'It was so odd, but when I first met her I would have sworn that she looked just like you,' Colin said, pushing through the bystanders in a panic.

Annabel followed in his wake, her stomach twisting as his words sank in. 'Like me?'

'God, I hope she isn't still inside,' Colin said, staring upwards.

Tiny fireworks floated on the gathering breeze, miniscule embers, each of them as hungry as the next, looking for more to eat.

An almighty explosion from behind the hotel sent the crowd cowering to the ground. Unseen, the fire had slipped round the back of the building, seeking the spirit barrels stored there. The alcohol proving to be the best fuel.

'Up there, look!' yelled a bystander.

Annabel and Colin looked towards the windows of the upper story of the hotel to see several faces pressed to the glass, eyes wide with fear.

'Why don't they climb out?'

'They should jump—'

'Where's the army? They should be here helping.'

'Get a ladder—'

The suggestions came thick and fast, but the fire flew faster than any of the solutions, blistering the paint on the weatherboards and pushing the bystanders back even further.

'There she is!' Colin pointed to the far left window.

Annabel saw her own face mirrored back. *Sarah.*

'Break the window,' someone yelled up to the windows, pantomiming the suggestion.

'Sarah!' Annabel cried, ignoring everything around her, even the baby in her arms. 'Sarah, break the window. Jump,' she screamed, her voice hoarse with the effort and the suffocating smoke.

The window next to Sarah's exploded open, the glass littering the audience. A sturdy chair poked through the hole, clearing the remaining shards from the wooden frame. Moments later the occupants of that room — two middle-aged men, waistcoats askew, their heads bare, clambered out onto the narrow ledge, their bootless feet providing poor purchase on the anorexic ledge.

The falling embers landed on the shoulders of a man lurking within earshot of Annabel's cries. A huge man, intimately acquainted with the layout of the hotel, Jimmy Jowl.

The face at Sarah's window struggled again to lift the sash window, but to no avail and she vanished from view. Fire was devouring the building's far side with the ease of a biblical whale swallowing Jonah.

The hose truck finally appeared, and as the volunteer firefighters rolled out their hoses, Sarah reappeared at the window, brandishing something in her hands. The crowd gasped in unison as they watched her striking the window.

'Why doesn't she just open the window?' someone asked.

'They're nailed shut, those upper windows,' replied a portly man, resplendent in gleaming white long-johns and a matching vest which barely constrained his mammoth belly. 'Heard it from the barman,' he added, stroking the snowy beard which completed his outlandish outfit.

Just then, one man lost his footing on the ledge, plummeting to the ground as the women in the audience shrieked, and the men surged forward. Whether it was for a better look or to offer help, it didn't matter because the man's skull had broken in half upon impact, his face unrecognisable in the dirt.

When Annabel and Colin returned their gaze to Sarah's window, no one was there. The only occupier of the room now the creeping caress of orange and red flames licking at the window and the curtains and the bed, sipping at the kerosene in the lanterns and nipping at the wicks of the candles.

'Sarah!' Annabel screamed.

'I'll find her,' Colin said, but the acrid smoke forced its way down his throat, and a coughing fit doubled him over as his lungs struggled to function.

Annabel swung her head around until she spied someone suitable, a matronly looking woman clucking over a small tribe of children staring at the carnage.

'Please, please hold the baby?' Annabel begged, thrusting Sophia into the woman's surprised arms before running off without waiting for an answer.

A line of bucket-toting locals sprang up, filling leather buckets from every available water source, the line of grabbing hands tossing the water over the nearest burning building. It seemed as if they were fighting a hundred different fires at once such was the confusion and lack of coordination.

Annabel intercepted one bucket, emptying it over her head and soaking the blanket wrapped around her shoulders. She shoved her handkerchief into another and, holding the sopping wet cloth over her face, she took a deep breath and dashed into the open mouth of the hotel.

Ignoring the men who tried to stop her, Annabel ran through the dark smoke-filled building, trusting her memory of the layout to get her upstairs to her daughter's room. She slammed her thigh into a misplaced chair, the pain barely registering in her mind. *Sarah was here, and she needed her.* The thought of her daughter enough to propel her up the stairs, the sodden blanket protecting her from the burning embers dancing with joy throughout the corridors.

'Sarah?' she coughed through her handkerchief. 'Sarah?'

She'd never have heard if Sarah had answered her, the sound of the fire sucking the noise from the air and replacing it with a loud crackling and splintering and spitting and groaning. Sounds which could have been mistaken for the screams of a young woman and the grunts of a deranged man struggling with his latest victim.

Annabel fell over a suitcase abandoned in the middle of the hall, blistering her hands on the super-heated floorboards. She pushed herself to her feet, the pain of no consequence with her daughter's life in peril. The stench of the fire stung her eyes making it all but impossible to see where she was going. Using the edge of the blanket as a protective glove, she felt her way along the wall, bent double, trying not to breathe, counting the doors, *Room 9, Room 10, Room 11 — Sarah's room.*

She reached round the edge for the doorknob, just as the door opened.

A giant stumbled from the room, a hulk of a man with a wet handkerchief obscuring his face, carrying a limp bundle.

He barged right past Annabel, the only noise his deep coughing in the smoke, the bundle unmoving in his arms.

Annabel grabbed his arm, desperate to see that it was Sarah he carried.

Thwack

The giant swung his fist throwing her backwards. If Annabel had been standing upright, it would have knocked her out. But as hunched over as she was, it only clipped the top of her head. The knock enough to send her sprawling to the ground, dazed and confused leaving the man's back a dark retreating shadow as he disappeared down the corridor with her daughter in his arms.

Annabel tried to stand — the blow to her head, coupled with the smoke and the flames reflection on the walls, more than disorientating. She didn't know which way was out, the bedroom doors as indistinct as the walls and the floor and the ceiling. She crawled towards the staircase, the thunder of the fire louder with every inch. The damp blanket had fallen off, and she'd lost her handkerchief, certain she was inhaling the hot sparks with every breath.

Every inch took an hour, two hours, ten hours. Time stood still. Was she crawling in the right direction? One more inch, that's all she could manage. It was too hot. Too late. She couldn't breathe. There was no air left.

THE HERO

*C*olin sank to his knees in absolute agony, not physical pain but mental anguish. Too late he'd seen Annabel dash into the burning hotel, the cries of the people alerting him to her folly. *Damn and blast these lungs* he thought, wheezing. *The stupid, stupid woman, if only she'd waited a minute.*

The army had arrived and were assisting the volunteer firemen and directing the gawking onlookers. Within a matter of minutes it looked like they would beat the fire. Soldiers and sailors had scurried onto the roofs of the surrounding wooden buildings, training hoses and beating out smaller fires with wet blankets. The bucket brigades were making headway, and the horses freed from the burning stables were no longer rampaging through the city. It was incredible what military coordination and discipline could achieve.

Colin spied Joe Jowl standing nearby. *Of all the men here, he'd be able to save Annabel, and Sarah,* Colin thought as he pushed through the crowd.

'Help me, please?' he wheezed. 'They're both inside.'

'Who?' Joe Jowl asked.

'Sarah, and then Annabel went in after her,' Colin gasped, his lungs almost incapable of speech.

'Who's Sarah?'

Colin tried replying, but nothing came out, the smoke too much for his body. He grabbed at Jowl's jacket, his eyes wide, gasping like a fish flapping next to a bucket of water.

'Save them...' he gasped before collapsing at Jowl's feet.

The army had commandeered a hose and a team of men to saturate the burning hotel. They couldn't save the hotel, but it was possible they could rescue anyone left inside if they got the flames doused.

Jowl's mind was overflowing with jumbled data and supposition. His brother was somewhere not by his side, which was a concern. Jimmy had unusual tastes, and in a disaster like this, victims were ripe for the picking. Joe had always covered up his brother's activities, cleaning up any mess he left behind, but tonight, with the army crawling over the city, his ability to conceal Jimmy's crimes would be slim. Bribing the army wasn't the same as paying off a miner or silencing a witness. No, he needed to deal with whatever Jimmy was doing himself, and quickly.

Joe stepped away from the unmoving body of Colin, and vanished, ducking between buildings, his huge body parting the crowd without having to resort to violence, the inferred threat of his bulk enough to make them move.

Jowl doused himself with water and forcing his way through a side door, he entered the burning building. He had to get to Jimmy before anyone else did. Making his way up the stairs, the heat trying to force him back. But like Annabel's quest to save her daughter, Joe's only thought was of his brother. It was just them, and if he lost his brother, he didn't know how he could go on, but he didn't let himself think that way. He'd find him, he always did.

By the time Jowl reached the top of the staircase, the heat seared the hairs from his arms and face. He took a hesitant step into the hallway where flame leaked from the door frames, the wood bulging. Jimmy must have come to look for the girl. As soon as he'd heard Colin say her name, he knew at once who she was, and seeing her face at the window of his own hotel had almost sent him careering into the building himself. He'd hesitated, not realising until too late that

Jimmy had seen her too. Stupid. His stupid brother. He took one more step and tripped over a body on the ground.

Although it wasn't Jimmy, it was someone else he knew, the woman travelling with the kauri gum carver, the boy he'd sent to Neumegen.

A door exploded open ahead of him, showering them both with wooden fragments, the hall completely engulfed in flames now. If Jimmy was still there, there was nothing he could do. He grabbed the unconscious body of the woman on the floor, hauling her downstairs.

Fire overran the hotel, leaving only the kitchen exit available. Jowl bashed through the connecting door, stumbling into a kitchen clogging with smoke, still carrying Annabel like a sack of potatoes. Grabbing a coat from a hook, he smothered his own smouldering jacket as he broke through the kitchen door into the night air.

A fireman saw him exit the building and loosed his hose over the pair, as Jowl stumbled from the now unstable building. A soldier ran up to him, relieving him of his burden.

'Is she okay?' Jowl coughed, smoke in his lungs.

'We'll get her straight to the hospital,' the soldier replied, not answering Jowl. There'd been too many bodies, what was one more?

Relieved of Annabel, Jowl focussed once again on the whereabouts of his brother. He was certain he'd have known if Jimmy had died in the flames. There was a connection between them; peas in a pod. But there was no way anyone could have survived the fire on that side of the building, no one. Even the foolish woman he'd rescued from the fire hadn't made it to the end of the hall. No, he'd know if Jimmy was dead. He was somewhere, and Joe felt that wherever Jimmy was, he wasn't in a good way. He had to find him fast.

'You saved that woman!' someone gushed. 'You're a hero.'

Jowl sniffed. He wasn't a hero; he didn't want anyone dying in his premises, especially since he'd ordered the windows nailed shut. Too many miscreants had tried climbing out the windows to avoid paying their bills.

'Excuse me, I have to find my brother,' he replied, pushing past the jubilant man. He had an idea where he would find Jimmy, he only hoped he wouldn't be too late.

Joe Jowl cursed whoever started the fire now consuming the city. He'd lost more than just the hotel, with another three of his buildings damaged beyond repair, and two more were perilously close to the fire. If the wind picked up, there was nothing anybody could do to save them. He could stay to pass buckets along the chain, or stamp out hot spots with a sodden blanket, but that was for the workers, not him. There would be many conversations with the insurers in the coming days, and they would pay to replace the old buildings, at little cost to him, delivering gleaming new buildings far more attractive to a well heeled traveller or digger, a lucky silver lining.

People streamed past him into the city environs, ghoulish sightseers chattering, worried about their jobs or their businesses. A team of horses flew past, the carriage behind them engulfed in flames, the whites of their eyes as bright as the fire they were fleeing from. Jowl jumped back, and a woman screamed as the carriage clipped her going round the corner. Her cries drowned out by the groaning of the Morrin & Co. Building collapsing in on itself with a thunderous sigh. The town was an inferno. They'd be lucky if there was anything left by daybreak. By the time the sun rose in the morning, the magnitude of the disaster would be obvious — one entire block of the city destroyed including the Young Men's Christian Association, the Greyhound Hotel, Mears' Store and the old theatre. Brunswick Hall was only spared complete annihilation by fortune of being one of the few brick buildings in the vicinity.

Jowl had no time to spare to help the woman, or anyone else trying to save their stock, and their families. He had his own family to find.

Jowl broke into a run. They kept a block of stables on the outskirts of town. He liked horses, they were the one thing which never disappointed him. And he'd spent a great deal of money ensuring he had the best horses. Which was why the stables were out of town, to avoid drunken louts scaring his horses, or any tomfoolery endangering his investment. His deepest desire was to race them. For an indefinable reason, he hadn't shared that vision with his brother. He shared everything with his twin, but not his intense love for the beasts. Perhaps because he knew that if Jimmy felt anything threatening their relationship, including the horses, it would end badly. What Jimmy did to the women he found didn't concern Joe. Everyone needed an outlet for their proclivities, and besides, the women were usually whores, no loss to society. But his horses were a whole different matter.

As Jowl approached the stables, he could hear the nervous shuffling of the horses, the confused snorts and the bubbling snickers of panic. Even here, the smoke hung heavy in the air, twisting its tendrils around everything in its path as the increasing wind wafted it southwards.

The door was open. He never left it open — open doors invite trouble. He'd told Jimmy that a thousand times. And not for the first time, Joe cursed his brother under his breath. He assumed his twin was inside, but it paid to be cautious. Cautious in business and in private, that's what kept him alive.

Grabbing a long-handled shovel hanging outside the door, Jowl entered the darkened stables, memory guiding his way. Most of the stalls were full, but the last three were empty, waiting for a delivery of fine stallions he'd ordered from Australia. He'd once found one of Jimmy's girls there, in pieces, but still alive. He'd put her out of her misery before burying her at the back of the stables, moving a mountain of horse manure to cover her grave. Joe didn't care about Jimmy's activities, as long as no one else knew. But, he wanted to deal with Sarah himself.

The horses whinnied a greeting, his presence spreading a blanket of calm through the building. Although the stables were of wooden construction, they were far enough away from the fire to be unaffected, keeping his horses safe.

'Jimmy, you in here?'

The horses moved nervously in their stalls, their stomping feet masking whatever answer he heard.

Jowl moved along the row of stalls, checking each one as he went. He'd left the door open behind him to see. He didn't want to risk lighting a lantern with so many people on the streets. The moonlight and the light from a city on fire was enough to see what he needed to see.

'Jimmy?' he tried again.

"Down here," a voice replied, competing with the sounds of nervous horses.

Jowl lowered his spade, and strode towards the end stall, muttering calming words to the beasts he passed. He was sure they'd picked up on his mood and were becoming even more agitated. One of them kicked at the wall of their stall, cracking the wood. Jowl whispered to the wild-eyed horse, but didn't notice the thickening smoke drifting into the stables, his mind focussed on far more important things.

'Calm down, beautiful one. Shh, it's okay,' he murmured in the horse's velvet ear. The horse stilled as Joe held its bridle, the supple leather smooth under his fingers. He stroked its neck, the strong muscles under his hand as familiar as his own. Giving the horse a final pat, he returned to the task.

'Jimmy, that girl better still be alive,' he said, steel in his voice.

A thunderous crash came from the outside, as another building succumbed to the flames. Jowl spun round, the flames visible through the open door. The fire much closer than he'd expected.

'Jimmy, you bring that girl out here, right now. Stop mucking around,' Jowl directed. He didn't have time for Jimmy's games. They'd need to move the horses and then they'd deal with the girl, at home, away from any prying eyes, or ears. He didn't want her anywhere near his stables.

A muffled *thump* came from the end stall.

'Jimmy, I swear, you get off that girl right now. We've got to get the horses out,' Jowl said, rounding the corner of the final stall, mindful that the only exit was at the front of the stables. He'd need to work fast now the wind had picked up. 'Jimmy?'

The light was almost negligible, but there was enough for Joe to see his brother slumped on the ground, his arms embracing himself amidst the prickly hay. There was a second body, a smaller one, curled up unmoving in the far corner. In the light it was impossible to see whether it was the girl from the window — Sarah, the girl who'd vanished with Wiremu Kepa, the miller. The girl they'd spent fruitless weeks searching for, before business drew them home.

'Jimmy, you okay?' Jowl asked, abandoning the shovel and bending over his twin.

Jimmy moaned through lips which weren't there anymore, his face a grotesque mask of what he used to be. Jowl recoiled in horror, the darkness lending a gruesome slant to his brother's ruined face.

'What happened?' Joe asked.

There was no answer from Jimmy. The answer came from a man standing behind Joe. A man left for dead, but who'd left his hospital bed to help fill buckets and wet blankets, together with the able-bodied men in the ward with him. A man who'd recognised the face in the window and who'd gone to help save her, only to find out he was tracking a monster.

Warden Price picked up the abandoned shovel and answered.

'The fire caught him, but that's not what will kill him,' Price said, testing the weight of the long-handled shovel. 'The burnt face and hands aren't a problem. He'll be as ugly as sin for the rest of his days, but he's not likely to survive the hole in his stomach, not with his guts hanging out, amongst the hay and horse manure you've got lying around.'

Jowl tugged at his brother's arms, almost vomiting as the burnt flesh sloughed off in his hands. The man wasn't wrong. Jimmy's guts were spilling out of a huge gash in his belly.

'How...' Jowl started to ask, before he spied the three-pronged pitchfork near his brother. And it became clear. This man had stabbed his brother, his only brother, in the stomach. Jowl roared to his feet and lurched for the pitch fork. He didn't need answers, he needed revenge.

Price struck first, wincing at the pain from the old bullet wound in his shoulder. The heavy shovel collided with Jowl's hip, sending the man into the rough wall of the stable. To Price's surprise, Jowl launched himself off the wall as if nothing had happened, the prongs of the fork landing dangerously close to Price's thigh before he twisted away just in time to avoid being impaled.

The fork stuck in the stall's wall, giving Price enough time to swing again. Movement was difficult in the confined space and the impact wasn't as great as he'd expected, allowing the giant in front of him to wrench the fork from the stable wall and try again, like a Greek javelin thrower in the early Olympics.

The horses in the stalls reared up in fright as the fight moved from the stall to the centre of the stables. Joe's throw of the pitch fork missed Price when he tripped over a piece of tackle left carelessly on the floor. The fork found a target though, imbedding itself in the mare's flank in the opposite stall.

The horse's anguished screams joined those of the man suddenly upon him, and they struggled on the ground, the larger man wrapping his hands around Price's throat, trying to strangle the life out of him.

'You killed my brother,' Joe screamed at Price, spittle flaying his face.

Price tried prising Jowl's fingers from his throat, but he didn't have the strength, the weakened muscles in his shoulder no match for Jowl's physical power. The gloom inside the stables deepened as the man's grip intensified.

'He didn't kill your brother, I did,' a soft voice sounded above him.

Joe looked up.

Standing over them both was Sarah, a small pistol in her hands, trained towards Jowl's head. A pistol she'd secreted after finding it hidden among the arsenal inside Neumegen's trunk. An arsenal stored by Neumegen on behalf of the Jowl's, part of the cache of guns stolen by the army deserters, guns which Jowl planned to sell back to the army for a profit. Or to whoever paid the highest price got the guns. He wasn't fussy.

Jowl rolled off Price, hatred spilling from every pore.

'You little bitch,' Jowl said.

Sarah's face was a shadow of what it had been. Her eyes swollen, lips bleeding, and her hair singed from half her head, but mostly she was intact. Her saving grace was that Jimmy enjoyed playing with his toys, giving her an opportunity to defend herself. And defend herself she did, after finding the fork on the ground obscured by the hay. When Jimmy had paused his games to relieve himself, she'd lunged upwards with the fork, straight into the flesh of his exposed belly. Weakened by the pain from his serious burns, he'd tried retaliating, but his body gave way. The rush of adrenaline from abducting Sarah replaced with the inevitability of going into shock. And he'd fallen to the ground as Sarah twisted the long-handled fork backwards and forwards and backwards and forwards, leaning all her weight behind her efforts.

'That may be, but I'm also a good shot,' she said.

Sarah pulled the trigger, the tiny pistol exploding in her hands as the shot flew true into the centre of Jowl's forehead.

A look of surprise flashed in Jowl's eyes, before a nothingness filled it, and he slumped to the floor. As dead as his brother, his mother, his father. As dead as Jimmy's dozens of victims, and as dead as Wiremu Kepa, and countless others who'd fallen foul of the brothers over the years. Sarah had done the community of Auckland, and New Zealand, a great favour.

THE MORNING

The sun rose over a decimated Auckland, where untidy piles of stock lay in huge mounds guarded by soot-covered owners. Newly homeless families lay huddled on corners, the stench of waste thick in the air.

There were extensive views across the Waitemata Harbour, where only the morning before, large buildings blocked the way. The owners of buildings untouched by the fire, thanked God and their lucky stars they weren't mourning the loss of everything they had, like so many others in town.

Auckland's only hospital was bulging at the seams, with the Albert Barracks taking the overflow. Most of the injuries were serious burns and broken limbs from people falling from windows through lack of adequate fire escapes.

Sarah sat at the bedside of Annabel, her mother, her own wounds of no consequence — they looked worse than they felt, and they'd heal. Her mother unconscious, her breaths shallow and her skin pale. The doctors had all but ignored her, certain there was nothing they could do, with death imminent.

After releasing the panicked horses from their stalls, and shepherding them from the stables, she'd watched as Price used his

291

flint to start a small blaze among the tinder-dry hay strewn about the floor. It would be better for everyone if they believed the Jowl's had died trying to save their horses, and each other. Sarah had even thrown dry hay onto the flames as they left the stables.

At her mother's bed, she couldn't speak to Price, uncomfortable in his company. So much had happened since she'd last seen him. A lifetime had passed for her, and for him it seemed. He'd barely left her mother's side, apologising to Sarah with pained eyes. Sarah had run the gamut of emotions. Delight at being reunited with Price and then confusion at the obvious depth of feelings Price had for her mother. Thoughts of her father clouding every other emotion she herself felt. She was at risk of being sent mad by everything washing through her body.

'I'm popping out for some fresh air,' she announced.

Price looked at her with guilt in his eyes.

'It's fine,' she said. 'Honestly, I understand.' Sarah left before the tears toppled over, standing outside on the steps of the hospital. The tang of burnt wood, and horse flesh, still strong in the air.

A dark figure loomed over her, Neumegen.

'You're hurt,' he said.

'Not badly,' Sarah replied, forcing a smile.

'And Colin?' Neumegen asked.

Colin was also in hospital, confined to his bed by a smitten matron, and reunited with baby Sophia, who was entertaining the nurses with her happy-go-lucky smiles and easy nature. Colin was a different story.

'He's inside, but won't speak with anyone. Maybe he can't? He's in a bad way but the matron thinks he'll recover.'

'I'll speak to him,' Neumegen said.

Sarah shrugged with nothing to add, she barely knew the boy. He'd looked at her blankly when she'd gone to see him after hearing the nurses talk about the young lad with the wee babe. She'd tried talking to him, telling him about finding her mother, but at the mention of Annabel's name, he'd turned away, refusing to engage. So she'd left, going back to Annabel's side, and the uncomfortable silence between herself and Price.

'I'll see you when I come out. Please wait for me,' Neumegen said, tipping his black hat and entering the busy hospital.

That was her life. Every man in it telling her to wait, or wanting something from her. She was her own person, capable of independent thought and action. There was no use fighting it. Without Neumegen or Price, and their protection, she was as useless as a newborn lamb.

She watched as uniformed soldiers roamed the streets together with the volunteer firefighters, pulling down still smouldering walls, training their hoses on hot spots, ensuring that the fire was out. Reporters flitted through the crowds, angling for a juicy story or some devastating tidbit for their papers. *Not at all different from reporters in the modern day* she mused.

Neumegen reappeared at her side, clutching a piece of paper in his hands. He motioned for her to follow him, and they crossed to the street to a small inn, unscathed by the fire, doing a roaring trade of handles of ale and hearty meals.

The pair slipped into a vacant table in the corner and after ordering for them both, Neumegen explained to Sarah the woes of the young man in his hospital bed.

'It seems your friend, the Warden, had promised to send a letter for the lad, many months ago. A letter he just discovered in your mother's pocket. He's devastated. He's been operating under the assumption that his mother knew of his whereabouts. There's a sense of... betrayal, I feel.'

'Can I read the note?'

Neumegen handed her the note written a lifetime ago by a young man filled with the promise of adventure, and the joy of reuniting with a brother he loved. A note addressed to the same woman in Wales on the note Sarah had in her own pocket, nestled next to a large gold nugget, burning a guilty hole in her conscience.

'He talked to you then?'

'He did.'

'And he knows Annabel is my mother?'

'He does.'

'Will he speak with me?'

'Perhaps? But not today, maybe tomorrow? Where will you stay tonight?'

Sarah looked up from the note, the realisation hitting home that she couldn't stay at the hospital, which was overflowing at its seams. Accommodation in the city now hotly contested, and priced at a premium, and she had no funds for even the smallest of rooms. She shrugged again.

'Then you will come home with me today and leave the boy to his introspection. Your mother knows in her heart that you have been with her. And she has the Warden to stay with her. You will convalesce from your injuries at my place. This town isn't in any fit state for a young woman on her own. Leave word with the matron, yes?'

It was the only solution. There was nothing she could do for her mother and watching Price's obvious love was distressing. Of Colin's heartbreak over letters not sent, she could at least remedy that with a letter of her own to his mother. She didn't think it would break any time travel rules, if there were any around time travel? *Doctor Who* was the only time traveller she was familiar with, and some girl called Claire who travelled back in time and fell in love with a red-haired highlander. But those books weren't guides to time travel. No, she'd send a letter to Colin's mother, explaining about Isaac, and Colin's injuries, including the two unsent letters. And the gold nugget she'd send that too. Heaven knows what life was like for Colin's mother now, with her sons so far away.

'Let me tell the matron,' she said, brushing down her skirts. She slipped the second note into her pocket, where it joined Isaac's one.

The matron was far too busy to listen to Sarah's babbling explanation of where she'd be if her mother's condition changed. And when she looked in on Annabel, Price had fallen asleep with his head resting on the edge of the bed. She backed away, a lump in her throat. If she ever thought she had feelings for the man, he'd never reciprocate them now.

Joining Neumegen outside, they walked down Queen Street, the stark morning light highlighting the night's devastation. Already the sound of sawing filled the air, the fresh lumber scent replacing that of the fire. Gangs of men in heavy duty boots and corduroy trousers worked tirelessly either shoring up damaged buildings, or tearing down those too far ravaged by fire. The army was out in force, keeping order, lending manpower to speed things up.

'Best thing for the town,' Neumegen said, pointing at the ugly shell of *Sheehan's Hotel*, its timbers still smoking.

Sarah chanced a look at the man. *Did he know about the Jowls'?*

'Trouble from the day they arrived here. The whole family,' he added. 'No great loss, it'll be better now,' he concluded.

Sarah's heart hammered in her chest. They were nearing a group of army officers milling around a gutted building. *Was Neumegen going to hand her over as a murderer?* But he did nothing more than to tip his hat, greet them politely, and carry on his way. Sarah didn't know what to think.

Back at the shop, Neumegen disappeared into the workroom, asking her if she wanted a cup of tea. She trailed behind him, noting that he'd reorganised the cabinets to fill the space of the damaged cabinet. The shop looked cleaner, more elegant with fewer cabinets in the space.

'Please relax, Miss Lester. Everyone has their secrets. As a pawnbroker, I am privy to more than most. I'm a keeper of secrets, even yours. We drink our tea now, yes?'

'Thank you,' Sarah said, her shoulders slumping with relief, excusing his odd turn of a phrase as a matter of translation.

They sipped their tea in silence, each of them considering their own issues.

'Do you believe in God, Miss Lester?'

Sarah considered his question. Her parents hadn't raised her to be religious, but she still appreciated that a higher power existed, whether it was God or Mother Nature or some other all-powerful being, she didn't know. She sensed however that Neumegen believed in God, so she smiled and nodded.

He seemed satisfied with her answer and disappeared out the

front, reappearing moments later, a long leather-covered jewellery box in his hand.

'Then I should like you to have this,' he said, passing her the box.

Sarah released the catch on the small box and found an ornate jewel-encrusted crucifix attached to a slender gold chain. The light from the lanterns on the wall infused the gems with a life of their own.

Swallowing her surprise, she murmured her thanks, the ostentatiousness of the piece overwhelming. 'It's quite something.'

'It is. I'd like you to have it. You have an angel sitting on your shoulder, but it pays to have extra protection,' Neumegen explained. 'I must get back to work. Trade will be brisk today. A calamity is good for business you see,' he said shrugging. 'Take yourself upstairs to rest, but no more going through my trunk. It's empty now, there's nothing there of interest.'

Neumegen left her sitting at the workbench, the cooling cup of tea in her hands. Her mouth agape at his last comment. The man was either a mind reader or had surveillance equipment installed. *How did he know?*

With a creeping unease, she abandoned her tea, and made her way upstairs to light the fire to boil the water to use in her bath, before returning downstairs to locate the water pump. A bath would help clear her head. It was too much to take in right now. Delayed shock perhaps?

The old fashioned hand pump stood outside the door, surrounded by an incredible amount of detritus. It was as if she'd stumbled into the backyard of a hoarder shown on American television. Curious, she poked around, turning things over, and peering underneath abandoned carriage seats and into cracked stone crocks. *Did the man throw nothing away?*

Sarah filled a bucket and wrangled it back up the narrow staircase, tipping it into the large copper she'd set over the fire. Heating enough water for her bath would be a long and laborious process. After several more trips, and burning herself once in the transfer process, Sarah decided a quick dip in the quarter-filled tepid water would be more than enough for her needs. Why anyone bothered to bathe in the 1800s was beyond her.

After drying herself off, she shuddered at the thought of wearing her soot, sweat and blood stained clothes, before remembering she'd left her jeans and shoes in Neumegen's room. *Perfect!* She dunked her filthy clothes into the still warm bath to soak... no point wasting the water and dashed into Neumegen's bedroom to hunt out her clothes.

His bedroom looked more or less the same as it had the last time she was here — sterile and sparse. Her clothes weren't still on the bed, and nor did she expect them to be. The travelling trunk was the most likely place he'd have stored them, unless they'd joined the innumerable cartons on the shelves downstairs.

Although he'd inferred that the rifles were no longer in the trunk, it still surprised Sarah to find that they'd gone. The only items the trunk now contained were hangers of identical black jackets and pressed trousers. Curious, she opened the little drawers, and found pairs of fine cufflinks and matching shirt studs lined up like soldiers. Neatly folded gloves filled another drawer, and undergarments filled the large bottom drawer. If they weren't in the trunk, that only left the washstand, itself blessed with three large drawers under the marble basin.

Sarah found nothing of interest in the first two drawers — winter clothes — thick knitted garments, almost too warm for Auckland's temperate climate. The bottom drawer contained something entirely different.

Not only were Sarah's jeans and shoes in the drawer, the *Converse* circle and star clearly visible, but there were two other pairs of jeans and a pair of *Reebok* trainers, not hers. An old style cellphone sat next to a modern wallet and a set of car keys. Stunned, she sat there staring at the motley collection, until her near-nakedness made her reach for her clothes.

As Sarah pulled her jeans and shoes from the drawer, she dislodged a small beaded purse. Almost art deco in its appearance, it looked brand new. The clasp made of sterling silver, and even without checking a silver hallmarks reference book, the marks on the clasp dated the purse to after 1890, or rather that the lack of the duty mark combined with the hallmarks for Birmingham, dated this piece some thirty years in the future.

Too scared to open it, she shoved it to the back of the drawer, and scrambled to her feet, sliding the drawer shut as quietly as she could. It was too late to get dressed into her *local* clothes, they were all in the tub, sodden. She needed to put her things back in the drawer, but until she found something else to put on, they'd have to do. She only hoped that she could source suitable clothes from the storage room downstairs before Neumegen recognised that she'd been prying through his things. Neumegen was a man of many secrets. But was she prepared to share hers to find out his?

THE PATIENTS

*C*olin refused any contact with Price, instructing the nurses that he didn't want to see him under any circumstances. The betrayal of the man, his disregard for Colin's one request. The broken promises were inexcusable.

This whole time, Colin had been operating under the certain knowledge that his mam knew where he was. The double blow was that Price knew about Isaac's death and hadn't told him until now. Letting him convalesce in Dunedin, in utter ignorance of his brother's murder. Even allowing him to go gallivanting off to Bruce Bay in search of his murdered brother. *Who did that?*

No, Colin wanted nothing to do with Price, or Annabel. He had baby Sophia, and together they would forge a new life together, somehow.

Convalescing in a ward with other sufferers of respiratory illnesses, the coughing from the various beds formed a relentless backdrop to Colin's thoughts. The coughing no less loud than the lapping of waves against the shore in Bruce Bay, and he castigated himself for ever leaving. If he'd known Isaac was dead, he would never have left Dunedin. He'd never have met Aroha, nor been the harbinger of death to her, for that was what he was, he was as sure as the sun rose and set. It was his fault that she'd died. She was travelling to her people, and her journey to the Māori fort had only been to help him. Well, he wouldn't be responsible for anyone else's deaths. It would be just him and Sophia from here. He had a job, and he'd find them a place to stay. There'd be plenty of young girls around who'd be able to care for Sophia whilst he was at work. They would be fine, together, the two of them. He didn't need Price, or Annabel, or anyone else. He didn't even need the Jowl's, although he felt the weight of their expectations settle on his shoulders as he remembered Joe Jowl's last words to him. Never mind, he'd work his way out from underneath that debt and then he'd be free.

Colin lay back against his mountain of pillows, the nurses made him sleep upright to relieve the pressure on his lungs. He'd spent more hours than he cared to contemplating the ceiling, and his life. Once again he was counting the nail holes in the ceiling, when the visage of Price loomed over him.

'An honest mistake,' Price said.

Colin turned his head away, his skin prickling at the effrontery of a man who broke his promises.

'I wanted to tell you, but it just didn't happen that way,' Price tried again.

Colin tried biting his tongue, but there was too much anger bubbling up. He'd trusted Price, looking to him for guidance in a new country. 'But you knew my brother was dead, and you never said a word,' he said, twisting the sheets in his fists.

'I wanted to, but—'

'But you ran off with your girlfriend instead?'

'That's not entirely true,' Price said.

Colin didn't see the faint smile cross Price's face at the mention of Annabel.

'She's married to someone else, Annabel is,' Colin spouted, his words aiming to hurt.

'Was. *Was* married to someone else.'

The patient turned to face the man who'd let him down.

'The husband's still alive, just ask Sarah,' Colin said, enjoying the discomfort on Price's face.

'No one knows if he is alive,' Price said. 'Too many years have gone since they were last together, and India is a wilder place than here. The church said there can be an annulment—'

Colin's laughter interrupted Price's explanation.

'Your job was to protect people, to help them. But as soon as a pretty lady flounced her skirts in front of you, you...' a coughing fit took over, forcing the matron to hold Colin as he coughed up blood-flecked phlegm.

'Mrs Lester meant to send your letter, Colin. It was a terrible circumstance she found herself in. I'll resend the letter for you now, will that make amends?' Price cajoled.

The nurse leaned Colin back against the pillows, his face as pale as the linen.

'And you'll tell my mam about Sophia? Tell her that she's mine?' Colin whispered, taking in the blood speckled sheet before moving his gaze to Aroha's infant daughter gurgling in her crib by the matron's desk.

Price squeezed Colin's limp hand. 'I'll write today. Trust me, nothing will stop me sending that letter now, I promise.'

The matron ushered Price away as Colin slipped into a troubled slumber, his chest barely rising. The young man almost disappearing before their eyes, melting like the winter's ice on a warm spring day.

Price stood in the doorway as the matron hurried back to her patient, and as the door closed, he couldn't help but wonder if this would be the last time he saw the boy.

THE LETTER

*P*rice left the hospital and made his way to the post
office, his head full of half-baked plans and ideas,
undelivered promises and formal orders. There was only so much
time he could claim to be convalescing before they ordered him back
to work.

He rolled his shoulder, trying to ease the stiffness. He didn't think
his body would ever return to the way it was, but he had more
mobility than he'd imagined, and he was alive, which was a miracle.

Left for dead after the ambush on their camp, the army had
discovered Price two days after they first came through to clear up the
mess, and transported him straight to Auckland, delirious,
dehydrated, and near death. When he'd come to, no one could tell him
where Annabel was or who'd attacked the camp — the imminent
attack on Auckland a greater concern. Life in any small town is full of
gossip, which flies faster than the wind. And it wasn't long before he
heard strange whisperings about a woman at Sheehan's Hotel,
travelling with a man and a baby, not of her own. The gossip was wild,
but the nuggets of truth coalesced into his utter belief that they must
have been talking about Annabel. When the fire overtook the city,
and the army forced him out of his hospital bed with the rest of the

302

able-bodied patients, and pressed him into service, he'd stumbled upon Sarah and Jimmy Jowl.

Despite their hurdles and mishaps, and although Sarah had reappeared, momentarily sending his heart into the heavens, it was Annabel he found himself drawn to and her wellbeing he wished for. Her touch that he needed. And his childish thoughts of Sarah, from so long ago, vanished like a sunset, subsumed completely by the light of another woman. That Annabel was Sarah's mother, didn't feel strange. He'd felt a kinship with Annabel from the first moment he'd seen her. It just made sense. He'd talk to Sarah at some point, but like a coward, it was easier ignoring the elephant in the room, and Sarah had disappeared from the hospital. No one had told him where, but for the time being, her absence suited him. It was unsettling having the mother and the daughter together. There was still something undefinable which set them both apart from every other woman he'd met. But he wanted to spend a lifetime with Annabel figuring it out; if she would have him.

The queue at the post office wove its way out the door. Harried-looking men clutching handfuls of paper, no doubt missives to their insurance company, detailing the stock losses they'd sustained in the fire. Or pleas to their families to send money to pay to rebuild stores not insured. The lines of worry on their faces a sign of how awful things were.

Price joined the queue with what he considered, to be a heartfelt letter to Colin's mother, detailing the death of Isaac, and the health of Colin. He believed it unlikely that the woman had the means to come to New Zealand to visit her son and his *daughter*, so he'd included a short postscript explaining that should anything happen to Colin, he would take it upon himself to care for the girl until she became old enough to return to Wales for schooling, should that be what the family wanted. He'd had to stop twice as he wrote that section, knowing in his heart-of-hearts, that Colin's health wasn't good, and he couldn't help but wonder if he'd be writing a second letter to Colin's mam in the coming days, advising her of his passing.

His palms grew clammy holding the letter. Perhaps it would be better if she didn't know about Colin and Isaac? Would she be any more wretched if she lived the rest of her days *not* knowing about her sons? The baby wasn't Colin's, but there was no point explaining that both her parents has been murdered. Would the baby be better off being raised by himself and Annabel, close to her tribe?

The line moved forward and before he knew it; he was inside, the clamour of the customers unceasing with their demands. The *clink* of metal stamps, the rattling of coins, and the clomping of boots adding to the chaos. And then he saw Sarah at the front, waiting her turn, an envelope clasped to her breast. The livid bruises on her face causing murmurs of interest in those around her, as they whispered behind mean hands and smaller minds. As she stepped up to the window, the clerk recoiled, causing the audience to titter in response. Price watched her straighten her shoulders, ignoring the comments from the captive audience behind her.

With the postage for her letter secured, she swept from the counter, intent on escaping as swiftly as she could. She faltered as she saw him in the queue. Price started to greet her, but she hurried past him onto the street. He had to talk to her; the situation weighed heavily on his chest, he'd had been so sure Sinclair had done away with her, that he'd moved on. His grieving done.

A decision made, he slipped out of the queue to hurry after her, the letter still in his hand.

'Mrs Bell! Mrs Bell, wait!'

She kept walking, head down, avoiding the stares of the other pedestrians on the street.

'Sarah!'

She stopped and turned towards him, her face a mask of pain.

'Mrs Bell, please, can we talk?'

She looked as though she was about to decline his request, but agreed to talk and followed him to a café unaffected by the fire — the St Mungo Café, opened by the gregarious Charles Canning and advertising itself as especially for the *discerning lady*.

'Tea?'

'Yes please,' Sarah said, fiddling with the condiments on the cloth-covered table.

With a pot of tea in front of them, Price talked. He had trouble getting the right words out, struggling to even forming them in his mouth. How did you tell the girl you loved that you'd fallen out of love, almost as quickly as a tide turns?

Sarah reached out and put her hand on his. 'It's okay, don't worry.'

'I beg your pardon?' Price said, staring into Sarah's blackened eyes, searching for the truth.

'It's fine, I'm happy you've found each other. I've been looking for her for so long, that I never thought about what would happen when I found her. But I don't need her anymore, not the way I used to, anyway. I'm all grown up now, and she has her own life to lead. And if that's with you, well, I won't need to worry about her.'

Price felt himself falling for her again, but differently. Not in the your-heart-races-and-you-can't-breathe way, but more in a grateful-she-exists way, that the world is a brighter place with Sarah in it.

'Thank you,' he said. 'There was never any intention to hurt you. But when Sinclair abducted you, I resigned myself to the fact that you weren't coming back, that you were dead. How did you escape from him?'

Sarah shuffled in her seat, her eyes sliding away from his. There was something she wasn't telling him.

'Is he still alive?'

'He was, but I'm not sure if he is now...'

'Damn it,' Price exclaimed. 'And the candelabra, from the church?'

A blush crept up Sarah's cheeks. Had she been in cahoots with Sinclair this whole time?

'Ah, those I know he sent to England. There was nothing I could do to stop him, sorry,' she said, the contrition obvious in her voice.

Price's nerves resettled. The last thing he wished to believe was that this young woman was part of Sinclair's web.

'Then I shall write to the church and advise them of this, thank you—'

Sarah interrupted him

'Thanks for... you know, taking the time to chat, but I should get back to Neumegen. He's putting me up till I can sort myself out. I don't enjoy everyone staring at me while my face looks like Picasso threw up on it to be honest, so I'll head off and see you at the hospital. Can you send word when my mother wakes? I asked the nurses but they're kind of busy.'

Price nodded, his brain stumbling over Sarah's peculiar comments.

'And can you tell Colin that I wrote to his mum, on behalf of Mum and I?'

'Yes, yes, of course,' Price said, conscious of the letter in his own pocket.

Sarah got up, smoothing her skirts. Her hand paused. Price watched as she seemed to argue with herself, before she withdrew a small rock from her pocket and thrust it into his hands.

Price had worked in Bruce Bay long enough that he could tell the difference between what was a rock and what was gold, and this rock was a gold nugget.

'This belongs to Colin now,' Sarah said, pressing Price's fingers closed around the nugget. 'It was Isaac's, and he asked me to send it to his mother. I was going to, but Colin needs it more. Will you see that he gets it? Can I trust you?'

The nugget was worth at least a year's worth of wages and yet Sarah had kept it with her all this time. Sinclair hadn't made off with it, and she hadn't spent on baubles and trinkets. Price held it tight in his fist.

'Yes, you can trust me,' he said.

THE GIFT

Sarah returned to Neumegen's shop, which was humming with customers. Neumegen had been correct when he'd explained that a calamity was good for business. Her father said the same thing after the Black Monday stock market crash in the 1980s. Those riding high on the dividends of their stocks, needing to liquidate their portable assets to keep their heads above the water and food on their tables.

She slipped through to the workshop. Being amongst the boxes of pawned articles, stacked haphazardly atop of each other, was akin to being at home, mooching around *The Old Curiosity Shop* in the school holidays. There was nothing in particular she needed to do, so felt adrift — rudderless and directionless.

Sarah tidied some boxes, straightening them on the mismatched shelves. Pocket-watch parts spilled from a broken carton, so she stuffed them back in, stacking the convex glass faces carefully. Next she turned her attention to the scrimshaw — carved sperm whale teeth. Neumegen had them lined up on the bench, sitting on black velvet bases, and all featured images of three-masted sailing ships and Māori maidens. One sported an impressive coat of arms, complete with the words *DIEU ET MON DROIT*, Latin for *God and my right*, the motto of the king.

Scrimshaw never turned up these days, families being far more savvy about the value of items hidden in attics and basements thanks to the internet. She'd never seen one in the shop, although her father had mentioned buying and selling them in the past. Neumegen's collection was extensive, perhaps someone had pawned a collection?

She picked up the piece with the coat of arms, turning it slowly as she examined the intricate drawings on the huge tooth. A scene from Auckland's busy harbour adorned the other side, highlighting the grand wooden buildings decimated by the fire only days earlier. Already it had a place in history as a record of what Auckland once looked like.

Replacing it on the bench, she reached for the second tooth, when Neumegen opened the door, an assortment of lanterns hanging on his long arm.

'Can you take these and shelve them out back?' Neumegen called out.

Sarah rushed forward to relieve him of his burden.

'Is there anything I can do to help?' she asked.

Neumegen shook his head as he cast his eyes over his workshop.

'It's best not to interfere with things out here,' he said. 'Everything has its place, it's where it should be, unlike you.'

'Pardon?'

A voice bellowed for Neumegen from the counter, sending the man scurrying back to his customer.

'Never mind what I said, just put those lanterns on the bottom shelf,' he said, pushing through the door. Something made him pause as he looked back at Sarah, but the impatient grumbles from the men waiting to pawn their goods interrupted whatever he wanted to say.

Sarah struggled with the heavy lanterns. Her father only ever pawned gold or silver jewellery, because of storage issues. Neumegen would be better off doing the same. He didn't have enough room for the stuff he'd already loaned out on. These lanterns weren't anything special, basic kerosene lanterns, made in England, and shipped out to New Zealand by the thousands. Still, she found room for them on the shelf, and shoved them in until they fit, some still had kerosene sloshing in the bottom which spilled on her hands.

Washing her hands under the pump, she considered her life, but it didn't pay to give it too much thought. There was never any sign or flashing neon light telling her what to touch to travel through time. If there were, she'd be a damn sight wealthier than she was now. She'd stock up on all the gold jewellery, sterling silver necessities and ancient pewter dishes which were a dozen to a penny here. She spent half her life in terror of touching the wrong thing, and the other half wishing she'd find the magic chalice to reunite her with her parents, preferably in modern day London, equipped with hot water and the internet.

Drying her hands on her skirts, she returned to the workroom. If she couldn't tidy in here, there was no point mooching around. Neumegen had a small shelf of books on display, she might read one of those to fill in her time. A far more exciting prospect than doing the laundry which was at least two hours hard labour once she'd boiled the water, rinsed the clothes, wrung them out, hung them up, and then ironed everything. She never ironed clothes at home. It's also why she never bothered buying linen, because that always *needed* ironing. Who had time for that?

The books were a disappointing collection of tomes written in what appeared to be German or Polish or something similar. Finnish maybe? Not a single one was in English. She had a smattering of French, and Latin, but neither of those languages equipped her to read Neumegen's books. She was just about to go upstairs for a nap, when Neumegen poked his head in.

'A telegram for you,' he said, stretching his arm out towards her. 'You aren't wearing the necklace I gave you,' he admonished. 'It will bring you luck if you wear it.'

Sarah muttered an apology, promising to put it on straight away as she grabbed the telegram from Neumegen's fingers stained with ink from the elegant records he kept, detailing the pawns and their redemption dates.

Neumegen smiled at her apology before returning to the counter, and once she was alone, she tore open the telegram which was short and to the point.

"Your mother is awake. Come quickly. Price."

Her world exploded in a kaleidoscope of colour and joy, her mother was awake. She needed her hat and her jacket, which were upstairs.

Sarah raced upstairs, her excitement giving flight to her feet. She wouldn't have bothered about a hat, except for the curious glances she'd got earlier at the post office. She didn't enjoy being a spectacle. A thousand thoughts crowded in on her. What should she say about her father? How would they talk about time travel with Price there? Had her mother already shared that with him? *So many questions.* How had her mother survived so long? What had happened to her? And most importantly, had she tried to return to her husband and child?

The last question gave Sarah pause, and her knuckles tightened on the top of the bannister. Of course her mother had tried to come home to her. They were the best of friends, two peas in a pod. Sure, she was daddy's little girl, but she was best friends with her mother, and needed her, no matter what she told herself.

Sarah dashed downstairs, running straight into the ramrod straight figure of Neumegen.

'It's my mother, she's awake,' Sarah gushed.

'Wonderful news, but please, can you mind the shop for a moment while I deal with a personal matter, yes?'

Sarah was champing at the bit to get to the hospital, but the pawnbroker had been so kind, peculiar but kind. He had his secrets and had kept hers. One day she'd ask him, but today wasn't that day. She didn't want to destroy the delicately balanced life she now had, so removed her hat, and reluctantly took his place behind the counter, trying not to pace the now empty shop. She had no wrist watch to check the time, nor a phone, and the pocket watches on display showed different times.

'Jesus Christ,' she muttered under her breath as the second-hand of one watch made a complete circuit of the opalescent face, then another, and another.

After an eternity, Neumegen reappeared, his face flushed and a smudge of dirt on the collar of his jacket.

'Thank you, sometimes personal business just will not wait. It was good of you to look after things for me and now you must go to your mother,' he instructed, passing Sarah her hat.

She beamed, her foul thoughts vanishing like dew in the morning sun.

'But first, the necklace, yes? As I explained, it will bring you luck, and that is what your mother needs. Surely you should look as though you are doing well for yourself? Any mother would want to see that of her daughter, yes?'

Sarah clenched her jaw. *That bloody necklace.* Nothing at all like her style, but the man was so insistent. And she'd left the thing upstairs.

'It's upstairs,' she tried.

'I'm certain, yes certain, that it would make your mother happy to see you wearing it,' Neumegen said, immovable on the subject.

'Fine,' Sarah snapped, and ran upstairs. It was just as well her belongings were few, so it only took a few seconds to locate the jewellery box. Without opening it, she all but slid down the bannister, brandishing it at Neumegen as she sailed past.

'Please, put it on,' his voice louder than she expected, his grip tightening around her wrist as he stopped her from passing. 'Please, before you leave. You need to wear the necklace,' he said, his long fingers like handcuffs on her wrist.

Trying not to scream with frustration, she stood stock still, hands clenched around the innocent black leather box, her knuckles white. She flipped the lid open, revealing the ostentatious pendant, with ill-fitting gemstones and crude workmanship. The cruciform pendant was so out-of-place in 19th century New Zealand that she had a hard time wrapping her head around how it came to be in Neumegen's shop.

She was still puzzling over the incongruousness of the necklace, when Neumegen pulled the pendant from the box by its woven hair cord and prepared to hang it around her neck.

Sarah wasn't to know that Mughal craftsmen made crosses such as these after the Jesuits visited India intending to convert Emperor Akbar to Christianity. Without diamond testers and the other miracle tools she used at work, she had no way of knowing that what she assumed were glass pieces inset into the centre were in fact rough cut diamonds.

By the time she remembered the eclectic collection of items in Neumegen's bottom drawer, and the penny dropped, it was too late. The pendant was around her neck, and as soon as Neumegen connected the two ends of the necklace's clasp, she couldn't do anything other than scream. A scream no one heard, not even Neumegen, who was standing alone in his shop, a sad smile playing across his face. It was better she wasn't here, and safer for them all.

THE BROTHER

*B*en Grey stepped from the ship's deck to the solidness of the wooden wharf, his sea-addled body as fragile as a newborn foal. Tripping over an uneven plank, he cursed as he continued his ungainly shuffle and the other passengers buffeted him from behind, their own limbs as unused to land as his.

With no knowledge of Auckland, Ben Grey stood at the end of the dock forcing his fellow travellers to mutter under their breath as they tried to avoid his stationary figure.

He'd made no friends on board, except for the unsavoury types. It was tempting to disembark in Australia — a country far more settled and civilised than the one he found himself in now. But that didn't fit his psyche. He preferred the roughness of a new country, unshackled by rules, and New Zealand was a far better fit. His mother and his conniving brother had done him a favour by sending him to the furthermost reaches of the Empire. But he'd never forget how they'd treated him and in time he'd have his revenge. But a new life beckoned, and he looked forward to enjoying the opportunities ahead.

Money filled Ben Grey's pockets, cash won during the long sea voyage, which was partly why his fellow passengers hadn't shared a heartfelt goodbye with him on the wharf. Their reluctance to acknowledge his existence entertained him even further and without a backwards glance he left them, the prospects of the city fuelling his grand ambitions.

It wasn't difficult to find accommodation; the signage adorning the streetscape a riot of copperplate advertising. *The Imperial Hotel*, on the corner of Auckland's Queen Street and Fort Street appeared to be one of the better options and so he strode into the darkened interior, lush carpets muffling his footfall. With his lodgings secured, Ben Grey washed away the taint of the ocean and weeks of stolen glances from people whom he suspected knew who he was, and why he was onboard. But now he was his own man; his heritage no hindrance or help. What a boon it was to be free of one's family obligations and expectations. Released, he could indulge in his passions and primal urges, just like he had in India, before his brother had put an end to it.

'Thank you, gentlemen. It's been a pleasure,' Grey bowed as he collected the pile of notes from the centre of the table, his companions looking on in quiet defeat, their purses emptied, their egos deflated.

Ben Grey left the tavern, his pocket a hundred times heavier than it had been before he'd entered. The tang of smoke all pervading despite the demolition of most of the damaged buildings.

Without the Jowls around to control the seedier side of colonial life, gambling ran unmitigated in every establishment. The town ill-equipped to house the newly homeless, address the risk of invasion from the natives, manage the ever-increasing numbers of immigrants *and* worry too much about gambling or petty theft.

Not that Ben Grey needed to lower himself to that level; he'd inherited his father's penchant for cards, and it was this that he excelled at, cleaning up at every table he played. He expected his reputation would soon precede him, with the tables at the more salubrious establishments, the ones unmarred by the fire, turning him away. But until that happened, he'd take his success where he could.

He'd been well away from the conflagration, entertaining himself at a pleasure house on the outskirts of town, where they were oblivious until the dawn skies turned dusty with ash, and sooty patrons turned up at the door asking for a place to sleep instead of looking for something to fuck.

With the cash burning a hole in his pocket, Grey was on his way to the sale at the rooms of auctioneers Mabin and Graham, who were also agents for the Royal Fire and Life Insurance Company. Grey had his eye on a block of land on Queen Street, a fire damaged hotel. Damaged but repairable. After living what he would describe as a pecuniary lifestyle, with his funds cut off by his older brother Edward, revenge was a motivating factor. He'd show that bastard of a brother, and his shrew of a mother, how successful he could be without them. He hadn't been drunk since his last night in England, preferring to nourish his quest for revenge instead of drinking his bodyweight in whiskey every week.

Grey strode up the busy hill, the harbour behind him disgorging more soldiers, and adventurers and settlers, with all of them needing accommodation and food and the entertainment his unique experiences could provide.

As he took his seat, Grey spied several acquaintances made over the preceding weeks. They either greeted him with a hat tip or a turned back, depending on how much they'd lost to him at cards.

'What piques your interest today?' asked a portly man falling into the seat next to Grey.

'Oh, this and that,' Grey replied, his poker face in place.

'Typical, you playing your cards close to your chest,' the man chortled, his neck wobbling dangerously in response.

The auction started with the bidding brisk from the first lot — the fire sale bringing out the sharks and scavengers. Dour faced men stood along the walls, men without insurance selling off their ruined lives before the bankers stripped even the shirts from their backs.

Grey only needed to raise his hand twice to bid, despite the *Sheehan's Hotel* being prime real estate. Although the constabulary had declared the Jowls dead, the charred corpses found in the stables presumed to be theirs, a virulent rumour persisted that the Jowls were alive meaning few bidders wanted to risk the Jowls returning and demanding their property back. The gossip didn't deter Ben Grey, and with the drop of the auctioneer's hammer, he was the proud owner of the smouldering remains of the *Sheehan's Hotel*.

'You canny bastard. That was a good buy,' Grey's neighbour said, spraying his words over Grey's face.

Grey smiled. *If only the fat prick knew his plans,* Ben Grey and Jimmy Jowl had very similar tastes in their after hours entertainment. And once Ben had his own place up and running, he'd be able to indulge as much as he liked. Fresh fodder stepped off the immigrant ships berthed at Waitematā Harbour every week, so there was no chance he'd run out of stock in the foreseeable future, until he deigned to return to England a wealthy man, when he'd ruin his brother's life, just as Edward had tried to destroy his.

And in the back of the room, Neumegen sat watching, making the occasional note in his pocketbook with a tiny silver pencil. He knew how this ended, which was why he held back, refusing to get involved in Ben Grey's wicked web. That would come later, in a different time, in a different place.

ENGLAND

~

THE DOLL

*W*hen Edward Grey married the American heiress Mary Bellamy, it was with the tiniest of regrets that it wasn't the enigmatic Grace Williams walking down the aisle towards him. But the birth of a daughter eclipsed everything. Elizabeth Mary Grey, the apple of Edward's eye. Adored by her grandmother, and lavished with gifts, the child wanted for nothing. Save for a sibling, which was not to be.

'Happy birthday, dear Elizabeth, happy birthday to you. Hip hip hooray! Hip hip hooray! Hip hip hooray! Happy birthday, my love,' Edward Grey leaned in to kiss his daughter's forehead, his eyes crinkling in pleasure.

Young Elizabeth gazed up at her parents — Edward and Mary, their proud faces reflected in hers. She removed the cream ribbon and placed it behind her before moving on to the crisp tissue paper. The unbalanced weight of the package confused her. Slowly, the luxuriant hair of a child's doll emerged. The matt bisque face exquisitely hand painted, her feathered brows frozen in arched surprise.

Elizabeth's heart sang. A gift from her father, from one of his forays overseas — a *Kammer & Reinhardt* doll, from the workshops of Germany. Manipulating the doll's composition ball-jointed body showed a fluidity of movement none of her other penny dolls had. The closest thing to a little sister she'd ever have.

'Her name is *Gretchen*, and I'm assured she is of a limited run. There'll only be a handful of girls sprinkled throughout Europe with this very doll. Think of that! You could be playing with her at the same time as those children are playing with theirs. It's magic.'

Elizabeth smiled at her father, still marvelling at *Gretchen's* glass eyes and real human hair tied in adorable braids. And twinkling in the doll's ears were a tiny pair of diamond and pearl earrings. As Elizabeth touched the petite jewels, her mother passed her a small velveteen box. After laying *Gretchen* on the tissue paper, Elizabeth opened the package—a child-sized pair of matching earrings.

'We thought this a fitting gift for your tenth birthday, so I had the jeweller in Germany match them to *Gretchen's*. Do you like them?'

'Oh, Father, yes, I love them. They're divine, thank you!' Elizabeth flung her arms around him, sinking her face into his strong shoulder. Her mother joined them, none of them realising this would be their last moment of true happiness.

THE ACCIDENT

*E*dward Grey pulled at the heavy rudder, laughing at his wife, her long hair in a frenzy behind her as the wind whipped at them both. Mary Grey yanked hard on her hat, its maroon ribbons slippery under her cold fingers.

'I've no idea why you're grinning, Edward, it's not fun. It was when you were thirty, but you're in your sixties, and this is a young man's sport. And I'm cold. Can we please go in?'

'Come now, Mary, let's live, before we're too *old* for living. I need practice before the regatta this weekend.'

Mary gave up on her hat, clamping it between her knees, concentrating instead on holding onto the sides of the dinghy, her fingers white.

'Why on earth you want to take up racing at your age is a mystery. Isn't being a race official sufficient excitement? All this damnable practice. Don't blame me if you catch a chill in this air.'

A gust of wind rose, pummelling the boat with sprays of icy water. Mary Grey gasped in shock, the frigid Atlantic trickling down her neck. Her teeth chattering, she glared at Edward, oblivious to her discomfort. For too long he'd played the City game. He missed the outdoors, the camaraderie of war. He had his family, but he missed his men, his command. Being a leader was a drug, at once both intoxicating and terrifying. The reliance you had on your men and their absolute obedience to your commands was like depending on drugs to transport you to nirvana.

The wind picked up further, rattling the sails on the small skiff, the fabric roiling like the sea beneath them. Mary ceased to be cross with her husband, worry replacing anger. She noted a tightening across Edwards's features as he struggled with the tiller. Mary lurched to her husband's side, placing her tiny white hands next to his. Together they wrestled the tiller against the angry waves who tried snatching their wooden rudder away.

The tiller loosened, becoming docile in their hands, lifting from its supports, until one strong wave sucked it away from beneath their hands, leaving Edward staring after it in utter miscomprehension.

The horizon, a strip of dark blue water against the pastel-blue sky when they'd set out, was now a filthy stain, indistinguishable from the sea. Alone on the sea, there was no one to help them. Mary fancied she could see the rocky shore, although she was so disorientated she couldn't in all honesty identify what was north, or south, or the shoreline they'd left.

They dropped the sails, with Edward gathering up the waterlogged fabric before the wind stole it. A rogue wave hit them broadside, tipping the vessel almost ninety degrees on its side. Laden with the heavy sails, Edward stood no chance.

The wave washed Edward Grey from the yacht, dragging him into the brutal ocean. Tangled in the sails, he struggled to surface, gasping for air that never came.

Mary screamed, her voice lost to the wind. Relentless waves obliterated all signs of her husband. Shock overcame her, and she stilled, resting on the sodden seat, all her former urgency hidden beneath the ocean with her husband. Some suspected she let the sea take her, a noble decision to be with Edward in his last moments. But for whatever reason, when the next wave came, Mary's fingers let go, allowing her to welcome the quick death the water delivered.

Unseen on the far shore stood Benjamin Grey, newly returned from colonies. Dressed resplendently in fine woollen trousers with a thick gold watch chain hanging from the waistcoat hidden beneath his winter coat, his hand tightened around the objects in his hand as a smile danced across his face.

Opening his hand he admired the two fat screws which lay in his palm. Screws formerly from the tiller mount of his older brother's yacht. What a glorious day it was, despite the inclement weather.

Benjamin Grey turned on his polished heel and sauntered to a waiting motor car, the driver wrapped up against the conditions.

'To London,' Benjamin said. 'To home.' Wouldn't his mother be surprised to see him on the doorstep, ready to console her on the loss of her favourite son. He hadn't decided whether to come clean about his role, but that would add a delicious flavour to their reunion. Yes, it was a glorious day despite the English weather.

LONDON

THE RETURN

*S*arah sniffed the air. The atmosphere was stuffy enough to tell her she wasn't in Auckland any more, the smell a secondary indicator. She was home. Sarah left her eyes closed a fraction longer, hoping that this last slip through time had returned her to the real present, to Warren Brooke.

Beyond the patch of carpet she'd landed on, she could hear movement. Someone was nearby.

Sarah wrenched the monstrosity from her neck, certain now that the magic only worked once. It wasn't the same as buying a return ticket to Honolulu. The precious jewels weren't a fair swap for her mother, not by any stretch of the imagination. Despite its obvious value, there was no way to sell it or keep it. To do so would invite a thousand questions she didn't know the answers to.

At least she'd answered the question which had haunted her. Her mother hadn't abandoned her, running off with a mysterious stranger for a better life, as so many people had inferred. If she could have, Sarah was positive her mother would have returned.

A part of Sarah mourned that she'd never see Annabel again. After everything she'd experienced — the love she'd found and the loss she had caused — Isaac, Seth, Christopher and Patricia, she wanted no further part of this crazy travelling through time. She needed her life back. And if that meant living it without her mother or her father, then that's what she'd do. And Sarah's heart broke once again.

Hemmed in between the wall and a Queen Anne style mahogany cabinet filled with cheap imitations of Royal Doulton Toby Jugs, their ghoulish faces mocking her from behind the glass, Sarah stood up, stretching the kinks from her neck. She dumped the hateful necklace into a set of bamboo bowls stacked on top of the cabinet. She did not care if the next customer stole the hideous jewels. Good luck to them. She wanted nothing to do with the past. She thought she'd struggle more with leaving her mother behind but what bothered her the most was Neumegen's role. He'd knowingly sent her back. She assumed he'd figured out how to travel backwards and forwards in time, and if he had, why hadn't he just told her instead of tricking her into returning to the present day? Would he now send her mother home too?

'I wasn't expecting you to be here,' came a voice from behind.

Sarah spun around to find a complete stranger.

'Is that the key?' he asked.

'The key?' Sarah said, frowning. *Who was this man?*

'The key to you disappearing? Is that how you do it?' he asked, pointing to the jewelled crucifix filling the bamboo bowl.

'I'm not following...' Sarah stuttered, searching the shop for any sign of Brooke or Nicole.

'It's funny that I don't recall Grandmama ever mentioning that piece, but I presume it must have once belonged to my family, like everything else you've brought back from the past,' Richard Grey surmised.

'I don't...'

'Come now, Miss Lester. There is no reason to play dumb with me. Answer the question. Is that necklace the key to travelling back in time? For that's what you've been doing isn't it, stealing valuable artefacts from the past and selling them in here? And your father did it before you, yes? Quite the racket. A real family affair. Well, Miss Lester?'

'Who are you?'

'Yes, sorry. We haven't met. Grey, Richard Grey.'

Sarah instantly recognised his name — the man from the *katar's* auction, the killer of the clerk.

'How are you here?'

'What? Where in this shop? Simple, you left the door unlocked, and I walked in. Very remiss of you leaving doors open. Any miscreant could have robbed you blind. It's lucky I only want the one thing from you. The key, Miss Lester, hand it over.'

Trying to collect her thoughts, Sarah hesitated before edging her way towards the counter and the phone.

'It won't work,' she said, hugging the bowl to her chest.

'But it worked for you,' Grey said, shadowing her movements, blocking her entrance to the counter.

'It only works once.'

'Is that so? Then it won't matter if you pass it to me.'

Sarah swerved behind a table laden with chinaware, using it as a barrier between her and Grey. Anything in the shop could be the key to the past, as she'd found to her detriment, but she wasn't going to hand him the precious jewels.

'I'll ask another way. Did you steal that necklace from my family the way you stole the *katar*? Because if you did, I want my stolen property returned.'

It made sense now, a distant relation to Edward and Benjamin Grey. He had their look, although he leaned more towards the sly cunning of Benjamin.

'You're related to Benjamin Grey?' Sarah asked, regretting the question the instant she asked.

Richard Grey clapped his hands, laughing.

'See, that proves it. There is only one way you could know the connection between the *katar* and my great-grandfather, you must have met him. I never had the privilege, but Grandmama used to tell me about him and how his family disowned him, sending him away to the colonies for mere *youthful* transgressions. I've spent my life trying to return my family name to its former glory, replacing all the treasures my great-aunt sold off despite me begging her to sell them to me — at a family discount. It's incredible to believe that the stupid old bat lived as long as she did. Great Auntie Elizabeth, who wanted nothing to do with me even though I was her only remaining family. And then I hear that you bought her entire estate, my inheritance. See, all you've done is steal what is mine. It's time now for you to pay. And you can start by handing me that necklace.'

'Elizabeth Williams?'

'Crazy old bat. War widow, hoarder, thief. Appropriate words to describe her. But yes, otherwise Elizabeth Williams was her name. Now, pass me the necklace, and we can continue our civilised conversation, otherwise things will get... how should I say this? Messy?'

'The necklace won't work for you,' Albert Lester said, materialising from the stairwell, his old-fashioned clothes not one whit out of place amongst the homage to Victoria's reign which abounded in the shop.

'Dad!'

'Ah, the mysterious father. How wonderful to meet you,' Richard Grey enunciated, every syllable slipping from his lips.

'I don't know who you are, but if you touch my daughter, I will shoot you.' Albert raised a small percussion muff pistol and pointed it at Grey.

'Now that is a lovely piece. Only shot though.'

'I only need one shot,' Albert replied, moving closer to Grey.

'The necklace.'

'I'm telling you, it won't work,' Albert said, taking another step towards Grey. 'It's not a return journey thing.'

Grey cocked his head to the side. 'Then how do you explain the *travel* you and your offspring have done? Hmm?'

'I can't, and even if I could, I'd hardly share that with a man threatening my daughter. Now get out of my shop.'

Grey raised his hands in mock defiance and laughed. 'Even if that thing could fire, I doubt you'd hit me. They're terribly unreliable.'

Albert took another step forward, joining Sarah behind the table. 'You okay?' he asked her.

Sarah nodded. She was more than okay now that her father was home.

'If the necklace isn't the key to time travel, there's no harm in handing it over, is there? We could call it a down payment on the real key.'

'Give him the necklace, Sarah,' Albert ordered.

As Sarah passed the bowl holding the necklace to Grey the rough cut gems flashed under the fluorescent lights.

Albert's eyes bored into Grey's avaricious face. Giving away a priceless, museum quality piece tore at Albert, and although he was the one with the gun, he'd always told his daughter to do whatever an armed intruder told her to do, that her life was worth more than what was in the jewellery cabinets or safe.

Grey grabbed for the necklace the same way a man dying of thirst would grab a water bottle.

'What a beauty,' Grey remarked, holding the necklace up to the lights. 'But you're right, it's not a key because otherwise I wouldn't still be standing here?'

Albert backed up, motioning to Sarah to follow him, and the father and daughter duo moved closer to the cluttered front door.

'This isn't over. Between the two of you, you know which piece of tat is the next key. And I want it. You've never dealt with someone like me before, have you, Lester?'

'I've dealt with a plethora of your kind,' Albert responded.

'Dad, no.'

'Men who think their wealth protects them, that it makes them better than the rest of us. Men who act as if the world owes them even more. Yes, I've known plenty of men like you. But I know them later, when it's come crashing down and they can't afford the payments on the sports car; when the wife has to sell her diamonds on the sly to stump up for the school fees. Men like you come grovelling to me to bail you out, Mr Grey.'

'What a pretty speech but sadly no prizes for public speaking today. The only prize will be the clothes on your backs after I've finished crushing your little enterprise, *if* you don't tell me how you've been able to travel through time, smuggling in such exquisite pieces. They've wasted this on you both. A two-bit pawn broker and his daughter, gifted the magic of time travel, and you've achieved what with it?' Grey screwed up his face as if he'd just sucked on a lemon. 'Nothing. You've achieved nothing.'

Grey stopped and frowned, looking around and noticing Albert and Sarah's flight through the shop. 'Why are you down there? What is it you are trying to draw my attention away from? There's something back here, on the shelf?'

Albert's face didn't change. It was his shop but given the time he'd been away, nothing was familiar and the place looked like Marie Kondo herself had tidied the place. He had no idea if there was anything behind the counter.

Grey must have seen something in Sarah's face though, because he stuffed the necklace in his jacket pocket and began rifling through the shelves.

'There's something here isn't there? But you don't want me to have it. You're as conniving as the old woman. She was as batty as hell, giving stuff away for the war effort, selling valuable antiques to raise funds for the local dog club, donating *our* family money to some piss pot Roman archaeological dig up north. It was *my* inheritance. She'll get the fright of her life when I go back in time. I'm no longer the timid little boy she once shunned, slamming the door in my face.'

'Did you say *Roman* archaeological dig?' Sarah asked, her hand tightening on her father's arm.

'What of it?'

'Nothing, but there's a statue behind the counter.'

'Sarah—' Albert started.

'A Roman statue. From the Williams' estate. I didn't unpack it, Nicole did, but...'

'Roman antiquities? Yes, I'll have myself a piece of that,' Grey muttered as he searched the shelves, greed sinking any rational decision he might have made.

'In the middle, next to the old shoe box,' Sarah suggested.

Grey straightened after he flung the pink shoebox onto the floor, the mother-of-pearl fragments inside shattering into nothing more than dust.

'This statue?' he asked, turning to look at Sarah, before returning his gaze to the small Roman bust. 'Wait for me here,' Grey instructed.

Albert started to speak, but Sarah increased her grip on his arm, the pressure enough to silence him. They both knew that if Grey disappeared into the past, it could be aeons before he returned. If he returned.

'I will restore the family name, Grandmama. I promise,' Grey announced, reaching for the Roman statue.

Albert and Sarah flinched, ready for the inevitable. Neither of them knew whether their disappearances and reappearances occurred with flashes of light or rolling thunder, but nothing happened. Grey stood in the exact spot as he had before lifting the statue. The only change was the expression on Grey's face.

'Do you think this a joke?' Grey screamed, hurling the statue towards Sarah and her father. 'A damn joke?'

Albert yanked Sarah away, propelling her towards the front door, as Grey abandoned his search to pursue the Lesters.

With the door open, Sarah and Albert raced outside, straight into Nicole Pilcher and Major Warren Brooke. It took only seconds for Brooke to assess the situation, taking stock of the small pistol still in Albert's hand and the look on Sarah's face, before Grey appeared in the doorway, all but frothing at the mouth.

What a curious sight the group made, Brooke still wearing the remnants of his 1860s uniform, whilst Albert's fine suit dated him to the same period. Sarah and Nicole both sported jeans and comfortable shoes, against Grey's dishevelled trousers and shirt.

'Give me the gun,' Brooke ordered, and Albert obeyed without question.

The gun exploded.

Nicole screamed.

Grey stopped dead.

And pandemonium broke out amongst the shoppers on the street.

A small Indian man detached himself from the morbid onlookers and approached Grey's unmoving body.

'Call for an ambulance,' someone cried.

'He can't be dead, I only winged him,' Brooke said, his marksmanship unquestionable.

'We don't require an ambulance,' the good samaritan said, checking Grey.

Brooke paled, and Nicole stifled another scream.

'He's dead?' Albert asked, his arm around Sarah's shaking shoulders.

'No, not dead. But you don't need an ambulance. Get him inside, no good having all these people watching.'

Albert and Brooke lifted the unconscious man, dragging him back into *The Old Curiosity Shop*, leaving a trail of blood behind. Sarah and Nicole followed behind, with the small Indian man in tow, locking the door after them. The wail of far off sirens almost audible.

'First, the question of the pistol,' the stranger said to Brooke. 'It was a prop which malfunctioned, if they ask, and they will.'

'Who are you?' Sarah asked, holding up her palm to stop Brooke from speaking.

Before answering, the Indian man stroked a prominent scar running down the side of his face, hiding the pinched skin at his jawline with his hand, the gesture one of contemplation. He appeared to be in no hurry to answer, unaware of the approaching sirens.

'My name is Sanjay. I'm of no importance, but the man on the floor cannot be let loose. In time, his motives would destroy us.'

'I know you,' Albert said, stepping forward.

The man nodded. 'Yes, we've met. I trust you still have the carving you chose? You're where you're meant to be now. I'm only sorry it took so long to right the wrong.' He stroked the scar on his cheek, a scar from so long ago now he barely remembered the silversmith who'd caused it. There'd been so many men over the years — chasing him, chastising him, threatening him. But time had also taught him that not all men were evil. That the world was still full of good people.

331

'Right the wrong?' Sarah yelped. 'You knew my father was in India, and you did nothing about it?'

He shrugged, ignoring Sarah's concerns. 'We can't be everywhere.'

'We?' Albert asked incredulously. 'Who's *we* and where were you when my wife vanished? Where were you when I disappeared, twiddling your thumbs?'

'History complicates things. Time even more so. But now I must go,' he said, rummaging in his shoulder bag.

'You can't go,' Sarah said, 'until you've told us what's going on.'

'The ironic thing is, Miss Lester, I don't have time to explain. The police are coming. They'll want to interview your father and question you about the gun shot. Mr Grey won't be here for them to interrogate. He'll be in a place where he can cause no further damage to the present, or to the future.'

'I'm confused,' Nicole muttered, her eyes fixated on the man bleeding on the tattered carpet.

The peculiar man withdrew a small wooden carving from his bag, that of a coiled snake. At first glance, it appeared to be a cobra, but on closer inspection it had the face of an animal and a head full of human hair.

'That's *Glycon*,' Nicole said, her voice infused with knowledge. She had no idea what else was going on, but she knew her ancient Roman gods, including the snake god they thought even the great emperor Marcus Aurelius worshipped.

'Very good, Miss Pilcher,' the man smiled, the smile only moving one side of his face because of the hideous scarring on the other side. '*Glycon* will take our friend on a journey, from which he cannot return. He will not come to any harm, I can assure you. Time is a perfect leveller. As you walk through it you appreciate the goodness in people, and you find it easier to identify the evil.'

With those final words, he leant towards Grey who was now stirring on the ground.

'I have the key you wanted,' the Indian man whispered as Grey struggled to sit.

'You shot me,' Grey hissed, holding his hand to the wound where it was obviously only a minor graze and not a life threatening injury.

'The means to time travel, Mr Grey. I have it here,' the stranger said, offering the small wooden statue of the snake god *Glycon* to Richard Grey. Grey's eyes widened with greed and he reached for the sculpture.

A hammering on the door interrupted the strange tableau.

'The key to my future,' Grey whispered as he took hold of the snake, unperturbed by the noise outside.

It wasn't the key to his future, but a ticket to a past he'd never lived.

Richard Grey vanished.

There were no bells or whistles, or puffs of magic smoke. With the thump of one heart beat, he'd disappeared, leaving only a smear of blood and a void on the floor.

'New beginnings, Mr Lester, with your daughter. But not with your wife, that is something I cannot change. Time is a great healer, and I think now your grief has already passed. I'm only sorry we didn't know in time.'

As Albert went to reply, the man rummaged once more inside his bag, but whatever he used would remain unseen, as he vanished, leaving not one shred of evidence that he'd ever existed outside of their collective imaginations.

'I'll get the door then,' Nicole offered, shock etched on her face.

When no one replied, she unlocked the front door, and armed police swarmed the tiny shop.

THE AFTERMATH

*L*et off with a warning for discharging a firearm in a public place, Albert Lester limped upstairs to the apartment above *The Old Curiosity Shop*. Life would not be the same, and already he pined for the days when others sought his counsel. Here, he was an old man standing in the path of his daughter's future. Or at least that's how he felt as he watched Sarah running the sales figures with Nicole.

Life in the *future* was benign, utterly predictable with no room for excitement or experimentation. For Brooke, life here would be different. He was experiencing the present as a visitor from the past. Everything for him was new and miraculous, and much less life threatening. But for Albert, the past held everything he needed to complete him.

After the police seized the unlicensed muff-pistol, they vacated the premises, leaving the remaining adults in a silent huddle.

As Albert lowered himself onto the couch, Nicole's quiet voice broke the uneasy tension.

'I've never lied to a police officer...'

Sarah started laughing, and before long Albert joined in. Then

Nicole laughed and Brooke smiled. The scene too surreal for anything other than an attempt at humour.

'I know what I saw, but I'm not sure I saw what I saw...' Nicole started.

'It's best not to think too much about how it works, or why. Just accept it. It's the only way,' Sarah said.

Albert nodded his agreement.

Nicole swallowed. 'If we ignore that thing that happened downstairs, which I'm still not sure really happened, can you say what will happen to me now? Now that you're both back?' Nicole's voice broke.

Albert and Sarah looked at each other. Albert not one hundred percent sure who Nicole was or what she did in the shop, but he had taken an educated guess.

'That's up to Sarah,' he replied.

'What do you mean?' Sarah asked.

'It's your shop, it's up to you.'

'But you're back now?'

Albert sighed. He was back, but couldn't live this life. Everything in the shop, the business, this life, reminded him of Annabel and their life together. A life he could never be part of. As he'd walked up the stairs, each footfall had hammered home the only decision which made sense. He had to return to India, to his home. This wasn't his life to live any more.

'I have to go back,' he whispered to Sarah. 'This is your life now, your business. I'll only get in the way—'

'Never,' Sarah interrupted.

'I've decided.'

'But the Indian man said you were in the right place now, you heard him. We heard him.'

Albert tipped his head. 'This may be the right place for you, but it's the wrong time for me now. I'm sorry, sweetheart.'

Sarah pouted, the petulant child coming through loud and clear.

'So, you'll run around the shop touching everything until you find a key to take you back? You could end up anywhere, just like I did,' Sarah said, shaking off Brooke's hand as he tried calming her.

'I have one of his sculptures, a tiger which will take me back to India, to the very moment I left.'

'You can't know that for sure.'

'I do, Love. I do. We've already said our goodbyes so many times before. But this time I have something to say before I go, about business I'm afraid. There's an old garage, or shed, out by what I guess is now Heathrow, on Harlington High Street. Next to a stately home, but on its own title. There's some stuff there for you. God knows what condition it's in now, if it's still there, but it should be. Paid more than an arm and a leg for it back in the day. Sell it. Don't keep any of it for a rainy day, not any more. I want you to live your life. Promise me that?'

Sarah nodded, tears streaming down her face.

Albert knew all she wanted was her dad, but he couldn't give her that. Not now. Sarah was an adult, a big girl on her own in the world. All children lost their parents at some stage. Most of them never got a second chance at saying goodbye, of settling scores or healing old wounds. But he had. And as he pulled Sarah into a giant bear hug, crushing her head to his chest, he couldn't help crying himself at the joy she'd given him and at the second chances they'd had.

'I love you, Dad.'

'I love you too.'

Then Albert Lester slipped his hand into his pocket, curling his tobacco-stained fingers around a tiny wooden carving of a recumbent tiger, and disappeared.

THE END

A number of the characters asked for more adventures, and so their stories continue in *Ithaca Bound*, the first book in my next time travel trilogy. [Click here to read]

ITHACA BOUND

What if Rome never fell?

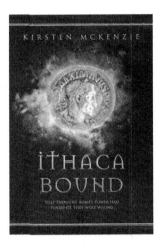

When ancient ruins are discovered on Lillian's family farm, emotions boil over as treasure seekers and the government descend like locusts. But ancient altars aren't the only riches lying beneath the soil at Ithaca Farm.

History lurks beneath the thin veneer of time. And when the past colludes with someone much closer to home, the greatest threat to Lillian's family and friends isn't necessarily the Roman army...

Unless she can halt the formidable march of ancient Rome into her time, she'll lose the only family she has left, and that isn't an option.

A sweeping saga of friendship, love, and the corruption of power.

Read Ithaca Bound - the first book in the spinoff series from the *Old Curiosity Shop* time travel trilogy, featuring a number of the same characters, and the continuation of their stories.

READ ITHACA BOUND HERE

THE FORGER AND THE THIEF

Five strangers entangled in the forger's wicked web, each with a dangerous secret, and an apocalyptic flood threatening to reveal everything.

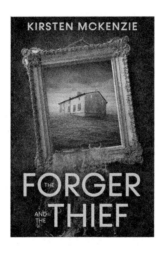

A **wife** on the run, a **student** searching for stolen art, a **cleaner** who has lined more than his pockets, a **policeman** whose career is almost over, and a **guest** who should never have received a wedding invite.

In a race against time, and desperate to save themselves and all they hold dear, will their secrets prove more treacherous than the ominous floodwaters swallowing
the historic city of Florence?

Dive into a world of lies and deceit,
where nothing is as it seems on the surface…

Read The Forger and the Thief now

REVIEW

Dear Reader,

If you enjoyed *Telegram Home,* could you please consider leaving a review on your favourite digital platform?

Reviews are invaluable to authors, and only need to be a couple of lines, or more if you like.

A number of the characters from the *Old Curiosity Shop* series have asked for more time on the page, more of their stories to be told, and for more adventures. Their stories can now be found in *Ithaca Bound,* the first book in my next time travel trilogy - the *Ithaca Trilogy.*

Thank you.

Kirsten McKenzie xxx

AUTHOR'S NOTE

- The Viceregal Lodge in Simla (Shimla) was not built until 1888. For the purposes of this narrative I had it constructed twenty or so years earlier. In 1863, the Viceroy of India, John Lawrence, shifted the summer capital of the British Raj to Shimla. He lived in a rented house, which didn't really suit the story, hence my poetic licence.
- The Indian Rebellion took place in 1857. The casualties across both fronts were huge, and appalling atrocities were committed by all those involved. This isn't a book on military history, it's a book which sits firmly in the time slip genre. I tried not to delve too deeply into the how's and why's of the Rebellion, but it sits behind the story as a volcanic backdrop. If there are errors or injustices in the story, they are mine. This is fiction, loosely based around fact.
- Imam William Henry "Abdullah" Quilliam was a real person and founded the first mosque in England after embracing Islam in 1887, aged 31 years old. On Christmas Day in 1888, Quilliam's mosque opened its doors to feed the poor in the morning and again in the evening. The premises at 8

Brougham Terrace in Liverpool have been restored and
turned into a museum. You can also book accomodation
there through the Abdullah Quilliam Society. I hope that I
have depicted Abdullah Quilliam as respectfully as possible.

- Governor Grey persuaded the Colonial Office in London to
  send more than 10,000 Imperial troops to New Zealand and
  General Sir Duncan Cameron was appointed to lead the
  campaign. Cameron used soldiers to build the 18 km-
  long Great South Road to the border of Kīngitanga territory
  and on 9 July 1863 Grey ordered all Māori living
  between Auckland and the Waikato take an oath of
  allegiance to Queen Victoria or be expelled south of the
  Waikato River; when his ultimatum was rejected the
  vanguard of the army crossed the frontier into Kīngitanga
  territory and established a forward camp. A long series of
  bush raids on his supply lines forced Cameron to build an
  extensive network of forts and redoubts through the area. In
  a continual buildup of force, Cameron eventually had 14,000
  British and colonial soldiers at his disposal as well as
  steamers and armoured vessels for use on the Waikato
  River. They fought a combined Māori contingent of about
  4,000.

CAST OF PLAYERS

THE OLD CURIOSITY SHOP SERIES

Sarah Lester/Grace Williams/Sarah Bell/Betsy

Art Loss Register
Gemma Dance
Ryan Francis

Auckland, New Zealand
Aroha Kepa, wife of Wiremu Kepa
Henry Neumegen, a pawnbroker
Jimmy Jowl, a publican
Joe Jowl, a publican
Moses Robley, collector of artefacts
Sophia Kepa, daughter of Wiremu
Wiremu Kepa, a miller
Clarence Whittaker, a surveyor

Bruce Bay, New Zealand
Bryce Sinclair, ferryman
Christine Young, wife of Reverend Young
Felicity Toomer, daughter of John Toomer

Frederick Sweeney, publican
Grant Toomer, shopkeeper
Isaac Lloyd, a gold miner
Margaret Sweeney, wife of Frederick Sweeney
Samuel Sinclair, son of Bryce Sinclair
Saul Hunt, ex convict
Seth Brown, a gold miner
Shrives, a bullock driver
William Price, Warden
Reverend Gregory Young

Christies Auction House

Andrew Harvard, Senior Specialist Costumes and Textiles
Don Claire, Senior Partner
Hamish Brooke
Hannah Gardner
Jay Khosla, Senior Manager of the Indian Art Group
Leo Hayward, a clerk

Dunedin, New Zealand

Amos Wood, army deserter
Annabel Lester, mother of Sarah Lester
Colin Lloyd, younger brother of Isaac Lloyd
Edwin Sutton, Sutton's General Store
Graeme Greene, police constable
Howard Cummings, a clergyman
Jack Antony, army deserter
Jock Crave, police sergeant
Mervyn Kendall, Collector of Customs
Norman Bailey, assistant to Bishop Dasent
Thomas Dasent, Bishop of Dunedin
Una Neville, on the boat with Colin Lloyd

England

Abdullah Quilliam*, opened England's first mosque

Adelaide, maid to Lady Laura Grey

Arthur, a silversmith

Arthur Sullivan*, composer

Audrey Grey, mother of Richard Grey

Barry Wentworth, a farmer

Benjamin Grey, brother of Edward Grey

Daniel Shalfoon, a clergyman

Edith Grey, ancestor of Richard Grey

Elizabeth Williams (née Grey), daughter of Edward Grey

Garth Moodie, photographer

Grace Williams, daughter of Robert Williams

Jessica Williams, sister of Robert Williams

Jonas Williams, foster father of Robert Williams

Josephine, a prostitute

Lady Laura Grey, mother of Edward and Benjamin

Lord Edward Grey, brother of Benjamin Grey

Lord Henry Grey, husband of Laura Grey

Mary Bellamy Grey, wife of Edward Grey

Melissa Crester, an American

Mr Sutcliffe, manservant to Lady Grey

Mrs Phillips, housekeeper to Lady Grey

Nicole Pilcher, the manager of *The Old Curiosity Shop*

Noel Glynn, brother of Sally Glynn

Patricia Bolton, a fashion designer, friend of Sarah Lester

Paul de Lamerie*, a master silversmith

Philip Williams, husband of Elizabeth Williams

Ravi Naranyan, security guard

Rebecca 'Betsy' Jane Williams,

Richard Grey, businessman and collector

Robert Williams, illegitimate child of Sarah Williams

Samer Kurdi, a trader

Sally Glynn, a converted Muslim in Liverpool

Stokes, employed by Richard Grey

Tracey Humphrey, Royal School of Needlework

Wick Farris, a knocker

W.S. Gilbert*, dramatist

Customs and Excise
Alan Bullard, Surveyor of Customs, London
Clifford Meredith, a customs officer
Mervyn Bulford, Collector of Customs, Liverpool
Paul Shaskey, a customs clerk

France
Clara Bisset, resistance fighter

London Police
Fiona Duodu, Constable
Owen Gibson, Detective Sergeant
Sean Jones, Corporal
Tania Foster, Sergeant
Victor Fujimoto, Inspector

India
Abe Garland, army officer
Ajay Turilay, assistant to Patricia Bolton
Albert Lester, husband of Annabel Lester, father of Sarah Lester
Alice Montgomery, Anglican Missionary School
Amit, servant to Simeon Williams
Christopher Dickens, army officer
Elaine Barker, Anglican Missionary School
Jai Singh*, the Maharaja of Jaipur
James Doulton, army officer
Kalakanya, servant to Sarah Williams
Karen Cuthbert, Fishing Fleet Girl
Layak, servant to the Raja of Nahan
Madame Ye, an opium dealer
Maria, Fishing Fleet Girl
Naomi Abbott, wealthy wife
Navin Pandya, a stonemason

Nirmala, servant to Sarah Williams
Raja of Nahan
Ram Singh II*, the Maharaja of Jaipur
Reverend Montgomery
Sally Brass, Fishing Fleet Girl
Sanjay, a street urchin from Jaipur
Saptanshu, driver for the Raja of Nahan
Simeon Williams, brother of Sarah Williams
Warren Brooke, army officer

Victoria and Albert Museum

Brenda Swift, curator
Eliza Broadhead, Department of Furniture, Textiles and Fashion
Jasmine Gupta, manager
Steph Chinneck, intern

Wales

Annwr Lloyd, mother of Isaac and Colin

* Real historical figures. Their names have been used in a fictional sense, although their achievements mentioned in this novel are real.

BOOK CLUB DISCUSSION QUESTIONS

1. What was your favourite part of the *Old Curiosity Shop* series?
2. Do you think the author sufficiently tied up all the threads? Or are there loose threads?
3. Which scene has stuck with you the most?
4. Would you want to read another book by this author?
5. What surprised you the most about the series?
6. How did your opinion of the series change as you read it?
7. If you could ask the author anything, what would it be?
8. Are there lingering questions from the series that you're still thinking about?
9. Which character did you like the best? And were you happy with their story arc? Why?
10. If you had to trade places with one character, who would it be and why?
11. What do you think happens to the characters next?
12. Would you want to read more books set in this world?

ACKNOWLEDGMENTS

The publication of *Telegram Home* ended up being a long and convoluted road, and I would like to thank each and every reader for staying with me, for your patience.

Thank you to Squabbling Sparrows Press. You have been a dream to work with.

I want to acknowledge my daughters, Sasha and Jetta, for being my listening posts when I've randomly asked them what they think about the death of X, or the treatment of Y. They may be young but they did steer me away from taking the easy route! Thank you also to Fletcher who kept me on track.

As always, thanks to the star of the book, the inspiration behind *The Old Curiosity Shop* — *Antique Alley*, the antique store on Dominion Road in Auckland, New Zealand my father started in 1971, and which my brother now runs. My grandmother did indeed wallpaper the upstairs room before my parents were married, and you can still see remnants of it on the walls in the Frame Room. It's still as messy as it was when my father was alive, with cartons and plates stacked precariously throughout the rooms. It's well worth a visit.

ABOUT THE AUTHOR

Kirsten McKenzie fought international crime for fourteen years as a Customs Officer in both England and New Zealand, before leaving to work in the family antique store. Now a full time author, she lives in New Zealand with her family and alternates between writing time travel trilogies and polishing her next thriller. Her spare time is spent organising author events and appearing on literary panels at various festivals around the world.

Her historical time travel trilogy, *The Old Curiosity Shop* series, has been described as *"Time Travellers Wife meets Far Pavilions"* and *"Antiques Roadshow gone viral"*. Audio books for the series are available through Audible.

Kirsten has also written the bestselling gothic thriller *Painted*, and the medical thriller, *Doctor Perry*. Her last thriller, *The Forger and the Thief*, is a historical thriller set in 1966 Florence, Italy, with some ghostly links to *Painted*...

She is working on her second time travel trilogy, which begins with *Ithaca Bound*, and features many of your favourite characters from the *Old Curiosity Shop* series.

Kirsten lives in New Zealand with her husband, her daughters, and one rescue cat. She can usually be found procrastinating online.

You can sign up for her newsletter at:
www.kirstenmckenzie.com/newsletter/

Printed in Great Britain
by Amazon

45340518R00209